South Georgia Blues

South Georgia Blues

DB CAP

KISSBOOKS
Atlanta

KISSBOOKS

Atlanta

Copyright © DB CAP, 2005
All rights reserved

Publisher's Cataloging-in-Publication
(Provided by Quality Books, Inc.)

Cap, D. B.
South Georgia blues / DB CAP.
p. cm.
LCCN 2004116993
ISBN 0-9746200-0-9

1. Murder--Fiction. 2. African American accountants
--Fiction. 3. Georgia--Fiction. 4. Mystery fiction.
I. Title.

PS3603.A636S68 2005   813'.6
                QBI05-800259

Printed in the United States of America
First Edition

Text set in New Caledonia LT Std
Designed by ZZ Geronna, LLC

TO THE READER

To have known love with you is to have lived
in the best of all possible worlds with you,
snuggling in the warm glow of true bliss with you,
sipping from the cup of love with you—
a companion, a mate,
a match with you—
THE BEST
OF TIMES
with you!

A Love Note to Stanford

CONTENTS

PART ONE

THE NIGHT THAT NEVER HAPPENED

PROLOGUE

GEORGE COUNTY

SATURDAY, JANUARY 16

THE TALL MAN parked the Ford Thunderbird behind a crumbling stick tobacco barn in Twofer County, South Georgia. The sky was black, ominous, and shot through with thunderclouds boiling over the treetops. Outside, the night sky growled and barked and spat, as the tall man sat listening to the last few bars of "Bitches Brew" leaking out the stereo speakers.

Miles Davis was his favorite Jazzman, but he was also deep into Wynton Marsalis, the combination Jazz master and intellectual.

The weatherman broke in with his dreary forecast. "It's gonna be cold tonight, folks," the weatherman said, shivering into the mike. "Cold and wet. The—"

Click!

The tall man sat thinking about the time he had almost been struck by lightning, the time the hairs stood up on his neck. Sneering the memory back into place, he jingled the keys before getting out the car and locking it. He hunched his shoulders to loosen the thick trapezius muscles of his upper back, and then he started his mile-long walk to the farmhouse in the next county.

The night ticked like an old clock.

The moon rose high and full. And as thunderclouds cruised the countryside like alien ships, and lightning went slicing through the clouds like a snake in the grass, thunder was pounding the moment like a drum.

The tall man moved purposely across the hay field. His long strides were steady and quick, his rhythm in tune with the tick-

3

tock, ticktock of a metronome unwinding inside his head.

Through gaps in the surging thunderclouds, the bright white face of the moon appeared and disappeared as if playing a game of peekaboo with the tall man. The night sky flickered and lit up the face of the tall man. He moved at a steady pace through the cedar trees, beyond the pine trees, across the front yard and past a Chrysler Fifth Avenue parked in the driveway.

He stopped near the first window he came to and pulled on his gloves. Slipping a jimmy through the rubber seal, he forced the window up. Reaching overhead, he hooked his fingers atop the window frame. Lifting his weight, he swung his feet through the window opening and lowered himself inside. He landed inside a room crammed with dolls and dollhouses and doll accessories. Drizzles of cool light glowed from a night-light stuck in the hallway.

He took out the big .44, stole across the hallway, ducked inside the bedroom, and he froze.

His trained eyes honed in first on the lump in the center of the bed, then swept across the room. His gaze locked onto the huge plate-glass window. He took out the penlight.

The chaos brewing outside was like on a movie screen.

He could see lightning flickering like a tease and then exploding in the gut of clouds pushed along by strong winds. He could hear the gushing wind howling and see it whipping the tops of 100-foot pine trees like hula girls whipping their lovely hips.

The tall man stood staring over at the woman in the bed, and he was wondering how she could sleep through all the hell-raising going on right outside her window. He flicked on the penlight and went straight to the bed. He jerked the bedspread back.

Steadying the light on the woman's face, he saw the beam slide off her sightless eyes. The hairs on his neck tugged at the skin.

Instinctively, he spun away from the window and dove for the floor. A lightning bolt streaked past the window. The room exploded in light. Thunder shook the walls down to the foundation. The noise went rollicking through the house like a train.

A bolt of pain punched the tall man behind his right eye like a fist. As he toppled over, he glimpsed the shadow of a man eight feet tall. He tried hefting the .44 at the same time another bolt of pain punched him behind his right eye. This time, the jolting blow slammed into his head like a cannonball.

His muscles twitched, the .44 fired, and he crumbled.

Inside the house, not a soul stirred.

Outside the plate-glass window, the top of a pine tree snapped off and jackknifed to the ground. Smoke curled up from the splintered white wood like ghosts. Hot sap boiled up from the wound.

The tall man stirred. His head felt as big as a six-foot hole in the ground, and weighed as much as a headstone.

The big gun laid near his hand. He lay on his back, dazed. As the confusion cleared, he slowly lifted his head and scanned the room. Seeing no one, he relaxed and lowered his head back down to the floor. Then he remembered the giant, grabbed his gun, and rolled desperately into a corner, ending up on his knees. He held the big gun out in front of him, his throbbing eyes searching around the room.

Then he remembered the dead woman in the bed. Slowly, he rose to his feet, feeling a little dizzy along the way. Hugging the wall, listening for the giant, he edged near the door leading to the hallway. He peeked around the doorframe, saw a foot, and ducked his head back. He took another peek. The foot hadn't moved. It was a small foot, like a woman's foot. Near the foot laid a book.

He felt a slight tingle near his right eye and cringed, expecting the worse the beast in his head had to give him. His forehead was swimming in sweat. He flicked the sweat away.

That was the worst migraine he'd had since...that was a bad one. Stepping slowly into the hallway, he made his way over to the body and knelt beside it. Two baby-doll eyes stared up at him. A ragged hole the size of a belly button was stamped in the center of the boy's forehead. The tall man made mournful noises.

He stared crazily down at the blood circling the small head. The goo looked like a black halo had leaked from the gaping hole where the back of the boy's head used to be. He made more mournful noises. Pressing his palm to the boy's eyelids, he rolled the lids shut.

The tall man's pupils had shriveled to pin pricks and now looked tiny inside his 1,000-yard stare. He bent forward, touched the bible, glimpsed the shadow of the giant, and heaved up the big gun.

His trigger finger froze!

He was pointing the gun at his own shadow.

Another wave of confusion clouded his thoughts. The tall man looked over at the night-light, and then looked over at the shadow. He stared down at the boy, and then stared back over at the night-light. He fell back on his haunches, making more mournful noises. Suddenly, a switch flicked on inside his head. His heart stopped pounding; his lungs stopped heaving; his mind stopped spinning.

He moved swiftly.

He snatched the bible off the floor again and squeezed it back on the bottom bookshelf. He pulled a spiral notebook from his inside coat pocket and hustled back inside the bedroom. He reached for the telephone and stopped his hand when he saw a nickel-sized hole in the thumb of the right glove he wore.

He picked up the telephone with his left hand and dialed with his right forefinger.

When the answering machine finished its spiel on the other end of the line, the tall man whistled into the mouthpiece seven times then he hung up without speaking a word.

The tall man turned on his heels and beat a hasty retreat. He slipped back out into the night from which he had come, leaving behind the dead wife and the dead son of his best friend.

But, in his freaky mind, tonight never happened.

1

STANFORD ROME STEPPED off the stainless steel elevator on the fifteenth floor of the Richard B. Russell Federal Building in downtown Atlanta.

The air outside was broiling hot. It was ninety-two degrees. The humidity was stuck on ninety percent. The wind was dead on arrival, and the misery index had shot up from unkind to unmerciful.

It was just another hot dog-day afternoon in the capital city.

Like he had done every Monday for two months, Stanford walked into the FBI's Atlanta office. On Mondays, he ate lunch with Clayton Westwood, a close friend and the FBI Atlanta chief.

Clayton's secretary led him into her boss's office. Clayton turned away from the computer screen and grinned at him. They shook hands in the hearty way of old friends. But Clayton didn't grab his coat, and they didn't head downstairs to grab a bite. Instead, Clayton slumped back down in his chair and pointed him to a chair in front of the desk.

Stanford's suspicions shot up like the hackles on the back of an old yard dog. He watched Clayton prop his thick forearms on the desktop as if anchoring himself in place to deliver bad news.

"I talked to Shelley about an hour ago," Clayton said and cleared his throat. "That Shelley, he sure sounds great these days, huh?"

Shelley was Stanford's best friend and Clayton's former boss. He and Shelley had been best friends since they were two skinny little boys growing up together down in Twofer County, South Georgia. Shelley had been Clayton's mentor in the FBI until Shelley quit as

FBI Atlanta chief three years ago.

Asked why he'd quit the FBI at the height of his career, and Shelley said, "So I can kick back and stomp the goddamn roses."

Stanford's suspicions shot up another notch when he realized Clayton was dancing around what he wanted to say. But what the hell, he would cut a step or two to humor a friend. Clayton had been working long hours over the past two months, trying to find the man who murdered Stanford's wife and son.

He slumped down into the chair. "Are we having lunch or not?" he asked Clayton.

"We're having lunch," Clayton said. The FBI chief steepled his fingers to his lips as if trying to keep from uttering the very words he knew he was about to speak. For the first time since he walked into Clayton's office, his friend looked him squarely in the face.

"We've shut down the case, Stanford. I'm sorry." Clayton fished his pocketknife from his pocket and sighed. "Thorpe, he's still the boss around here, you know. I am so sorry, Stanford."

Click-clack. Click-clack.

The steady rhythm of Clayton snapping the knife blade open and shut, click-clack, filled the small office.

He knew he should say all the right words and let his friend off the hook. But he didn't feel up to saying the right words. He was not at all unhappy to see Clayton wiggling on his own hook either.

The click-clack slowed then abruptly stopped. Clayton turned, looking at him sideways like one of them was a backstabber.

"Ahh, hell, Stanford, don't look at me like that; like I'm something you stepped in, like I'm shit. I'm a good guy. Damn, I feel bad about it. But I'm just a pawn in this game called the FBI. For Christ's sake, give me a break."

He wanted to kick something. His right leg kept bouncing up and down as if Christopher had broken an unbreakable law, as if his son had sprung back to life like Lazarus supposedly had done.

His leg kept bouncing up and down as if his son were back riding that bouncing knee like he was the only pearl found in a whole world of oysters. But that was not the reality. Christopher was not back alive just because that bouncing leg wanted him to be—back alive so he could hug him, so he could hug his dead son.

Instead, his dead son was still buried down in the cold ground.

While his son lay dead, pushing up daisies in a Twofer County dirt bed, the FBI had stopped looking for his killer. Not good. Now, no one was out there hunting the killer who blew out the back of his son's head and strangled his wife to death. Not good at all. He grunted to himself and pushed up on his feet, staring down at Clayton.

"Stanford, wait." Clayton pushed the pocketknife back into his pocket and rose from behind his desk. "Stanford, you know, if anyone could've nailed this killer, it was Shelley. He worked this case like it was a full-time job. We have all tried so hard because…you know…I mean—we care for you, man; you know what I mean. You're a stand-up guy, Stanford. We did it for you, Shelley and I. We did it for you. Believe that. Don't blame Shelley. Thank him."

He nodded, his anger waning. It was not Clayton he wanted to drop kick. It was Shelley he wanted to smack—the traitor. The whole FBI set-up smelled like crap Shelley stirred up. And he should have seen it coming. Now it all made sense to him. Now he knew why the FBI started investigating the case two months after Stacey and Christopher were so savagely killed.

Shelley had brought pressure to bear on the FBI. He had manipulated Clayton and the FBI to look into the murder case. Shelley convinced them the killer had committed the crime in Georgia but had escaped into Florida. Shelley's scheme to lure him back to Atlanta worked because Shelley knew him so well.

Shelley had tried to get him to stop acting like a PI in Twofer County and return to Atlanta and start acting like a CPA again. His best friend knew if the FBI worked the case, or pretended to work the case, then he would do as Shelley wanted him to do. He would leave Twofer County and return to Atlanta to start putting his sorry life back together again. That had been the plan—Shelley's plan. And it worked.

"Stanford," Clayton said, "I know you're going back down there, back to South Georgia. I know you're going to start right where you left off two months ago. If I can help in any way, you just call me, you hear?"

"Sure, Clayton." He extended his hand. "And thanks a million. By the way," he added, releasing the handshake, "Shelley may sound great, but he's in a little trouble. It's those migraines, the ones he's been having since he was a kid; they're back with a vengeance."

"Is he seeing a doctor?" Clayton asked, cocking his head.

"No. No, he's not. Here's the deal on that. Shelley, he tells me, 'yeah, make the appointment, and I'll go.' I know a doctor here in Atlanta, a neurologist. The doctors he used before, they are all down in Miami. Anyway—"

"So you figured it was easier to get Shelley to a doctor here than to get Shelley on a plane down to Miami," Clayton said.

"Exactly. He'll rather shit out a brick than fly in an airplane. Anyway, so I make the appointment. But, first, you know Shelley, I tell him upfront, hey, he's a white guy. Shelley says, 'that's cool; white's cool.' So, I make the appointment, and he was a no-show, three times a—No, four times a no-show."

"Jesus," Clayton said. "Can I help in any way?"

"Sure, you can. Do you know a neurologist, who's female, drop-dead beautiful, pumps iron, pops steroids, got boobs the size of cantaloupes, a butt the size of an ass's butt, and loves to screw?"

Clayton chuckled. "It's a fantasy; she doesn't exist."

"Or she's a nightmare if she does," he said. "Anyway, Clayton, the next time you see Mr. 'Sounds Great,' tell him to go see David Harte. He has an open appointment for anytime."

"Now, that's first-rate service," Clayton said. "What are you hold-ing over this neurologist's head to make him so cooperative. He cheating on his taxes or what?"

"No, not a client. He's my neighbor out at Lake Arrowhead."

"Oh, yeah, you live up there in the mountains of the gods, I hear. Are you guys up there scratching your heads and searching for the Theory of Everything?"

He chuckled. "I wish I were a physicist. Those are the high gods of the numbers game. Me, I'm just a lowly numbers cruncher."

"I know better," Clayton said, his face now a picture of concern. "Stanford, don't you think it's time to come down from the moun-taintop. I mean, you are shutting out everyone, including me."

He thought about it. A sharp image from his childhood popped into his mind. The image was of Aretha and Franklin, QueenBee's two bull mastiffs—and her bodyguards. Back then, he would watch them lick a bowl of food clean in thirty seconds. He timed them. Now thinking about it years later, he didn't feel at all like the dogs felt—full. He felt like the bowl looked—licked clean.

Well, Clayton," he said, "I'm going to figure out why they were killed, and then I'm going to find the man who killed them."

Out came the pocketknife again. Click-clack, click-clack.

"Yeah," Clayton said, "I hear you. But let me tell you, Stanford, you want to kill somebody. And you don't even know you want to kill somebody."

§

The empty elevator was waiting for Stanford.

The doors bumped shut behind him. The car started its downward plunge, and only by clenching his teeth did he keep from screaming to the top of his lungs for as long as he could stand it.

He hung his head, and grief spilled out at his feet.

Licked clean. He felt licked clean. Empty.

First, the local cops threw in the towel, then the GBI took a hike, and now the FBI had whimpered off. At that rate, they may never catch the killer. But that did not mean the killer would not be caught. Clayton was right, and Clayton was wrong.

Clayton was right; he wanted to kill somebody, but Clayton was also dead wrong; he knew he wanted to kill somebody. He was going to catch the killer, and he was going to kill him. Of that, he was sure. He could accept that the cops may never find the killer.

But he could never accept that he never found the killer. Their deaths had been devastating. His nervous system had taken one hell of a hit. But it was not knowing why they were murdered that deepened his despair, intensified his pain, and made him bitter. And the guilt. How could he ever overcome the guilt of not being there for them when they needed him to be there for them?

The elevator doors sprang open.

Stanford strode briskly across the pavilion, pushing on through the revolving doors, and back outside in the jungle again, soaking up the Atlanta heat. The images playing around inside his mind gave him great pleasure.

He was imagining how he would first torture the killer, and then how he would, second, blow out the back of his fucking head.

He chuckled, bitterly.

2

TWOFER COUNTY

MONDAY, MAY 16

STANFORD PARKED ON the grounds of the Twofer County Dirt Beds. He sat listening to raindrops pelt the roof of the sedan.

He watched the silver drops sprinkle the headstones and the cement slabs, and stir the dead flowers. But he was a South Georgia boy. He knew the evening showers would soon run their course, blowing away on the first passing wind.

Twofer County was located four hours and 250 miles due south of Atlanta. When Stanford was thirteen, he and Shelley and Justin and Jud and Jake and Colt literally changed the name of the cemetery. They removed the word *cemetery* and welded two four-letter words across the metal arch spanning the entrance. Twofer County Cemetery became Twofer County Dirt Beds.

As the last raindrops splattered the windshield, he opened the door and got out. The sun had already punched a hole through the clouds and was now squeezing a rainbow from the water drops.

Stanford walked past his grandfather's grave.

QueenBee's husband died August 24, 1949, the night Stanford was born. He stopped at his father's headstone. Odis Rome was born on June 12, 1925; died September 15, 1953. His father was twenty-eight when a stranger shot him dead; the murderer never caught. He stopped next to the headstone of Laurel Carter Rome. Like his grandfather, his mother had also died on August 24, 1949, the night he was born. She was eighteen years old. Not knowing his mother was a hole in his life that could never be filled.

Stopping at Stacey's grave, he stared out across the tombstones, his mind fumbling back through the memories. He continued to hurt. He heard a car pull into the parking lot behind him.

He turned and saw sunlight glistening off raindrops beaded up on the sleek front grille of a black Jaguar coupe. Then, Jocelyn Slade emerged from the driver's side like the birth of the blues.

Standing tall behind the open door of the beautiful automobile, the "darling of Atlanta's airwaves" took off her sunglasses. She watched him watching her.

The sight of the WTNT-TV News evening anchor pounded pain deeper into the chambers of his heart like a stake. The sight of her provoked memories of a night that haunted him like a boogie man from the dark. Wisps of steam rose from the concrete slabs and hung over the dirt beds like a shroud. Or like spirits.

He turned and stared down at the small grave. This couldn't be happening to him. That was his son down in that hole.

The car door clicked shut, and the sound made him shudder. Footsteps crunched slowly, almost cautiously, behind him. Each footfall made his heart pound a beat quicker. The footfalls stopped. His pulse rate stabilized. But her perfume rode waves of her heat, heat that reached out and touched him.

Shivering from conflicting emotions riding him like he was a horse, or a mule, he turned. He looked at her, drinking in the liquid brown eyes of the one woman he had to hate. He had to.

His eyes yelled at her—Stay the hell away from me!

But her presence was so much larger than his grief. His chest tightened, seeming to close around his heart like a fist. He walked past Jocelyn Slade to make good his getaway. In his rudeness, he escaped the source of his guilt.

§

Stanford crossed the winding Timseesee River. He drove for the homeplace where QueenBee raised him.

He grinned at seeing Aretha and Franklin racing lickety-split across the pasture. The dogs were as thick and heavy as runt-sized Clydesdales. The two massive bull mastiffs helped Bubba Bazin guard the mile-long road winding up to the farmhouse perched on a rise in the distance. As usual, the homeplace was all dressed out in color-bursting flowers of every stripe and description.

The landscape was a showcase of colors.

The fertile grounds blossomed with fruit trees, pecan trees, oaks and pines and cedars, and every flower and shrub known to the county. This was home, and the hardy roots were already tugging gently at the soles of his feet. This was home. No matter how bitter; no matter how sweet; this was home. Forever.

Each time he came visiting, he saw that his grandmother's eyes had dimmed a little more. It was as if she were wasting away as some prerequisite to dying altogether. Maybe she was already hearing footsteps in the dark. Except for Stanley—living in Paris with his mother—she was the only kin he had left in the whole world.

Bubba Bazin nodded and waved him on through the checkpoint with a thumb's up. He stopped and got out.

The two huge guard dogs strutted around in high spirits before sitting on their haunches on either side of him, as was their habit. He squatted and hugged them, stroking their big heads and running his fingers over the short hairs of necks as thick and wide as their skulls were broad and wide. They snuggled him with short black muzzles so evident of their bulldog heritage. He gave them a final pat, waved to Bubba and got back in the car.

As far back as he could remember, the homeplace has had an Aretha and a Franklin. This pair was the fourth, and they were also the darkest brindle, and they had the blackest masks across their muzzles. They were fierce-looking, and had the size to back up their appearances. Both were nearing the end of their typical eight- or nine-year lifespan.

In another two or three months, there would almost magically appear a fifth generation of bull-mastiff pups roaming the homeplace. Aretha and Franklin would train the pups to replace them as QueenBee's personal bodyguards, as they themselves had been trained by the bull mastiffs before them.

From a half mile away, he saw the ever-present Big Flossie, still wearing that gun on her hip like she was born with it there. She may have been born that way. No one really knew where she came from as a pregnant 12-year-old kid, not even QueenBee.

He parked and got out. Big Flossie was eyeing him like he was an enemy and not to be trusted. He walked past a white Ford Crown Victoria wearing government license plates and spoke to Big Flossie in passing. They didn't care for each other. Long story.

"Bertha's gonna pat you down, today," Big Flossie told him.

Bertha was a tall stout woman, who treated him like family. She led him to the sunroom without patting him down. Aretha and Franklin had already taken up their positions inside.

But now the bodyguards were all business. Aretha sat on her haunches on the left side of the rocking chair, and Franklin took up the same position on the right. Their folded ears gave their huge heads even more of a square shape. The dogs were intently alert, their ears raised until the v-shaped tips were at eye level.

QueenBee rose from the depth of her rocking chair and opened her arms to him. He moved toward his grandmother.

He heard a low growl coming from Aretha's throat, as he hugged his grandmother with all the tenderness demanded by an eighty-three-year-old body. Aretha's growl deepened. QueenBee looked over at Aretha. "Go to work," she said.

Franklin bolted through the doggie door. But Aretha only reluctantly sulked away, glaring back over one shoulder and then back over the other shoulder, eyeing him suspiciously.

"Go to work," QueenBee said again. This time Aretha turned, bolting through the doggie door, and was gone.

"And Aretha was so eager to see me on the way in," he said.

"Ah, don't worry yourself about Aretha. She's just ornery in her old age. Like me. She especially doesn't like anyone touching me for some reason. Has she ever gotten nasty with you before?"

"Never," he said.

"Well, forget Aretha. How have you been?"

QueenBee was dressed as she was mostly always dressed. She wore a cotton pantsuit, white boat shoes, and a single strand of pearls with matching earrings. She wore her white hair shaped in a round three-inch Afro. Her back was more tilted than straight, and her shoulders were a little more slumped than when the last time he was there.

Bertha served QueenBee peppermint tea. He sipped a strong cup of coffee. QueenBee rolled the dice from her hand and picked up the teacup. She eyed him over the teacup as he told her about the FBI quitting the case.

She set the teacup down, and she kept studying his face.

"Shaft, what will you do different this time, may I ask?"

Ignoring the sarcasm, he shrugged. "I don't have a clue. Yet."

"Answer me this," QueenBee said. "Will you shoot James Kelsey before you leave, or will you shoot your partner after you leave?"

"QueenBee, I didn't know you knew James so well."

"Well, I do. And I know Juanita Robeson's the soul of that outfit. And I know Greg Lang's the geek. And I know you're the conscience. And I sure know James Kelsey's the shark of that crew. Don't play me, Son. I may be old as dirt, but I'm still a player. I've been around here longer than that turnip truck most folks can only brag about not falling off of."

QueenBee sipped her tea. Her hand trembled a little. Her eyes seemed to focus in front of his face rather than focus on his face. His grandmother was listing to the side like the sinking of a mighty battleship. Another pruning of his already skimpy family tree.

QueenBee set the teacup down and scooped up the dice.

"You and Stanley, you two still on the outs?" she said.

He shrugged. "We communicate. That's something, I suppose."

"Well, he just couldn't stand around to see his daddy suffer no more. Who can blame him. We talked before he left." QueenBee rattled the dice and frowned at him. "I hate preaching to the choir. You hate listening? Good," she said before he could answer. "And the next time you see that knuckle-headed Shelley, you tell him to come see me, PDQ."

Then his grandmother changed the subject completely.

"Jocelyn Slade, she came visiting yesterday. Her words are as pretty as her face, and she's one tough sister. She's writing a piece on a local personality, as if we have such a creature with such a personality around these parts. She played coy with the truth is what she did. She wouldn't say who she was talking about. She's a sly one, I tell you. That Jocelyn Slade, she's a real sly one."

QueenBee rattled the dice. "She's got the hots for you, too." A smile puckered her cheeks, adding sparkle to her dull eyes. "I saw clean through those deep tannin brown eyes she's got. Such pretty eyes. Eyes, they make a woman, you know."

He clammed up. She was picking him again. It was better to say nothing and let her make of his silence what she may.

QueenBee rattled the dice. "Are you gonna talk to me or what?"

He smiled at her feistiness. A good sign. But he stayed mum.

"I said, 'are you gonna talk to me or what?'"

"QueenBee," he said, "Jocelyn Slade has the hots for a story, not the hots for me. Nothing but a story."

"Huh-huh," QueenBee said, rattling the dice. "You think maybe it's Shelley she's after?"

"Now, that's a story," he said. "But, of course, Justin has roots in Twofer County, and he's only one appointment away from being nominated to sit on the Supreme Court."

He saw a glint in his grandmother's eyes. She was proud of Justin, as were they all.

"You know, QueenBee, it could be you she's doing a story on."

Her eyebrows lifted. "You reckon?"

Her reaction tickled him. "Just kidding, QueenBee. Just kidding."

"Oh," QueenBee said. "I don't want that woman bothering Shelley. You keep your ears to the ground on this for me. If she goes after Shelley, you let me know, pronto. Got me on that?"

"Got you on that," he said.

"Good," QueenBee said and rose stiffly to her feet. "Got to go tend to my company. On your way out of town, do drop by the Computer Shack and see Colt before you go."

He and QueenBee hugged good-bye as they hugged hello.

QueenBee squeezed his arms feebly. Her eyes moved powerfully across his face, her brow a ruffle of ridges.

"Stanford, you do be careful. Don't you trust nobody; you hear me?" Her grip tightened then wavered as if strength had deserted her. "And don't be trusting Shelley all the time either."

He cocked his head at that. He heard tons of dread in her voice, and he knew something important was left unsaid. What was between those two?

"Yesterday," QueenBee said, "when Jocelyn Slade was yapping about this and that, I kept thinking of Shelley. I thought of what a troubled boy Shelley was back then, and what a troubled man Shelley is now. There's something about that woman that's as troubling to me now as Shelley was troubling to me way back then. It's those eyes, I tell you. It's those eyes. They're troubling to me."

§

Stanford parked the sedan in front of Colt's Computer Shack.

Thomas Jefferson Lee, aka Colt, was Twofer County's computer

God. No database in the world hooked up to a telephone line was safe from Colt's prying eyes. He was now curious about Jocelyn Slade's intentions in Twofer County. Colt could ferret out all he needed to know about the darling of Atlanta's airwaves.

He replayed his conversation with QueenBee. Her mind had wandered a little, enough to concern him. The most precious part of QueenBee was her mind. But she'd kept talking about Jocelyn and Shelley as if they were one and the same person.

He didn't know much about Jocelyn Slade, except what he read about her. But that was information cranked out by a news media of which Jocelyn was a star. He wanted the scoop on the real Jocelyn Slade, she who complained when the toilet seat was left up rather than down, she who stood naked in front of the mirror and marveled at her own reflection in the looking glass.

Thinking of Jocelyn Slade triggered memories of that night at Lake Arrowhead. She had been flirting with him, and he had been loving every minute of it. The memories faded.

Colt's Computer Shack was a square cinder-block building. He got out and waved up into the surveillance camera staring dumbly down at him like a bird of prey, or a vulture. The door buzzed.

He pushed inside, and the cool air sucked at his face.

Colt looked like a bear in a man suit.

At first glance his friend looked retarded. But the opposite was true. They greeted each other like the old friends they were, old friends who had grown up together. The name "Colt" didn't fit the burly man. Colt was not frisky. Neither was Colt much of a pistol.

When he told Colt what he wanted, Colt picked up a binder with a white label stuck on the spine. "You wanted it yesterday, right?" Colt said and tossed him the binder.

He looked at the name printed on the label: *Jocelyn Slade*.

Smiling, Colt cracked his knuckles. "It's not like that. I'm not a mind reader. Yesterday, QueenBee, she asked me to do the same thing you just asked me to do. That's my book on Jocelyn Slade. So fresh off the press, the ink, it's still dripping wet."

Colt kept smiling.

"Now, ain't I a pistol and a son-of-a-gun?"

3

STANFORD HEARD THE car tires crunching across his gravel drive-way. Seconds later, the Thunderbird's powerful engine shut down. The car door slammed then he heard footsteps.

The door to the cottage swung open. Shelley Lester stood in the doorway looking like nothing but trouble. Shelley stepped inside, closed the door, and then he knocked.

"Hey, Roscoe," Shelley said.

"Hey back," he said, watching Shelley get comfortable.

Shelley took off his suit coat and slipped off his upside-down shoulder holster. He draped gun and coat across the sofa chair. He kicked off his boots and left them where they dropped. Stepping up to the bar, he flexed his shoulders. He lined up three one-shot glasses on the bar top, poured a finger of Hennessy in each one, recapped the bottle, propped a foot on a barstool, looked over at him and beamed.

"Do you join me or do you watch me, Roscoe?" Shelley said.

He looked at Shelley without answering.

"That bad, huh?" Shelley said.

He nodded.

"Okay, Roscoe. You pissed. Show your feminine side and get it off your chest. You're on the clock. And it's ticking."

"For one, QueenBee's more than a little upset with you. She wants to see you, like, yesterday. PDQ. What's with you two?"

Shelley held the first glass at eye level then gulped the cognac down with a quick toss of his head. He flipped the empty glass

19

upside down on the bar. "One down, two up. Next gripe."

Shelley's eyes were as inviting as empty graves. He was two feet wide, shoulder to shoulder. He looked like a powerfully built Jim Brown. But at six-four, he was a taller version of the great Cleveland Browns running back, who Shelley considered the greatest running back ever. Shelley showed the world a gentle, sad-faced, and slightly cross-eyed look. His thick body could still run two miles in ten minutes or less. Clean-shaven, he wore a box-cut hairstyle clipped short on the sides, thicker on top, and sprinkled with gray.

His best friend projected a calm manner. But an attentive person could tell by the depth of his eyes that inside that man, clouds gathered, winds picked up and stirred, and pretty soon shit would hit the fan and stick like grits.

"Ticktock," Shelley repeated. "Next gripe. Let's get on with it."

"For two, you were a no-show again yesterday. That's not good."

"Oh?" Shelley wriggled his toes, squinting up into his face.

"Oh," he said. "Oh," he repeated. "Shelley, I made the same appointment four times because you said you were going to go see David. And four times you lied. And all you can say is 'Oh'?"

Shelley lifted the second shot glass. "Roscoe, you have this here eroticism with the number 'four,' huh? The Four Tops, the Four Seasons, the Four Corners, the Four-Forty. What gives? Lighten up on the fours, why don't you. Ten-Four?" Shelley grinned.

"Don't grin at me, you—you jackass. Losing your memory is not funny. Your head coming apart at the seams is not funny at all."

Shelley's black eyes glazed over, and his pupils sharpened to hollow points. "Roscoe, now don't you go badgering me like maybe I'm sweet on you or something like that. Because I'm not sweet on you. We'll tie up, me and you. Big-time. You got me on that?"

"The last time you tried, I put you on your butt," he said.

"Yeah. I had a gut full of moonshine, and I was sleeping."

"Like hell you were sleeping."

"Well, then, how can I dream that you put me on my ass if I'm not sleeping, Mr. Pocket-protector-wearing man; tell me that?"

"Shelley, I'll put this in real terms even you can under—"

"You're gonna print it in *USA Today*? Then, it must be about sex, the only reality I know," Shelley said. "Hey, why don't I just whip it out and beat you to death with it."

He glared at Shelley.

"Alright, already," Shelley grumbled. "Get it off your chest or you'll burst." Shelley grinned. "Then I'll have crap all over me."

"You are a trip, Shelley," he muttered. "A fucking voyage. But, it's my humbled opinion that you need to go see David Harte."

"Opinions are like dick strings, Roscoe. Every man's got one."

Shelley gulped down his second Hennessy and flipped the empty glass upside down on the bar beside the first one.

"Two down, one up," Shelley said, eyes on the third shot-glass.

He leaned forward, exerting his will. "Okay, you cretin. Answer me this. What happens when a migraine pops your happy ass when you're doing—whatever it is you do to some chick, and you forget what the hell you're doing to said chick? Then whacha gone do, Roossscoe?" he mocked.

Shelley's guffaw exploded up into his throat like a sonic boom, and his shoulders shook as he laughed and laughed.

"Now, Roscoe, you pulling my hanging thang like it's your hanging thang when it's mine. Who needs a mind to do some chick? A mind, that's a complication; it gets in the way, don't you know that? Craps you out, shrinks your balls, makes you whimper. Don't you know anything about birds humping bees?"

He felt defeated. "You mean the birds and the bees," he said and hung his head.

"That a boy," Shelley said, grinning. Shelley reached for the last shot of cognac, but he beat him to it. His fist closed around the glass, and Shelley's big hand closed around his fist. Shelley glared at him. He glared back.

"Cretin, huh?" Shelley said and withdrew his hand.

He gulped down the last shot of cognac, banged the empty glass down beside the other two, and smirked at Shelley.

"Don't you wanna just pack up your shitty attitude and go ruin someone else's day?"

"You bet," Shelley said, snatching up his gun and coat, scooping up his boots and turning for the door. "Cretin, huh?"

He grabbed one of Shelley's thick wrists in a viselike grip and blocked the door with his body.

Shelley stopped in his tracks and glared down at the offending hand clutching his wrist. Then Shelley looked up, those reptilian eyes slashing across his face like teeth. He saw a viciousness he'd seen many times before. But this was the first time Shelley had directed his meanness straight at him. Always in the past, Shelley had come at him from the side. This was a frontal assault. A first. The past two days have been full of firsts.

"One more thing," he said, still holding firm. "That so-called FBI investigation was a paper tiger, wasn't it? You used Clayton to get me back to Atlanta, didn't you, asshole?"

Shelley wrenched free as if his grip were a child's grip.

"Move yourself or I move yourself," Shelley growled.

"If you can't help me, don't you hurt me, Shelley. I mean it."

Shelley's face muscled up a soundless grin. "Roscoe, I'll go see the shrink when I go see the shrink. As for you, go fuck yourself."

Shelley stepped around him and out the door.

"Asshole."

"Your grandmama."

When the roaring engine of the Thunderbird died away, Stanford took his throwing knives outside to unwind.

Throwing the knives did for him what sitting beside a pond with a fishing pole did for other folks. He spotted a fox squirrel and her kits meandering through the branches, heading for the creek, and he started missing his sons—the dead one and the living one.

Two months ago, when Stanley's mother Chris said she was moving them to Paris, France—a career move she said—he nearly begged his thirteen-year-old not to leave. Stanley left and said he wouldn't be back until Stanford got his act together.

His own mother died birthing him into the world—she was checking out when he was checking in. He was just cursed that way, he supposed. He was only five when his father up and died, leaving him an orphan in the world. Just him and QueenBee back then. Before Shelley came to live with them. And now she was hearing footsteps in the dark like she too was packing to leave.

He snapped the last knife into the pine tree with a viciousness. The blade sank deep into the soft white wood.

The handle quivered and sang. The killer was out there, and he was going to find him and cut out his fucking heart.

He spat, and rubbed it in the ground with his boot.

4

CANDICE BERGENS JOGGED through the North Georgia woods like a sleek black cat. Her lips were full and dangerous, her hair long and limp, and her eyes cheetahlike and tombstone gray.

So this was the South, the almighty Dixie, where grown men called cute southern girls steel magnolias and Georgia peaches. On the Front Range in Colorado, where she came from, men called a woman like her an iron fist in a velvet glove.

Her breathing ran deep and steady like in feel-good sex.

Spring was everywhere in the air.

Her hormones were just humming up a storm inside her, and all that sassiness left her damn near swooning, as she ran north of the huge lake. She was heading for her listening post located 100 yards south of Stanford Rome's cottage. She used to be a cross-country runner in high school, and she'd jogged in terrain much worse than Lake Arrowhead before.

But that was back in her other life, back home in Denver. But for now, for a while anyway, Atlanta was her new home in her search for a big payday and big money. The Mile-High City was a distant memory in her long-ago past, except for her memories of Frank— her first real lover.

Once upon a time, she had big money, but that money was long since gone. Quicker than a magician's trick the money got sucked away, leaving her with less than six figures in the bank. Coming to Atlanta wouldn't change that any time soon. She felt great. Her breathing matched the rhythm of her gait so well her coaches often bragged that she ran "with the grace of a goddamn deer!"

She wore a skintight cotton jumpsuit and hard-soled moccasins. The outfit protected her from the hostile environment of weather, plants and animals as she jogged along the firebreak. An Atlanta Braves' baseball cap sat snug on her head, her hair spilling from beneath and all across the backpack. Not only did that Anaconda holster keep her Beretta .380 snug and tight to her hipbone, but that "sHOOTERs bra" hugged her tits like a man's firm hands.

What a wonderful day!

She thought about Shelley again and how his gruff voice made her all wet. Today, maybe, she would finally get a good look at the man with the voice that turned her on like she was a gutter slut, available to him for nickel bags or for free.

She stepped down on it—her ankles wore wings as she ran.

She was still over a mile from Stanford's cottage and out in the open when she heard a car racing fast toward her. She dropped flat behind shrubbery, crouching like a scared baby rabbit. Her heart was motoring, sweat boiling from her pores.

The car stopped, the idling engine grumbling like a race car.

She pulled out her binoculars. She heard the door open and stole a peek. Through the shrubs, she saw him standing by the front bumper, his back to her. She watched and waited for him to turn.

He turned, the thing wiggling like a snake in his hand when he shook it. By the time she raised the binoculars from his crotch to his face, he was already back behind those tinted windows.

Had she ever seen a longer one? Yes. Had she ever seen a thicker one? Yes. But she'd never before seen such a long thick one.

As soon as the car sped away, she was back running again. She was back thinking about Frank and Denver. After a short fling with Frank, he up and disappeared one day. They made a date. Frank never showed, and she never saw Frank again. When she graduated from college, she left Denver for good. When she went home the last time to visit, her mother, surprisingly, asked for a favor.

She agreed because the mystery of what her mother told her and the mystery of what her mother did not tell her got the best of her. Her mother wanted to know if Stanford Rome had killed his wife and son. She asked her mother why, and her mother told her she would find out soon enough. And she did know soon enough.

She knew the instant she saw a photo of Katie Kane.

That one picture had been worth a thousand explanations.

Candice Bergens pressed on down the road, picking up speed as she ran. She'd never whacked a black man before and swore on her daddy's grave she never would. But times were hard. Besides, in every town with a Styles by Candy beauty salon she'd killed a man. The city-too-busy-to-hate would be no different. Her heart seemed to be pumping pure adrenaline, she felt giddy, running in a quiet zone. The sky was so blue, the trees so green, the moment so sweet, and she was just a sex machine getting off on herself.

Good gracious! She refused to be mounted and conquered by a man—she wanted to hop on and ride.

Her mind exploded in ecstasy, as she ran on and on.

When she reached her listening post, she slumped against the old sprawling oak and kept sucking air for a full minute, her hot, tired muscles shuddering in free fall from her runner's high.

After assembling the Gatman gun, she shoved an ammo clip up into the mechanism. The Gatman gun had the range of a buffalo rifle and the punch of a small tank. Suddenly, the treetops came alive, a herd of squirrels racing down to the creek for a drink.

When the chatter faded into silence, the wild smell lingering, she went back to work. She had planted six tiny transmitters inside Stanford's cottage. She recorded everything said inside.

Hoisting the recoilless rifle up to her shoulder, she sighted it. She set the lightweight weapon aside. Fitting one earphone in her ear and plugging the other end into her receiver/recorder, she tuned in to what was going on inside Stanford's cottage this time.

Planted on a tree stand up in the branches of the huge oak tree were three tiny amplifiers. They boosted the transmitter signal before pumping the sound down to drive her earphones.

She had to go back inside Stanford's cottage one more time. She had to plant a bug inside that room she couldn't get into last time.

The room was padlocked. Iron rods barred the window as if the room were some sort of macabre shrine to his dead wife and son.

Over the earphone, she heard him singing that blues song again. "You gonnnna maaake me cry..."

She listened and waited.

5

TWOFER COUNTY

WEDNESDAY, MAY 18

BUBBA BAZIN RAKED a shell into the Thompson Pump shotgun as soon as he saw the white Pony Express delivery step van turn onto QueenBee's 1,000-acre Twofer County homeplace.

The van was speeding toward the guardhouse.

Aretha and Franklin, the two bull mastiffs, pranced at Bubba's feet. The three of them manned the gate blocking the only road leading to the farmhouse. QueenBee had enemies who long ago threatened to kill her and all her kin. The why of it nobody knew, and nobody asked.

Aretha and Franklin kept circling Bubba's feet like planets orbiting the sun, awaiting instructions. Bubba studied his two companions. Their necks were as large as their big heads, and they had dark gray coats overlaid with darker stripes. The coloring allowed them to be almost invisible at night and was perfect camouflage for what the bull mastiff was bred for—chasing down night poachers.

The bitch Aretha was ten pounds lighter than the heftier 130-pound Franklin. They were a whole lot of dog. It seemed to Bubba the dogs too expected the letter that came May eighteenth every year for as long as Bubba could remember. QueenBee stayed in a funk for days after getting the letter, and a few times the funk lasted weeks.

"Go to work!" Bubba barked.

The dogs' powerful hindquarters dipped like those of a quarterhorse leaping from the starting gate. They bolted, racing lickety-split down the middle of the road like they were going to rip off

26

the tires and shred them. Instead, they veered to either side at the last possible second. It was a sight to see. The bull mastiffs wheeled around, the slowing van between them.

"Damn fool dogs," Bubba said, cradling the Thompson Pump.

When the van stopped at the gate, Aretha and Franklin kept their dark eyes locked on the driver's face while Bubba searched the van. Satisfied the van presented no danger to QueenBee, Bubba raised the gate.

The van drove through.

Big Flossie, pearl-handled .45 hugging her hips, pointed for the driver to park away from the house, between the oaks and the pines. Then she led the driver into the foyer. She patted him down for weapons and then made him take off his boots before leading him into the sunroom where Bertha took over.

Bertha led the driver into the sitting room.

QueenBee waited. Aretha and Franklin sat on their haunches on either side of the rocking chair.

When the driver moved toward QueenBee, Aretha gave a low menacing growl and rose powerfully off her haunches.

The driver jumped back and cowered.

Franklin growled low in his throat but stayed on his haunches.

Bertha stuck out a hand. The driver handed over the envelope.

Aretha dropped back on her haunches, eyeing the driver.

Bertha eyeballed the outside of the envelope before she handed it to QueenBee, who sliced it open with her pocketknife. She pulled out a color photo and a small 3x5 note card. After studying the photo for long seconds, she read the three words printed on the note card.

For the first time in over thirty-three years, the Twofer County matriarch smiled on May eighteenth.

§

Flossie led the driver back outside. She watched him as he walked back toward the trees and the van. Aretha and Franklin tore back toward the guardhouse, racing, kicking up dirt.

Once back inside the van, the driver reached down and twisted the heel of his cowboy boot. A three-inch, two-shot .41 caliber derringer fell out of the hollow heel into his sweaty hand.

The driver cursed his bad luck. The big guy didn't tell him he would have to take off his damn boots before he gave her the letter. And how could the big guy have forgotten to tell him about two of the biggest, meanest-looking bulldogs he had ever seen in his whole life. That chick goon with that gun on her hip was walking toward the van, but she was too late. He revved the engine to a whining pitch, 4500 rpm, then slammed the pedal to the metal.

The van leaped forward, lunging, and plowed ahead, picking up speed as he aimed it straight for the farmhouse. The chick goon dropped into a two-fisted shooting stance, the speeding van barreling down on her at forty miles an hour and racing.

Bending low, he hugged the wheel and prayed. A fusillade of .45 slugs peppered the windshield. The glass exploded, the shards pelting his head like hailstones. The van skidded precariously on two wheels. The driver gawked at his world flying by, the steering wheel locked in his hands.

The driver felt the vibrations of the front bumper ripping down into the dirt like a plow. He felt the rear rubber wheels losing grip with the ground. The heart-stopping sensation of the van becoming airborne and the heavy Gs he felt hurling through space made him lose touch with reality. He released the steering wheel and threw up his hands like he was waving good-bye to the world.

The white Pony Express step van slammed into a stout oak tree and exploded. The core of the explosion spat out a spinning fireball that hit Big Flossie in the chest.

She burst into flames.

§

QueenBee sat grim-faced in her sunroom.

Aretha and Franklin sat on their thick haunches on either side of the rocking chair, their black eyes trained on the sheriff. The bull mastiffs' ears were held higher than usual, the dark eyes even more penetrating.

Sheriff Jake Keller was trying to explain Big Flossie's death.

QueenBee loved Big Flossie.

Her heavy heart had already sank down into her stomach like the Titanic must have slid under the sea. She swallowed another lump that had just taken place of the previous lump she'd swallowed. She knew who did it. The same man who killed Stanford's wife and son had tried to kill her.

What good could come of this?

Why after all these years would he try to kill her now? She was too old to be killed. Why now? She needed more muscle. He had threatened to kill her and all her kin. There were only three of them left: Stanford, Stanley, and yours truly.

She needed some big-time help. But she could no longer depend on Shelley to carry out her wishes. And Jake over there was just not mean enough. She needed more muscle, and more bite. Fred Junior, her lawyer, wouldn't do because his only bite was an overbite. Stanford was too burdened with the blues to be of much help to her. Again she squeezed the dice in her fist. The people she cared about and loved the most, why were they all the time dying?

Jake was talking again, and she tuned the sheriff back in.

"QueenBee, we'll never identify the pieces of that driver. The van was stolen. The car tag and the license were phony. So, you're our only lead, QueenBee. Who's after you? You have to tell me."

"Never you mind, Jake," she said. "Never you mind about that."

The sheriff persisted.

"These are pros after you, QueenBee. Those bombs were buried inside the walls of that van. I've seen that type of thing done before. With napalm. That's what killed Big Flossie—napalm. The van is called a Trojan horse. And for good reason. The van even fooled Bubba, and he's thorough in what he does to protect you. These are professional killers, QueenBee. I need your help."

"Jake," she said, locking eyes with the Twofer County sheriff. "Jake, I want you to keep the lid on this...this Trojan horse. For the record, we blew some stumps for Hercules is what happened here today. That's all that happened here today. See to that for me, won't you, Jake."

She rattled the dice, the bones clattering angrily.

Jake Keller studied his hands, looked up, studied her face, and then the Twofer County sheriff nodded.

"Thank you, Jake," she said and pushed up sighing on her feet. "And do make sure Stanford hears none of this. If Stanford gets any bluer, we'll lose him, and he'll just become more fresh meat for that Twofer County dirt bed out yonder."

Jake Keller nodded again.

She studied Jake's face. He wanted to ask her something.

"Okay, Jake," she said, "you go ahead and ask me. You've been wanting to ask me that one question for the longest."

Jake Keller's lips tightened. On anyone else's face, it would have passed for a smile. For Jake, it was only a tightening of the lips.

"Are you sure it's okay, QueenBee? It's personal."

"Shoot," she said. "Ask your one question. Aim high."

Jake steadied his gaze. "QueenBee, I just wanna know why is it that every year, you get a snapshot of Justin Grimes? Every year. Same time."

"It's not a snapshot of Justin, Jake. You're wrong about that."

The sheriff looked dubious and tried to hide his skepticism.

She smiled at his confusion and rattled the dice.

"Jake, I know you feel better for the asking. And I feel better, too, that you asked that one question. Now, I've got other company to see to. You do take care, and Jake…"

She waited for Jake to look at her before she spoke. "Do keep Stanford in the dark about all this…this Trojan horse business. He already has troubles enough."

6

LAKE ARROWHEAD

THURSDAY, MAY 19

"STANFORD, YOU'RE THE best damn CPA Lake Arrowhead has ever had. It's been a pleasure working with you all these years."

Richard Stoole spoke with the heat of a preacher wailing fire and brimstone at a tent revival down by the railroad tracks.

"So you can't up and just quit on us like you're doing, Stanford. You just can't leave Atlanta for another whole two months."

The Lake Arrowhead president squawked like a crow. Stanford still didn't get it. Why was Richard overreacting that way? He was just taking another leave of absence from his own damn firm.

"Stanford, don't do this," Richard pleaded. "That's all I'm asking—hell, who am I kidding, I'm begging you, for Christ's sake."

Richard flapped his arms and kept crowing, while he watched and kept listening. He hoped to hear Richard say something that would give him some clue about what was going on here.

"Stanford, if you take another leave of absence, we're fucked right in the ol' fart hole. We are screwed. Have a heart, Stanford—hell, have a heart transplant if it'll change your mind. Just don't leave us hanging like this, our assholes exposed for any prick happening along with a hard-on, and just waiting to just ram it on home."

Richard's office door opened, and Mark Davis walked in.

The Lake Arrowhead attorney had a brandy glass in his hand, his face flush with drink.

"Hey, Stanford," Mark Davis said in his casual way.

"How are you, Mark?" he said, puzzled at Mark's condition. That was something else unusual besides Richard's carryings-on.

31

"It don't get as hard as it used to," Mark said, chortling. "It just hangs heavy now. That's par for the course. And yours?"

"Hanging," he said, trying to lighten the moment. "Just hanging."

Mark's youthful face was topped off with jet-black hair. His big bright eyes lit up his face whenever he smiled. Mark was so well-rounded. He was tough, arrogant, able, and some cold fish, almost cruel, when it came to looking out for Lake Arrowhead.

Lake Arrowhead was RKL's largest client. His partner James Kelsey had been Richard's and Mark's CPA in Kansas City for fifteen years. Seven years ago, when they moved Lake Arrowhead to Atlanta, James Kelsey followed his largest client to Atlanta.

In Atlanta, Lake Arrowhead grew like weeds. James Kelsey had to get bigger to keep his growing client. Otherwise, he would lose Lake Arrowhead's booming business to a larger CPA firm.

Stanford was surprised when James Kelsey cornered him in his small office one day and suggested merging their two firms into a partnership. Two months later, they merged Stanford Rome, CPA, and James Kelsey, CPA, into Rome & Kelsey, CPAs of Atlanta.

A year later, Greg Lang, a computer geek, became the third partner, and the firm was renamed Rome, Kelsey & Lang, CPAs (RKL). A year ago, Juanita Robeson, a tax lawyer, became the firm's fourth partner. Five years after he and James first became partners, Lake Arrowhead had grown to become a $500-million land company with a $100-million cash reserve stashed in the bank. And Rome, Kelsey & Lang, CPAs was the premier midsized CPA firm in the city.

RKL billed Lake Arrowhead three million dollars a year, one-fourth of the firm's income of twelve million dollars a year.

A month after he and James Kelsey first merged the two CPA firms, James asked him to take over the Lake Arrowhead account. James wanted to spend more time developing CapCity Investments, a new client 100 times smaller than Lake Arrowhead.

For five years, he'd been partner-in-charge of the Lake Arrowhead account. He helped Richard and Mark run the company.

"And how does the new Lake Arrowhead president feel today?" Mark said and held up the brandy glass in a mock salute.

He looked at Mark, puzzled, then turned to Richard, frowning.

"Mark," Richard said, "Stanford, he turned down our offer. He won't run Lake Arrowhead. He's taking another sabbatical."

"What is this?" Mark spat. "I don't believe this. Stanford, you promised."

"I—," he stopped himself and studied Mark's reddening face. Mark was lying through his teeth. He had made no such promise. His first impulse was to tell Mark to go jack off. His second impulse was to just walk away from the brewing fight. His third impulse told him to stand and fight this battle, no matter the odds, and no matter on whose turf. But he'd seen this dynamic duo in action before when he'd been on the other side—with them. They were relentless. He was already feeling the pressure. He couldn't just turn tail and run, but neither could he let these two muscle him this way. Not good, either way.

He was not into getting muscled around, especially by two white guys. But if he lost the Lake Arrowhead account, he would have to fight James Kelsey, a black guy. Either way, he was in a pickle.

"I don't know what to tell you, Mark," he said. You're a liar is what he didn't say. He looked to Richard. "Aren't you guys making too big a deal out of this? I mean, you two run Lake Arrowhead. I'm just the CPA. I keep an eye on the checkbook, bless the books, and keep the IRS at bay. And I make suggestions, especially on how you can cut cost and bring in more dollars; that's what I do; that's all I do. I'm just a hired gun."

"Ahh, Stanford," Richard said, "that's bullshit and you know it. You blowing your nose when you should be blowing your horn. You know more about Lake Arrowhead than Mark and me put together. Sure, you make suggestions, and we do what you suggest every time you suggest it; or haven't you noticed?"

"Yeah," Mark chimed in, "that's why we pay you the big bucks, too. You run the damn place, Stanford. Richard and I, we are just the rainmakers. Richard's the president, sure. But he doesn't run anything around here. Have you ever wondered why we don't have a chief operating officer to run this place? Have you ever wondered why we don't have a CEO to deal with the banks and money managers and the insurance companies and the pension funds and such as that? Stanford, have you ever stopped and asked yourself why is it we don't have a huge office staff?"

He had noticed, but so what. Of course, they paid him the big bucks for a reason, and he just told them what they were. In a way, they were right. He had been running Lake Arrowhead for the past five years. James Kelsey had done for Lake Arrowhead in Kansas City what he was doing for Lake Arrowhead in Atlanta. As QueenBee would have said: the knuckleheads were right.

They had gotten much richer because they had done what he suggested they do every time he suggested it.

"Stanford," Mark said, "we've made some promises. One promise was you would be around to help the new guy when he shows up." Mark scratched his head. "Stanford, I don't get this. You're turning down $500,000 for one year's work, plus stock options, to boot. That's crazy, Stanford. When we go public, you'll make millions. What's wrong with making millions?"

He swallowed the number whole. Richard hadn't said anything to him about money. His jaw went slack but he held it in place. A half million bucks? What new guy? What are they talking about?

"Guys," he said, "I'm confused. Help me out here."

Richard said, "Mark, I never got around to telling Stanford the details, the salary and the stock options, and whatever else."

"Ohh!" Mark said, the fire in his eyes flaming out. "I see. And you're worth every damn penny, too. You're the only CPA I know who's worth a damn and not a fucking oddball to boot."

"Stanford," Richard butted in, "we're only asking for one year. That's all we're asking, Stanford. One year."

"You know, Stanford," Mark said, smiling and slapping him playfully on the back, "we've been good for one another, your firm and ours. Rome, Kelsey & Lang, CPAs and Lake Arrowhead. We've all worked damn well together, the four of us—you, James Kelsey, Richard and me. A couple of black guys and a couple of white guys doing our own thing and making damn good money at it. You're a good guy, Stanford. So is James. Richard and me, we're good guys, too. We do need your help on this one, big guy. Don't leave us out here hanging. Help us out with this new guy."

"What new guy are you talking about, Mark?" he said, reaching and gently lifting Mark's heavy hand off his shoulder.

"His name's Tartuffe," Richard said. "Tartuffe Jitt. He should be here already. But he'll be showing up any day now."

He rubbed his neck, grimacing, and moved away from Mark.

"Listen, guys," he said, "I hear your problem. Here's mine."

He told Richard and Mark about the FBI quitting the case. As he spoke, he saw Mark withdrawing into himself like a clam in a shell. That shrinking away was Mark at his most belligerent.

Mark glared at him. "You promised, Stanford."

"Mark, stop saying that," he said. "It's not true."

"It's true!" Mark insisted.

His face stung as if Mark had punched him. His eyes drifted over to Richard, who simply looked unhappy. The pressure to hit back at Mark reached such a feverish pitch that all his big muscles shuddered in restraint. Richard kept shaking his head, no. His eyes kept moving from Mark's face to Richard's face, and he kept telling himself, no.

Mark snarled. "Stanford, you walk. We sue."

"No, no, Stanford," Richard sputtered, almost hurling himself between them. "Nobody's suing anybody." Richard glared at Mark. "Right, Mark? Nobody's suing anybody, right, Mark? Right?"

"Wrong," Mark said, icily. "Walk on us, Stanford; we walk on you."

"Shut up, Mark!" Richard bellowed, trying to push Mark away from him and having a hard time doing it.

"That's bottom line," Mark spat. "You walk, we sue." Mark was backing away reluctantly under Richard's firm nudges.

His eyes stung from his effort to control his rage.

So there it was. Mark had broken protocol and picked a fight.

His self-control felt gut-wrenching, as his heart sank through his stomach and down into his scrotum, snuggling up next to his shrinking balls. Mark, the weasel. Sweat oozed into his palms. He strained to keep his cool under fire.

How could he possibly leave there with his dignity intact, and the Lake Arrowhead account still in his pocket? He had to concentrate on doing both, or he could end up with neither. Focus.

"Stanford," Mark said, "we need CPAs we can rely on. If James don't straighten you out, we're hiring CPAs who will be here for us when we need them to be here for us. We have a contract."

"There is no contract, Mark." He ground out the words.

"Let's let the courts decide," Mark said coldly.

Again, he looked at Richard, who looked pale and browbeaten. Richard held out his white palms like flags. "Stanford, Mark, he's made it a legal issue. Mark's the attorney. It's out of my hands."

"Stanford," Mark said, "you know how I operate. If you walk out on us, then I would be derelict in my duties as the corporate attorney if I don't look out for Lake Arrowhead's best interest."

Sweat trickled from his armpits. Why were Richard and Mark offering him a small fortune to run Lake Arrowhead for one year, and a shitload of grief if he didn't run Lake Arrowhead?

"There was no contract, Mark," he repeated, the words sounding hollow even to his ears.

"The courts will decide," Mark repeated. "And, your checkbook, don't leave home without it. This breach of oral contract will cost you and your partners. You and your employees and their families. Everybody loses something for the decision you make, or everybody wins something for the decision you make.

"Stanford," Mark continued, "you're the managing partner of Rome, Kelsey, and Lang, CPAs. Your main concern should be for your firm. Instead, you make your personal life your main concern. So, how can we trust you to put Lake Arrowhead's interest above your personal concerns when you fail to put your own firm's interest above your personal concerns. I know this is harsh, but these are harsh times for Richard and me. We have a lot on the line."

Mark stood flat-footed, fists tight at his sides. "Stanford, harsh times demand harsh measures."

He watched Richard hang his head at almost a ninety-degree angle, making him look like a flesh-and-blood rendition of Rodin's sculpture the "Shade" on display over at the High Museum of Arts.

He stared at Richard until the Lake Arrowhead president met his eyes. When Richard made a slight shrug with his shoulders, he turned and looked at Mark Davis again. Was he going to leave there with his dignity and empty pockets? Or was he going to put his partners and his employees first, and his self-respect second?

Mark looked unmovingly resolute.

He turned toward the door. "See you, Richard."

"Take care, Stanford," Richard said. "Sorry about all this."

He brushed past Mark Davis. "Fuck you, Mark."

Richard Stoole groaned.

7

LAKE ARROWHEAD

THURSDAY, MAY 19

STANFORD'S EYES POPPED open. The ticktock of the grandfather
clock dominated his senses. The cottage was pitch black inside.
He lay on the sofa, ears cocked, listening. As his eyes adjusted to the
faint light in the room, he tried to remember what woke him. Was it
a dream, or was it real? Not a sound…but movement. The wind?

He squinted at the clock: 2:02 a.m.

Yawning, he rolled off the sofa. He picked up his rifle and flashlight, and went outside. He stuck his arms out in front of him and
flexed and stretched his tight back muscles.

The sky reached high and deep, and it was so black and starry.
Months ago, a sky like tonight would have impressed him. Tonight,
a sky like tonight was just a lid on top of the world, a world from
which there was no escape. Or was there?

Out the corner of his eye, he glimpsed a flicker of light. Turning
his attention in that direction, he sensed faint sound waves prick-
ling his ears. With a suddenness, all the bits and pieces floating
around in his brain came together in his mind. He had been jolted
awake. That had been an airplane gliding over the cottage, and that
airplane had just crashed north of the huge lake.

Stanford turned back toward the open door, spun back around
and ran, throwing himself out into the night. He ran in the rut of
the firebreak, the cool air lapping his face like a grateful pet.

§

When he stumbled up on the wreckage, the orange-yellow flames
were dying out. The fire was barely hissing over the twisted metal.

37

The twin-engine plane had plowed into the ground nose first.

Stanford heard a rustling behind him.

He slunk back into the shadows and the underbrush, his eyes aimed toward the sound. A light beam came cutting through the darkness, followed by a man carrying a rifle.

The man was unsteady on his feet. Stanford watched him study the burning plane. Then the man propped his rifle against a tree and set the lantern on the ground beside it. The man aimed the beam up at the sky like a beacon. Then he crossed his legs and tried to sink to the ground; instead, he dropped hard on his butt and grunted. He had a bottle in his hand. The flames of the dying fire danced off the face of David Harte. The psychiatrist, his nearest neighbor.

A twig snapped behind Stanford, and he jerked around. He saw David turn and look over to where he stood out of sight.

Caught between the unknown behind him, and the known in front of him, Stanford chose the known and spoke out.

"David, it's Stanford Rome!" he shouted out. "Coming in!"

"Yo, Stanford!" David shouted back. "Get yourself on down here and pull you up a stump."

David Harte lived two miles from him. David was mostly retired at age forty-five—burned out in his professional prime. They met a year ago on the jogging trail. Over months, they warmed to each other. He told David about Shelley's migraines. David said he could help Shelley and wanted Shelley to come by his cottage for an evaluation. But Shelley kept breaking appointments.

He and David sat and drank from the whiskey bottle. He soon felt warmer and a little lightheaded. David had already reported the crash to the Civil Air Patrol, and they were on their way.

The bottle was empty when they heard the whoop-whoop of a helicopter flying in low over the treetops. Floodlights lit up the ground as the helicopter landed thirty yards away.

Ron Aubrey, the pilot, talked to them, while the other two men scratched through the wreckage like chicken digging for worms.

"A roadside druggist," Ron said, whiffing the probe. "I smell the smack. This crate had a dynamite load, too. A bad combination."

Ron taped their statements.

Half an hour later, the machine angled up off the ground like a monster dragonfly and went hurtling back the way it came, the winking lights fading over the treetops, the big night sky slurping up the sounds.

David staggered and said, "I tried calling you but found out you don't own a telephone. I'm throwing a small party next Friday night. About a dozen close friends. I want you to show up."

He nodded. "Sure, I'll definitely drop by."

"Good," David said. "And Stanford…" David hesitated then said, "Stanford, Shelley's folks, are they still living?"

"I don't know. Shelley, he was adopted. The Lesters adopted him. They're dead. There's no one but Shelley."

"His real parents? Where were they from?"

His mind backpedaled through the years.

The Lesters adopted Shelley. But Shelley kept waking up in the middle of the night screaming. The Lesters told QueenBee to stop his screaming, or they were hauling him back to the orphanage. QueenBee did ease Shelley's nightmares, but by then Shelley had been spending nights with him and QueenBee for so long that he stayed. He never went back to live with the Lesters. They stayed his guardians, but Shelley lived at the homeplace. QueenBee said Shelley had so much fear and hate in him that he had to scream.

"David," he said, "QueenBee, she raised Shelley. We grew up in the same house. QueenBee, she raised us as brothers."

"You two saved his life," David said. "You and QueenBee. What happened to his real parents, the Whitfields you told me about?"

"They were institutionalized. They both had mental problems."

"Not good," David said, shaking his head. "How did your grandmother stop Shelley's screams? She did something special?"

He shrugged. "Maybe she did. QueenBee and Shelley would go into her bedroom for ten or fifteen minutes, not longer than that. QueenBee said that was the limit of Shelley's attention span."

"You never asked Shelley what went on in the bedroom?"

"Sure, I asked him. Shelley said all they did was talk. QueenBee, she said she was telling Shelley what a wonderful person he was, saying good things to balance out the bad things said to him."

He smiled to himself. "I'll tell you what, David. One time I did put my ear to the door. I heard QueenBee talking to Shelley in a real low voice, but Shelley, he never said a word."

"What was she saying to him?" asked David.

He thought about it. "Well, I remember hearing QueenBee say, 'I am who I am. Comfort me,' or something crazy like that."

"Hypnosis, probably," David said. "That's how your grandmother stopped Shelley's screams. She hypnotized him."

§

On his way back to the cottage, something shiny on the ground caught Stanford's eye. It glimmered in the moonlight.

He shined the flashlight on it. The beam bounced back off a piece of cellophane. Then he noticed small tracks in the rut of the firebreak. He bent down for a closer look. Old tracks. Smaller than the tracks he made when he ran past. Small like a woman's tracks or a child's. The distance between the tracks were wide like his. So that person was running, too. He switched off the flashlight and walked back to the cottage by the glow of the moon.

He kept shaking his head as he walked.

He had told David things he'd never told anyone else. He had never told anyone that he and Shelley had lived a brotherly past stitched together like a quilt. You had to have been there in his childhood to know that. Only people who knew them both knew that, for the most part. Their friendship was not a public affair. Their friendship was almost like an affair in its secrecy. The fact was that he and Shelley had been two orphans growing up in the world together. He and Shelley were best friends bonded together by the memories, the sweet and the bittersweet.

He felt a kind of relief rehashing the past with David.

A screech sprang from the dark like an "I got ya!"

He caught sight of a barn owl soaring silhouetted against the backdrop of the moon. The hunter was cruising the night skies with mouse in hand. Those talons were full of life on the one end, full of death on the other end. That was life. You were born into life. You lived life. You died out of life. End of story.

He would never understand what it meant to die and to be dead. He was born from death—from the womb of his dead mother. But still he would never really get the hang of death.

Stanford saw chunks of light streaming from the open doorway of the cottage. He just wanted to lie down and rest. He was not so much tired as he was weary—the weight of his sorrow still so heavy a load to bear. He dragged inside the cottage. He had taken two steps inside when his head vibrated. His wide eyes honed in on the biggest handgun he'd ever seen from the ugly end.

"Drop the rifle," the intruder said.

The diamond drilled into the man's left earlobe reflected light beautifully. The ticktock of the grandfather clock told Stanford time hadn't stopped at all, no matter how much he thought time had stopped dead still. The intruder could shoot him twice before he lifted the rifle a half foot.

He felt strangely out-of-body but not scared. He was perhaps disappointed in himself, but he was not afraid of the dire circumstances now facing him. His lips twisted into a knowing smile. He could easily turn the tables on this intruder. He could force this stranger to become his executioner. He could make this intruder shoot him, end his sorry existence, and break his circle of pain. All he had to do was to raise the muzzle of the rifle, and he was out of this life forever, just like Stacey and Christopher. In one deliberate move he could be free of guilt and pain and grief. He could be free of Mark's threat. He could be free of Shelley's betrayal. He could be free of Jocelyn Slade's—whatever. Free of the new guy. Free of the whole ordeal of waking up to face a new day jam-packed with the same old pains of yesterday.

A calm washed over him.

"Don't," the intruder said, reading his mind. "Don't!"

But he did. He slowly raised the rifle, giving the intruder all the time in the world to execute him. Then the muzzle of the rifle was aimed at the intruder's face. That he was still alive pissed him off. He fought back the impulse to just pull the trigger.

"Drop it," he said, almost apologetically. The damn coward.

The intruder smiled then opened his hand. The pistol thumped to the floor. The grandfather clock ticktocked.

Alarm bells vibrated inside both his temples an instant before a smothering force enveloped his head in a vise of muscularity.

He felt his body evaporating from around him like smoke. And before his very eyes, the intruder's smiling black face vanished into a flash of white oblivion.

8

THE WHINING NOISE of the Lockheed L-1011 Tristar filled the first-class compartment of Delta flight 317 from Atlanta to Miami International Airport.

Shelley's ticket read coach, but he was flying first-class. The captain, a Vietnam veteran, upgraded Shelley's coach ticket when he recognized the Medal-of-Honor winner boarding his ship.

The runway lights blurred when the three Rolls-Royce turbofans roared for take-off. The big jet started a slow almost graceful roll down the lighted runway as if shoved reluctantly along by a strong wind. Then, as if on a whim, the metal bird scooted ahead like it had been kicked in the tail fin. The 250-ton tube rose into the sky on wings that didn't flap.

Shelley gripped the armrests and held on for dear life. It was the getting up above the clouds that torched his brain to no end. He hated flying, but he hated worse what the migraines, his beast, had done to his mind and to his memory over the past four months. He was cracking up in the head and possibly losing his mind for all times. His thoughts were scary thoughts now. He no longer rode an unbroken stream of consciousness like everyone else with good sense. No, his thoughts didn't flow like a river from cradle to grave like the average Joe Blow, like the 250 other passengers flying to Miami with him. No, his thoughts were nothing like that at all.

His thoughts were now grotesque still pictures of ugliness and death. His thoughts were now snapshots with huge gaps of time stretched between each photograph. His world was weird and different and stuffed with all kinds of weird-looking people.

It was a freak show!

Some people looked like they had just stepped off a Pablo Picasso canvas and lived in a house of mirrors. Some people had eyes stuck in the backs of their heads. Some people had asses stacked on top of their shoulders. Some people had minds invisible to scrutiny. His world had changed from the real to the weird.

His world was now a freak show.

The jet shuddered like it too felt Shelley's discomfort and pain.

The L-1011 had leveled off, five miles up into the troposphere, and they were cruising along at 600 miles an hour. Shelley eased his grip on the armrests. Now-now, big chicken. This was his last chance to kill the beast. If his Miami doctors couldn't help him, he was down to his last straw. He would go crawling back to Queen-Bee for the relief she'd been giving him since he was a boy.

The thought of going back to Twofer County snarled and snapped at his small piece of mind. He and QueenBee were at cross-purposes. One day, she would send someone for him. Maybe Jake. Maybe Colt. Maybe Justin or Bertha, maybe even Stanford.

The beast was defiant. He had never defied QueenBee in his life and he never would. He had always carried out her instructions to the letter. Always. The beast was defiant. The beast did it!

He shuffled his thoughts back to the present. He eased out The Brain to recharge his memory. He didn't want to forgot why he was flying down to Miami. His memory had gotten just that bad. He opened the screen. The tip of a thick finger tapped out today's date. The names WEBB and PEARSON appeared on the screen. He remembered, closed the screen and stuffed The Brain back in his pocket. He thanked the flight attendant for the vodka she brought him. He eyed her backside as she twisted away.

Butt too small. Lots of butt was his liking. He emptied the vodka in a cup and spiked it with a bite of Black Russian from the leather flask he smuggled aboard. He sipped the smooth liquor and closed his eyes to suffer those images again. Death reared its head.

He'd seen enough death to know death on sight.

He'd seen death etched in the face of a Vietnamese girl roaming into a camp of sleepy GI's. The girl exploded, and the GI's died.

He'd seen death emanating from the scowling face of a Vietcong male pouncing from a tree with a Ho-Chi-Minh dagger clenched in his teeth. He shot the male dead. He'd seen death stalking battlefields like pimps stalking flophouses, and he'd seen American GIs and NVA Regulars fighting over rice paddies like whores fighting over johns. Shelley opened his eyes and blinked.

Is that you, Frank?

§

Miami was such an ugly town.

But Cicely Webb certainly was a beautiful woman with a two-foot trophy to prove it. She was Miss Florida in 1980, and she still wore the same size dress today that she wore back then.

Cicely locked the South Florida Theater doors and set the alarm at her usual prompt time of 9:30 p.m. She stood waiting on the steps, arms folded beneath her breasts, one high heel tapping the concrete. She looked both ways as if waiting for a speeding car to come roaring past so she could fling herself in front of the grille. Then she could become just another boring statistic of Miami life. She had to get out of this stinking town.

Miami smelled too much like fish and salt and Cubans and old folks. But the Cubans and old people were the worse of the lot, because they were so one-track-minded in their hatreds.

The Cubans hated only Fidel Castro, and the old folks hated only being old. There had to be a better way to waste away your lifetime while waiting to die. Or just waiting on Castro to die when he had outlived all who, at one time or another, had tried to shove death down his throat. And to think she missed her true calling in life. Cicely Webb just wanted the simple things life had to offer her. She just wanted to service people.

She just wanted to be a mortician—an undertaker—someone serving the living by burying the dead. What's wrong with that concept, for crying out loud?

The security guard hurried toward her and Cicely relaxed.

"Sorry, Mrs. Webb," he said. "Just making my rounds. Ma'am, you should buzz me when you ready to leave."

She raced home like she had a hot date waiting to sweep her off her feet. But she didn't have any kind of a date, especially a date with a broom. She wasn't even sure she still had a husband at home waiting for her like a bottom feeder. A sucker. Him or her?

Cicely Webb parked the BMW in the garage, feeling unusually tired. The lights blazed in the rear pool deck that was the envy of the neighborhood, but their ten-foot privacy fence kept all prying eyes at bay. Besides, no one needed to know what her weird husband and his weird friends did in their own backyard.

She padded on through the door, calling out for Clarence, who didn't answer, thank God. She pushed on upstairs to the bedroom. She was so tired. At the top of the stairs, she stopped.

"Clarence?"

She stepped onto the second-floor landing. She looked one way, then the other way. Where was that weird husband of hers and his weird friends? She sensed someone behind her and spun around.

A tall man stepped from the bedroom with a—

"Frank! No!"

§

From the seventh floor of a Miami high-rise apartment, Shelley aimed the long rifle at the building across the street. He pinned the cross hairs on the face of the pretty young girl massaging the ass of the man she was with.

The girl looked sweet sixteen, not much more than a kid in the face, but that gorgeous body squirming on that bed looked like she'd lived those sixteen years ten times or more. The pretty young thing, all dressed up in her cute little face and her perfect little bones, could rip out a man's soul between heartbeats.

The beast reared its ugly head.

The girl's baseball tits did push-ups when she pulled the drapes apart, so he could see his mark. The man was hung like a horse, and the she-tramp, she was all smiles, squirming over that bed like a cold-blooded snake. She was slithering and coiling around that cock like it was the first course of a ten-course meal. In one choreographed motion, Shelley worried out the slack in the trigger and squeezed off a perfect shot. No one could shoot better.

The rifle jumped and spat out a dumdum. Jackie Pearson's head exploded in a red halo of blood and gore—and bullshit.

The girl leaped off the bed, her face matted with brain soup and skull bone—and bullshit. He turned from the window. The beast turned from the window and went lumbering back down into the deep caves of his mind, like Godzilla dragging back into the sea.

PART TWO

STANFORD

9

CANDICE BERGENS GRIPPED her Atlanta Braves baseball cap with her left hand to keep it pinned to her head, and she dropped the dollar token into the slot with her right.

Hurrying through the Lenox station turnstiles two steps in front of a WTNT-TV News camerawoman, she sprang onto the south-bound MARTA train just as the doors closed.

It was noon in Buckhead.

Before the MARTA train picked up cruising speed, Candice was already back to thinking about Shelley. Why did Shelley help the intruder escape from Stanford the night the plane crashed? Weren't they best friends? They fussed like husband and wife, or best friends, take your pick.

She had not learned a whole lot about the two middle-aged men from listening to hours of recordings made whenever Shelley was around. They never talked much about anything except things that happened when they were boys. There was a joyfulness about them, and there was also a lot of unspoken sadness and loneliness. At times, they seemed to be mothering each other, for lack of a better word.

She supposed that had to do with the fact they both grew up without their mothers. And she suspected a lack of motherly love was what made them such "hard" men, so to speak. Tenderness, as she knew it, had to come from the mother, and maybe something close to tenderness came from everyone else. She was an expert on tenderness; more specifically, the lack thereof.

Eavesdropping on Stanford had convinced her that he was too hurt, too broken up, almost suicidal, to have conspired to kill his wife and son. It just didn't happen. Sure, he could have hired someone like her—but not her. She would never kill a kid, no matter what. That was just dead wrong—killing a kid.

But Stanford could have had them killed, and he was now having second thoughts. But she suspected he didn't harbor too many second thoughts about anything.

Perhaps the Atlanta Public Library held answers to questions about Shelley as well as answers to questions about Stanford. But business first. Then her pleasures would follow. Later, she could find out what the big guy looked like, to see what he really looked like from the neck up. For that, a face shot would do the trick for her. But, for now, back to the business of business—and Stanford.

By 12:30 p.m., she sat alone in a lavender reading room at the Atlanta Public Library, curled up in a chair, reading and copying articles about Stanford Rome. Then she lined up the newspaper photo of Katie Kane side by side with the 5x7 snapshot of her own mother she brought along for that purpose. The family likeness was not only unmistakable—the two women could have been twins.

Well, well, what have we here?

Stanford's mother-in-law and her mother were twins. She and Stanford's dead wife were first cousins. Ain't that a hoot?

That mystery solved, she fled the library with a pound of copies and a plan of what to do next. She had to find out if Stanford had a woman on the side. That would be the most common motive for a man to dispense with his wife—but not necessarily dispense with his son, unless he was a sadist or something inhuman like that.

Most men, in her experiences anyway, had an "other woman" out there somewhere in their lives. She had gotten her hands on a guest list for the Lake Arrowhead banquet and had already talked to three of the twelve caterers who served dinner at the banquet. All three say they saw Stanford in the company of several women. One had openly flirted with him, which eliminated that woman. She was looking for an old flame, not a shameless flirt.

§

Two hours later, back at Lake Arrowhead, Candice drove to David Harte's cottage. She used her key to let herself in. She changed into running gear and strapped on her backpack. Then she took off jogging through the loblolly pines, her hair spilling from beneath her Atlanta Braves baseball cap.

Two miles later, she heard voices up ahead of her and stopped running. She stepped off the jogging path and hid behind some trees and shrubbery until she pinpointed the voices. Then she duck-walked into thicker growth and took out her binoculars.

She watched the men.

Sid, the Lake Arrowhead security chief, and two other guards were searching the grounds, hunting for something. A fourth man sat in a Jeep Cherokee; she couldn't see his face. One guard spoke to Sid then got into a second Jeep Cherokee and sped away.

A lazy breeze made the grasses quiver and soothed her moist skin in passing. Bored with watching the guards walking around with their eyes on the ground, her mind drifted back to the night the plane crashed. She'd been bombed out of her mind at David's place after having snorted the most wicked cocaine she'd snorted in years. She passed out on that huge wall-to-wall sofa.

When she woke up, David Harte was gone. She got pissed about that and left the deserted place.

Driving back to the Lake Arrowhead Hotel, she'd spotted a black Jeep Cherokee racing hellbent down the road toward Stanford's cottage. She doused her headlights and tailed the speeding Jeep. She parked in the thicket about a quarter of a mile away and ran the rest of the way. She got to Stanford's cottage just in time to see a big man put a martial-arts hold on Stanford's head and hold it until Stanford passed out. Then the big man heaved Stanford up on his right shoulder and hauled him inside the cottage.

Then the big man, and a man with a lame leg, and Sid, all three piled into the Jeep Cherokee and sped off. After they left, she went inside the cottage to check on Stanford. He was sleeping it off, so she left him there on the bed.

A loud ruckus jerked Candice's attention back into the present, back to Sid and the guards out there hunting for something.

One guard held up a stick. Dangling on the end was a dead snake. She looked down and scanned the ground around her feet then forgot about it. She was used to killing snakes. Sid yelled something, but she only caught the last two words: *duffel bag*?

Whatever they found, it was not what they were out there looking for, so they kept looking for it. The sun was drifting down toward the horizon, a red-pink-orange smudge streaking the sky. Bored again, Candice's mind drifted back to the past.

Since quitting the CIA seven years ago, she'd bought her way into ten beauty salons in six states. She became fifty-fifty partners with each owner, then she ran the business like she owned the whole shebang. She ended up remodeling the drab decor to her high-class standards before she slapped her name out front in hot, bright neon lights: Styles By Candy.

She ran in-house gyms where her spoiled patrons worked out and sweated. She installed plush lounges where her loyal but still quite-spoiled customers pampered themselves. Or they just simply hung out with their favorite soaps, alcoholic beverages, or daydreams. She ran her salons twenty-four, seven, and her motto told the whole story: We Never Open Because We Never Close.

Styles By Candy was her day job. Now she owned a beauty salon in twelve cities, and the head count for her night job was eleven men. But her night job was on hold for now; she had to take care of that matter for mother dearest. A loud hubbub snapped her thoughts back to now and the Lake Arrowhead security guards.

The man sitting in the Jeep Cherokee now stood outside. He wore a hard cast on his left leg. She wasn't sure but he looked like the same man she had seen at Stanford's cottage that night. The man turned, and she caught his profile and the sparkling diamond in his left ear lobe. That clinched it for her. She was certain he was the same man. That man was the intruder.

She frowned. Who were all these people masquerading as rent-a-cops? Drug smugglers? More memories—bad ones. She back-pedaled. Not spooked. Just worried.

Drug dealers were savages. They cut off your hands and threw away your fingerprints. They stuffed your own tits down your own throat to gag you, and to send a message. More bad memories.

Candy girl, you best pack it in and haul your ass up outta here.

10

TWOFER COUNTY

MONDAY, MAY 23

"WHAT ELSE DID you find out about Jocelyn Slade, Colt?"

Early Monday morning found Stanford back in Twofer County conferring with Colt at the Computer Shack.

"Give me a minute or two," Colt said and disappeared into the back room.

A drizzling rain fell outside in the bright sunshine. To country folks, that meant the devil and his wife were going at it again. Although the conflicted weather was considered a phenomenon in other places, it was quite a common sight in Twofer County. There was running commentary in other counties about more than a few devilish husbands in Twofer County getting beat up by their angelic wives.

For his own sanity, he had taken another day off from the office. He felt a change creeping up on him like a thief in the night. He felt himself changing—from what to what, he didn't have a clue. But he was certain someone would point those changes out to him sooner or later. Else, he would possibly never know he'd changed. It was just so hard to tell from the inside.

Too much was happening too fast right now.

Last week had started off all wrong. Monday, Clayton told him the FBI was off the case, and Jocelyn tried to corral him in the Twofer County dirt beds. Tuesday, Shelley dogged him. Thursday, Mark threatened him, and a plane limped over his cottage and crashed. Then two intruders, at least, rendered him unconscious, laid him out in his own bed like in a coffin and just left him there, otherwise unharmed. What more could possibly happen to him? His son had deserted him and flown off to Paris with his mother. QueenBee was hearing footsteps in the dark, and Shelley was becoming unglued.

Hello! What else was out there? Hey, bring it on.

Bored—he was not. Just distracted. And saving his strength for the hunt. He felt disconnected inside, unplugged. But he had to stay focused, and he knew that. Otherwise, it would become all too easy to tell the rest of the world to just "kiss off!" Then he would start his hunt for the killer and to hell with everyone else. He just had to stay focused for a while longer.

He relaxed his muscles and shuddered from the sudden release, the burst of tension fleeing his muscles.

The most troubling part of last week was Mark's threat.

The threat affected the livelihood of too many people for him to take the threat lightly. That was Mark's ace-in-the-hole. Despite all the rhetoric Mark spewed that day, Mark knew he was going to put his employees and his partners first. Mark knew he would do what he had to do to keep the $3-million Lake Arrowhead account. For sure, the threat worried him immensely more than even the FBI quitting the hunt worried him. He didn't understand why Mark would make such a threat. The dread of losing the Lake Arrowhead account felt like a dead horse in his chest. If he could only figure it all out. Mark's threat seemed more a smoke screen than anything else.

But a smoke screen to hide what from whom? Why would they turn him into an almost instant millionaire for a year's work? Was James already a rich man? If James owned stock in Lake Arrowhead, then there was a major conflict of interest for the firm.

He thought about all those things, but the real reason he'd come back to Twofer County was not to find out about Jocelyn Slade. He came back to revisit the crime scene.

"I'm ready," Colt said, tossing a paper towel in a wastebasket.

Stanford broke his reverie and turned his attention back to Colt.

"Your Jocelyn Slade," Colt said, "she once had herself a very serious medical problem."

"Oh?" he said. "How serious was it?"

"Kept her off the tube two months. I'll say pretty serious."

He remembered. It was about a year ago. "Tell me," he said.

"Well," Colt said, "she took this medical leave of absence, and the TV station's PR people dressed it up like it was a contract dispute that kept her off the air. That was a smoke screen. She and the TV station colluded to fool the public. Whatever she had, the treatment for it was on the pricey side. She yanked $400,000 from her savings and put zero dollars back. She paid all medical bills with cash money and took all medical records with her when she left the place. Her insurance company didn't even get involved. She carried the whole financial load on her own shoulders. Now, is that there strange or what?"

He whistled. That was a new one on him. He had never heard of such a thing. He whistled again.

"Could it have been cosmetic surgery?" he said. "A face-lift or something like that?"

Colt gave him a skeptical look. "Think about what you're saying."

He thought about it and nodded. "Yeah, Colt, you're right. What improvements could be made to that face. But it's still so weird."

"That it is, Stanford. So true. Weirdness also slams the door on snoops like me. No insurance company means no paper trail to follow. No paper trail means we don't know the name of Jocelyn Slade's mysterious sickness. But that's a small strange. I've got an even bigger strange for you. Jocelyn Slade, she ain't really Jocelyn Slade either."

"She changed her name," he said. "That's public knowledge."

"It's public knowledge that Jocelyn had changed her name from Alice Cooper. But the orphanage where she was raised—well, it burned to the ground eight years ago. Went down in the books as arson. All records went up in smoke. The state doesn't even have records for a Jocelyn Slade or records for an Alice Cooper. Alice Cooper's past died in that fire is what I'm saying to you, Stanford."

He cocked his head and smiled at his friend. Whenever Colt said, "what I'm saying to you," it meant there's something he was not saying to you. So you played along and asked what that something was.

"But what did you find in the ashes, Colt?" he said.

Colt leaned forward and whispered conspiratorially.

"I just got lucky; that's about all. Our Alice Cooper, the real one,

55

she went on a class field trip once. And she got an impacted tooth. The dentist she went to, well, this dentist had a 64K computer. So, I found out that back then Alice Cooper had *O* positive blood."

Colt milked the moment further before he said, "But, our Miss Jocelyn Slade, she's got a rare *AB* blood type."

"You mean—"

"I mean Jocelyn Slade is not Alice Cooper is what I mean."

"Jesus Christ," he said.

"She ain't him neither," Colt said, deadpan. "She's prettier."

§

The sun was out, the drizzle had slowed, and a rainbow was promised when Stanford left Colt's Computer Shack.

He drove past the cedar trees and the pine trees, and parked in front of Katie Kane's farmhouse. When he opened the front door of the house where they were killed, stale air hit him in the face.

He opened the drapes and stood there thinking about those same drapes being open the night Stacey and Christopher were killed. He turned his attention to the bed where Stacey had been strangled. The open drapes still gnawed at him. Stacey never slept with the drapes open. She was a chicken that way.

Digging his driving license from his wallet he knelt. He studied the spot where three months earlier he'd found a piece of rubber the size of a fingernail wedged under a sliver on the hardwood floor. The cops had missed it when they combed the place for evidence a month earlier. He'd taken snapshots of the rubber, front and back, then given half of it to Clayton.

The FBI lab said it came from a rubber glove surgeons used in operating rooms, and it had no tissue, blood, or chemicals on it.

He didn't find any more slivers to lift, so he put the plastic back into his wallet. He spent the next two hours going back over every square foot of the house, looking for a clue in a haystack.

In the hallway, he stared at the spot where Christopher was killed. What was the last thing his little boy saw just before the bullet blew out the back of his head? He still winced at the thought. The second thing that gnawed at him about that night was that his son's eyes were closed after he was dead.

The coroner told him Christopher's eyes had been closed about an hour after his body had cooled. That bothered him as well. His son's eyes were closed when he got there that night and found the bodies. He went over to the cherry bookcase and scanned the titles on the top and next two shelves. Stepping back, he scanned the titles on the fourth shelf down by his knees. He did a double take. He bent down and slipped a book from its slot.

A bible. A bible?

He rubbed his fingers across the soft cover, stroking it and wondering. This was a miscarriage of justice.

What was a bible doing in Katie Kane's house?

He opened the Holy book. The stiff pages groaned with newness. Katie Kane did not keep religious books or guns on her property. His mother-in-law posted warning signs all over her property. His favorite read:

No Guns Or Bibles Allowed On This Property.
Violators Will Be Preached At Then Shot At!

How had he missed seeing the bible all the other times he'd scanned the books? Maybe some mean-spirited soul had only recently placed the bible there to mock his dead mother-in-law, or perhaps some well-meaning Christian had planted it.

But the reality was that the reason he'd overlooked the bible was the same reason the cops had overlooked the piece of surgeon glove—short attention span.

He had to do better.

He bent down to examine the space the book occupied.

The empty space was free of dust, which meant the bible had been there all the time. The bible was sandwiched about three inches farther back than the two larger books surrounding it.

He took the bible to the dining table and switched on the overhead light. He examined the faint smudge on the spine of the Holy book. Using Katie Kane's magnifying glass, he took a bigger look at the smudge.

He lightly touched the tiny ridges with his fingertips.

The impressions felt like and looked like swirls of a fingerprint.

11

AT ROME, KELSEY & Lang, CPAs, Janay buzzed to tell Stanford that Mark Davis had arrived for his appointment. A shot of adrenaline surged through him like electricity, and that was a bad sign. For Mark. For him. For the future of the firm.

"Give me a few minutes, Janay," he said. "I'll let you know."

Standing at the window, he stared down onto Peachtree Street, rubbing the nape of his neck, thinking about the plane crash. But what worried him most of all was the intruder, and the fact the stupid move he made hadn't gotten him killed. He had been feeling mighty low. That accounted for his own stupidity. What about the intruder's stupidity? Why did the intruder let him get the drop on him like that? Maybe he wasn't the only one with a death wish that night. Strange.

When he woke up, the intruder was gone and had left behind no signs he had even been there.

He still hadn't told anyone about the intruder, not a soul, and he still couldn't say why he hadn't.

He took one last look out over the Atlanta skyline and turned around to go deal with Mark Davis. It would not be pretty.

Mark Davis wore bright Arthur Ashe LetNet sneakers on his feet and dark rings under his big brooding eyes. They sat in armchairs at right angles to each other. Mark was cordial and tried hard to make peace, but he was having none of it. He wanted Mark to remove the threat, then they would make the peace.

"You've made your point, Mark." He spoke evenly. "I will not serve as president of Lake Arrowhead. To do so would mean I'll have to resign as managing partner. It won't happen. I owe you my loyalty as your CPA, as you so eloquently stated, but you don't have the right to tell me I must resign my firm to run your firm."

Mark was seething but controlling it. He could see the effort it took for Mark not to explode.

"You'll sink both ships, RKL and Lake Arrowhead, just to hunt a killer neither the GBI nor the FBI can find? Come on—"

Mark backed off the trigger and gave him a pitying look. There were hints of moisture in his eyes—crocodile tears of frustration. The croc was unable to swallow his victim whole.

"I'm such an asshole, Stanford. I'm not even listening to you. For a second there, I actually put myself in your shoes, and there was just no way I wanted to walk a mile in those shoes. I mean what man would not want to do what you're going out there to do. I can't imagine you not doing what you're doing. But, Stanford, can't you do what you have to do, and leave us in a position to keep doing what we're doing?"

Mark spread his arms in a gesture of openness. "I mean, our two companies feed a lot of mouths and pay a lot of mortgages in this town. You have to do what you have to do. I got that now. Believe me. I got that now. But, Stanford, so do we. We have to keep doing what we're doing, and we have to grow to do it. Now, to grow, Richard and I have rolled the money dice big time. Maybe, we were rash—hell, let's be real. We were rash, taking you for granted, not consulting you about our plans. That was my blunder, not Richard's, but all mine."

A half-smile tightened Mark's lips.

"As you pointed out, I am demanding that you resign from your firm to run our firm. That's past arrogance. That's mega-arrogance. I understand that. So, let's do this, why don't we.

"Why don't you hire you two of the finest private investigators in the country, not in Atlanta, but in the whole country. Hire them to do the grunt work; hire the pros. And Lake Arrowhead will pay the freight, the whole kit and caboodle. I guarantee it. We'll set up an escrow account, and it won't drop below six figures."

He couldn't believe what he heard. And that was Mark's intent, though the attorney's sincerity was as plain as the strain on his face.

"Stanford, you can't beat that with a stick."

He looked away from Mark. It was still more of the same thing. Just another attempt by Mark to change his mind. He looked at Mark again and saw disbelief etched in his strained face. The attorney's confidence had begun to shrivel.

"Whoa," Mark said, throwing up his hands, "don't say a word." Mark lowered his hands. "Why don't you just think on it, Stanford. Think on it. Talk it over with your partners. Talk it over with your wi—Ah, Mary, mother of Christ, I'm sorry, Stan—"

"Forget it, Mark. I make the same mistake; me thinking I still have a wife."

Mark paled, as if all the blood had drained from his face; that could not be faked. What trouble could they be in when they had 500 extra, extra large in the bank? Mark was full of crap. Money may not buy you love, but money could surely buy you freedom from the stress Mark was suffering. He looked genuinely pained.

"Alright, Stanford," Mark said, "just think on it, and I'll call you, later, in a few days. Okay, Stanford?"

He nodded. "Sure thing, Mark."

§

After Mark Davis left his office, Stanford still felt stressed. He sat on his office sofa and leaned his head back, closing his eyes for a breather. Tomorrow, he started the challenge of becoming a single parent again.

That meant manipulating, cajoling, threatening, housing, promising, pleading, wishing, compromising, encouraging, feeding, loving, clothing, hugging, punishing, nursing, transporting, educating, scrutinizing, trusting, distrusting, bullying, exploiting, kidding, horse-playing, learning, understanding, and whatever else it took to teach, discipline and live with a teenage son. Yes, tomorrow, he would sign the lease on a downtown Atlanta loft he and Stanley would call home this summer. Just the two of them.

He covered his face with his arms and sank deeper down into the cushions. He thought again of Mark's unbelievable offer.

Events in his life were becoming so weird, and he felt so alone.

But, really, what would a private detective do that the FBI and the GBI hadn't already done? Private investigators would be more of the same thing. Someone needed to try something the FBI, the

GBI, and the locals hadn't tried. Someone needed to try something new. That someone had to be him, and not private detectives. He didn't know what new something he would try this time around, but he would know what that new something was once he tried it. He rolled over onto the floor and stood. He made his way over to the window.

A weariness moved in on him, creating a weakness in his gut, as a lump of sadness settled in between his heart and his stomach.

§

At Lake Arrowhead, Richard Stoole took in his friend's worsening mood. Ever since Mark got back from meeting with Stanford, he'd been in a funk. He figured Mark had just learned something about Stanford Rome he, himself, had learned years ago.

Stanford Rome didn't have one forgiving bone in his body.

Piss Stanford Rome off today, and Stanford would still be pissed off tomorrow, and the next day, and the next day. Obviously, Mark had gotten himself squirted with a large dose of "Stanforditis," and he hated the taste.

Richard doubted Stanford even had a heart, despite being one of the nicest people he'd ever worked with before. He got no small pleasure out of knowing Stanford was a rock Mark had stubbed his big toe on. He could not understand why a white guy like Mark almost always made the mistake of underestimating a black guy like Stanford. On the other hand, a black guy like Stanford rarely made the mistake of underestimating a white guy like Mark.

Mark had "white man" disease. He underestimated the sophistication and tenacity of his black male counterpart.

"Richard," Mark said, "you give any thought to what we need to do about Miss Bitch over there?"

"Mark, I don't see why we should have to do anything. So what if your IRS snitch said Juanita requested a copy of Lake Arrowhead's tax returns? She's the one who filled them out, remember."

Mark stared at him but didn't answer. That meant he had missed a point in the conversation, a point Mark was trying to make.

He tried again to feel his friend out. "Mark, this is not about Juanita or the tax returns. This is still about Stanford, isn't it?"

Again no response from Mark.

"Mark, you just gotta get over your beef with Stanford. You were drunk and got a little too aggressive with him. Stanford is not one to be manhandled, as you obviously found out.

"So just get over it. We are here for a reason. We've got a debt to work off, remember? Me, I'm ready to blow this isolation camp and get back to real living. Mark, get over your beef with Stanford, and let us get on with what we gotta do. This isolation is for wild animals. I'm not so wild. I'm tamed. I want out of here. So, let's don't get bogged down in personality clashes with the natives."

"The bitch, she's snooping where she has no business snooping," Mark growled. "Now she knows something she shouldn't know."

Again, Mark hadn't listened to a word he said. Mark had let him say his piece, but had not heard a word. "And what's that, Mark?"

Mark looked at him with more than a little pity in his eyes. "That we don't file those tax returns she prepares for us. That's what."

"And how bad is that, Mark?"

"Damn bad. She'll know we file tax returns James prepares for Lake Arrowhead, not the ones she prepares, not the ones Stanford signs off on. She's in the loop; she shouldn't be in the loop."

He shrugged. "So what, Mark? Let's just let James Kelsey handle her the way he's always done. So what if she's snooping? Let her."

Mark snorted. "She's gotta go, and that's just the way it is."

"For crying out loud, Mark, she's a partner. She doesn't have to go anywhere. She owns a piece of the rock. This is no employee you're talking about here. This is Stanford's partner. Believe me on this, Stanford will not let you walk all over her. She's a woman—a black woman. He's a man—a black man. Stanford is not James Kelsey. Besides, Mark, we're law-abiding citizens. We ain't gangsters, okay?"

"Yeah, yeah," Mark growled again, "you go tell that to the man holding 500 extra large of our bad paper. That's what you do. You go tell that to Jocko Jitt, and see how far that gets you. Go tell that to Jocko Jitt."

§

"I hate dumb employees."

Juanita Robeson, the junior partner of Rome, Kelsey and Lang, CPAs, limped into partner Greg Lang's office. She eased the door shut behind her and slumped back wearily against it.

"I hate dumb employees. Dumb know-it-all employees I hate

most of all. I need some relief from all this aggravation."

Greg Lang spun away from his computer keyboard and stared at the tax partner from over the top of his wire-rimmed eyeglasses. Then he leaned back and clasped his pianist hands behind his neck like a pillow, and he grinned at her with even white teeth.

"You look awful, J. R. You been playing titty-grab with the IRS again?" Greg chuckled then flashed his TV grin again.

"Behave yourself, Gregory," she said, pointing her finger. Greg was such a machine person. She knew a few computers with more human qualities in their off-on switches than Greg had in his entire six-foot frame. But she'd entered Greg Lang's space with a mission to carry out. She'd come to find out where Greg stood on Mark Davis' threat to dump the firm as their CPAs. She intended to do exactly that before Greg got under her skin so bad, it would jeopardize the mission.

Greg said, "J. R., a long face, no matter how pretty the face, will not change Stanford's mind about leaving the firm and going back down there to Twofer County. I know why you're here. So, let's get at it."

She groaned and pouted. "We have to stop him, Gregory; don't you see that?"

"Now, J. R., whining gets you nowhere." Greg beamed that TV grin again. "Be real, J. R., we're just glorified bookkeepers in the scheme of things. And I've got a news flash for you. Neither do we eat at the top of the food chain. Besides, the FBI's off the case, and it's just killing Stanford, being here and not out there acting like Steve McQueen in 'Wanted Dead or Alive.' A man's gotta do what a man's gotta do, J. R. That's the law of the male gene."

"That's testosterone hogwash," she shot back. "We need Stanford here. Right here. We're still catching up from the two months he took off to look after Stacey's poor mama before she left us."

"J. R., J. R.," Greg cried out, clucking his tongue. "Stanford, he was hunting the killer; that's why he was down there two months. Besides, her mama was comatose. The old woman was in a coma. She could've done ads for Campbell Soup—she was a veggie."

"You—You insensitive lil' brat," she said, stopping herself from slapping him silly. She was scared she would break those fragile-looking bones in his face. "Gregory, you're so despicable. Stanford, he cares for people; Stanford, he stayed down there until she passed away, and—"

"Your euphemisms are too nice, J. R.," Greg said. "People, they don't leave us. People, they don't pass away. People, they die, they croak, they drop dead, but people, they never ever pass away or leave us, J. R."

She clenched her teeth, peeled herself away from the door and plowed ahead with her plan. "About Mark's threat?" she said. God, she was tired. "Your thoughts on that, Gregory?"

Greg shrugged his bony shoulders up to his ears almost, then he leaned back in his hydraulic chair. The light dimmed in her partner's eyes, and the TV grin had receded into his mouth for a checkup. He was finally getting serious, and Greg Lang, at times, rare as they were, could become very serious.

"Well, J. R., the way I see that is this way. We need to add a $3-million client, not lose one. Technology is passing us by. We're still doing too many things the old-fashioned way. In some ways, we're still using the old tried-and-true hammer and chisel."

Greg spread his arms. "Hey, J. R., the bigger this joint gets, the better my chances of getting my greedy little hands on bigger and better machines to tinker around with. That's bottom line for me. I would hate to lose a $3-million client, for sure. I would hate it as much as I would hate losing a thumb. Hell, there are CPA firms in this town cutthroat enough to kill me, you, Stanford, and James for a plum client like Lake Arrowhead. I support James on this one. I lust for bigger and better whistles and bells around this joint. And I'd rather stick my hand up a constipated alligator's rump than to run off a $3-million client, believe me."

She snorted her disapproval. "I guess you're saying we shouldn't sue the city for our $60,000 either. Since you favor caving in to outside pressure and all, I guess Atlanta can keep our sixty grand. Is that your thinking, Gregory?"

"I ain't that generous," Greg said, looking up, studying the ceiling for a three-count before leveling his don't-mess-with-me gaze back on her. Oh, boy, maybe she had pushed him too far. He was tough and no pushover, or Stanford would have never added his name to the firm's letterhead.

"J. R., You should be very particular about what you ask for—

but since you asked, I see that like this. Since black folks started running the airport out there, white folks have called it a nest of thieves and petty crooks. As a black man, I resent that to the core of my bones. That airport has always been a haven for thieves, and especially for white thieves. Those white CPAs, they saw the same crooked dealings back then that Stanford found and exposed. But those white CPA firms, they just collected their big audit fees and looked the other way."

Greg cackled and shook his head.

"Hell, J. R., even Ray Charles could have seen all those sweet-heart deals, the double dealings, and the kickbacks going on out there at the airport when good 'ol white folks were running things out there. When RKL audited the airport, we didn't whitewash the sweetheart deals like the white CPAs did when white folks were stealing. We exposed those black thieves for what they were. In our eyes, thievery's colorblind.

"Stanford nailed their asses but good. And when the city stuck its nose in to defend those crooks, Stanford told the mayor and the council to go fly a kite. I liked that. Loved it. Stanford, he's a stand-up dude. That took guts, standing up to pressure like that. And now the sons-of-bitches won't pay us our paper. But—"

Greg sighed and went back to gazing up at the ceiling like it was the *Sistine Chapel* in Technicolor.

"But what, Gregory?"

Greg lowered his eyes again. "But, today, I wouldn't put this firm through the hassle of fighting that airport gang. Frankly, today, I'll just take that $60,000 check and run like hell down to the bank to cash it. We've got better things to do than to stand around pissing in the wind with bootlicking politicians who all get a regular pay-check. We don't get a regular paycheck around this joint. We've gotta meet a $60,000 payroll every two weeks around here before me, you, James, and Stanford get one red cent. We gotta bust our balls—," Greg grinned, "and bust our ovaries around here—"

"But, Greg—"

"No buts, J. R. When I was a boy, I worked in chicken houses, and fighting Atlanta politicians is like slipping and sliding around in chicken shit. Black-and-white chicken shit is the worst shit—"

"Stop grossing me out, Gregory. Please."

"Well, J. R., it's my opinion that Stanford can do us all a big favor if he'd just go run Lake Arrowhead for a year as their president. That would give us the time we need to get over the hump, so in the future, threats like Mark's won't make us or break us."

"Gregory, we can't let our clients threaten us," she said.

"J. R., you asked my opinion and bam—there it is. I don't wanna bust butt replacing a $3-million client we lost because our fearless leader took a leave of absence instead of taking a vacation. That's what Gregory Hines Lang is about, J. R. I may be from a bump in the road called Cogdell, GA, but this good ol' South Georgia boy still dream his big dreams. I still dream of one day driving myself a Cray computer up and down this superhighway, and I ain't whistling Dixie neither, Bubba."

Her partner was back grinning again. Serious conversation over. Greg Lang: one. Juanita Robeson: zero.

She sighed, hugging herself. Now, she knew that Gregory had been sucking up to James Kelsey. "Okay, Gregory, I know where you stand. Now, tell me that you have a good friend working over at CapCity Investments."

Greg hunched his bony shoulders again. "I don't. But—hey, go ask Consy Torrey. I think his friend, you know—," Greg held up a limp wrist. "He runs the computers over there."

"Greg, you're as lame as your wrist."

"What the interest in CapCity, my lovely partner?" Greg said.

She gave him a coy smile and flicked a careless wrist. "Well, let me see. I keep running across the name CapCity a lot lately.

"How so, J. R.?"

"It's lending loads of money to over half our clients," she said.

Greg smiled. "Got another news flash for you, J. R. That's what investment companies do. Plow money into other companies."

"I know that. But it goes beyond investments in my opinion. But it's no big deal. Since they are such a big part of the balance sheet, we're going to give them a good looking-over anyway. I just want to get a head start. Now, can you help me out or not, Gregory?"

"J. R., hello—I told you about Consy Torrey's friend, remember that?"

"Oh, yes, you did." She pulled at her hair. "It's those damn dumb employees. They are driving me up the frigging wall."

Her partner was looking at her kind of funny. "What, Gregory?"

Greg Lang's eyes narrowed. "I was wondering. Since CapCity is James' pet client, this could also be about James Kelsey, right?"

Greg dropped his feet down to the floor. "Juanita, shouldn't you and James kiss and make up? I mean, we've got a lot going on around this joint; we really do need to stick together."

Juanita studied the sincere and thoughtful look on Greg Lang's face. She said, "Greg, that's another battle. Let's fight that one to-morrow. Me, I'm going to hotfoot it on home, pour me a glass of warm wine, and cuddle up to my cold remote."

§

Dissolve the firm.

Stanford couldn't believe James Kelsey threatened to dissolve the firm if he took another leave-of-absence. That threat was a hard swallow. When James cut and run, Greg Lang would cut and run, too. James Kelsey, the rat, he's abandoning a sinking ship.

He swallowed hard a third time, now massaging his throbbing temples with his fingertips. He looked at his desk and over at the credenza. He had tons of work to do. The stack of audit reports he had to review and sign loomed as tall as Stone Mountain before his tired eyes. Now, not only did he have to deal with Mark's threat. Now he had to deal with James' threat. He was certain Mark pressured James Kelsey to pressure him. That was why James Kelsey threatened to dissolve the firm if he took another leave of absence and lost the Lake Arrowhead account.

To hell with Mark. To hell with James.

He opened the cover of an audit report, and soon his anguish dissolved peacefully into his work.

Two hours later, a frowning Juanita Robeson poked her head in Stanford's doorway. "Hey, get a life."

He smiled at her frown and shut down his office for the night.

During this morning's partners' meeting when he told them that he was taking another leave of absence, he saw the hurt look on Juanita's face. Of the three other partners, she was the one most able and willing to take his place as managing partner. James Kelsey hated the responsibility of running the day-to-day operations, and Greg Lang hated any work not connected to a computer.

But James Kelsey disliked Juanita Robeson, so the two months he was gone, nobody really ran the show. The firm limped along. And it took him two months of sixteen-hour days to right the listing ship once he returned from that first leave of absence.

"Here's one for the books," Juanita said, shattering his reverie. "I get this letter from the IRS. They're asking us to resubmit Form 6115 that had been illegible on the tax return. But when I checked our record, I find out that we did not send a Form 6115 in the first place. I asked the IRS to send us a copy of the tax return. But the jerks up in Chamblee told me my POA was invalid. And you know why it was invalid? Well, because Lake Arrowhead filed a consolidated tax return, and not the tax return I prepared for them. So my question is this: are we their CPAs or aren't we their CPAs? In other words, in ghetto-speak, what's up with them?"

"But, Juanita, why did the Feds notify us? The consolidated tax return would not have had our address on it."

"I just assumed the obvious; that it was just another bureaucratic SNAFU. Do you think there's something sinister going on here beyond my own suspicions?"

He shrugged. "I doubt it. But I'll give Henry Finch a call and find out what it's all about."

He glanced at the clock and picked up the telephone.

"Who's Henry Finch?" Juanita said.

He shrugged again. "He's a multiethnic. White on the outside, yellow on the inside, and shot black through and through. Actually, he's the guy who's going to tell me the name of the company that filed a consolidated tax return with Lake Arrowhead."

"Good to know. Stanford, I'm telling you. There is something screwy about that outfit. I smell it. They are just too smooth."

He shrugged a third time. "Proof, Juanita. That's what we CPAs are all about. Proof. Otherwise, James Kelsey would have long ago chewed me up and spat me out in little bitty pieces."

"And we most surely can't have James Kelsey putting you in his mouth. Now, can we?" Juanita said and grinned.

"We sure can't," he said.

For a blink, a sleazy look glowed in Juanita's dark eyes. She was telling him something without really telling him something. He knew that to be Juanita's way of gossiping without really gossiping.

"Okay, tomorrow," Juanita blurted out, as if reading his mind and waylaying his curiosity. "If I live and nothing bad happens."

She got in her car, started the engine, and powered the window down.

"One of these Sundays, Stanford, you should come to church with me. Couldn't hurt, you know. Might help."

He smiled. "Take care, Juanita."

He watched the car vanish around the corner. He wished his two warring partners would kiss and make up. Well, at least make up. He rubbed the nape of his neck and thought about her. Now he had to go meet a woman he'd been successfully dodging for four months now. But he could no longer dodge her because this time she'd nailed his butt down—but good.

§

From her perch in the shadows, Candice Bergens watched Juanita and Stanford. Was she the other woman, the goose to Stanford's gander? When Stanford left the garage, a dark sedan crept from the shadows and followed him.

Candice followed the dark sedan following Stanford.

What have we here?

What have we here indeed!

12

TUESDAY, MAY 24

TARTUFFE JITT LOOKED like hell warmed over twice. He kept seeing images of his father flashing before his eyes.

He kept seeing images of Jocko Jitt.

He leaned back against the damp rock wall. Drawing his knees under his chin, he locked his arms around his legs and continued to suffer. He wished he was already burning up in hell. But he was not burning up in hell. He was still waiting to die. There was such a long wait between waiting to die and actually walking through those gates of hell.

He rarely slept, fearing he would not see death coming for him. He wanted to see death come for him. Shackled in semi-darkness twenty-four hours a day had driven him close to the edge. One of these mornings, those animals were going to drag him out in the courtyard, and tie him up to a hitching post so he couldn't move, and slice off his eyelids so he couldn't blink. Then those animals were going to shoot him in the head and make him dead.

He had the routine down pat. He had heard the screaming, the shooting, and the dying. He knew what to expect.

These people were no joke.

These were evil people.

These Nigerian soldiers were the ultimate madmen.

Tartuffe felt like a big sardine stuffed down in a small tin can. His mind was feeding on itself, quick little nibbles and bites. Soon there would be nothing left slouching around inside his skull but liquefied insanity. Nothing left over to kill. Now, more than ever he wanted his mommy. A mommy was all he ever wanted from life. He'd never known a real mommy. A nanny had always cared for him in a nine-to-five way. He thought that was the normal way to grow up until he butted heads with real normalcy. He attended boarding schools, and that was okay. Summers and holidays were times enough to hang around with a father like he had, a father like Jocko Jitt.

He had never known he had a living mother until just three years ago. The truth was blurted out when he and Jocko got into one of their many confrontations. The latest setback in their fragile relationship happened all because he refused to go to Atlanta to run Lake Arrowhead for Jocko. Then Jocko had slapped him in the face with the cold, awful truth. Jocko bragged to him that his mother had not died in childbirth. Jocko had lied to him all those years about his mother.

Jocko told him his mother was alive. That was bad enough.

Then Jocko said that his mother had never wanted to see him. That was when he snapped for real. But hitting Jocko in the mouth turned out to be a mistake—a big mistake. The old man surprised him. Shocked him really. Jocko was old. Jocko's muscles were old. Jocko's mind was old. Jocko's movements were slow. But he still had to settle for a draw with a man twenty-five years his senior. He wanted to throw up.

That happened three years ago. They talked a few times on the telephone, but he hadn't seen Jocko since then and hadn't wanted to see him. Until now.

Grand images of his father kept circling his brain, his magnificent father riding at the head of a calvary coming to rescue him from the gates of hell. Now he would be thrilled to death to run to Atlanta to run Lake Arrowhead for Jocko. Again he was aware of the plop-plop of the water drops. He squinted to see beyond the semi-darkness. His seeing brain cells were mostly dead or retarded. Shafts of light piercing the gloom lit up human shapes strung up and down the long craggy room. Here he was, a rich man's son buried inside a Nigerian rock prison with fifty starving prisoners like himself.

Plop-plop went the water drops.

Water dripped continuously through the rock crevices.

But he had learned to turn off the sounds like he had a built-in switch to do it with. He had changed a lot, especially his thought processes. He even liked some of the many changes in himself. He kept squinting in the direction the sound kept coming from. He couldn't see much. The dim light bulbs cast more shadows than light. A good thing, too, because who wanted to see the misery of men claiming only twenty square feet of space in which to eat, to sleep, to be miserable.

But he was very vigilant. The darkness was both hothouse and cloak for men and their dreams, for men and their fantasies and their madness, their sucking sounds, and their grunts. All through the lonely days and miserable nights, they stroked each other to sleep all nightlong.

Silence fell in the dungeon like a guillotine falling on a neck. The water drops exploded on the rocks like artillery shells falling on the troops. Then came the footfalls.

The massive middle door to the dungeon opened up. New air rushed in ahead of two soldiers toting machine guns. The soldiers took up threatening positions facing in opposite directions. Guns were not really needed down in the dungeon. Few, if any, prisoners had the strength necessary to do more than resist the force of gravity to stand from a sitting position.

In popped a pompous third soldier with two stars pinned on each shoulder. The general stepped beyond his two underlings to speak.

"Good evening, gentlemen," the general said, clasping his hands behind his back like a black Napoleon.

"Bad for you. You broke Nigerian law. We will punish you. We will shoot you. But good for you. Justice is so slow here in our country. So a relative has been contacted for you, and this relative will come free you from your troubles."

The general scowled, did an about-face and strutted out. The two soldiers fumbled through a poor imitation of the same maneuver and stumbled after their leader.

The heavy door closed.

"What you in for?" the voice of darkness wanted to know.

Tartuffe didn't answer. He had no intentions of answering.

The voice continued.

"Me. I am here to pay for the sins of my father. An Igbo doctor, you see, he fought for our Igbo freedom. The soldiers, they got my father's name one day, and the soldiers, they came for my father one night. But my father was not home, so the soldiers, they took me. The oldest son, I must now pay for the sins of my father. It is written somewhere in the land that all sons must one day pay for the sins of the father. It's the way, I don't know. What you in for?"

The sins of the father, Tartuffe wondered. Was that why he was here, the sins of his father?

Life had been one of bliss and ease for him until he hooked up with Preacher. Jocko warned him to stay away from that Miami drug lord. But if Jocko was against Preacher, then how could he be anything but for Preacher. He was already in too deep before he knew Preacher also ran the best mule network in the southeast.

So when Preacher complained that small-time mules were nibbling his operations into a slow death, he persuaded Preacher to let him put a high-tech spin on his cocaine mules. He was first going to hookup each big shipment with a GPS.

That was when his troubles really started—a woman, no less.

He'd caught a red-eye flight from Miami back home to Paris when he bumped into tall, redheaded Victoria. It was love at first sight. She was the most gorgeous woman he'd ever seen. He ended up tailing Victoria to Lagos. There, at the airport, Nigeria's military police found $1-million of heroin stashed in her bags. The thuggish cops then beat him unconscious and dumped him inside their rock prison.

He imagined the police fed Victoria's fine corpse to the hyenas.

If he would have listened to Jocko. But, really, what son listened to his father—of all people? Every son knows that if a father were so wise, then why did he have sex with the mother in the first place. Worse than even that, he knew Jocko's gangster past. He found it impossible to listen to a man who had once been a Kansas City mob boss—and all those nasty things that entailed.

After gambling, prostitution, loan-sharking, and crooked politicians made Jocko filthy rich, his father moved them to a North Miami Beach mansion.

There, Jocko secretly bankrolled deep-sea fortune hunters under the name of L. A. Trust. The business made Jocko one of the richest men in Dade County. Still, the old-monied Miami rich snubbed Jocko and his very successful L. A. Trust.

But being a quick study, it hadn't taken Jocko long to see that he had yet to succeed much in the world if all he had to show for it was mere money. Jocko had to do something big. Big and daring, like solving a huge problem plaguing society in a big way.

In the meantime, he, himself, graduated college and law school.

For eight years after finishing law school, he had climbed the corporate ladder, jet-setting all across Europe, his happy feet firm-ly planted in Paris, the City of Lights. Then, at thirty-two, he got his first $200,000 annual trust-fund check. He spent the past three years wallowing in the jolly lap of luxury. Now, he was shackled to a rock wall, his glitter world as stage a galaxy away now from where he lay. But Jocko would come for him. Then, he would gladly fly to Atlanta to run Lake Arrowhead for his daddy.

Images of Jocko riding at the head of a calvary hurrying to res-cue him from this madness kept circling his brain.

A decrepit man waddled toward him wearing just enough rags for a G-string. The man squatted beside him. Looking like a fox, the man's head looked frail like an eggshell. His skin looked like melted wax.

"You American, right, chap?" the Fox said.

He was startled but nodded slightly, not knowing who to trust.

"Was she redhead or blond?" the Fox said.

He placed his lips close to the Fox's ear, whispering. "What you mean?"

"The girl. The one with you when you got pinched. Don't you know, chap? You been grabbed. Snatched for bloody ransom. Two million yanks, or they shoot you full of holes at dawn."

He squinted at the waxy-looking man. Kidnapped? Had Preach-er set him up to somehow get back at Jocko for some old grudge? He doubted it, but he HAD been set up. The only question was a simple one: who did it?

A bitter bile leaked into his throat.

But if not Preacher, then who? Stretching out his long legs, he tugged his chin with his left hand.

Without warning, the door opened up.

Two soldiers strutted in, one carrying a rifle, and one carrying a pistol and a blackjack. The first soldier stopped directly in front of

Tartuffe and swung the blackjack at his head. He ducked and the soldier missed with the blackjack. When the first soldier reloaded for another swing, the Fox flung his puny body at the soldier and floored him. The second soldier cracked the rifle butt across the Fox's egghead.

The blow was the most sickening sound Tartuffe had ever heard.

The first soldier fired at the Fox but the bullet missed its target. The bullet ricocheted. The soldier aimed for a second shot at the Fox, but Tartuffe lashed out with a foot.

His kick cracked into the soldier's throat and snapped the man's head back hard.

Then his own head exploded in pain. He dropped in a heap.

13

STANFORD SPED DOWN I-85 South for the airport. After nearly four months of trying, the woman had finally nailed his butt down—but good. He begrudgingly thought about her.

If she were not Alice Cooper, then who in the hell was Jocelyn Slade?

He cruised under the huge jets now roaring overhead for touchdown at Atlanta Hartsfield International Airport. A scattering of powerful light beams bounced and glittered off all the sleek metal birds. A big lumbering Lufthansa Lockheed L-1011 screamed overhead seconds in front of a Delta McDonnell Douglas MD-88. And circling as far out as thirty miles, more big jets lined up to land at one of America's busiest airports.

Stanford wheeled the sedan down into the underground parking garage, Level 2N, and whipped into the first vacant space near the wall. He sat there, deciding what to do next, his mind churning out questions about what this woman really wanted to see him about. He was certain it had something to do with Shelley and, if so, he had to alert QueenBee, as she had insisted he do. The car headlights across from him flickered once.

He took a deep breath, again wishing he hadn't come, and got out. He went over to the Jaguar, opened the door, and slid down onto the soft leather seat.

Jocelyn Slade beamed at him so warmly he almost smiled back. Almost. Instead, he nodded and buckled up.

The Jaguar fled the airport like a bat out of hell, west on Camp

Creek Parkway and racing hard for the Loop. Suddenly, the car shot from sixty to ninety in a gasp, Jocelyn threading traffic, in and out, a few miles before backing off the throttle.

"In case we're being followed," she explained.

When his partner Greg Lang first moved to Atlanta from South Georgia, Greg talked about the major expressways as if they were extensions of NASCAR. He called Interstate 85, I-8500; he called Interstate 75, I-7500; and he called the Loop, I-28500. Greg said he so named them in honor of Atlanta's favorite pastime—speeding.

He settled back and tried losing himself inside the aching blues of Billie Holiday. Lady Day was letting the whole world know that her man just didn't love her anymore.

Jocelyn sped them out beyond the Loop and into Cobb County, past Dobbins AFB, hightailing it toward Dalton, the so-called carpet capital of the world. They rode in silence. He was now agreeing with the powerful voice of Wilson Pickett begging Sally to slow that Mustang down. From where he sat, he sensed Jocelyn's unease. Whatever was going through that creative mind of hers was powerful stuff. Headlights from oncoming cars illuminated the tension that was bundled like ropes of gold in her face.

He didn't want to tear his eyes away from her face. Even if the flesh melted away from that face, leaving behind just a skull, the skull would still be beautiful. Jocelyn's beauty was etched in the structure of her bones—her beauty was bone-deep.

Even as he thought those thoughts, he shied away from her. She was nothing but trouble. All his senses told him so. She was nothing but trouble to him.

The shadows of her cheeks flowed down into her chin, and her hazel eyes were set hard under a brow shaped secure like a ledge on a cliff. Jocelyn was all things beautiful in a woman. But he refused to fall under her spell. What choice did he have, really?

"Thanks for coming," Jocelyn said and broke his reverie. "I hate playing hardball. Be a gentleman and believe me on that."

Her face was so easy on the eyes. He looked away.

Jocelyn kept glancing over at him every few seconds.

"You're not such a bad hardball player yourself," Jocelyn said. "You use your silence as viciously as we women use their tongues, and as recklessly, at times, I might add."

The tension in the car crackled and popped like a downed electrical wire in a rainstorm. He kept staring out the window, his muscles not as tensed as when he first sat down in that seat next to her.

"I can accept you avoiding me, Stanford." Her voice had a tinge of a tremor in it. "But I won't accept you not speaking to me."

He turned his head and looked at her to see if she was joking. Instead he saw resolution in her face. He saw fire-engine red.

"Listen, lady," he ground out the words, "when you sell yourself as a tramp, expect to be trampled."

The shocked look on her pretty face pleased him. In fact, he was so pleased with himself that he felt more than a little smug about what he'd said.

"Well, aren't we one moralistic SOB," Jocelyn said with emotion. "You're not much of a gentleman if you must resort to pointing out how much of a tramp I am. In fact, you're a butthole."

He leaned his satisfied head back on the headrest, ignoring her lightweight jab. They rode in complete silence awhile. Nearing Lake Allatoona, the first twinge of regret bit into his chest. A few miles farther, his regret had moved down from his heart into his stomach. He felt embarrassed by what he'd said to Jocelyn. Why was he so mean-spirited these days?

He cleared his throat. "Listen," he said, "will the tramp agree to go along if the butthole calls for a truce?"

Jocelyn slashed her eyes at him like switchblades, then turned those knives back to the road. They now rode to the thumping beat of The Commodores' "Brick House."

"Whatever the shitty butthole wants," Jocelyn finally said.

"Good," he said, nodding. "And thanks for the backhanded promotion from simple butthole to shitty butthole."

"It was a demotion," she said.

He slumped down in the seat just as the Rome exit zoomed past on the right. They rode in silence for a few miles. He felt the tension inside the car ease, and he was about to ask where they were heading when Jocelyn spoke up first.

"Stanford, why are you so pissed at me? I—I mean, if you blame me for what happened, then just say you do."

Jocelyn's voice quivered but didn't crack. "Just say you blame me.

78

Just say we were just having too much fun together. Just say if it hadn't been for me, maybe you would have been there for them that night. Just say you blame me and get it over with. I can accept blame from you. But, God, I can't accept rejection from you. Blame, yes. Rejection, no. Go ahead and say you blame me."

He didn't speak.

"Say it, damn you." Her soft voice was demanding. "Just say it."

He kept his eyes closed. He didn't really blame her. Now, for the first time, it was clear in his mind why he agreed to meet with her. There was something he just had to know, besides whether she was investigating Shelley or writing a story about Shelley. He opened his eyes and turned his head to look at her.

"Jocelyn…?"

He waited for her to glance at him. Then before he continued, he aimed each one of his seeing brain cells at her face.

"Jocelyn, who hired you to keep me there that night for as long as you could keep me there? Who were you working for?"

Jocelyn shot him her most puzzling look so far.

But the puzzled look was all wrong. She should not have looked puzzled. She should have looked shocked, or maybe insulted—but not puzzled.

"Stanford, what on earth are you talking about? I was trying to seduce you that night. Wasn't that blatantly obvious?"

"So you were just out to get laid; is that it?" he said.

A shocked look squeezed Jocelyn's face as if she'd bitten into a forbidden fruit. "And what's wrong with getting laid?" she said.

He didn't answer her. But he sure felt better. Now she looked shocked and insulted. Good. Boy, was he a butthole, for real.

She glanced at him again, her eyes reflecting light like jewels.

"Stanford, FYI, I have wanted to make a move on you for three years running. And until that night, I kept myself in check. But that night I flirted with you and didn't care who noticed. I wanted to come right out and say I'd gladly be your piece of ass on the side without any commitment from you at all. That I was very available to be your little plaything if that was all I could be to you. But, Stanford, I never dreamed you would end up hating me for it."

Jocelyn's lips crimped and quivered the same way Shelley's lips crimped and trembled when he got emotional.

"I love you, Stanford. I can't help that. Do you think I can help that? Well, I can't. Neither could you if the roles were reversed."

The words deflated him as if he were a balloon full of hot air and they were pinpricks. He let his head fall back onto the headrest, and his eyes close. He sat listening to the rubber tires speeding across the asphalt. They were now surfing the blacktop to the bluesy tune of Otis Redding's "Sitting on the Dock of the Bay."

For the first time in four months, one week, and one day, he felt little hostility toward Jocelyn Slade.

Eyes closed, he spoke; his words were light and soft and seemed to hover above his lips before floating away to Jocelyn's ears.

"I don't blame you, Jocelyn. I blame the killer."

He couldn't have felt lonelier if he'd been stranded in deep outer space somewhere else in the Milky Way galaxy. Here he was sitting by one of the most beautiful and desirable women in his world, and he felt alone. He was a sick puppy; that's what he was.

A sick puppy.

Is there a doctor in the house?

14

JOCELYN SLADE HAD never before sat so proud in her Jaguar.

Cruising up I-75, she was high enough to have imagined sitting behind the wheel of a Learjet 31 cruising five miles high. It was as if the halves of her brain once disconnected were now joined again. All because Stanford Rome was now sitting close enough to her that she could just reach over and hug his neck. And, God, how she wanted to just reach over and hug that man's neck.

She felt whole, having Stanford so near to her. She had never met such bullheaded resistance from a man before, even one so heartbroken as her Stanford Rome. Yes, she was claiming him.

Stanford was hers. She wanted to help Stanford get over all his hurt. She knew damn well how to work magic on that testosterone slouching around inside any man. She was just so happy she told him how she felt about him. And what made her happier still was that he hadn't rejected her outright. He hadn't told her, "I love you, too," which is what any woman really wanted to hear after telling a man she loved him. But he did say he didn't blame her. That wasn't exactly, "I love you, too," but it was still four words, and the words even sounded alike.

"I love you, too" did sound like "I don't blame you."

The Jaguar seemed to be cruising the blacktop on a ribbon of helium, and the machine was chewing up the miles with a hunger bordering on ravenous. Stanford hadn't spoken since he said he didn't blame her. That was a big relief. But she knew expressing her love had been the right words to say.

She also knew that timing was everything in the ways of love.

She glanced over at Stanford again.

"Stanford, have you heard of a company called Life Jackets?"

Stanford reached over and turned down the volume on the radio. "A condom company, right; and you own half?"

She was both surprised and pleased that he'd been checking up on her. Expending energy like that definitely showed he had an interest in her.

"Well," she said, "I do own half the company. But Life Jackets, it's more than a condom company; it's a safe-sex company. I want you to audit the books for me. Can you handle that?"

They rode in silence for a minute or two. What was he thinking about over there? He'd done his homework on her. Her half ownership was hidden under two layers of lawyers and a holding company. But he'd gone behind that wall. He was checking up on her. That was what a woman really wanted to know, that her man was interested in her enough to check our her credentials. That was an investigative stage all careful men went through, and a careful man like Stanford was indeed her cup of tea.

"You suspect someone's stealing the company's rubbers?" Stanford said and shrugged. "A rubber robber, perhaps?"

"Wow," she said, "humor from a CPA; that's refreshing."

Stanford didn't say anything. He just sat there.

She glanced over at him. He wasn't smiling. He was not joking.

"No, not thievery," she said. "Let's just say, I'll much rather chew on push pins than face another IRS audit. Last year, Life Jackets lost, I'm told, about $500,000. I want that loss corroborated before I put my half, a $250,000 loss, on my tax return. You see, in my other life, the IRS audited me, and things got ugly. I hired two tax lawyers, one to keep me from paying more taxes and one to get back taxes I'd already paid. But, in the end, they were bulldogs, and I came out ahead. What's your fee for something like that; an audit, I mean?"

"Depends," Stanford said. "Tell me more."

They kept talking about Life Jackets, and she kept loving the moments. She was so happy—no, better than so happy, she was so thrilled, and she felt so loved. Just having Stanford's undivided attention was exhilarating to her. He explained what an audit was and what an audit wasn't. Things were going her way. Really going her way. And then she let her enthusiasm get the best of her, and she blew it. She blew it big-time.

"Stanford, are you seeing anyone?" she said, out of the blue.

"That's none of your business," Stanford said, his voice arctic.

"Then, are you fucking anyone?" she said.

The buzzing tires sped across the asphalt.

"I'm celibate," Stanford said, three whole minutes later.

"No kidding," she said and shot him a dubious look. "Then, who's Claudia from LaGrange?"

She wanted to reach up and yank out her own hair. She'd said the wrong thing and knew it. She wanted to snatch the words right out of the air and stuffed the little buggers right back inside her mouth where they belonged. The sinking feeling in her stomach slowly sank down to smother the glowing warmth in her loins.

Stanford gave her a look so cold it instantly depressed her.

"She's a married woman," Stanford said. Each word shot from his mouth like a bullet shot from a gun.

"The husband is impotent," she shot back. She lacked the guts to back away from a fight, even from a man she didn't want to drive away. "They're separated as well," she added. She just could not hush her mouth. Maybe her old boyfriend Bryce Boyd was right. She just didn't know when to put a cork in it. But he started it.

Stanford shot icicles at her, his eyes as cold as any eyes she'd seen before. "Why are you spying on me, woman?"

"For one, my name's Jocelyn Slade. Helen Reddy was woman. For two, I don't spy, I investigate. Like I'm investigating Shelley."

Boy, was she on one hell of a roll, doing what she did better than any woman—driving a man away from her. But, no turning back now. Damn the sex and full-speed ahead in screwing yourself.

"Speaking of whom," she said, hitting him right where it would hurt the most, "what exactly does Shelley do for our good governor these days? Isn't Shelley a bodyguard and not some troubleshooter the governor says he is? And what's between our bachelor governor and the *grand dame* of Twofer County?"

Boy, she was on a roll.

Stanford slumped in the seat, and she felt those cold eyes melt into puddles of slush. He stared ahead as he spoke to her.

83

"Jocelyn Slade, you listen to me. Shelley is grief you don't need in your life. No payday from WTNT-TV is worth the aggravation of tangling with that man." Then Stanford turned almost menacingly and studied her face until she blushed before he finally spoke.

"If you cause Shelley any more grief than he's already suffering, I'm going to turn this country upside down and shake it. And I'm going to keep shaking it and shaking it until I find out who the hell you really are. Then, we'll negotiate on whether or not I'll spread the news."

She shot him a dirty look, and she would have shot him a bullet if she had a gun—a bullet full of her love for him. Meanwhile, back at the fight.

"So, you're asking me not to investigate your friend Shelley because you're afraid I'll find out he suffers seizures, too?"

"Don't play me, woman," he said, glaring now. "I'm a player."

"Sounds like something your grandmother would say," she said.

"Huh-huh," he said, turning away from her.

She could almost hear the iron curtains slam shut behind his eyeballs. Conversation over.

"Stanford, I hope this personal disagreement doesn't mean we can't do business together—I mean, Life jackets and all."

"Dream on," he said, turning up the radio volume to Lady Day again; this time, the wounded Billie Holiday was wailing out her misery with "Good Morning, Heartache."

Stanford shot a suspicious look over at her.

"Crying-in-the-beer music," she said. "I burned it myself. Just for this very happy occasion."

§

Juanita Robeson opened the gate to her condominium compound. After leaving Stanford, she had stopped by the local supermarket and was now glad to have finally made it home.

She drove through.

The gate creaked shut behind her.

She parked her Taurus wagon inside the garage, disarmed the alarm and dragged inside. She was more than ready to just kick off her shoes, pour herself a glass of warm wine and curl up next to her cold remote.

The alarm rearmed itself.

Juanita sensed something wrong immediately. She did a double take at the fireplace. Somebody had stuffed real logs in her gas fireplace and a clock. A clock? She picked it up. Not a clock, but some kind of timer, and it was set to go off in another ten minutes.

Whack! Juanita saw pain—it was red. Whack! Whack!

The fireplace poker shattered her collar bone with vicious blows. Screaming pain. Whack! Pain knifed her chest. Whack! Whack! Every which way she turned, she felt pain. Pain was everywhere in the room. Ribs stabbed lungs. More pain. She opened her mouth but couldn't force air past her broken neck. She was suffocating. Lynched by her own neck. Whack! Whack! More pain. Her nervous system went haywire all over her body, her brain becoming a sizzling-hot frying pan of pain.

Then a weariness seeped into her brain. She felt a disconnect deep inside her body, releasing her soul to the sky as a child releasing a helium balloon to the wind. She faded and she thought of all the young cousins, all the young nephews, all the young nieces she had to live for. She was a role model—for Christ's sake! She can't be dead. Not yet! What about them! Sensations deserted her as she swelled with happiness and great ecstasy. She was dead. A goner. And a done deal. Whack!

The fireplace poker caved in her face, and the vicious blow left her giggling at the lunacy of watching a crazy man pulverize her flesh—now meat. Such a stupid man. He stuffed her flesh in the fireplace and doused her flesh with cheap gasoline. And she would have stayed to enjoy the cookout if it hadn't been for her brother. With an eye she didn't even know she had she saw Johnny point a beckoning finger at her.

She couldn't disobey her brother; now could she? Heck no. She had to go to him. Seeing Johnny alive for the first time in twenty years sent her happiness soaring up into the atmosphere of elation. Like her brother, Johnny, she too became one with the solar winds, and she just flew on away from there—at the speed of light.

§

Candice peeped from behind the hedges in front of Juanita Robeson's condominium. She saw a man wearing a Stetson hat step from behind the building. Mr. Stetson Hat moved with the cocky knowledge that he belonged in the neighborhood. But the vibes given off by the apish way he moved said he was a danger to her.

Suddenly, she heard a loud whoosh.

The inside of Juanita Robeson's condominium burst into flames.

Seconds later, fire alarms rang out. Lights lit up other units in the gated community. The gates to the compound sprang open to admit heard but unseen fire engines. She gawked at the burning unit, totally oblivious to her surroundings. She gasped at her helplessness when Mr. Stetson Hat popped up right in front of her.

He poked a long gun in her face, held it there for a two-count, then spun on his heels and walked swiftly away. When her mind returned from wherever it had ran off to, she wondered why he'd forgotten to blow her face out the back of her skull.

She trembled. Sucked in a deep breath and trembled again.

Her body hair again hugged her skin only when Mr. Stetson Hat was out of sight. She crouched in the shadows to calm herself.

Her eyes were wet, her neck wet, her brow wet.

The back of her hand skimmed across her brow.

She continued to tremble.

15

Friday, May 27

Tartuffe Jitt stared out over the Seine River. He had escaped that Nigerian rock prison. Thanks to Jocko.

Back home in Paris he couldn't eat or sleep. He could drink, and he drank a lot. He was moody, disoriented, detached. His Nigerian nightmare shattered his old-world beliefs to smithereens, and the pieces laid in the bedroom, in the closet, on the shelf, in a shoe box tied by a string.

He had put away childish things.

Finally.

He sipped the cognac. Preacher had set him up. And Jocko had saved his bacon. Jocko saved him from that hellhole and gave him forty-eight hours to recover from his ordeal, shut down his Parisian lifestyle, and beat it on down to Miami for further instructions. There he would be told the details of how he would repay his huge debt to his father for rescuing him from a firing squad. He glanced over at his luggage, packed and ready to go. He swallowed hard.

Jocko had paid a $3-million ransom for his release. He was the $3-million man for real.

He kept staring out over the Seine. Was he ready to leave, ready to pull it all back together again? Was he ready to go and meet his mother? Was he ready to do good for society like he promised God he would do if he could just walk out of that Nigerian rock prison alive? Was he ready to keep his promise to God Almighty?

Yes, he was ready. He'd lost heart with his Life-of-Riley lifestyle. His feel-good philosophy was deeply flawed for a man his age.

The Life-of-Riley lifestyle was a young man's game. He was nearing middle age, and he must now atone for a life he'd so far squandered. That Nigerian rock prison did what neither Jocko nor his lifestyle could do. The hellish experience had changed him.

The truth had finally gotten through to him. He was a motherless child. He had mothered himself his entire life. So much so he never allowed himself to really grow up. He had been a poor mother to himself. When the time came for him to kick himself out the nest, he hadn't done that. He had continued to mother himself. But how could he not? He was himself.

And his mother, too!

Talk about a catch-22.

It was just his luck of the draw to be born into such a screwed-up life, and to such a screwed-up father. Who could possibly be his mother but a screwed-up woman.

Yes, the truth had finally gotten through to him. He was screwed up in the head. But once he'd beaten this Prison City and Lake Arrowhead into shape for Jocko, then his father would arrange a meeting with a mother he had no memory of, with a mother he never knew he had.

That was the deal between father and son. If Jocko was lying to him again, he would just shoot the asshole and be done with it.

Tartuffe Jitt turned from the window. Time to go now.

§

The Gulfstream jet skirted the 5,000-foot runway at Lake Arrowhead in a perfect landing. Richard Stoole watched the sleek jet taxi to the hangar.

Minutes later, the Lake Arrowhead president was driving Jocko Jitt to the Presidential Suite. The suite was kept reserved for the owner and his son, the overdue Tartuffe Jitt. Jocko didn't say a word on the five-minute drive and was as distant, as aloof, as cold as when they'd first met in Kansas City a dozen years ago.

In the early days in Kansas City, Jocko had been called a wheeler-dealer. He would get his hands on a successful small business by cash, hook, or crook. He would quickly grow the small business into a medium-sized business by pumping lots of dollars into it, along with some much-needed management. Then he would sell the medium-sized business like it was a big business. The private sale made lots of cash that couldn't be banked in the usual way.

Richard and Mark's single job was to find other ways to turn Jocko's cash cows into land, buildings, equipment, and inventories, especially land. And the chef who cooked the books for Jocko Jitts' many enterprises was James Kelsey, CPA.

Jocko believed in sharing the wealth, and he paid top dollar for top talent. In Kansas City, Richard and Mark raked in $250,000 a year in salaries plus bonuses of at least another $150,000, and unlimited expense accounts. They both lived the rich life, and they both gambled a lot. The gambling became their downfall. Richard became so deeply in debt that one bookie put a hit on him. But Jocko had saved the day and his ass by buying up $500,000 of his bad paper, plus $500,000 of Mark's bad paper.

Jocko promised to erase their debts at the tune of $100,000 a year plus pay them $200,000 a year if they helped him buy up almost an entire South Georgia county down near the Florida line. In the past five years, he and Mark had almost worked off their combined $1-million debt. He had also saved a million dollars because he had nothing to spend his money on for the past five years.

Richard had stopped gambling. But Mark was still gambling bigtime and hadn't saved a dime. That was the root of Mark's anger at Stanford. Mark needed the $250,000 bonus money they would get for bringing Stanford on board as Lake Arrowhead president for a year.

Richard sighed at the thought of his past troubles. Once they were inside the Presidential Suite, Richard brought Jocko up to speed on Prison City and said they were running late because his son Tartuffe hadn't showed up yet.

"He'll be along in a few days," Jocko told him. "What about the CPA, Stanford Rome, you got him signed up and on board yet?"

"Not yet. But it'll work out."

"Nail him," Jocko said. "We need him for the politics. We need him to bless the dotted line when the time comes to seal the deal. Who can question the integrity of a guy who busts balls the way he busts balls, especially that airport scandal. He bust his own people. We need him, and I want him. I want you two to stay until you get him. You hearing me on that?"

"That wasn't the deal," he said, not liking the prospect of having to stay even one day longer than he'd planned on. "In three weeks, Mark and I, we're outta here. And we leave debt-free. That was the deal. The Stanford Rome bit was an add-on."

He braced for Jocko's counterattack and was surprised when it didn't come. Jocko eyed him thoughtfully instead of lashing out as was his modus operandi. Jocko was acting out of character and, to Richard, that was cause for concern.

"Okay," Jocko said, "you're right. It is an add-on. So here's a new deal for you and Mark. Get me Stanford Rome's John Hancock on a year's contract. Then you two guys stay on for another thirty days after Tartuffe shows up. If you do that little extra for me, I'll up that bonus from $250,000 to $350,000. Plus, I'll set you and Mark up in business and bankroll all of your quality deals."

Richard smiled.

"I don't mind sharing the wealth," Jocko continued. "But I expect results. I don't want to hear 'not yet,' and I don't want to hear 'It'll work out.' I want to hear, 'It's a done deal.' That's what I want from you two—results."

Richard kept smiling. The gaiety bubbled right up through the pores of his skin. The new deal made him a millionaire and a half. Richard kept right on smiling at his good fortune.

§

A pale Tartuffe Jitt strolled through Atlanta's Brown-Abernathy Airport terminal to wait for his luggage to arrive. He could have flown down on Jocko's jet but he wanted to drop in on Lake Arrowhead unannounced.

He was blind to the stares the other passengers gave him, having learned long ago the stares came with the territory of being over six and a half feet tall.

"Hi, Judge," a smartly dressed woman said in passing, the fourth person to call him *Judge*. Again he nodded and kept walking. Outside the terminal, he hailed a taxi. He spotted an elegantly dressed and very beautiful woman eyeing him as he neared the taxi. When she raised her hand and started walking expectantly toward him, he opened the taxi-cab door, popped inside, eyed the driver's nameplate on the visor and spoke quickly.

"Let's ride, Mr. Timbutu. Step on it for a big tip."

The boxy Checker taxicab shot from the curb like a tired old man on uppers, leaving the woman behind stamping her feet.

During the ride on the interstate that threaded the city, Tartuffe took a measure of Atlanta. The city was no Paris. That was plain enough to see. But what city could possibly compare to the City of Lights—a city where people wallowed in such high self-esteem that they looked no further than to themselves when seeking their equals in nature? The hour's drive to Lake Arrowhead took twice as long because of gridlock on the expressways.

Timbutu signed them in at the guardhouse. The security guard kept stealing a look at him, and doing a poor job of stealing it.

Sam, the guard, snatched up the telephone as soon as the taxi pulled away from the guardhouse.

"This is Sam at the gate. Let me talk with Mr. Stoole, right away."

Sam drummed his fingers while waiting to be connected.

"Mr. Stoole, this is Sam down at the gate. I thought you'd wanna know U. S. Judge Justin Grimes's on his way to see you...Sure, I know a federal judge when I see one—sir. I worked courthouse duty with the city. It's the judge, sir."

On the drive to the hotel, Tartuffe was feeling safe enough from Preacher already. Now, he had both the time and the space to think about where his life was headed. As the taxi approached, he saw a very large hotel stuck out in the middle of the sticks. Perfect.

He was thirty-five years old and alone. He'd been running from love and friendships for as long as he could remember. He cannot imagine a life without aloneness—a lack of love and friendship.

"Tell me, mister," Timbutu said. "At the airport back there, why you give the slip to the 'darling of Atlanta's airwaves'?"

"Who?" he said.

"Jocelyn Slade. She works for WTNT-TV. She's a TV star."

Timbutu stopped the taxi in front of the hotel entrance.

Two men waited under the awning.

Tartuffe stepped to the curb and faced the two men.

The two men looked at him, then they looked at each other.

Tartuffe said, "I'm the new guy."

16

FRIDAY, MAY 27

STANFORD SAT LOW in the pew. He was as stunned as when he'd first heard the heartbreaking news. He couldn't believe Juanita Robeson was dead, and he was attending her funeral.

The people mourning her death looked just a little less lifeless than the body stretched out dead inside that coffin. The mourners looked like death warmed over, but the mourners were very much alive. And Juanita was very much dead.

He was never really going to get the hang of death. No one really ever understood being dead but the dead.

And the dead, they told no lies about being dead.

He turned his attention back to the people inside the church.

The people, they all seemed to drag themselves reluctantly inside the bowels of the small country church. On the way inside, they filed past hundreds of white crosses already planted outside in the cemetery like a garden plot. And today a fresh hole gaped open in the earth to accept a new member to the "dead" club.

The oblong box entered the church through the north end, and the oblong box would leave the church through the south end. The coffin seemed so small—dwarfed by so many beautiful flowers and the, thankfully, competing smells. The church was decked out in enough flowers to start a florist business.

Stanford sat on the second-row pew staring at yet another coffin, death now such a constant in his life. It seemed to him. Every which way he turned, he stared death in the face.

Juanita Robeson was dead.

Like the other mourners in the church, he could not believe it was true. But the sniffles, the tears, the occasional wail confirmed the obvious—Juanita Robeson was stone-cold dead.

§

The tall gangly soloist walked to the front of the church like she owned the place and everybody in it.

She sent her bright eyes surfing out over the wave of people to shush them. She waited to hear a pin drop among the flock, so she could begin entertaining them. She had come to prime the mourners for the coming outpouring of grief—throwing out their buckets of sorrow.

Her heartbeat was so strong that she thought the muscle might bust right through the walls of her chest. But as she always did, she fought back the urge to just double over and puke right there in front of everybody. That was how scared she was, standing up there, alone and waiting. She'd stood there two hundred, if not three hundred, times or more, but she was still scared sick to her stomach.

Nevertheless, when the organist struck up the first loud chord of "The Old Rugged Cross," she was ready. She was so ready that all her doubts and her fears flapped their wings and flew wearily away. They hovered overhead, waiting for the show to end.

She was now ready to sing her heart out for these folks.

When she opened her mouth to sing, her lips didn't merely part to let the sound out, her lips fluttered open like butterfly wings. She unshackled her soul, as she sang. She stretched mere sounds into lovely notes rising from the depth of her music, as she sang.

She filled the church, bulging, with her song, swelling, with her song, her sweet, sweet song, as she sang. Her voice exploded with passion, as she sang on and on, she sang, she sang, she sang. The mourners, they were up on their feet, moaning and swaying, and singing and shouting, and weeping and clapping, and fainting and—just running away from the hard reality that Juanita Robeson was, indeed, dead…dead—dead!

She sang on and on, giving them all a rhythm to grieve by in their miseries, a rhythm to weep by in their sadness, a rhythm to scream by in their madness. She just kept singing her song to the rhythm of their hurt and to the beat of their loss until her song was over. The last long begging melody burst overhead like fireworks. Her lips fluttered shut like the sweet beaks of a nightingale. Then all the doubts and fears that had been hovering overhead, waiting, they again perched on her neck like an albatross.

Now, kind folks of Sparta, Georgia, she thought but didn't say, you go now and bury your dead.

§

Stanford and Clayton sat on the couch in Clayton's office.

"What have you got for me this time, Shaft?"

The FBI Atlanta chief softened his sarcasm with a smile. "Just kidding, and don't go giving me that look again, like I'm something you stepped in. Remember that?"

"I don't know what you're talking about," he said. "But, I'm sure glad that we're back sitting on the couch. Instead of me sitting in front of that desk so you can take potshots at me."

"Yeah, that was business," Clayton said. "A distasteful business, too. But today's different. We meet as friends with no FBI business between us." Clayton started rubbing his palms together. "Now, what can I do for you today, my friend?"

He handed Clayton three 8x10 blowups Colt had developed for him. The pictures showed the thumbprint taken from the bible he found in Katie Kane's house Monday, four days ago.

"Run this through your AFIS computer for a match," he said.

Clayton studied the prints. "Is this blood?"

"Don't know that," he said.

Clayton looked at him, bright-eyed. "Where did you get this?"

He let the question go begging. Clayton waited, looking at him, expectantly. "Well, Shaft, talk to me."

"I'd rather not say."

Clayton squinted at him. "This here has something to do with the case, right?"

"You said you would help. How long did you say it takes to run this through the FBI's fingerprint files?"

Clayton set the photos on the coffee table, meshed his fingers then looked at him, studying his face like he was a specimen under a microscope. "Stanford, I'm gonna stand by what I told you Monday before last. But answer me this, what makes you think you're so much smarter than the rest of us, we who do this shit for a living

94

every damn day? Answer me that, my friend."

"Not smarter. Harder. My dick's harder. Now, if you would just call me when you're done. With the prints, I mean. You'll never be done bitching at me. I bitch at Shelley, so he says; You bitch at me, so I say. Tell me, Clayton, who bitches at you?"

Clayton didn't answer.

"Oh," he said. "Her."

Clayton nodded.

§

As soon as Stanford left his office, Clayton laid the 8x10 blowup on his desk, unlocked his drawer, and flipped through the files. He pulled out a manila folder. From it he took out a dime-sized piece of rubber Stanford had given him three months earlier.

Clayton placed the tiny piece of rubber on top of the large snapshot of the thumbprint. He turned and twisted the piece of surgeon glove, first one way then another way, until satisfied with his labor. The shapes came together like pieces of a jigsaw puzzle.

"Shaft," Clayton said to himself, leaning back in the chair with a big grin on his face, "you do Richard Roundtree proud, my man."

§

Four hours later, Stanford was back at Lake Arrowhead, listening to Shelley give him the official read on Juanita's death.

"Roscoe, your partner was trashed by a pro—," Shelley said, then threw up a hand. "Hold one. Gotta hit the can."

Stanford poured two shots of liqueur into a six-shot glass, filled it to the brim with milk and stirred it with his finger. He thought back to the day Stacey and Christopher had been murdered.

He had been at the Lake Arrowhead Hotel when Stacey called at four-thirty that afternoon. Katie Kane, his mother-in-law, had suffered another heart attack, and the doctors didn't expect her to live. The next minutes were hectic as he hustled to be there for Stacey.

Lake Arrowhead had been in the middle of its annual banquet, and he was the keynote speaker to the business crowd. Many people in the audience thought his speaking role was a prelude to him dipping a toe into state politics and a possible run for governor.

He'd been approached by, encouraged by, and nudged by a cross section of Atlanta's deep-pocketed business leaders, especially after Rome, Kelsey, and Lang bust the so-called airport crowd. Uncovering the massive airport fraud triggered investigations in dozens of airports all across the country.

He was more amused by the attention than he was interested in joining the circus. He saw his keynote-speaker role as repaying a favor to Richard Stoole, who asked him to be the headliner. It had been as simple as that. Then Richard stacked the podium with the same people who wanted him to run for governor. If he knew who was behind the madness, he would take them behind Greenbrier Mall and flog them with a kudzu switch.

When he'd told Richard about his mother-in-law's heart attack, the Lake Arrowhead president made the company jet available for his personal use. The pilot flew him to Atlanta.

Several other people tagged along, including WTNT-News evening anchor, Jocelyn Slade. Earlier, the darling of Atlanta's airwaves had been flirting with him. And within the big picture of the banquet he had encouraged Jocelyn's little flirtatious scenes.

But he never would have suspected, in a million years, that all he'd been doing that night was setting himself up to suffer through the goddamnedest guilt trip he could ever imagine.

On the flight to Atlanta, he'd caught Jocelyn watching him a few times. Each time he caught her eye, she smiled at him a second too long before looking away. After the plane landed, he last saw Jocelyn standing at a bank of telephones, a receiver stuck to her ear, a cellular phone palmed in her hand.

Stacey and Christopher boarded the jet in Atlanta, and the pilot flew them to the Twofer County Airport.

They arrived at the hospital at 6 p.m. Katie Kane was sedated. Her condition had been upgraded from grave to serious. She was still hooked up to life support. After speaking with her mother's doctor, Stacey had sent him packing back to the airport.

He arrived back at Lake Arrowhead in time to give his keynote speech. After his speech, he called the hospital.

A deputy sheriff was preparing to drive Stacey and Christopher to her mother's house for the night. Stacey insisted that he not fly back to Twofer County until the next day.

So he'd spent the next two hours enjoying the hilarious company and undivided attention of beautiful, vivacious Jocelyn Slade.

The pilot flew him back to Twofer County just after midnight.

He took a taxi to Katie Kane's house and found the bodies.

"Roscoe!" Shelley yelled out from the toilet. "This shit's harder than my dick. It's gonna be awhile."

"The way you eat, you need a laxative," he said.

"Yeah, yeah. I need a bigger asshole is what I need."

§

Stanford and Shelley first met on the playground when they were nine years old. They fought and bloodied the school's most notorious bullies: Frankie and Johnny Boy. Shelley was the new kid in school. On his first day on the playground, Frankie and Johnny Boy jumped on him. By the time Stanford got there, the two bullies had ripped Shelley's shirt off his back and were taunting him with it.

"Gotta be a sissy, gotta be a faggggg. Sheeeeelee! Sissssy! Sheeeelee! Faagggg! Sheeeelee! Sissssy! Sheeeelee! Faagggg. Gotta be a sissy, gotta be a faagggg!"

Stanford socked Johnny Boy in the mouth, then kicked him in the nuts. Shelley put Frankie on the ground with the same two vicious punches—a knuckle sandwich and a nutcracker. They destroyed the two bullies. Upon that victory, they built the foundation of their friendship.

Since then, they had been best friends. They trusted each other, and when the chips were down, they stood up for each other.

Two days later, Shelley moved into the homeplace with him and QueenBee. The Lesters had threatened to take Shelley back to the orphanage because he woke up screaming all during the night. No one could get a night's sleep. QueenBee stopped Shelley from screaming so much, but he never went back to the Lesters to live.

He and Shelley forged a bond, and that devotion grew into their blind loyalty to each other as men. They later dominated school politics. He was the politician, and Shelley ran all his campaigns.

§

After Shelley sped off in his Thunderbird, Stanford went jogging. He thought about Shelley again as he ran.

He wondered if Shelley had something to do with the talk going around about him possibly running for some state office. Even in high school, Shelley, more or less, had talked him into running for student council and class president. He and Shelley always won.

They won because he kept things simple. He basically did exactly what Shelley told him to do. He was not a very good politician, but he was a stickler for details, and so was Shelley.

His elected offices always ran smoothly; things got done. He kept campaign promises. He never had much opposition. Rumor had it that Shelley intimidated potential opponents. That had only been a rumor. He sucked in a breath as his muscles heated up.

It was a pleasant day for a long run, the sky empty of clouds.

After two miles, he turned off the main road to run down one of the many foot trails on the Lake Arrowhead compound. Two hundred yards along the trail, he spotted a nest of snakes and stopped. The snakes were sunning on top of a faded canvas bag, the slimy bodies moving like ocean waves. One gaped its white fluffy mouth. Cottonmouths. South Georgians called them water moccasins.

Unlike other vipers, cottonmouths were awfully mean and cantankerous and would bite unprovoked. He picked up a stick to beat back the snakes so he could grab the duffel bag and see what was inside it. He was surprised when the snakes slithered off the bag and disappeared into the underbrush before he could whack them with the stick. That was strange snake behavior. He waited awhile after the last snake disappeared to see what happened next.

What happened next was worth the price of admission.

The thick underbrush slowly parted. Inch by cold-blooded inch, seven feet of snake crawled on the scene like African royalty. He had never before seen, or even heard of anyone seeing, such a large timber rattler.

The timber rattler's huge size fascinated him. With a quickness that sent him scrambling back on his heels, the snake snapped into a squirming coil. Its rattlers were a blur, a whirring blur of motion, the deadly sound loud and menacing. The foot-high pyramid of rippling muscles stood its ground. At the top of that cold pyramid was an arrow-shaped head larger than his fist. He backed up a few more anxious feet to put a little more space between him and that monster timber rattler.

Usually, the timber rattler was not so fussy. It was a wimp compared to the eastern diamondback, the largest venomous snake in the country. But the eastern diamondback was found in the coastal areas and not in the mountains. This was a monster timber rattler and maybe a record. But he was not into trophies.

Even as he retreated, he could see the syringe fangs glittering in the sunlight. He backed away until he figured it was safe enough to turn his back on the snake; then he turned on his heels and ran. He had to even up the odd a little before tackling that big snake.

Half an hour later at the cottage, he pulled on his boots, grabbed a throwing knife, a throwing spike, tape, snakebite kit, and rifle. Then he drove back toward the lake.

Fifteen minutes later, he was back at the duffel bag. He taped the sharp knife to a stick twelve-feet long and went to see if the timber rattler was still there.

The huge snake was still there and met his challenge with a nerve-racking singsong of agitation. Armed with a heat sensor perfected over hundreds of millions of years, the timber rattler could kill a rabbit in total darkness. Stanford kept his eyes glued to a head as steady as a gyroscope, forked tongue flicking the air like a sneaky left jab.

He leaned forward, poking the duffel bag with the spear. The big snake struck out, sending a stream of venom twisting through the air. The powerful head knocked the spear from his hand. The snake snapped back into its coil with a popping sound, its high-pitched rattle a steady singsong of menace. He slid out the throwing spike and threw it as he had thrown the spike thousands and thousands of times before.

The throwing spike hit the target straight on, striking the timber rattler at the base of the head, lodging there. The squirming beast attacked the spike, consuming the steel within its massive coils.

Game. Set. Match.

§

Back at the cottage, after making sure a snake was not hiding inside the duffel bag, Stanford dumped the contents on the floor.

He suffered an immediate flashback, the images forcing him to stare up at the ceiling. He could almost feel something big and slow sliding over the rooftop like a blimp.

He stared back down at the pyramid on the floor.

Bricks of cocaine—many bricks of cocaine.

Bundles of $100 bills—many, many bundles of $100 bills.

17

STANFORD FELT THE throbbing music energize him as soon as he parked the sedan next to five luxury cars glittering in David Harte's lighted driveway.

The sky was starry-eyed and endlessly black. The party sounded like it was already up to speed.

He hurried past a snow-white BMW 3000SX four-door sedan with the uniformed chauffeur stretched out on the backseat. Excitement strummed the air. He felt his muscles relaxing already. Today had been quite stressful. In the beginning he thought the confrontation with the timber rattler was the highlight of his day. And it had been the highlight until he dumped the contents of the duffel bag on the floor of the cottage.

He counted 22 bricks of cocaine, and 200 bundles of $100 bills. Even now, the memory made him want to stare up at the sky and imagine something big and slow sliding over his cottage that night, eight days ago. He jerked his mind away from the memory and turned his attention back to the music. He wanted to forget today, for a couple of hours anyway.

Janet Jackson's monster hit "Nine-Pound Steel" was jazzing up his sagging spirits in a big way, chasing away the blues he'd been feeling lately. He was buoyed by the pounding beat of rock. He was glad he came. No, he felt more than glad. It was a thrill.

SizzzzZap! Excitement was not the only thing humming in the air. So was a Bug Buster dangling overhead under the balcony. It glowed in a haze of soft violet light. ZapSizzzzZap! The killer rays lured and zapped bugs without impunity. Zap-Sizzzz!

"Heyyy, you made it!"

Stanford looked up to see David Harte leaning over the second-floor balcony, a dangerous twelve feet off the ground. The psychiatrist was grinning down at him.

He waved and shot David a thumbs up.

David greeted him in the foyer and ushered him into the great room, its hue a hip cool blue. Unlike the rest of the house, the great room rose to a cavernous cathedral ceiling.

David led him past shoes, socks, scarves, panty hose, hats, and belts. The clothing trail ended near a twelve-piece sofa group so velvety plush that it threatened to swallow its occupants in one easy gulp. In a separate corner loomed a wide-screened television displaying a huge picture of WTNT-TV News's color weather map.

The room throbbed with the excited voices of people enjoying themselves and the company they were keeping.

The heavy beat of music gave the close-knit gathering a heartbeat of its own, as couples drank their favorite beverages, coughed from what smelled like ass-kicking marijuana, and snorted cocaine cruising the room on a sterling silver tray. Then Stanford glimpsed catty eyes stalking him and David across the floor like they were two plump mice.

David turned down the music, and a stocky redhead leaped up, her brain as hot as her hair. "Don't touch that dial, David Harte!"

The others hooted until David's face turned as red as the helium balloon stuck to the ceiling. The redhead threw a shoe.

David ducked. The shoe sailed harmlessly past and smashed into a lamp that teetered but didn't fall over.

"Carrot Top hates your guts," he whispered into David's ear.

David leaned into him. "Her name's Jackie. I dumped the nymphomaniac and she's just paying me back with interest. She crashed the party. But you know how it is. Her mouth's not big for nothing. The wench got more suction than a wet vac. Come on, let's haul my woes outside, and air 'em out."

David cranked the music back up, grabbed a bottle of liquor, a carton of milk and headed outside.

The pancake moon reflected a soft light on the ground.

David sat under the gazebo.

Stanford stood a few feet away, stargazing.

"I've got the latest scoop on that crash," David said.

"Oh, yeah," he said, turning his attention back to David.

"The pilot—I mean, the passenger, he was dead before the airplane nosed into the ground," David said. "Drugs. It looked like somebody ripped somebody off—hey, did I tell you, Shelley, he's dropping by tomorrow. He called me this morning. He sounded motivated to show up. Good job. I thought you'd like to know that whatever you said or did—well, it worked wonderfully."

"Good. That's good to hear, David. I'm worried about Shelley."

"Well, anyway, back to that plane crash," David said.

They chatted about the plane crash, the implications of the missing pilot and the missing drugs, and the pissed-off redhead for ten more minutes.

David pulled Shelley's photo from his pocket and handed it to him. "I had a copy made. Thanks."

He stuffed the photo in his pocket.

David cleared his throat and rubbed his chin. "Stanford, I bet when Shelley's screams stopped when he was a boy, his migraines started. Is that about right?"

He flipped back through the memories like he was looking back through a dusty yearbook. "You're right, David. Is it important?"

"Darn tooting, it's important," David said. "Shelley, he stopped screaming on the outside. But he started screaming on the inside. Shelley's screams, more than likely, became his migraines is what I'm saying. Now, come on, let's go back inside."

The megahit "Coca-Baby" was shaking the walls when he and David strolled back into the great room. The lovers hadn't moved except that Cat Eyes was missing from the room.

David popped in a Michael Jackson CD and then cranked up the sound. "Let's boogie-woogie! Let's get it on!" David shouted, shaking his hips to the first thunderous beats of "BANG!" Michael Jackson's latest megahit.

The bass guitar rocked the cathedral ceiling, drawing the dancers up on their feet. The crowded floor became a swirling mass of gyrating bodies. The mad hypnotic beat of "BANG!" thumped and bumped, the dapper dandy stick man dragging pop music screaming to the next highest level. The pop superstar kept cranking it up, higher and higher until it seemed as if every molecule in the room was thumping and bumping to the same beat.

As David steered Suzanne toward the dance floor, the missing mystery woman, Cat Eyes, popped up at his side.

"Let's dance, old man," the pretty woman said, extending a hand.

Cat Eyes swept him up into her embrace before he could react, and he followed her smooth moves across the floor, as they danced toward the other dancers. Her waist was as tiny as Stacey's, and her chest was nothing less than trophy-sized. What a dinosaur he was.

"I'm Candy," she said and smiled.

"Cinnamon or peppermint?" he said and smiled back.

"Your favorite?"

"Cinnamon," he said.

"Then you can call me Candice Bergens, you can call me Candy, or you can call me Cinnamon. And what may I call you?"

"Well, Candy, I'm Stanford Rome, but you can call me Lucky."

"Lucky?"

"Yes, what else can I be—I mean having such a lovely woman in my arms on such a beautiful night makes me feel so lucky."

She laughed and seemed to melt into his arms. "A new twist on an old line," she said, speaking gently into his ear and then leaning away, looking at him, as they danced, hips locked together. Up close, her face almost made him gasp, his heart skipping a beat and a half. They fumbled out of step, like first-time lover the first time, she clamping his arms to keep her balance.

"I—I'm sorry," he stammered, their bodies again meshing snugly, their feet in sync as clumsy two now moved as smooth one. "Yo—You just look so much like my wife, Stacey, the way she looked, I mean." He swallowed. "You see, she...my wife, I mean, she was murdered, she and my son. About four months ago."

His mind went numb for a few seconds but quickly recovered.

"I'm sorry," she said and tightened her grip on his arm.

They danced in silence.

Finally he said, "Who's the white guy?"

"So you're into the color thing?" Candice said.

He hunched his shoulders. "Then who's the gay guy?"

She threw back her head, exposing her throat as if she trusted him already, and then she startled him when she smiled at him with Stacey's face. He jerked his eyes away; he couldn't bear it.

"Andre's his name; he works for me," Stacey's face said. "So you hung up on gay guys, too?"

"Depends on what you mean by 'hung up,'" he said, smiling at her and pulling her closer. As Shelley would have described it: he was busy playing around in the music. They danced slow and close, his pelvis snug to hips swaying to the last notes of the dwindling melody. He looked away from that face to contain himself. The scene was so uncanny that it seemed to have sucked all the joy out of the evening. He wanted to flee, run away and hide from Stacey's face.

"You didn't answer me," Stacey's face said, returning him to the moment. "What about Andre?"

"Oh," he said. "Andre, he's—ah, rather cute."

"So are you," Stacey's face said, lifting Stacey's eyebrow. "Let's do this again, soon. It's fun. Why don't you come up and see me sometimes." She held his hand softly. "Up in Buckhead. I own a beauty shop there: Styles By Candy."

Stacey's face slipped from his embrace like a dream. Stacey's lips said, "Stanford, I'm truly sorry about your wife and son."

Stacey's body walked away, stopped, rotated her shoulders and smiled at him, fluttering her fingers the same cute way Stacey used to do.

He flashed a *peace* sign and turned away.

§

The cottage was miserably quiet after the noisy hours he'd spent at David Harte's party. Stanford sat slumped in the sofa chair for an hour, images of Candice Bergens circling his brain like images of his dead wife.

He took Candice apart inside his mind, dissected her. How she looked. How she smelled. How she talked. How she danced. How she touched him. Who she seemed to be.

Did Candice make herself up to look like Stacey? Did Candice practice dancing like Stacey? Why was Candice doing this? Why did David let Candice do this to him? He thought about that last question. David had never met Stacey, and so David didn't see how much Candice looked like Stacey. Was this all a coincidence, or was someone trying to send him screaming over the edge?

He sipped the cognac, set the glass down and opened the photo album. He dug from his pocket the photo of Shelley that David had returned to him. He flipped through the album and slid the photo back beside the only other photo he had of Shelley.

He glanced at the second photo of Shelley, before zooming in on the soldier draping an arm on Shelley's shoulder. He slid the photo from the plastic sleeve and flipped it over to read Shelley's scrawl: "The 'Nam 1968. Me, the gang, and Fly Boy."

Holding the photo up to the light he studied the soldier's facial features. He lowered the photo, thinking. He held the photo up to the light again, studying it some more before lowering it again.

Flashbacks floated through his mind. His first inclination was to dig up the duffel bag and burn it.

His second inclination was to treat the duffel bag the same way he treated the intruder. Out of sight, out of mind; and "mum" was the word. He held the photo up to the light again, his eyes tracing the outline of the face.

There was no doubt in his mind.

The soldier leaning on Shelley's shoulder was the intruder.

18

LAKE ARROWHEAD

SATURDAY, MAY 28

A LAZY DAY at Lake Arrowhead.

It was a clear breezy spring day of seventy-three degrees when the Thunderbird bore down on Grant Tucker like a bat outta hell. The security guard was leaning in the doorway of the guardhouse, knowing what to expect. The speeding car slowed so fast the grille dipped to the ground like a bucking horse.

And when Shelley floored the V-8, the front end rose in the air as if the car were set to rear up on its hind wheels. That was how Shelley saluted Grant from behind the tinted window as he roared on through.

Grant shook his head. "Look out now!"

The tail end of the Thunderbird disappeared up the road, rear bumper level to the ground. Shelley must have gotten them there shocks fixed because last week Grant saw that the rear bumper was riding mighty low, like maybe Shelley was hauling moonshine inside the trunk. Or somebody's woman.

Grant done heard all the rumors about Shelley. But damn if he was going to believe any of that negative stuff. Shelley had been good to him. Not only did Shelley get him this cushy job, he also lets him tag along sometimes so he could do another kind of job. That job made him proud to be a black man because he was helping his race in a big way. Shelley had helped him change his sorry life by helping him to improve it. He sure wasn't about to believe no doggone gossip about Shelley.

Grant was now a positive thinker in his own mind, and like the lady preacher said last Sunday—Whoa! Grant stopped his thinking on a dime. What's this world coming to when you got a woman preaching to a man about how a man ought to live his life when that ain't her own man the woman be preaching to. Lordy, Lordy, what's the world coming to. Women trying to take over the world, trying to preach to a man.

"Who can you trust?"

When the lady preacher asked the congregation that question last Sunday she was looking right at Grant, like he was some special kind of sinner. The lady preacher said he was supposed to just trust in that Lord thy God. Yeah, right. That's what he was thinking at the time, that he should trust in that Lord thy God.

In the next life, maybe so. But in this here life on earth Grant was trusting nobody but Shelley Lester, the only man he knowed who won the Nobel Peace—nope, wrong one. Grant scratched his chin, thinking, grimacing—ahh, whatever it was, Shelley he won it and he didn't win it at no raffle either. Shelley won it on the battlefield. Shelley won it by killing a whole shitload of gooks who was out there trying to kill him.

Grant Tucker took one more admiring look in the direction the Thunderbird flew. "Look out now! Right on, brother-man. Blew them damn gooks away. Rat-tat-tat-tat-tat! Yeah, man."

§

Shelley Lester became one with the low groaning of the electric motor as David Harte leveled the recliner out into a couch. Shelley had taken off his coat, but he refused to take off his gun. The tiny recorder was attached to the small of his back with Velcro and hidden by his shirt, and the microphone was his belt buckle. Plus he was wired in so many ways inside his head that his skull was fit to be shrunk by the shrink.

Thoughts about that Miami goon he had sent to the Promised Land flashed in his mind. That Sturro fellow. But he couldn't exactly remember what he had done with the pieces of that Miami thug. Maybe all that kudzu ate him up, you reckon?

David closed the file folder and rattled his throat, the sound breaking Shelley's reverie. The psychiatrist leaned forward.

"Now that we know what hasn't worked in the past, Shelley, why don't you tell me a little bit about yourself."

Shelley's fingertips tapped a cadence on the side of the recliner. Nothing good was gonna come of this. But he would try anything to keep from crawling back to Twofer County and QueenBee for her help. But the migraines were turning him into more of a sex hustler than he'd ever been before. Still, he had to keep his distance from QueenBee; she could read his mind. That wouldn't do. That would ruin everything he had planned for Stanford's future as Georgia's next governor. But if he was unlucky enough to get close to QueenBee, she would uncover his plot.

David said, "Shelley, you seem uneasy. If you would rather see a black psychiatrist, I have friends who meet that qualification."

He sliced and diced the psychiatrist, scrutinizing him from head to toe. "Maybe it's you with the problem, Roscoe. You reckon that's the deal here?"

"My name's—"

The psychiatrist wet his lips. "I doubt that's true, Shelley."

"Then, we don't have a problem here; now, do we, Roscoe?"

"My name's—"

David cleared his throat. "Shelley, your records suggest no physical reasons for your migraines. Is it true that sex gives you some temporary relief?"

"I can fuck away the pain, if that's what you getting at."

"And, Shelley, how often do you have sex?"

"Everyday, two, three times a day. All day. Depends on the woman I'm poking."

"In what way does it depend on the woman you're poking?"

"Depends on whether she can take it or not."

David lifted an eyebrow. "Is that fact, Shelley or bragging?"

"When you poking her, it's fact. When you talk about poking her, it's braggadocio," Shelley said, adding, "Roscoe."

David nodded. "How long does…it last, Shelley, the poking?"

"Depends on the quality of the woman I'm poking at the time," he said, really enjoying unnerving the quack.

David flipped through the paper pile on his desk. "So, Shelley, if your libido drives your migraines, why not control your migraines by controlling your sex drive, like toning…ah, toning the poking down, not doing it so much, I mean?"

Shelley didn't answer. He was trying to figure out how this guy got to be a psychiatrist with such a deficiency in listening skills.

"Shelley, since nothing has worked for you in the recent past, don't you think you should be open-minded about your options? I mean sex and stress rest on opposite ends of the human psyche, like opposing ends of a seesaw. When sex is up, stress is down; the two are mutually exclusive like that. When sex is down, stress is up. An orgasm not only waylays stress, it also waylays a man, diluting his adrenaline, weakening his testosterone, and who knows what other chemical changes go on inside a man at the moment of orgasm."

He'd had enough of this impostor. Stanford was off his rocker if he thought *this* guy was any good.

"Excuse me, Roscoe," he said, rising on one elbow. "Are you a psychiatrist, or a fucking sex therapist, or a damn pervert who gets his kicks from talking dirty to a middle-aged man lying on his back alone in your office—with a gun!"

The big gun was in his fist, the ugly end aimed at David's face.

David Harte looked away from the muzzle. "Point taken. You may put away the gun now. We have a little work to do here."

"First, you listen to me," Shelley said, holding his aim steady. "I said *fucking* eased the migraines. I did not say *fucking* triggered the migraines. Do I make myself clear here, Roscoe?"

"Very much so," David Harte said. "Very much so."

Shelley stuffed the gun back into the holster and lay back down.

David picked up the clipboard.

"It says here, Shelley, that you went to Drake University in Des Moines, Iowa for two years before joining the Army. That you completed your schooling at Drake in '75 and joined the FBI's Denver office, spending a year in Chicago, followed by a year spent in DC. After that, you set down somewhat permanent roots in Miami for six years before you moved to Atlanta in '83 as agent in charge of the Atlanta office. You quit the FBI in '85." David looked up from his notes. "Does that accurately reflect your history, Shelley?"

"Pretty much," he said.

"Did the headaches force you to resign the FBI?"

"No. I started forgetting things. A bad mind."

"But, don't the two go together?" David said. "I mean the memory loss and the headaches?"

Shelley shrugged. "Depends."

"On what?" David said. "Depends on what?"

Shelley felt a throbbing pressure slowly building up inside his head. He tensed. "Well, Roscoe, I've sent colored people to hell by the boxcar load and I did it all for the good of this country. Now the same colored people I sent to hell by the boxcar load…well, those ghosts are now killing me with flashbacks worse than any napalm we dropped on those people over there."

"Oh. These flashbacks, Shelley, they trigger your migraines?"

"Sometimes they do; sometimes they don't."

"When did you first notice this connection?" David said.

"Five months ago. The middle of January."

"You sound so sure. Your memory about that seems okay."

"I write things down. I went over my notes before I came here. The old memory's shot. Trust me on that."

"Shelley, what was happening in your life around then?"

"Since—"His head started pounding behind his right eyeball.

David pressed the issue. "Shelley, did your migraines start after the Rome murders or before?"

He didn't answer.

David cocked his head. "Shelley, were you close to Stacey?"

He didn't answer.

David slapped the pad shut.

The motor whirred beneath him again, the recliner slowly folding back up into a chair.

"That's it for today, Shelley. Your migraines are not all chemical. The murders put a greater strain on you than you know. Have you talked out your feelings with your friend, Stanford?"

"About *the night that never happened*?" he said.

David looked at him sideways. "What do you mean by that?"

"One way to deal with it, Roscoe. Is that illegal or immoral?"

"No, Shelley, but it's an illusion. That night did happen."

He shrugged.

"Shelley, you may feel that your migraines exist mostly because you've killed people. But men have been killing men since Adam. It's not the high body count of Vietnam that's screwing you up in the head; your wounds are more recent than that. Even you said your migraines intensified five months ago. Shelley, you have to come to grips with what happened about five months ago—one way or another. You must, Shelley."

"Maybe," Shelley said. "Maybe not."

David shook his head and tugged on an earlobe.

"Shelley, did your investigation into the murders reach the same conclusion as the police?"

Shelley kneaded his cheeks with his thumbs. This was hard. He was falling apart at the molecular level, like dandruff falling from his head down to the floor at his feet. He had to get outta there. Remembering was too much. He was finally losing it completely. He gathered the shards of his shattered mind and pieced himself back together the best he could. But when he turned to David, the psychiatrist was gone.

In David's chair sat the beast. The beast was speaking to him, and he was listening to the beast speak.

"Shelley, you must listen to me. That night did happen. Neither you nor Stanford has dealt with this reality. Your denial, it's causing havoc in your lives. You can't let reality slide by like water under a bridge without you feeling it, without you dipping your toes in it. You must stay in touch with what's real out there in the world. It's unhealthy to do otherwise. Shelley, you must go back in your mind and deal with this tragedy like you're supposed to deal with your tragedies, like we all are supposed to deal with our tragedies. Put your tragedies behind you like we all must put our tragedies behind us.

"Shelley, take your tragedies out the closet, dust your tragedies off and do with your tragedies as you must do, but then put those tragedies back in the Hope Chest in the attic where they belong. Shelley, that night did happen. Shelley, deep down inside your mind, that night keeps happening over and over, and you're there that night, Shelley, over and over, that night keeps happening, over and over, and that night did happen, and you believe that night did happen and keeps happening, over and over, and you're sinking deeper and deeper into that night that did happen, Shelley, down and down and down into that deep black night that keeps happening, over and over, deeper and deeper down into that black night, Shelley, deeper and deeper, Shelley, deeper and deeper..."

19

SATURDAY, MAY 28

CANDICE BERGENS SOAKED her aching muscles in the bubbling warm waters of the Jacuzzi. She tried forgetting all about the voice that still turned her on like she was a gutter slut, available to him for a nickel bag, or for free.

She tossed the idea of bedding down a breeder bull like Shelley to the back of her mind for now. Too much trouble to even think about that man.

The next item on her long list of things to do was to find out where Shelley lay down his head at night. Once that was done, she could bug the place and find out what Shelley was all about. Even if Shelley, the intruder, and the security guards were drug smugglers, she was sure Stanford was not part of the gang. And he was the reason she was at Lake Arrowhead, and the rest was just fun and games.

Except for Mr. Stetson Hat, of course.

Mr. Stetson Hat could have shot off her face. But he didn't. That sure didn't pass the smell test. She had seen Mr. Stetson Hat's face, which meant she knew what he looked like, but still Mr. Stetson Hat let her live to tell about it. Why did Mr. Stetson Hat let her live when she could pick him out of a police lineup? That was crazy. Or, a better question: why was he certain things would not come to that, a police line up, that is?

Glancing at the wall clock, she gripped each nipple firmly and slipped under the bubbling water like a U-boat. One minute later, she burst back up through the surface for air. Her lungs were back!

As strong as ever, her lungs were back.

Leaning back against the wall of the Jacuzzi, she stretched her arms along the top and kicked the water. She was squealing like the little girl she used to be, a little girl growing up in Denver: her ponytails, her penny loafers, her braces, her giggles, and all the good things she loved about that city, her hometown. The Mile-High City was a great place to grow up in, but she couldn't live there anymore. Too laid-back for her taste.

Her mood sobered as more thoughts rippled through her brain. She gulped a breath and back under the water she dove. A minute later, she hurtled back to the top for air. A minute later, back under she dove…a minute…back up. Back down. Back up.

Why didn't Mr. Stetson Hat shoot her? Back under…a minute down…back up. Her lungs heaved like a blast furnace blazed. But now she knew. Finally, she again slumped back against the wall of the Jacuzzi. Now she knew.

Now she knew why Mr. Stetson Hat didn't shoot off her face. He hadn't seen her; he hadn't seen her at all. The man had not seen her. He had seen a ghost of Stacey Rome.

Of that she was absolutely sure. How could he shoot Stacey in the face—when Stacey was already dead. That explained the interval of perhaps two or three seconds when Mr. Stetson Hat was paralyzed.

But how could a man as brazen as he was be paralyzed by someone as small as she was, unless she scared the living daylights out of him by her very presence?

That made sense to her. She looked so much like a dead woman. Not any dead woman. But a dead woman Mr. Stetson Hat knew well.

If that was true, and it was true, it meant Mr. Stetson Hat knew Stacey Rome well. And he also knew Juanita Robeson well. That narrowed down Mr. Stetson Hat's identity to someone who knew Stanford quite well. Stanford was the common denominator between Stacey Rome and Juanita Robeson; one was his wife, the other his business partner.

Candice cupped her breasts roughly as a man would do, and she squeezed her nipples gently as only a woman could do. She was so caught up in pleasing herself—it was a pleasure dome!

But she was so thankful. Stacey Rome had reached up from the grave to save her dumb ass from Mr. Stetson Hat's gun. I owe you one, Cuz. She smiled at the thought and slid so silently and so completely back under the water—like an enemy submarine.

§

When Shelley parked his Thunderbird at the farthermost end of the Atlanta International Country Club south parking lot, next to a black BMW 300i, Candice was waiting in her black coveralls and black knitted hood.

This was where Shelley always parked the Thunderbird, a sure sign he felt safe here, and his guard would be down.

Shelley picked up his women from here, leaving minutes ahead of some married woman, or some married woman leaving minutes ahead of him. She had to find out where Shelley lived so she could bug the place and find out more about the man who turned her on like she was a gutter slut.

When Shelley doused the headlights, Candice quietly slid from under the BMW and wiggled under the Thunderbird, clamped a transmitter on top of the rear axle and quietly wiggled back out. It took five seconds. Her favorite childhood nursery rhyme was now navigating through the swirls of her excited brain.

"Everywhere that Shelley went, that Shelley went, that Shelley went, Cinnamon was sure to go."

She mouthed the name—Cinnamon.

20

QUEENBEE WATCHED THE hummingbirds feasting on the sugar-water feeders. On either side of her rocking chair, the bull mastiffs, Aretha and Franklin, squatted on their haunches like firedogs in a fireplace. She scratched the huge dogs' pointed ears and continued staring out across the fields. But the guard dogs' keen black eyes stayed focused on her visitor.

Setting the rocking chair slowly in motion, she closed her eyes and imagined the note card she'd gotten ten days ago. She'd also received her thirty-third snapshot of the boy, now the man.

She couldn't understand why the murdering, raping kidnapper denied murdering Stacey and Christopher at the same time he sent a car bomb to blow her to kingdom come. It didn't add up. But one day real soon she would find Rooster and have her way with him. Even if the murdering, raping kidnapper didn't murder Stanford's wife and son, that man still had a killing coming to him.

She opened the photo album and studied the first photo; the boy was two years old. The first photo she got from the kidnapper. She kept flipping through the years, one photo for each year, arriving the same time each year on May eighteenth. She flipped the page to the thirty-third photo, the most recent one. She reread the first three words on the note card that came with it: I am innocent.

She stared back out across the fields. For the first time in three years, Twofer County farmers had something to smile about. But the rain Gods rarely blessed a grinning farmer for long. She turned and looked at her lawyer and knew by his slack face he hadn't heard about the car bomb. It had been ten days since Big Flossie died, and Jake had kept the lid on as she expected him to. Good for Jake. She finally told Fred Junior what she wanted, and he left to take care of it.

She picked up the *Miami Herald* and again read the below-the-fold headline: IS THE MIAMI ASSASSIN BACK?

She got all her news from newspapers. She didn't listen to radio or watch television. She flipped through, scanned or read up to eight newspapers a day: the *Miami Herald*, the *New York Times*, the *Washington Post*, the *Wall Street Journal*, the *Pittsburgh Courier*, the *International Herald-Tribune*, the *Atlanta World*, and that other Atlanta newspaper. She just couldn't get over the bigotries and injustices heaped on her and her people by the racist folks at that other Atlanta newspaper when she had been a girl and a young woman and a middle-aged woman. A bigot always hid his stripes a long time before losing them. And that other Atlanta newspaper had yet to hide their bigotries long enough to be legitimate, in her mind, anyway.

QueenBee pushed off on the balls of her feet. The chair picked up speed, rocking back and forth, rocking back and forth, remembering the way things used to be in times gone past long ago.

§

At eighty-three, Queen Beatrice Rome had simply outlived the other big landowners in Twofer County, a once-poor county of 20,000 souls. The county was located a hop, a skip, and a jump from the Florida state line, and right next door to the Okefenokee Swamp. As the good ol' South Georgia white boys died off over the years, the only old-timer left was a good ol' South Georgia black girl.

Over the many years, she'd added the land of the dead to her own land. The young white heirs in the county were happy to sell the worn-out farmland, pocket the money, and skip the county for good. They eagerly abandoned the homeplaces of their ancestors. It took her only one generation to own more land than anyone else and to become the only power broker in Twofer County, South Georgia. Even though one-third of her land was swamp land, she owned two-tenth of one percent of the entire state. But expensive cedar trees grew inside that swamp—money did grow on trees.

Those trees grew more precious each passing day because the

land where such trees grew was disappearing all over the globe.

QueenBee was one of the 500 largest landowners in the state. Other than Colt, only one other person knew the extent of her wealth. But that one other person didn't know that he knew so much about her. Twofer County was the envy of other counties stuck down in the bottom of the state where gnats and pine trees ruled supreme.

South Georgia had once been in high cotton when it came to Georgia's racist politics. But like other small and poor counties in the bottom of the state, Twofer County suffered grievously when the courts outlawed the county unit voting system that propped up Jim Crow segregation in Georgia since that *Yankee farce* most folks so eagerly called Reconstruction (disguised re-enslavement).

The sole aim of Jim Crow was for Southern white people to enslaved Southern black people by other means. The money stopped trickling down so fast from Atlanta when white South Georgia politicians could no longer deliver the South Georgia white vote to offset the Atlanta black vote. The hateful county unit system allowed a majority white South Georgia county with only 5,000 white people to have as much say in state government as a majority black county with over 250,000 black people.

The large South Georgia plantations, led by the race-baiting Talmadges and their lot, masqueraded as small counties. But they lost much statehouse clout in Atlanta when the courts declared county unit voting unconstitutional because it so diluted the black vote all over the Empire State.

Atlanta, the mother city, now unshackled from the race-baiters of South Georgia, took off like a rocket to reclaim her seat at the table of America's prosperity. The capital city left South Georgians behind eating the dust kicked up by the galloping hooves of Atlanta men and women scrambling to catch up with the rest of the country. But QueenBee changed all that down in Twofer County when she took over power in the county.

QueenBee pumped lots of money, mostly her own money in the beginning, into the county's empty coffers. She lured businesses to the county with free land and low taxes. Those businesses hired the unemployed and the underemployed in Twofer County and other counties. Jobs, schools, libraries, computers, and a hospital got top priority in a county that now had a rock-solid economy.

In her mind, there were three Georgias out there, not two: One Georgia was Atlanta and the towns ringing her city limits like pigs suckling at a sow's tits. A second Georgia was North Georgia, orbiting Atlanta's sun like a planet and basking in the mother city's glow. Then there was a third Georgia; South Georgia counties below the gnatline that clung to a plantation mind much too long, and the people were now paying the ultimate price—generation stagnation.

In those South Georgia counties, sons and daughters of "poor white trash" and "illiterate black garbage" paid dearly and suffered severely for the blatant sins of the fathers, the false virtues of the mothers, and the deep ignorance of their kids. After Jim Crow bit the dust hard, South Georgia could have been a part of east Alabama or north Florida or west South Carolina or south Tennessee or even the Atlantic Ocean for all Atlanta and the rest of the state cared.

The state cast South Georgia adrift on a life raft of negligence in a sea of ignorance—to suffer and stew in its generation stagnation. They turned their backs on and ignored poor black folks and poor white folks still fighting over crumbs falling from the tables of those who profited from their ignorance and bigotries—ignored until election time rolls around. Then the politicians came around again begging for the vote and soft-pedaling the same bigotries that had worked so well for them and their forebears in the past.

Queen Beatrice Carter Rome was a player, and had been a player for over forty years.

For those same forty years, she had tithed a tenth of her good fortune to prop up every kind of politician the state had to offer up to serve the people, except for the bigots. Never support a bigot was her one true motto. Not even her own bigots did she support.

She banished Malcolm Xavier, Twofer County's worst black bigot, to Chicago. Twofer County had no time for bigots, regardless of race, creed, nationality, or religion.

She'd always had such big plans for the county, and until five months ago she'd had such big plans for Stanford as well. But then the murders happened.

The murders changed all that.

QueenBee stopped herself from putting Stanford in harm's way. Now she had to stop Shelley from putting her grandson in harm's way as well. She had only one grandson, but she'd played mother hen to six other boys who grew up with Stanford.

There was Shelley, Stanford's best friend; Twofer County Sheriff Jake Keller; Atlanta attorney Fred Wainwright Junior; Atlanta detective Jud Judson; federal judge Justin Grimes; and Thomas Jefferson Lee, Colt, a Twofer County detective and a computer legend in his own time.

Those boys had grown up much too fast for her taste, and they too soon left home for college. Only two returned home to Twofer County to stay. That was Jake, the snake and Colt, the gun.

QueenBee lived low when all her boys left home for college and grew into adulthood. Even as she pushed the boys away from Twofer County, she hated like hell to see them all go.

She bought Colt his Computer Shack. Colt stuck his computer gear and backup power supply inside a climate-controlled building with walls three-feet thick. Jake Keller, as sheriff, was the official power in Twofer County, as sheriffs were in most South Georgia counties.

QueenBee stopped rocking and sat still awhile. The *Miami Herald* didn't have to tell her something she already knew—he was back killing again. She already knew that. She had created that monster and had never imagined she would someday lose control of him. She had to deal with him, and deal with him, PDQ.

To do that, she had to first pry him away from the governor without raising the governor's suspicions. The governor was one of her heavy-hitting politicians; they operated on the same wavelength. They both believed that what was good for Georgia was also good for South Georgia, and that what was good for South Georgia was also good for Twofer County. She set the newspaper aside and scratched Aretha's ear.

When she did, Franklin's ears perked up. But the rascal Shelley hadn't come calling in nearly three months now. That was twice as long as he'd stayed away at any other time since the Vietnam War petered out. He was a problem, a dangerous problem. She knew of only two ways to solve such a dangerous problem once and forever. She would try the first way.

If the first way failed her, she would execute the second way.

She rattled the dice.

She had to get him back to Twofer County, so she could send those killing demons scurrying back down into the deep caverns of his mind like she'd been doing since he was a boy. But he wouldn't return to Twofer County; for good reasons, too. He knew what was waiting for him, and he knew damn well who was waiting for him.

Then she had a thought, and the thought brought with it a smile. Why not? He was the governor, and he did owe her one or two or three favors; she'd lost count. But enough thinking about that. For now her top priority was to keep on living.

Soon enough she would find that murdering, raping kidnapper, and she would drag him back to Twofer County to stand trial for his crimes, and to face a one-woman firing squad.

§

QueenBee was born in 1905 to John R. and Alice Mae Carter. She was christened Queen Beatrice Carter.

Her childhood traumas included getting swept up in the mad dash of sons and daughters of ex-slaves fleeing the South Carolina cotton plantations in droves. They streamed north to the big-city life in Chicago, Cleveland, Detroit, and New York to eat the fruits grown on the tree of life in the Promised Land. But her father, John R., turned his back on the northern passage. He chased his rainbow down into the Sunshine State, steering his family due south and full-speed ahead.

She remembered that day they had all stood on the South Carolina side of the Savannah River, waiting for old Uncle Buddy to step aboard the ferry that would carry them all over into Georgia. Her father had stood staring out across the water. Then she saw her father slump to his knees and sweep away their footprints with his bare hands. When the ferry drifted across the water, relatives and dear friends cheered, tossed hats and bonnets, and danced big-time jigs. Her father stood off to the side—alone.

His head hung so low.

"I was betrayed by this land. I gave so much of me," her father had said. The sad, sad words broke her young heart.

Then they all had turned their backs to the land they had been born on. Deeper and deeper into the bowels of the old Confederacy they went, making camp in the woodlands of South Georgia. Here, the pine tree was king and the pine tar, the royal jelly.

Work was plentiful, year-round, and back-breakingly hard. Her father worked for a railroad gang. Her mother Alice worked as a seamstress.

They shared a new life in the same old land.

She was ten when diphtheria fell her mother.

The doctor bills piled up and kept rolling in, forcing her father away from the railroad gang and into the life of a high-roller gambler. They needed the money for doctor bills. Lots of money for doctor bills. John R. became a fierce gambler. He teamed up with Frank "Royal Flush" Steele and Jesse "Animal" Campbell, two of the darkest, stealingest, lyingest, meanest hell-raisers in all of Georgia.

The three gunslingers rode lockstep with death in every town they rode into. Her father carried two handguns, was a crack shot with either hand, and he slept with both eyes cracked just a little. She would never forget that about him; the way he slept with both eyes cracked just a little.

She was eleven when Alice Mae died in her sleep in 1916, leaving her fifty gold eagles and a doll collection. Days later, her world took another big hit. This time an avalanche struck her. When in full stride, her father dropped dead in the middle of muddy Main Street.

Townsfolk gossiped "heartbroken," but the wise old doctor ruled heart attack. Her father left her 382 gold eagles. A week later, she married Stan Rome, a big, strong, handsome man thirty years her senior, old enough to have been her grandfather.

Her new mother-in-law, Carrie Rome, guardian of the hoodoo trade, spent her time righting the confused minds of freed slaves. She earned herself a small fortune for doing it. Carrie taught her new daughter-in-law the tricks of the healing trade.

Shunning magic chants and evil eyes as tools for chasing away demons, Carrie used wild herbs and roots in curing her sick. Mostly, she mixed ginseng with the toxic mushrooms that grew wild in the backwoods of the South Georgia Deep.

She and Stan had one child, Odis Rome, in 1925.

Odis married Laurel Carter in 1947.

On midnight June 24, 1949, a Sunday, QueenBee sent for Odis and his pregnant wife to hurry on over. That day became her own Black Sunday. It had all started when, first, seventy-four-year-old Stan Rome had his only stroke. In his delirium, Stan asked her to pull on his boots for him. Stan died with his boots on.

Standing unnoticed in the doorway, Odis Rome took in the entire scene played out in front of him. He saw QueenBee kiss his father's eyelids shut for the last time. He saw her pull the sheet over his cooling face for good. Her lips quivered, but she didn't cry. In the next room, the midwife snipped the umbilical cord of yet another man-child, and then the midwife screamed out for help.

"A blue baby!" the midwife shouted out.

"QueenBee!" the midwife screamed out the name.

Still standing rooted and unnoticed in the doorway, Odis Rome gawked at the stillborn child on the table, his child. He watched the midwife fight to stop the heavy flow of blood from between her legs—his wife's legs. He saw the midwife was quickly losing that battle. He saw the midwife throw up her bloody hands, horrified, and stand gawking miserably over at him.

Odis then stepped farther into the room, looking dumbfoundedly down at his dead baby, his child who'd yet to take his first breath in the world. Then he looked over at his dead wife, his wife, who had just taken her last breath in the world. Odis turned away and walked out the house. Not only did Odis Rome walk out of Queen-Bee's life, but he never looked back.

If he would have looked back, he would have seen QueenBee snatch the stillborn up into her arms and spurt water up the infant's nose. But he never looked back. He never saw his son take his first breath . He never heard his son scream bloody murder.

It would be a year before Odis Rome walked back into Queen-Bee's life to learn he was a father with a son to raise.

21

SHELLEY PARKED THE Thunderbird next to a BMW 300i at the farthermost end of the Atlanta International Country Club south parking lot. The lot attendant watched over it for him.

He pulled out the tiny recorder, ejected the cassette and popped it into the playback machine. He pressed "Play."

David's voice: About the time Stacey and Stanley were killed?

Shelley's voice: Yes.

Silence. Long seconds of static silence. Shelley fast-forwarded the tape to the end of the first session with the psychiatrist.

David's voice: How did Frank die?

A long silence.

Then his voice. He told him. Did he say that? He stopped the playback machine. He was perspiring. It felt as if huge bubbles of slick sweat had come squirming up through his skin like earthworms deserting the ground after a heavy rainstorm.

He'd told that quack everything!

David Harte had hypnotized him without his knowing he was being hypnotized and without his permission to be hypnotized.

He scowled.

Nothing good was coming of this. The two-faced quack would pay for his double-cross. Because of his worsening memory, the shrink now knew him better than he knew himself. Nothing good was coming from this. He knew he had to tell David everything, but it was not supposed to happen like that.

Telling David Harte everything was the only way to go; he knew

123

that. Otherwise, David couldn't help him. But it was not supposed to happen like that. The only way for David Harte to root out those old memories was to first know the old memories were there. Once he'd told David the old memories, then his recorder would record the old memories for him to later use. By listening to the recorded old memories, he reprocessed those forgotten events back through his brain. That was how he planned to somehow resurrect his vanishing and forgotten past.

His memory was bad; he was just trying to help it limp along awhile longer. But it was not supposed to happen like that.

He needed David's help to replant his old memories. But all the quack wanted to talk about was "the night that never happened."

If David failed him like those Miami doctors failed him over a week ago, he would have no choice. He would have to go crawling back to Twofer County, crawling back to QueenBee for the relief he needed. Or he would end up eating lunch from the barrel of his own gun.

He took action two years ago when he realized his memory was heading south on him. He pieced together a year-by-year history, a sketch, of his life from as far back as he could remember. Now he used that same history to recharge his fading long-term memory.

In the beginning, two years ago, he listened to and memorized the history once every two weeks. But, a year later, he had to listen to and memorize the history every week. And, now, today, he had to listen to and memorize the history every other day. Soon, he would have no memory of his past. And like his black people, who had no memory of their past, he would be lost. He would become easily manipulated by other people out there who had a strong sense of, both, their own past and of his people's past as well.

But, all too soon, he knew it would become an everyday thing. But he still plain forgot to keep hunting the killer who murdered the wife and son of his best friend. He plain forgot.

But whenever he tried thinking about "the night that never happened," he woke up the sleeping beast. He could not long survive many more of the beast's temper tantrums.

Shelley again stared out across the parking lot then glanced over at the black BMW. He adjusted the tiny tape recorder inside the special pocket of his suit coat. He got out and took another look at the black car—a BMW 300i. Nice ride, he thought, remembering seeing the same car parked there last night. He was pleased he remembered that. Still smiling, he headed for the AICC entrance. He made a beeline for the Jazz Room where a quality quintet was paying tribute to the music of Miles Davis—his favorite jazzman.

Half an hour and two Black Russians later, the trumpeter had blown and sweated his way through the first two cuts of the Jazz masterpiece "Kind of Blue." A woman walked into the Jazz Room and sat down four tables away. Soon, she was using her eyes like scissors to snip away his jacket, his slacks, his jocks.

He knew right away when a woman was undressing him.

When the quintet took a short break, the voice of the King waffled smoothly through the loudspeakers. Nat King Cole's silky soulful voice made his atmosphere, and that alluring woman over there now matching him drink for drink would surely make his night. For now, Shelley had all ten fingers stuck down inside Nat King Cole's tunes. He was lost and fumbling around inside the silky sounds of the most romantic voice the music world had ever known.

Two drinks later, Shelley was ready to call it quits. So he went over to the woman's table to make a bid for entertaining her for the rest of her night.

She looked up at him almost longingly and smiled as if pleased to see him standing there. He asked if he could join her, and she said he could, and he did. The woman's angelic face looked familiar, but after a few drinks, all women looked the same between the ears. In the same way that after a few cocktails, all cocktails started tasting watered down.

Shelley looked the woman straight in the eyes and swung for the home run.

"I don't know your name," he said. "But names are so unimportant. But tell me, pretty woman, give me a little idea about how many orgasms you can have in one night."

Shelley's face felt so deadpan he thought it might crack.

The pretty woman didn't say a word, and her eyes never once wavered from his gaze.

Shelley smiled at such a welcomed challenge. "I'm Shelley. My pad's only ten minutes away if you'd like to lie down and rest yourself. You do look a little tired and a lot sexy by the eyes." His facade fell apart, and he smiled. He couldn't help himself.

The woman was too cool. Knowing eyes seemed to rappel down his face to his crotch then undulate back up his torso to his face. Shelley was used to on-the-spot sizing up, but this eye examination bordered on the obscene.

With a slight nod, the gray-eyed woman covered her mouth with a smooth hand and let go an audible yawn. When she took her hand away from her mouth, she said, "I'm Candice. Ten minutes is way too long a time to wait for so long a thing. Let's do my place in nine." The woman pointed a delicious finger at him. "Me and you. Is that a plan, Frank?"

Candice's startling voice made him do a mental double take. The voice, it sounded so familiar to him. And didn't Candice call him Frank when he'd just told her his name was Shelley? Was she kooky or what? But she sure didn't look like a nut.

Shelley held out his hand and rose. "That's a plan, Rosetta."

§

Shelley so loved what Candice brought to the bed with her that he sent up a special prayer to heaven: Our sex, which art between our legs, long will be thy fame, heaven on earth.

Shelley's body throbbed in anticipation.

Every ounce of blood in Shelley's head was now pounding like mad deep down in his loins, his mind drooling with expectation. Candice came to him as if she'd waited years and years for just this chance to play sex games with him. Candice traced silky fingertips all over the curves and angles of his face. Her hands moved with the lightness of being. She poked him in the chest with fingers so gentle the touch had the force of a shove. He settled down on her bed on his back like a puppy to be rubbed.

Mirrors were stuck everywhere, absorbing, reflecting, and holding their images like footsteps quivering in raw cement.

Mirrors plastered adjacent walls from ceiling to floor. Stuffed cats of all spots and stripes occupied the pussy zoo. There was a jaguar leaping from ambush, a lioness stalking wildebeest, a cheetah chasing gazelles, a bobcat treeing raccoons, and a big lumbering earth-toned cougar pouncing down from rocks onto the thick broad back of a spooked mule deer. His nakedness was surrounded by an amazing zoo of pussies.

Candice was as quiet and smooth as she was raw and greedy, and the aroma of their sex just blew him away completely. She pulled away from him and stood tall at the foot of the bed. Her hands rode high on her hips, her breasts jutted from her chest like twin peaks, and her nipples poked out like extensions of her sex.

And softening a face that looked like it was chiseled from the side of a granite mountain was a field of coal-black hair. The long silky strands seemed to grow from the top of Candice's head and down into her skull only to emerge unscathed between her legs as pubic hairs weaving down long thighs like promises. The silky little pussy fingers raced down her knees in desperate search of man, rippling over diamond calves with long gorgeous bellies stretching all the way down to within inches of her cute little ankles.

The woman's legs alone were worth the price of admission to the rest of her gorgeous body.

Candice covered him with that body, her mouth and her sex, and if the woman wanted to chain him and put a whip to his back, he could very well go for that. She tamed his hard macho sex, so willfully, so maliciously, so mercilessly, so completely that he unraveled beneath her like a broken spring. She teased him to please him. And he nearly ODed on the appetizer.

When, finally, Candice opened herself up as a flower to him, he sank down into her like a big black bumblebee.

Her long smooth thighs drew him tight into her until he was snug as a glove. Her arms roped his neck, her calves hugged his back, and the last sane sound he heard was her ankles locking down on him clanging like a jailhouse door.

§

As Shelley's world filtered back in on him, he bumped into his own consciousness with a jolt. Suddenly, the hot wind rippling across his flesh turned icy cold.

The smell was unmistakable to him.

Shelley kept his eyes shut. He'd smelled enough death to know death when he smelled it. And death was close enough to kiss him on the lips. He smelled Candice somewhere nearby but not close, and she was clutching his .44 Magnum Blue in her hands.

The scent of the linseed oil he used to clean the gun had mere seconds ago waffled up into his nostrils. Shelley kept his eyes shut, and he lay there babylike. His left arm rested across his forehead, but his right arm was stretched out by his side. He had no choice but to turn that hot little cunt into maggot meat. He started a slow countdown and would move on the count of zero. Three. Two—

Shelley heard Candice padding across the floor away from him and stopped the countdown. He cracked an eyelid and saw Candice slap his gun back up into the Opossum and roll two bullets from his ammo belt.

She dropped the bullets inside her purse, looked up and gasped.

He was now staring right at her.

Candice clutched her chest, and her eyes closed.

"Why?" he said, unmoved from his sleeping position.

Sighing, Candice opened her eyes and looked at him. "I've just always wanted to do that. To screw a guy's brains out and then pretend to blow out his brains. Looking for a rush. No rush there."

She held up the purse. "But, I've got these. Two souvenirs." She winked. "You could've been dead, you know."

He eased his grip on the unseen derringer.

22

ATLANTA/LAKE ARROWHEAD

MONDAY, MAY 30

"GOOD NIGHT, BRYCE," Jocelyn Slade said, as they stood in the doorway of her split-level home.

The dinner had been pleasant enough. The meal was over with, and Bryce was leaving. She stepped back to close the door on Bryce, but her ex-boyfriend blocked the door with his foot. Their faces were inches apart like two boxers ignoring prefight instructions from the barking referee.

Bryce said, "Joy, can you tell me what happened to ol' Norman Gene? These two dudes from the apple, they came peeling down south looking for ol' Norman Gene about four months ago. Said ol' Norman Gene jumped down Atlanta way between Christmas and New Year's, but he never made it back to the big NYC. Did you see ol' Norman Gene while he was here in the ATL?"

She smiled around her annoyance. "I'm no baby-sitting service, Bryce. Now, move your foot before I claw your pretty face."

Bryce was unmoved. "Wait up, Joy. This is on the up; this is important. Norman Gene, he came to Atlanta to do a business deal with someone he knew here. You and me, Joy, we the only friends Norman Gene got who live this far south. He's never been south of the Mason-Dixon before. Do you see what I'm getting at, Joy? Norman Gene didn't come to Atlanta to see me, so maybe he came to Atlanta to see you. What you wanted Norman Gene to do that I couldn't do for you? Who done pissed you off so bad that you needed Norman Gene to set things right for you?"

"I don't know anything about it. Now move your damn foot."

Bryce smirked and she clawed at his face. With the slick move of a mongoose, Bryce weaseled out of range, but she saw a flash of panic in his eyes. Bryce's lifestyle of booze, coke, women had turned his once hard body a little on the soft side. Her punch nearly got through, and she'd never come that close to digging ditches in that pretty face before. Such a pity. Gone to pot.

She slammed the door on Bryce's grin.

Jocelyn flushed the cocaine Bryce had purposely left behind. She hadn't touched the stuff since she hit Atlanta five years ago. She hadn't needed the cocaine and the uppers, not since she left the unbelievable pressure of New York City behind her for good.

She soaked her weary body in bubbles for thirty minutes, threw on a pair of silk pajamas, grabbed her latest novel-in-progress and collapsed on the bed, exhausted. Getting on top in the news business was a battle—one small skirmish after another one. But staying on top was all-out war, and every engagement a major fight.

She lifted the bookmark from page 145. Richard Wright's *The Outsider* was hard reading for her, and she didn't feel up to fighting with this brilliant but obviously flawed black man. Not tonight, darling Richard. She had a headache. Excuses, excuses. She threw the book aside and returned to brooding over Stanford. She hadn't heard from him since their joyride. She was nearing the sixteen-month anniversary of her celibacy. She was ready to get laid.

On the sixteenth anniversary she wanted Stanford to knock the bottom out for her, even if she had to pay him to do it. And she was dead serious about that—even if she had to pay him to haul her ashes for her.

Jocelyn jumped bare-assed naked in her Jacuzzi and sulked. But in minutes she was back hatching plans to seduce Stanford Rome and to claim that heart-broken man as her very own.

She sank to the bottom and giggled underwater.

Bubbles shot up to the top. And she would use his best friend Shelley Lester as bait to first hook him, then she would reel him in by telling him how much she loved him and how much she wanted to please him. That always worked. She thought about that again. Maybe telling him how much she wanted to please him was going a little too far. Regardless, she was going to give an Oscar-winning performance that would woo any testosterone man into her bed.

Another giggle. More bubbles shot up to the top.

Damnit, she was tired of waiting on Stanford to make his move. It was time to sink her teeth into this man, to blow his mind—or to just simply blow him. Naughty, naughty. She giggled at the very real image of blowing Stanford up like a balloon. Whatever it took. That was kind of cute; she had to remember that one: to blow his mind or to just simply blow him. She took out her day planner to check not only her schedule but Stanford's schedule as well.

Naughty, naughty.

She always knew where Stanford was going to be at any hour on any day. She paid an informer in Stanford's office a weekly fee to give her a copy of Stanford's day planner. Her informer also called her every time Stacey Rome left town for an overnight visit to her mother down in South Georgia, some 250 miles away. But she had never before acted on the information received from her informer, except for that one time. Now it was time to act on that information a second time. Her number-one priority, for now, was to lose her virginity a second time. This time around, the honor was going to Stanford Rome whether he wanted the honor or not.

Bedding down Stanford Rome was more important to her than anything she'd ever wanted before. Well, not exactly. Her greatest lust has always been and would always be to become a TV-network superstar. She was nobody without her stardom. And he was treating her like she was nobody even with her stardom. Something just had to be wrong with that man. Or was something wrong with her? Nope, couldn't be her. Had to be him.

He'd been mean to her before, and she had forgiven him. It happened that night she trapped his elusive behind inside Peacocks The Restaurant. She was hot for him that night and he was mean to her. Goddamnit, would they ever be on the same page?

She sat, seething, remembering the night he was mean to her.

§

At Peacocks The Restaurant, the chandelier dangling from the ceiling doubled as a clock. The late-night hour found Jocelyn Slade sitting alone at a table for four, sipping red wine and watching the entrance into the dining area.

Her lips were chilled by the cool smooth rim of the crystal glass she was drinking from. Jocelyn had been waiting for Stanford to show up for a late dinner as Mr. Saint Simon had said he would. Stacey Rome was down south visiting her perpetually sick mother. He intended to dine alone tonight at Peacocks The Restaurant, but he would end up sharing a table for four with her.

She would make that happen.

The wine smoothed out the wrinkles in her nerves, strengthening her resolve to seduce this man, this night. To hell with celibacy.

At 9:45 p.m., Stanford entered the restaurant with the flourish and flair of a movie star. She watched him and caught herself licking her lips as if Stanford were a Popsickle searching for a mouth and tongue, and not searching for just any old mouth and tongue either—but searching for her willing mouth and tongue.

Stanford moved easily through Peacocks The Restaurant. Walking side by side, he and the maitre d', they were just laughing and talking and chatting it up like old war dogs. With every other step Stanford took, he glanced around the restaurant as he moved on through, like a bounty hunter with cross hairs in his eyes.

What did Stanford look like naked? She felt skittish; her wants and her needs were more fragile than crystal and just as transparent as glass. This anchorwoman, she wore no clothes. Not a stitch on the bitch! She wanted to shout out that rallying cry from her wild New Orleans days, a cry her and her drinking pals screamed out when a stud stepped onstage hung like a bull:

Who dat rode that bull in here like dat—Who dat!

Those times had been the wildest of the wild times, and they had been the wildest of wild women. Those had been her drinking pals, her hanging-out buddies. She had never had any real friends, the kind you told deep secrets to.

Who dat rode that bull in here like dat—Who dat!

The maitre d' ushered Stanford to a small table for two, pulled his chair back and waved him down in it. Mr. Saint Simon looked very much the precious toy soldier, all dressed up in his black tuxedo, ivory-white gloves, and pressed-on professional face.

Jocelyn had a perfect view of Stanford's table. She could see him through a mirror hidden from his view by latticed railings on the next dining level above him. She sized up her guy.

Stanford was a karate black belt which suggested stamina for the long haul, she supposed. And his ancestors, they had to have been royalty. That would make Stanford a prince, a fierce warrior, a leader of men, a breeder of women.

Stanford had that look about him, his eyes never still, constantly sorting out the world and his place in it. God, every woman should feel as lucky as she felt right this minute, to run across a man who just had that look and that feel about him that made a woman's toes curl up into little fuzzy balls.

Jocelyn knew she was going to give Stanford some the first time she laid eyes on him. But, of course, she didn't know it would take her five years to give it to him. If loving Stanford Rome was wrong, she didn't give a damn about doing right. That last thought had country song written all over it.

"Good evening, Miss Slade."

Her head jerked around. Stanford stood staring straight down into her face. She felt cold. She could feel her sexuality shutting down on her, body part by body part: her thighs slapping together, her ankles clamping down, and she was gonna come—unglued.

Her brain was a marquee of flashing lights blaring tomorrow's shocking headlines for everybody to read:

SEX ATTACK LAST NIGHT!!

> Last night at the Marriott Marquis, in full view of a dozen conventioneers from Ankeny, Iowa, Jocelyn Slade, a local television personality, assaulted and seriously wounded Stanford Rome, a married man and local CPA, with her sex. Mr. Rome's in the hospital with first-, second-, and third-degree burns over a private one-percent of his body.

"Stanford Rome," she said, nodding to the chair opposite her. She planted her elbows on the table, meshed her fingers into a bridge, and rested her chin atop the bridge, eyes piercing his face.

"I hope this is a pickup and not a setup," she said and smiled.

"Don't be coy, Joy." Stanford smiled then settled down into the chair across from her, still smiling like a winner.

"Miss Slade, Mr. Saint Simon, he's been on my payroll for years now." The winning smile turned a little smug. "Now that you have me where you obviously want me, Miss Slade, what's the next part of your diabolical plan? Perhaps flip me over on my back and stick me up inside you until I'm limp and wet, I suppose, Miss Slade?"

A kidder, she thought. He could be real fun. She leaned smartly back, fingers slipping apart as if finely oiled and greased.

"You have a high opinion of yourself, Mr. Rome. And your wit is quaint and obvious." She smiled. "And charming, I must admit."

"Call me, Stanford. I'll call you, Joy, if I may."

"I'll call you, Stanford. You call me, Joy, if you like."

"So, Joy, will we fuck each other figuratively, or will we fuck each other literally?" His face was as flat as a cookie sheet.

"Stanford, that's disgusting," she said. "But original BS."

"And, Joy, you're some foxy lady," Stanford said. "Or should I say you are one hell of a chick?"

"Stanford," she said, "you can say whatever you like as long as you keep talking. I find it simply amazing that you can, both, talk out of your butt and sit on it at the same time."

And that was the way the conversation had gone. No quarters had been given, none asked for. Yes, he'd been mean to her. And yes, one day they would be on the same goddamn page.

§

Jocelyn turned off I-85, thirty minutes shy of her destination and drove slowly around the mountain, enjoying the scenery. She stopped at the Lake Arrowhead guardhouse.

"Hello, Sid," she said.

The security guard held out the clipboard for her signature.

"Good afternoon, Ms. Slade. What a combination. A gorgeous day and a beautiful woman. Ma'am, if I had your hand, I'll throw my hand in and quit the game for good; I'll do it, I swear."

Leaving the guardhouse behind, Jocelyn veered left toward the Lake Arrowhead Hotel. But she circled the huge lake and took the winding road leading to the cottage that Stanford owned. Twenty minutes later, she rounded the last bend of a horseshoe curve and saw Stanford's cottage for the first time.

The place looked eerily quiet.

She parked and got out. Stanford's car was gone. She walked to the door and turned the doorknob. It clicked. She hesitated, then pushed the door open. She poked her head innocently inside.

"Stanford?" she said. No answer.

But she thought she heard a rustling inside.

She eyeballed the room from where she stood. But the rustling could have come from outside. She kept staring inside, eyeing the orderliness, the sparse furnishings, the mounds of books, the desk, the credenza, the swivel chair, the filing drawers, the small cassette player, the bar, the dummy, the grandfather clock, sofa, sofa chair, ottoman, books again, reading lamps, telescope, microscope, binoculars, rifle, dumbbells, weight bench, and chinning bar.

She sucked in all the room's telling details but something was missing. She stepped back and left the door slightly ajar.

She drove the 4x4 around back where it couldn't be seen from the road. She hurried back inside Stanford's cottage to snoop. As soon as the door clicked shut behind her, she felt an instant case of nerves, like maybe she'd locked herself inside the lair of a bear and was now at the mercy of that beast. But she fought off her dread and started nosing around. A photo album gaped open on the coffee table. She flipped through the pages.

A loud lingering gong boomed in her head.

Her heart jumped up into her throat, stifling her scream.

As the gong faded, she clutched her chest and glared at the culprit of her near fatal heart attack. Damn grandfather clock. She took a few deep breaths then went back to snooping. She ran her fingers over a mannequin wearing a bulletproof vest. Odd.

One of the two bedrooms was padlocked. She wondered what Stanford hid in that room. She heard a noise outside and darted to the peep-hole. She saw the two security guards getting out of a black Jeep Cherokee, and one had a ring of keys in his hands.

She whipped around in a panic, shot glances around the room and darted away from the door.

No place to hide. She bolted inside the bedroom, and squeezed herself inside the walk-in clothes closet. She eased the door shut behind her. Crouched down inside the dark closet she hugged herself. Did those guards see her truck? She felt sick.

She whiffed and thought she smelled—

A hand clamped her mouth. A deep voice spoke into her ear.

Jocelyn Slade fainted.

23

Lake Arrowhead/Miami Beach

Monday, May 30

Candice Bergens eased the woman's limp body to the closet floor. But she kept an ear cocked to the voices outside the closet door. She gripped the Beretta tighter as if it might try to shoot its way out of there without her.

The two men outside the door were talking loud to each other.

"You know, Larry, I'm gonna rent one of them Mercedes they rent out down at the hotel, and I'm gonna haul ass from one end of this mother to the other end, wide open, like a bat outta hell!"

"Yeah, right, Vern, I hear you, and I'm gonna be peeling your dead ass from around one of these black gum trees, too. Just like old Joe did last year when he wrapped that Jeep around a tree."

"Well, my name ain't no Joe. Besides, I know how to keep from breaking my fool neck. Hey, who's this in this picture here? Shelley, ain't it?"

"Let me see—yeah, that's my man."

Candice jumped when the woman on the floor moaned and stirred. She crept farther away from the closet door, shrinking behind a long wool overcoat. Outside the closet door, she could still hear the two men bellowing at each other.

"I bet you never heard tell of the Miami Assassin. That's Shelley since you don't know that. He's the one. He so bad the Mafia put a $1-million hit on his bad ass. You didn't know that, I bet you, Mr. Know-it-all. Bet you didn't know that."

"Yeah, right. Like I'm supposed to believe that malarkey. Man, if any man got a $1-million hit on his black ass, he won't have no black ass no more, and I don't give a shit how bad the black ass he be toting. He'll be too through. I don't care how many Medals of Honor he done won. Shoot, man, you crazy."

Candice's ears perked up. She had never hear about a $1-million hit. With a name like Miami Assassin, the hit had to be put out by the Miami mob and Preacher, that sociopath. She could always fly down to the Bottoms and ask Preacher about it. But that was a bad idea. She couldn't chance running into Preacher's sidekick, that evil midget, Little Bruce Wayne. She shuddered at the thought of crossing paths again with that certified crazie. But, she was moving up in the world. She had screwed a certified crazy before, and now she had bedded down a Medal-of-Honor winner.

The woman on the floor moaned again.

The voices outside the door abruptly stopped. Not a sound did she hear from the two men on the other side of that closet door. The stirring woman moaned louder. Candice stiffened and rooted herself deeper behind the clothes. The closet door flew open. Candice eased the slack from the trigger, waiting. If the clothes moved, she would roll out shooting.

"Outta there!" the voice shouted.

Candice didn't move, but she was ready to roll out shooting.

The groaning woman rolled around on the floor of the closet.

"Jocelyn Slade?" one of the men said.

§

Long sleek black limousines lined the curving roadway in front of Preacher's Miami Beach mansion as far as Mario could see. The flagship for that fleet of gloom was a silver Rolls Royce hearse.

The bodyguard was impressed and annoyed at the same time.

Preacher's huge mansion was set a hundred yards back from the street. The view was obstructed by tall palms with huge flapping fronds as green as the luscious lawn they were planted on.

Mario whistled. "Quinn! We ready to head out. Go tell 'em inside we ready to roll outta here!"

Mario shook his head. Quinn was on the slow side. He didn't want to hire the guy, but what could he do; they were cousins and all. He and Quinn, they grew up together. Also, Quinn's boss Carlos Martinez was serving nickel-and-dime time in the Pen up in Atlanta. Quinn did need somewhere to be for a while. He put Quinn on Preacher's payroll because Quinn knew his way around Atlanta. They had spent four days up in Atlanta looking for Preacher's missing son, Sturro. They didn't find Sturro.

But the two guys who went to Atlanta with Sturro, he and Quinn did feed those meatheads to the fish in that Chattahoochee pond. Preacher held those two nitwits responsible for whatever happened to Sturro. Preacher even paid him and Quinn a bonus.

Even without a body, Preacher declared that Sturro was dead, and now they were all going down to the cemetery to bury, of all things, an empty damn coffin. Mario kicked the ground then held both arms out in front of him. His arms shook. His fucking hands were trembling like he had palsy or something, and he couldn't stop them from shaking like crazy. It was Preacher. He was up to something. Preacher was scheming again. He could feel it in his bones. And he just knew he was going to be pulled down into one of Preacher's harebrained schemes. What would it be this time?

Mario kicked the ground again—harder this time. He'd never before seen Preacher in such a dangerous mood. But planting an empty coffin in the boneyard was a little too much.

Even for Preacher. What will he do next, resurrect the dead?

§

It was late evening when the twenty-limousine procession ended its hour-long crawl through Miami Beach traffic.

At the grave site, Mario felt a chill pass between Preacher and that six-foot hole in the ground they all stared down into. Preacher was doing the "ashes to ashes, dust to dust" bit while gazing at the dirt trickling through his fingers as if that were his life he was looking at. The scary part was that Preacher was grinning like a sinner who'd somehow wormed his way into the pearly gates of heaven.

"Myyyy, my!" Preacher cried out.

His voice was as mean as it was loud, as mournful as it was bitter. The words rang out across the cemetery like a pitiful wail. But Preacher kept grinning like a sinner.

"Damn those who took from me!" Preacher's voice roared.

Preacher stood gazing down the long line of drivers dressed in tuxedos and all standing at attention alongside their black shiny limousines. Preacher grinned, his cheeks bright in the sunlight. Large teardrops streamed from his eyes as he kept on grinning.

"Marioooo!" Preacher's voice boomed.

"Go to Hugo's, Mario. Go to Hugo's and get broads for all my shooters who weep with me here today. Bring tents, bring broads, bring bands, bring booze…"

§

Thirty-one hours later, Mario watched Preacher peel off his limp tuxedo like it was a suit of armor.

The fake funeral was over, the real party winding down. Only a sprinkling of people still hung around. The celebration had been a nonstop party. The loiterers seemed unable to accept that something so glamorous, so magnificent as Preacher's funeral bash was not a circle on which they could chase the good life without end.

Preacher's parties were the standard by which all other parties for miles around were judged. The Looney Tunes, the fourth big band that played, wound down as Preacher loosened the buttons on his shirt and unclasped his cuff links, looking irritated.

"Preacher," Mario said, "can I say something?"

Preacher studied him. "Sure, Mario, go ahead, say something."

"Well, Preacher. I was thinking that—I mean, are you okay? Can I do anything for you? To help you, you know? You seem so sad."

Preacher shrugged. "Nah. I'm okay. People, they die every day." Preacher tossed him a pair trunks. "Let's take a dip."

Mario cocked his head. "With or without sharks?"

§

At the Olympic-sized swimming pool, Preacher took a toehold and dove in, slicing through the water like a diving loon. He was floating on his back when Mario dove in. Mario swam two laps and stroked over to where Preacher hung onto the side of the pool. Mario felt those vibes again, stronger now. Even in the water he felt those vibes. Something was all wrong.

Preacher pulled himself out the water and sat dripping on the edge of the pool, his feet dangling in the water. Mario sat beside his boss and draped a towel over Preacher's shoulders.

His boss was sad. That was when Preacher was most dangerous. Whoever offed Sturro in Atlanta was in for troubles beyond anything they could ever dream up. He had a sick feeling Preacher was set to "go off" and do serious damage to a lot of people.

Preacher pulled the towel tighter around his shoulders.

"Mario, a swim do you better than a fuck, you know that?"

"I'd rather get laid," Mario said; and not wanting to prolong the agony of not knowing, he added, "what's up, Preacher?"

Preacher sighed and didn't speak for almost a minute.

"Mario, get me Bruce. I got a job for Bruce up Atlanta way."

Mario shook his head, his mind spinning. He stared at Preacher stupidly. Bruce Wayne was the shortest distance between a cradle and a grave. Preacher knew that better than anyone else because Preacher and that baby-faced killer used to be tight. But, these days, Bruce Wayne hung around with a psychopath whose idea of fun was to slice out your spinal cord. A chill seeped through his gut and down his legs to his cold, cold feet.

"Preacher, you said no sharks," Mario whined.

"No grief, Mario. Not now."

"Preacher, are you kidding me? Bruce, he's not only a shark, he's a fucking Great White with teeth on both ends. Preacher, you told me no sharks."

Preacher sniffled. "No grief, Mario."

"But Preacher, Little Bruce—"

Preacher was facing him now, his eyes filled with tears.

"Shit!" Mario spat out the word and looked down at the floor as if expecting the word to lay squirming at his feet.

Tears were streaming down Preacher's face.

Mario glanced out across the Miami Beach flatness like he was looking for a hill to head for. Then he gawked down at the water, looked back up at Preacher's weeping eyes, turned and dove in.

Mario sank to the bottom of the pool, safe as long as he held his breath. Why did Preacher need Little Bruce Wayne?

He let his body go limp, and farted.

Bubbles shot to the top.

24

JAMES KELSEY PLOPPED down on the sofa in Stanford's office, crossed his legs, and rested both arms across the back of the sofa. Stanford knew that pose as James Kelsey's fuck-you pose.

"What's on your mind, Stanford? CapCity's got an SOS out for me. So let's hear it and be quick about it."

James rolled his wrist, making an exaggerated effort to look at his watch.

Stanford told himself he was doing this for Juanita because he promised her he would do it. Even though she was dead, he felt obligated in a way to keep his promise. He said, "CapCity Investments is what I wanted to chat about, James. They sure are herding tons of business our way these days."

"That's right. We get all their business. In the beginning, they farmed it out for low bids. But while you were gone, for two whole months, I might add, the folks over there felt sorry for us. They dumped the whole thing in our laps. Great bunch of guys, huh?"

He toyed with the pencil. "And obviously they're good at what they do," he said.

"They're tough," James Kelsey said. "No doubt, and they're really picky about who gets their greedy hands on their money. No loan applicant borrows a dime from CapCity until they first stand a clean audit from us. That I like. In fact, that I love. Our take on these loans comes to $40,000 a month, averaging about $5,000 an audit. Not only that, we prepare CapCity's quarterlies, their tax returns, the year-end stuff, the computer work, the whole ball of wax. You're right, for once, managing partner. CapCity herds lots of business our way. Lucky us, huh?"

James stood before he could respond. "Anything else? I really got to get going. I'm a busy man."

Stanford cursed himself and his motives. Why was he stirring up even more trouble with James Kelsey now? Juanita was dead. The thought of Juanita being dead flashed in his mind. His timing was wrong. James was alive and now he needed his cooperation. He rubbed the nape of his neck, studying his partner's stern face.

"No, nothing else," he said. "Thanks for dropping by, James."

James stood pat. "You still taking that leave, I suppose?"

"I suppose," he said and shrugged.

He saw James' lips tighten, and he braced himself.

"You know, Stanford, I wish you would stop risking the future of this firm over what you think is right. Who gave you the right to go shoving our faces into your shit pile of morality? No one gave you that right. It bothers the hell outta me when people who don't put one thin dime in our pockets are so quick to pat us on the back for some good deed they feel we done did. We should say, 'fuck you, you backslapping, tree-hugging, ass-kissing sons-of-bitches. We're no morality police, Stanford. We're a business, and we in business for the money, m-o-n-e-y. Are you listening, Stanford? The m-o-n-e-y. The money. It's always about the money!"

James wiped his mouth with the sleeve of his coat as if his own words left a bitter taste in his mouth. He knew it was better to let James get it all off his chest, again, and be done with it. That was the downside of being the managing partner. He had to be the glue that held the separate parts together. And, sometimes, like now, he had to be a punching bag for the good of the firm.

But it was much tougher when catching hell from the client and catching hell from the partner.

"Another damn thing, Stanford," James said, "it makes my heart pump pure piss when Fortune-500 companies don't come kicking down our doors to do business with us. And, we're supposed to be famous now because you busted that so-called airport gang. Oh, we get tons of government business, but, they pay on the cheap, and we can barely recover our labor cost. But we haven't gotten one call from a Fortune-500 company. And you know why, Stanford?

"Because Fortune-500 companies don't want their warts exposed all over the six o'clock news; that's why. They don't want grand-standing from their bookkeepers. And now you've got Mark up in arms, threatening to snatch away our $3-million client. Stanford, our clients are not our enemies. Our clients, they pay the bills around here. Are we on the same page here, Stanford?"

He shrugged. "I'm listening," he said.

"You better be listening!" James blurted, jabbing a finger at his face. "That so-called airport gang, they didn't do one damn thing their predecessors didn't do—not one damn thing!"

He held up his hands. "James, you're preaching to the choir."

"Then hear it again, buddy. Where in the hell were people like you when those white boys were out there at the airport ripping off the system? Where were people like you when all those white boys were hauling their white asses on back to the suburbs dragging their booty behind them in their cute lil' red Corvettes?"

James hissed and stepped toward him.

"Now the same thieving white bastards have the goddamn auda-city to call us crooks when it was they who sacked and looted At-lanta. At least when William T. sacked the bitch, he had the decen-cy to torch it to the ground. Now, good day, Mr. Morality Police. I've gotta go to work so we can pay the bills around here."

James jabbed the same finger at his face again. He was tempted to bite the offending digit off at the knuckle.

"Don't you forget what I told you. If you walk, I walk." James Kelsey snarled. "And Lake Arrowhead walks —and Greg Lang."

Stanford smiled and shook his head. Had he been whipped like a dog, or what?

He drew back his fist as if he were going to throw it through the closed door and smack James in the back of the head with it. But instead of breaking his hand, in utter frustration, he poked out his tongue so far he thought he might dislocate it, and then he felt like weeping. Not fighting back, sometimes, it simply broke his heart.

James Kelsey was a pain in his ass. He should just kick him in the balls and watch the bastard hurt and puke. And while he was kicking ass, he could add Mark Davis to the mix, and fuck him up, too. Thorpe Henry, Clayton's boss; he should just dropkick that bastard upside his fucking head for quitting the case, and then he should…well, he'd run out of asses he really wanted to kick.

He smacked his fist in the palm of his hand so hard, it vibrated his not-so-funny bone, and it stung like hell, but it felt so goddamn good! He did it again, and it stung like hell again, but it felt so goddamn good! And he did it again, and it stung like hell again, but it felt so goddamn good!

He no longer felt like weeping. He felt like going for a walk, taking a stroll along Peachtree Street.

He had read somewhere that the earthworm felt secure only when touched on all sides of its body by the ground it lived in. That was the way he once felt. He had always wanted solid ground under his feet, a sky over his head, and surrounded on all sides by folks, coming and going. That used to make him feel like the earthworm felt—secure. He wanted to feel that feeling again.

He wanted that feeling back—a feeling of security.

After splashing his face with cold water for about a minute, he had calmed himself. He now stood by the window, staring down on Peachtree Street. He'd come a long ways in the two months he'd been back running the firm. He looked northwards where the mountains lay, thinking.

A WTNT-TV News helicopter swept past the window, vanishing behind the skyscrapers.

The sky was clear over the capital city. But he could see distant thunderheads gathering on the horizon. Trouble was heading his way if trouble hadn't already arrived.

Shelley told him that Richard and Mark had been big-time gamblers, and a bookie once put a hit on Richard for not paying his IOUs promptly enough. Sure, Richard and Mark's buying-and-selling business in Kansas City could have been a money-laundering scheme. But neither man had a criminal record, and neither man had been indicted for any crimes.

Shelley said something else that got his attention.

There also had been a rumor in Kansas City that one of those three—Richard, Mark, or James—was a killer more dangerous than a two-headed snake.

25

ATLANTA

WEDNESDAY, JUNE 1

ATLANTA WAS A soggy eighty degrees when night clamped down hard on the capital city, trapping the smog between the clouds and the concrete, the asphalt, the steel.

Atlanta stewed in sweat and misery.

The MAPD patrol car shot across Peachtree Lane like in the movies, hit a jagged pothole on Joetta Drive and bottomed out. Sparks went flying, and a steel wire got caught in a wheel and raveled around the rear axle. The black-and-white zoomed down the rutted street, the wire clicking against the wheel—clickclickclick-clickclickclickclickclickclickclick.

Garcia Chavis slowed the patrol car, turned left onto Auburn Avenue and crept closer to the curb—clickclickclickclick, click-click click-click, click-click, click-click, click, click, click, Click, Click, Click.

§

Wednesday morning, 2:41.

Shelley Lester was cruising Auburn Avenue. The proud street of black capitalism in the Deep South was nearly comatose. The lip-smacking sound of Sweet Auburn Avenue no longer graced her name, her future now cloaked in dust and rust.

Shelley circled the city, gritting his teeth and enduring the tapping sound inside his head. He felt Stanford's pain. Every agony, he felt. He had to find some way to help Stanford. But every time he tried to think of some way, he woke up the sleeping beast.

He couldn't much longer survive the temper tantrums. He dragged the back of his hand across his brow and swore to do better.

Shelley exited I-75 onto Capitol Avenue, and the tapping sound exited with him. The Trust Company Bank sign flashed 2:47 a.m. Wednesday. Seventy degrees.

Shelley slowed near Georgia State University, and the tapping sound in his head slowed right along with him. Candice Bergens popped into his mind or what was left of his mind. He was glad he didn't have to waste that broad. But she was trouble to him. Hell, at the AICC, he smelled trouble with that chick as soon as she called him Frank when he'd just told her his name was Shelley.

Was she a Bronner Brothers blond or what?

He turned onto International Boulevard just as a MAPD patrol car shot across Peachtree Way. He kept cruising the city. A left turn onto Auburn Avenue sent him racing to the east side of town, the tapping sound racing right along in him.

§

Wednesday morning, 2:53.

The patrol car slowed at THE CHURCH in Atlanta: Ebenezer Baptist Church. Click-click, click-click, click, click, click; click; click; Click. Click. Click.

Garcia Chavis parked the patrol car and waited.

The uniformed police officer, the new guy, dismounted from the shotgun side. He went into his slick two-minute, honor-guard routine with the practiced moves of a professional. Snapping to attention, he clicked his heels. Staring beyond the ancient Mother Church, his gaze locked onto the steel-and-glass Ebenezer, II.

The magnificent offspring was capped off by twin 200-foot spirals popping up out the roof like a devil's horn. The tall rising bulk of the church graced the sky like a modern-day Tower of Babel.

Atop that sleek monument to God, two fifteen-foot orbs topped off spirals that vanished on gray hazy days. On clear days, the twin spheres pierced the Atlanta skyline as if in search of the illusive heavens.

The new guy paraded around the reflecting pool and crypt, doffed his hat, made a snappy left turn then beat it on back toward his waiting partner.

The new guy stopped dead in his tracks, puzzled. The patrol car went squalling into an ugly U-turn—the new guy started running—and the patrol car zoomed off into the night without him.

Click, click, click, click,clickclickclickclickclick.

The new guy stopping running and cursed.

"What the fuck?" said the new guy.

He kicked the ground.

§

KabooOOMMmmm!

The old Ebenezer Baptist Church erupted like a volcano blowing its top. A towering fireball blew the roof off Ebenezer II and made it disappear.

Flames shot up into the sky like a gigantic blowtorch, the 100-foot flames screaming like a siren. Ruptured gas lines fed an endless stream of fuel to the fiery blaze that soon turn the holy house into a great big screaming ball of hellfire.

Wailing sirens wah-wahed the woeful cries of the city.

Explosions erupted like thunder.

Flames leapfrogged from one church to the other church until a smothering sheet of fire had transformed the two holy houses into an inferno. Firefighters, racing on the scene in record time, could only stand and watch in record numbers.

The fires twirled and whirled, whipping the night and consuming the two churches in hours. A weary groan shrieked through the air like a banshee. Ebenezer I crumbled in on itself like a gutted buck rolling over to die.

Black smoke billowed into the sky. Floodlights lit up a whole city block when the twenty-four-inch gas pipelines were capped, robbing the fire of its powerful engine and its roaring sound. A swelling crowd pressed in on the stench of hot rubble.

Overhead, a helicopter hovered, a bullhorn warning the crowd to stay back, keep away.

The city was stunned.

On foot, Shelley skirted the fringes of the destruction.

The tapping sound in his head was gone, but he felt a migraine coming on like a cacophony of galloping hooves. A MAPD helicopter swung in a wide arc, circling the destruction like a vulture, a teetered camera operator leaning out the side door for his shots.

Then the machine swept the photographer away with satisfaction or annoyance, Shelley couldn't tell which.

Biting smoke gathered about his head like dark thoughts. He coughed, a dry hacking cough, and the beast stirred deep within him—a warning.

Smoke clawed at Shelley's eyeballs; sweat balls bubbled up from his pores, pooling between his shoulder blades before trickling down the vertebrae of his spine and dribbling into the crack of his ass. He watched the police, fire and EMTs dig through the debris, hunting bodies, survivors and clues.

Fire engines, EMT wagons, police cruisers, ATF vans, FBI cars, and assorted vehicles glistened in floodlights lining two city blocks.

Shrieks, screams and shouts cut through the chaos and the madness. Shelley plowed through the crowd, looking for Markus Striker, the MAPD bomb expert. He pushed his way deeper into the swarm of flashing lights and milling bodies.

Shelley spotted Markus Striker. He adjusted the sensitivity of the recorder to account for the loud hubbub.

He and the MAPD bomb expert huddled near an ATF van.

"What the hell happened here?" Shelley said.

Markus took off his hard hat, dabbed his brow with a dirty handkerchief and said, "whoever set this off, they knew *A* from *B*."

"Arson?" Shelley said.

"Clearly arson. But it looks and sounds a hundred times worse because those ruptured gas lines fed the flames."

"So, pros firebombed these churches is what you're saying?"

"Right," Markus said. "And they were good, too—"

"Ca—Cap'n!"

Shelley turned to the sound of his old military rank.

Gerald, the MAPD cop looked like Casper the Ghost.

"Oh, Cap, it—it's Garcia," the stricken man said. "Oh my God! Cap'n, somebody, they cut his spinal cord. Som—Somebody, they butchered him. Crippled him. Oh, sweet Jesus."

PART THREE

SHELLEY

26

THREE MILLION PEOPLE were stunned into a solidarity unknown before in Atlanta. The city choked in sympathy, as support poured in from all over the country.

The Georgia governor, a Protestant, walked shoulder to shoulder with Muhammad Ali, an American icon and a Muslim with arguably the best known face on the globe. They and hundreds of other religious honchos toured the MLK ruins with rabbis and priests to lament the destruction of a monument devoted to a Christian Protestant. What a country.

Yes, the governor thought, what a country.

The governor called up his crisis management team for action. They piled into his war room to wait for "the man" to show up. The governor didn't see his media-shy public safety adviser. Except for Clayton Westwood, he didn't have much confidence in the rest of the people in the room.

The governor settled down to listen to the nincompoops and to wait for the real deal to show up. Boy, he hated politics, but he was in it for the money. His own money, that is. The governor still marvelled at the political animals in Atlanta. They so envied his bachelor lifestyle that they were forever sniffing out ways to run his butt out of that governor's mansion. Fat chance of that happening. QueenBee would skin him alive and feed him to those damn bull mastiffs of hers if that ever happened. He hated the sight of those bigheaded beasts. They looked like weightlifters. Anyway, it would never happen.

The governor had spent $4 million of his own money to buy the four years he was serving, and he was going to damn well serve every second he paid for. The job cost him three cents for every second he served, a buck-ninety for every minute, $114 for every hour, $2,740 for every day, $19,000 for every week, and $83,000 for every month he lived in that governor's mansion. Besides, he loved Atlanta like nobody else ever did, and he didn't give a damn who knew it. If he had his way, he would incorporate everything inside the Loop into the city of Atlanta. He would slash taxes down to the bone. But the buffoons would rather tax the people up to their eyeballs than be tied to Atlanta. Crabs, the lot of them.

The haters and the baiters. Damn crabs.

The governor let go a sigh when the real deal finally settled into the vacant chair next to him. "You're so late," the governor said.

"Yeah," Shelley said, "I may be late but you the man."

"What's that supposed to mean?"

"My point exactly," Shelley said.

The governor loved having Shelley close by. It was like having an extra set of balls dangling between his legs. He ignored those naysayers who said Shelley would sabotage his administration one day. But QueenBee knew what she was doing when she hooked him up with Shelley. Or did she hook Shelley up with him?

Whichever. Sure, Shelley was a piranha, but as long as that fish swam in his pond, he wouldn't too much worry about an invasion of snakes and naysayers. Besides, Shelley had lived a life most men only dreamed of living. Shelley was the quintessential American hero, a model of bravery and machismo.

Any man who had killed as many dangerous men as Shelley killed, any man who had loved as many beautiful women as Shelley loved, then that man could call him Roscoe any day.

The governor nudged Shelley and whispered near his ear.

"QueenBee sent for me. And you, too," the governor said and cocked his head. "Y'all feuding, you and QueenBee?"

Shelley looked through the governor. "Does whale shit float?"

"What's that supposed to mean?"

§

"Woman, it's that way!"

Phyllis Smallmon gripped the steering wheel tighter. Timothy

Smallmon glared at her like he was a starving man and she was the food he intended to eat—alive. But she didn't have a problem with that at all. Her husband could eat as much of her as he wanted to eat, and he would get no resistance from her. None.

Timothy looked like he'd been knocked down and stepped on. He was tugging at a necktie he said made him feel like he was getting lynched. The only thing holding up his dignity was the hangman's noose from which he claimed he dangled.

Timothy was all but foaming at the mouth he was so pissed-off at her. But it was his own damn fault. When it came to business, he was weak as water. Since Timothy was hard in all the right places, she didn't mind taking up the slack on the business end of their lives together as husband and wife.

Timothy said, "I told you to stop by the Phoenix, woman! I don't care about no CapCity Investigation. Th—"

"It's CapCity Investments," Phyllis said in an even voice. "I keep telling you that. It's CapCity Investments."

Timothy glared at her as she weaved through the Atlanta traffic. "I'm a workingman," Timothy cried. "I ain't no pimp; I got blisters on my hands. See 'em!"

Timothy thrust his hands near her face.

She cut her eyes over at her husband. She was mad again. "Ahh, hush up, Tiny!" The stress of being penniless and helpless to do anything about it had frayed her nerves. "Griping gets you nowhere but beside the highway picking up cans for a living. Now hush up, and I mean it, Tiny. A woman's gotta think. So hush that noise over there."

She'd listened to Timothy's noise ever since she beat up on him like a natural woman and took over their broken-down marriage. That was what a good woman was supposed to do when her man wouldn't do right. She was supposed to take over. But she had no intentions of trading Timothy in on any unknown model out there. She knew what she had in her Timothy. They were damn near penniless, she and Timothy, when she took over the household. But now they could rub two nickels together and get a quarter instead of just getting blisters on top of blisters.

"Tiny," she said, "we're somebody; we'll get the money; you just wait and see; we'll get the money." She loved her Timothy.

153

"Woman, don't you be trying to jive me. I know what we is and I know what we ain't. We equal opportunity beggars is exactly what we is. These here white bankers got the equal opportunity to look at our black ugly faces with our big ugly noses and our big ugly lips, and the fucks, they just lean over them big shiny desks and start grinning at us with them big pretty teeth, mocking us cause we ain't grinning and all white like them. Them peckerwoods, they don't even talk to us like we folks, like we humans, like we got a brain. The sons-of-bitches be throwing out them highfalutin words like we hookers turning cheap tricks for them and such as that. And now that young sissified punk down at the bank—"

"Tiny!"

She gritted her teeth almost down to the gum line, counting the hours before she could judo-flip that little man down on the bed, grab him by that tight round rump and put his big mouth to work. That was his work—hauling her ashes outdoors for her. Thinking was now her work, not his. Timothy's work was to be there in the bedroom when she needed him to be there in the bedroom.

"Tiny," she said, in the sexiest voice she could muster, "talk like that ain't gonna get us nowhere. His name is Mr. Rawls, honey."

"Young punk is what I mean, woman—young punk! I know a punk when I see a punk! He's a punk! A punk! A punk!"

Phyllis pulled into the parking lot and jammed the brakes.

"Whoooa!" Timothy shouted. He barely kept from kissing the windshield. He glared at her. She cut the engine, asked forgiveness from the Lord God in advance, and then turned on him. She swiveled in her seat, her head swaying hypnotically.

"Tiny, don't you go in there dissing nobody, or so help me, I'll put a lock on this monkey like you've never seen before, and then I'll beat the living crap outta you." She snatched up her shoulder bag and smiled. "Now come on, Honey," she said, sweetly.

When Phyllis first stepped into the mint-scented office at 1120 Harris Street, she knew they had found their sugar daddy.

For nearly two months, she and Timothy had gone around begging, pleading, and scheming to borrow $200,000 to pay for equipment sitting at Tapps Trucking's receiving dock. But they could not come up with a $200,000 certified check. With that money, they could ship out the order backlog of 105,000 boxes of Honey Dew, their honey and sesame seed snack, at a buck a pop.

Those orders poured in when Mr. Olympia Lee Haney plugged their Honey Dew snack on his bodybuilding TV Show. She hated being turned down by every bank, every insurance company, every S&L, and every finance company in town. Even loan sharks sneered in her face: "Nothing honest, Honey!"

But CapCity Investments was different.

She could smell the difference in the room they sat in.

The cute Afro-wearing receptionist wore a $200,000 smile. Phyllis listened carefully while Miss Cutie Pie explained why they had to wait before the vice president could see them. The woman acted embarrassed they couldn't be seen right away. Phyllis marveled at how Miss Cutie Pie's fingers raced across the keyboard like, maybe, little bitty minds were stuck under her fingernails.

One time she saw Freddie Cole play the piano just like that over at Paschal's Lounge on the westside of town.

The receptionist took off her headset, turned and smiled. "Mr. & Mrs. Smallmon, the vice president will see you now."

The vice president sprinted from behind his glossy desk like a track star. The man's big hands were warm. She was impressed.

"Mr. Timothy Smallmon, Mrs. Phyllis Smallmon, I'm Ted Summers, your loan counselor." The vice president spoke in a flourish. "I'm managing your loan."

The vice president pressed his hands in front of his crotch like a satisfied child. "Pete Rawls over at the Bank of Atlanta, he faxed your application over his morning. You got the money."

"Thank you, Jesus! Thank you, Sweet Jesus!"

Phyllis threw her shoulder bag up in the air. It hit the ceiling and dumped the contents on the vice-president's desk.

Timothy slumped in the chair, palmed his crotch and gazed at the vice president. "You mean I can keep the ol' family jewels—"

"Tiny!"

§

Shelley couldn't believe it. Some bastards had bombed his city. He drove away from the Royal Peacock Hotel parking garage and raced for Auburn Avenue. So much was happening. The mutilations, the bombing, and now bodies popping up all over town.

And none of this civil unrest was his own doings. It felt so odd being on the outside looking in on the chaos. This was all new territory for him—on the outside looking in.

Yesterday, scuba divers found two Miami thugs peacefully decomposing on the bottom of the Chattahoochee River. The same thugs were with Sturro the night the Miami drug lord was wasted, so he'd heard. Who had the guts to bomb Atlanta like this? Who nipped Garcia Chavis' spinal cord and dropped the cop in a wheelchair for life?

Shelley parked the Thunderbird, adjusted the sensitivity of the tiny recorder, and stood watching massive excavators biting into the ground like grazing brontosauruses, gouging out tons of dirt and debris. He stared down at workers repairing the underground utilities until the thud of a wrecking ball drew his attention.

The north wall of Ebenezer II collapsed, sending a dust plume splashing skyward. A grayish mushroom cloud curled around the fell building like a shroud and engulfed the rubbish like a mouth.

Shelley turned to the man who had walked up beside him.

"Why the 9-1-1, Roscoe?" Shelley said.

Striker, his face caked in dust and sweat, unclipped his hard hat and dragged out a dirty handkerchief. The MAPD bomb expert wiped his brow then spat on the ground.

"It's unreal," Striker said, looking around at the destruction. "Old Civil War shells did all this damage. Fucking Rebel duds."

"And that gas pipeline," Shelley said.

"That too," Striker said. "We've found four live shells. No telling how many of those suckers blew. This explains why there were so many explosions. The Civil War strikes again. Ain't that a shit?"

"You mean the bombers got a bigger bang than they intended?"

"Way bigger than they intended," Striker said.

"Hmm," Shelley said. "What was the bombers' original intent?"

"This is very preliminary," Striker said. "But I believe they meant to blow the crypt. The bomb was deep. I'm guessing fifteen or twenty feet. I don't think the bombers knew about those pipelines or about those old Civil War shells. There was a water department truck here yesterday working on some underground utilities. My guess is that was how they planted the bomb."

"Only one bomb?"

"So it seems," Striker said.

"That figures," he said. "Civil fucking War shells. So," he continued, spreading his arms, "all this was accidental. Just bad luck. If what you say is true, then this was not a direct attack on religion or the churches. It was a direct attack on the city."

Striker nodded. "Yeah and what better represents this town than that crypt?"

"Right on," Shelley said. "Now, all we have to do is figure out who the city of Atlanta has royally pissed off."

§

"Avondale Station!"

The bullet-shaped MARTA train rolled into the MARTA rail station as if gliding on air pockets. The doors sprang open. The riders poured out onto the platform.

Near central control, a MARTA police officer aimed a flashlight down the dark tracks, then she slipped the radio from her belt. She spoke into the mouthpiece.

"Jesse, it looks like somebody's hugging one of them hot rails near the platform. I'm checking it out; send some backup."

Irene eased out her .357 Magnum, aimed the flashlight beam and edged closer. She stopped. "Hey, mister...Hey, mister!"

Roosevelt, her partner, joined her. Their combined flashlight beams lit up the ghoulish face on the ground. The flesh from nose to chin was missing, and an oblong bloody object protruded from the twisted mouth. The two MARTA police officers gawked at each other, then they stared back down at the dead man.

§

Four hours later, Shelley followed Clayton to an isolated spot in the shadows, away from the corpse on the ground. Clayton's eyes were hard and set.

"Okay, Shelley," Clayton said, "as you know, these folks are very territorial. They let me in here as a favor. So, let's keep this under your hat. Here's what we've got so far. The dead man, his name was Edward Shaw. Went by Eddie Shaw..."

"Fortyish black male," Clayton continued, "no record. Wearing a cat-burglar garb. Hands gone. Diamond earring in left earlobe. Face gone. Chewing his bone."

Whap! The beast snapped its tail.

27

JOCELYN WAITED PATIENTLY for the red traffic light to turn green. Two fortyish men strapped in a red Corvette and wearing Atlanta Harlequin caps whistled at her.

They blew kisses at her like zit-faced teenagers smoking cigarettes would do. She wanted to scream at them. *Grow up!* Then she remembered that, on rare occasions, she enjoyed acting half her age, too. She threw up her hand and waved; then she ignored the boys.

The capital city sweltered in an unseasonable June heat wave that felt so much like an August heat wave. The spring rains came, and the spring rains went away. Three and four times a day, everyday, the spring rains came and the spring rains went away. All-day long, the heavy soggy heat marched up and down the city streets, scaled the skyscrapers, rode the expressways and the trains and the buses. But it was the million or so cars that were the hottest rocks in the steaming sauna that threw off so much of Atlanta's humidity and heat.

Like a knee-crawling drunk, the misery index rose unsteadily to intoxicating levels. Jocelyn dug the advertisement from her coat pocket. She had to get away from the city and out in the country somewhere, so she could hide from her failure to get Stanford Rome into her bed. The bombing chaos sure didn't help her frame of mind, and the city was way too crowded for her to let her hair down, so she could relax and unwind.

The red light blinked green.

The Corvette screeched ahead. Jocelyn punched numbers into her phone and chased after the Corvette. A pleasant male voice answered on the other end on the second ring. Jocelyn told him of the pleasant male voice she wanted to tour Lake Arrowhead with hopes of buying a lot there. Then she settled back for him of the pleasant voice to deliver his spiel.

Meanwhile, she was quite busy bullying her way through the thick bumper-to-bumper downtown Atlanta traffic. Minutes after breaking free of the mass congestion, she leaped on the I-7500 speedway and raced hard for the mountains and her freedom. Cruising ninety, she punched a single digit on her cellphone.

Her secretary answered on the second ring—such efficiency.

"Hi, Della, listen up. One, hold messages. Two, I'm out for the day. Three, cancel all appointments, give the usual excuses, and reschedule as you see fit to do so. Four, get me a profile on Lake Arrowhead Development Corporation. The basic stuff. A quickie and shoot it through the fax...thanks, Della." Laughing, she said, "have yourself a good one, ya hear!" and she clicked off, laughing.

She completed two more calls before calling it quits. She killed the power to the phone and tossed it over in the passenger seat.

Half an hour later, Jocelyn was speeding along the twisting drive leading to the entrance to Lake Arrowhead. Atlanta's movers-and-shakers (some say loan sharks-and-hustlers) fled here to escape the Atlanta riffraff.

She stopped at the guardhouse.

Her visitor's pass was waiting as him of the pleasant voice had promised. The guard was not bad looking. She sneaked a last peek in her rearview mirror, then gunned the engine for the thrill.

§

"I am Lou Houston, the Texas city variety, not the Atlanta street of the same fame," the very tanned man of the pleasant voice said and smiled.

She just loved that smile. Those lips could make any dildo obsolete. Now, now. Naughty, naughty.

Lou sported a bald spot in the top of his head, the male pattern kind, and it was as gorgeously tanned as every other exposed inch of his sturdy frame. Lou was handsomely tailor-made, and he looked so much like Ken of Barbie doll fame. His necktie was dotted with honeybees, and if there was a message there, Jocelyn missed it completely.

Lou's perfect teeth flashed Lou's perfect smile that never once sagged during their two-hour tour of Lake Arrowhead in a black Jeep Cherokee. It seemed all Lake Arrowhead employees drove Jeep Cherokees. She enjoyed the tour. Lou was not only gorgeous to look at, but he was also the perfect gentleman. But being with Lou Hudson only reminded her of how much she wanted to be with Stanford Rome.

Later back at the Lake Arrowhead Hotel, Jocelyn sat in the lobby enjoying the interesting outdoor decor and waiting for Lou to return. That was when she spotted a very tall man bounding down the curving staircase leading from the second level.

The judge walked right past her. She was surprised then angered by the snub. Lou Houston appeared at her side.

"That was Judge Grimes," she said. "He owns property here?"

The pained expression on Lou's face raised her eyebrows. "You okay, Lou?"

Lou muscled a smile and shrugged, lifting his palms. "I can't divulge that information, Ms. Slade. We protect the privacy of our members and guests. I'm sorry. We will be just as discreet when others inquire of you."

Lou's forced smile softened into his much more pleasing store-bought smile. "Ready for a refresher? The oyster bar, perhaps?"

"That was Judge Grimes, right, Lou?" Jocelyn said as all sorts of news possibilities danced around in the ballroom of her reporter's brain. Unlike all her nay-sayers, she saw herself more as a reporter than as a talking head on the boob tube. She was nobody's Bronner Brothers blond. Lou's discretion was all well and good, but she was hot on a story, and she wanted answers from him, not platitudes.

Lou led the way. "Let's sit at the oyster bar, Ms. Slade."

Why not? She might bite into a pearl or she just might be lucky enough to spot the judge again.

Jocelyn coated another oyster with cocktail sauce, then bit it in half. No pearl there. No judge here. Lou kept preaching the virtues of living at Lake Arrowhead, but she was more interested in Judge Grimes, and why the judge snubbed her the way he did. She scanned the cozy room with the huge fireplace, seeking her target.

Where was the judge?

A woman entered the lounge, looked around, and then fled to a vacant corner like a rabbit down a hole. The woman's face made her heart flutter. Jocelyn steadied herself. She knew that if she sat there a moment longer she would panic.

She stood on wobbly legs, eyes locked on the corner where the woman sat. A man approached the woman's table, smiled and sat across from her. Jocelyn looked away from the table to better calm herself. She felt warm and light-headed.

"Anything wrong, Ms. Slade?" Lou Hudson said.

She looked at him. "No," she managed to say. "I have something important to do back in Atlanta. I'll call you later, Lou."

She had to make it outside to fresh air before she fainted. She was losing touch with reality. And it was a scary feeling.

That woman just couldn't be her. How could it be her?

God, she had to pee.

28

SATURDAY, JUNE 4

CANDICE STRAPPED HERSELF into the window seat of the Delta jet flying her down to Miami and sighed. She felt miserable without a gun close at hand.

Another deep, heavy sigh sent her thoughts drifting all the way back to Lake Arrowhead and Thursday. She had spotted Jocelyn Slade sitting alone in the lounge. When the newswoman stood and started toward her table, she nearly panicked. And then Horace had showed up at her table, a one-man cavalry, and saved her from that newshound. That night she rewarded Horace and gave him some. And now Horace the Conquered had bought her a diamond brooch and was now shopping around for a mink stole.

What would Horace buy her if she blew him, she wondered. A 747 with hubcaps? Or a Lamborghini with a coon tail? Maybe she would venture to find out.

Why was she always bumping into the darling of Atlanta's airwaves? Obviously, Jocelyn Slade didn't remember being inside Stanford's clothes closet with her.

Candice shook her head, chuckling. That experience was right out of a paperback novel. Before Jocelyn showed up at Stanford's cottage that day, she'd just picked the lock and gone inside to plant a bug in that locked bedroom.

A glass pencil holder shaped like a swan had drawn her attention. When she looked inside it, she found one of her audio plugs. She remembered losing the same plug near the oak. Stanford had obviously found it. She put the audio plug back inside the swan and started thumbing through the photo album laying open on an end table. She was studying a photo of Shelley and his Vietnam buddies when she heard the Jeep Cherokee stop in the driveway.

She thought it was a Lake Arrowhead security guard, and she hid inside Stanford's walk-in closet. She later heard someone park the Jeep out of sight. Then Jocelyn had snooped around like she'd been doing until the guards showed up. The woman then hid inside the same closet she was hiding in. She wondered what lie Jocelyn had told those two security guards.

The security guards fell all over themselves helping the news-woman out the closet. She had waited, expecting Jocelyn to tell the two men about her in the closet. Instead, they all just left.

Candice sighed again and sank deeper into the airliner seat.

She was taking a big gamble meeting Preacher on his own turf. She pushed up the window shade and gazed at the clouds floating past. What a week. She still hadn't connected Stanford to another woman. She'd followed him to the airport nearly two weeks ago and saw him and Jocelyn Slade together.

That woman had better watch her step. Stanford was still Stacey's man. To repay Stacey for saving her from Mr. Stetson Hat, she promised to keep Stanford's mind focused on finding Stacey's killer. He could screw Jocelyn Slade later.

Candice popped two ranitidine tablets to soak up all that greedy acid nibbling on her stomach walls like teeth. She had to think positive. She had the inside track on a $1-million payday if what she'd heard was true. She wanted Preacher to put a name to the money man, the paymaster. Still she was risking her life going to Miami, since Preacher was still tight with Little Bruce Wayne. But for $1 million she'd even risk running across that pathetic runt.

She pinched the bridge of her nose and expelled another long sigh. It seemed strange how things had turned out for her. But she remembered her father's advice and his "Anything" poem:

> If your life's in a rut, doing anything, even the wrong
> thing, is ten times better than doing nothing at all.

She took one last look out the window at an endless sea of stark blue sky before she pulled the window shade back down. The ranitidine tablets were starting to kick ass down below. Now her thoughts were not so strained. She shook her head, remembering. Shelley was Frank, by God. Shelley and Frank were one and the same. How about that. But he didn't even remember her. How sad.

Candice thought back to the first time she met Shelley back in Denver. She'd been a seventeen-year-old hot piece of ass, a seething pot of bubbling hormones. Before Shelley, then Frank, she'd only screwed around with her friends, male and female. She really enjoyed practicing the theory of sex education. Shelley was Frank, so from now on she was calling him Shelley-Frank, so she would never for an instance forget they were one and the same person.

At thirty-two, Candice was just as confused about who she was now as when she'd been only seventeen. She still suffered adolescent thoughts about men and women; still not knowing if sex and love were the same thing or not. She'd screwed her boyfriends and a few girlfriends, who could never get enough of her. She shoveled sex out of both drawer legs with zip, zeal, and zest. Her boyfriends all said sex and love were the same thing, and she marveled at how smart they all really were. Anyone who made her feel as good as they made her feel had to know everything about anything! Then along came Frank.

That was when she learned how dumb her boyfriends had really been. The flight attendant touched Candice on her shoulder.

"We're about to land, ma'am."

§

In his private 100-seat movie theater, Preacher sat slumped in his director's chair, a thick unlit cigar clamped between big teeth exposed in a wide grin. Preacher's close-set eyes were locked on the silent explosions flashing on the movie screen hanging down from the ceiling.

Until then, Candice hadn't realized what was unfolding on the screen before her. Now she did understand. It was disgusting. She was struck by how huge the fire had been that destroyed those two famous churches. But why would someone torch that place? The dream had died with the dreamer. Didn't folks know that?

The Civil Rights nonviolent movement shot its wad in the sixties. It's over, folks. With the exception of those civil rights groups now institutionalized like slavery was once institutionalized, like racism

164

today was institutionalized, that movement was as relevant now as the pet rock. Not fighting back was for losers, not winners. No way the meek would inherit this earth she was living on. Earthworms would rule Earth before meek humans would rule the planet.

The giant movie screen flickered once and faded into white.

Seconds later, a different, calmer scene flashed on the movie screen. Six figures dressed in white smocks huddled around a body stretched out on an operating table. One man lifted his head and faced the camera, and waved. Preacher. A second man lifted his head and faced the camera, and waved. Candice felt her blood turn to ice water. The Surgeon. She slowly looked around the room. She instinctively pressed her hand to the new pistol.

That lil' runt Bruce Wayne was close by. She then saw Preacher strutting her way.

"Take off the shades, Babe," Preacher said, as 360-plus pounds flopped down in the theater seat next to her. "I look like a pig from a distance, I know." Preacher said. "But up close, I'm a real doll."

Candice had never seen the walrus so friendly. She didn't like him acting out of character, so she pushed his "oink" button.

"I've seen one pig, so I've seen all you swine," she said.

Preacher recoiled from the bombshell. "Listen bitch! I—"

"Oops," Candice said after planting five inches of steel beneath the dewlap dangling under Preacher's double chin. The gun barrel was nearly lost within the folds of his fat throat. Preacher was red-faced. That meant Preacher was back in character. She felt better already that Preacher was back in character.

She glimpsed Quinn itching for his gun and threw up her left palm like a traffic cop would do.

"Don't," she warned Quinn. "Drop the piece and move back."

Quinn dropped the gun and stepped away from it.

"Now, Preacher," she said, screwing the muzzle deeper into the man's throat, "you tell me who put one million pepperonis on the Miami Assassin? Is the contract still open?"

She felt the slight nod of Preacher's big head. She relaxed her grip and stepped away from Preacher, keeping Quinn in sight and the muzzle aimed point-blank at Preacher's piggish face.

"Who's the Miami Assassin?" she said. "The ground rules for collecting the kill fee, what are they?"

Preacher rubbed his throat and glared at her. She glared back. She could almost see through his buttermilk eyes. His gears were just grinding away, winding up his springs of hate. She'd screwed up big-time. She made this so difficult when it could have all been so easy. But there was no turning back now. The swine was gonna sic Bruce on her. She should just blow him away now and be done with it.

The thin corners of Preacher's pursed lips dipped low. "Bring him in alive," Preacher said. "The best proof there is."

"Who do I collect from if someone gets all happy and blow your shit away first?" she said.

"My Miami lawyer," Preacher said. "Alfred Warner."

"What's the lawyer's cut of the kill fee?"

Preacher smirked at her. "Always angling, huh? Warner, he's on the payroll. No cut for him."

"Why spend a million on those old Miami killings?" she said.

"It ain't about money, honey," Preacher said. "It's about respect."

Her hot enthusiasm for bagging a $1-million payday had cooled somewhat. The Miami Assassin and the $1-million hit could just be a ruse by mobsters to stop the Miami killings. She had fell for ruses before. Now was worse. Now she had gone and pissed Preacher off and had gotten nothing back in return.

She lowered the gun and put it away. She and Preacher watched each other with almost benign curiosity.

Preacher rubbed his throat. "Candy Girl, ain't Little Bruce stalking your pretty ass these days?"

Candice took small side steps toward the door.

She was convinced of one thing for sure. Preacher, he was the money behind the Atlanta bombing. And Bruce was the bomber. She saw no profit in that for Preacher, who was always interested in profit. Unless, of course, someone had done something stupid like what she had just done and pissed Preacher off in a big way.

But, it didn't matter now. Preacher was no concern to her now because his life span rivaled that of a Mediterranean fruit fly.

Preacher was dead meat, for real.

You just didn't go around blowing up American cities.

End of story.

29

SATURDAY, JUNE 4

SHELLEY DROVE UNDER the looming arch of the Atlanta Pen. He parked the Thunderbird in the visitor's parking lot and adjusted the tiny recorder in the small of his back.

He sucked in a long weary breath. He needed some help finding the bomber and the butcher.

By the time he'd walked across the yard and into the administrative building, he was already sweating bullets in the soggy ninety-degree heat. Carlos Martinez, the real warden of the Atlanta Pen, could help him stop both the bomber and the butcher. Getting his help would not be easy. They were not the best of pals anymore.

Carlos Martinez's living space was slightly smaller than a $400-a-night suite at the Ritz-Carlton. It was a luxury granted the real warden of the Atlanta Pen because of his clout, inside and outside those iron bars that both confined him and did not confine him.

"Eh, welcome, Cap'n," Carlos drawled and hugged him. "You damn gook killer, you. Carlos welcomes all two of you, or however many there are of you this time, eh?" Carlos let loose another deep-rooted guffaw and tapped a forefinger to his own temple. "I remember how you used to do. You kill lots of gooks that way, eh. Welcome all y'all to the University of the Atlanta Penitentiary!"

Another rollicking guffaw shook the air.

Shelley waited until Carlos wound down before he spoke. "The bombing, Roscoe, who's behind the bombing? I need names."

Carlos worked his jowls then jabbed a forefinger at a chair. "Eh, you take a load off."

Shelley sat down. "Who's behind the bombing, Roscoe?"

Carlos' eyebrows knitted together like two crossed stilettos.

"Now, Cap'n, do Carlos look like he don't never wanna eat lunch in this joint again? You know, it's not so easy running a prison these days, what with so many uppity assholes strutting around with guns and keys and rules and regulations and such nonsense like that, you know. I'm too old for all this bullshit. I think I'll just kill me somebody if they go and mess with me. You know that, Cap'n?"

"I know that, Roscoe. You go right ahead and you kill you somebody. But tell me about the bomber. And about the butcher."

Carlos studied his face then squinted. "Eh, you fight like Smokin' Joe Frazier used to fight, you know that? Pressure. You jam a man; you keep jamming a man like Smokin' Joe jam a man. That's good. Good for you, the jammer. Bad for me, the jammed."

"Cut the sermon, Roscoe. I need some answers, PDQ."

Carlos' squint widened into a glare. "I hate your attitude, Cap'n. Why crack on me like you do?"

"You ain't hearing me, Roscoe. We all hear voices. Don't you go fucking with us. Talk to us, Roscoe. Use real words this time."

He reflected Carlos' glare back at him.

Carlos' face darkened like he was turning around and around inside his own head, searching for the right words to say or looking around in there for a big rock to throw out at him. Carlos' eyes twitched twice before settling back under his prominent brow.

"When I say what you want me to say, Cap'n, then you—I mean, you all get outta my face, right?"

"We all get outta your face, right," he said.

Carlos' big head rocked in agreement. "The money man's from the Bottoms. His name's Preacher."

He nodded. "Two more things I need, Roscoe."

"I don't owe you no more. Now you all get outta my face."

"The gun who did Eddie, who bought that gun, Roscoe?"

Carlos' hard scarred face turned almost sorrowful. "What's done's done," Carlos said. "Eddie was wrong; now, Eddie's dead. In this business, you wrong, you dead. Eh?"

"Ed Shaw was our friend, Roscoe," he said.

"Your friend!" Carlos snapped, trembling lips snarling. "When you steal from the wrong people, you stop being Carlos' friend."

"Eddie deserved better, Roscoe."

"Eddie—" Carlos bit into his lower lip, eyes closing ranks as if trying to bridge the wide gap between them.

"Who was the gun, Roscoe? Who did Eddie?"

"A thief has no hands. Eddie had no hands. You go figure."

He nodded. Eddie died in the line of duty and enough about that. Eddie died the death of a good soldier.

"One last thing, Roscoe, those two floaters in the Hooch, the Miami goons, who offed the two floaters?"

Carlos stroked his brow, studying him, and shook his head. "Nobody local. Maybe from the Apple. Maybe from the Windy City. Maybe from the City of Brotherly Love. Maybe from the Bay City. Maybe from the Twin Cities. Maybe from the Quad Cities. Maybe from the Mile-High City. Maybe…"

§

Saturday, 2:57 a.m. Atlanta night was cooking like Atlanta day on medium. The heat was gone, but the warm air hovered over all the concrete and steel and sheet metal, and the all-too-few trees.

Timothy and Phyllis had celebrated the $200,000 business loan they had gotten from CapCity Investments with a $10 meal and a $5 wine. They went strolling down Martin Luther King Jr. Drive.

At the crosswalk they waited for an EMT van to pass, then they crossed onto Marietta Street and walked past the MAPD substation. Phyllis waved at the cop she saw through the plate-glass window.

The policewoman inside waved back and circled a pencil over her head like a lasso. Phyllis twirled her shoulder bag in return, as she and her husband walked on down the street on cloud nine, their heads filled with dreams.

"So, this is how it feels to win one," Phyllis said and leaned into Timothy, squeezing his hard biceps. "I love you, Tiny."

"Ditto," Timothy said as they neared the Phoenix.

They clasped hands and eyed the mythological bird that burned itself up, and then rose from its own ashes 500 years later as if it had never died. What a story. The EMT van rolled up to the hugging couple. The rear door opened, and two bulky men stepped to the ground near Timothy and Phyllis Smallmon. The two men took them from behind. Seconds later, the EMT van crept to the corner, made a right turn and drove toward Grady Hospital.

The shoulder bag laid at the base of the Phoenix.

§

Shelley ground his teeth. The beast was back stirring around inside his head again. The pain squeezed tears from his eyes. He was out of control and at the mercy of his emotions, and the pain that so easily triggered them. The beast was back for its pound of flesh. He tried but couldn't shake away the popped eyes of death—the woman—the eyes kept coming back. He couldn't hide from those wide eyes of death—the boy—the eyes kept coming back.

He parked the Thunderbird at the Royal Peacock Hotel.

Panic pounded Shelley's brain. The beast would not be denied this time. Of the seven routes leading from the hotel to his house on Avenue B, Elvira Street was the quickest route, and he headed that way. He had to hurry and reach the safety of his sanctuary.

When he unlocked the door to his house hidden behind a thick kudzu jungle on Avenue B, he was almost blinded by the pounding pain in his head. He stumbled downstairs into the basement.

He locked himself inside the padded soundproof room and tore off his clothes. He sank on top of huge pillows littering the carpet like stuffed animals moments before the first big pain slammed into the side of his head as if he'd been kicked by a mule.

Whap! The beast snapped its tail.

He fell over, landing on his back, shaking. Drool puddled in the bend of his neck. The overhead camera clicked on and whirred.

Shelley clamped his head, howling, the soundproof room soaking up each decibel of every wail until his vocal cords collapsed under the strain, and his brain blinked out from the stress.

Whap! The beast snapped its tail.

§

Time: 3:17 a.m.

The MARTA Midnight Express bus made a looping right turn off Auburn Avenue and cruised up to the bus stop at the front entrance of Georgia State University's Arts Center building. A middle-aged man and a teenaged boy stepped off the bus and dallied down the street, hugging and squeezing. The man stroked the boy's bouncing ass as they strolled down the walkway.

The MARTA bus driver slammed the doors shut, and the heavy

bus groaned away from the curb. The driver slid the side window open and shouted, "Fags!" He slammed the window back shut.

The boy mooned the driver, and the man flashed a bird.

The driver steered the MARTA bus to a stop next to the curb. He slid the seat back as an EMT van parked two spaces behind.

Time: 3:20 a.m.

The man nibbled at the boy's lips, coaxing him down the crumbling concrete steps of the boarded-up building to a door. The man opened the door, and the lovers stepped into a wide cavern with hay pallets strewn all about. The man fell to his knees, ripped open the boy's fly and consumed him whole.

From a dark corner, two homeless men watched the action.

"Come on, Po' Boy," one man whispered. "Let's git; don't like the company."

Po' Boy clutched the brown paper bag to his chest, gawked at the man and the boy, and didn't move a muscle.

"Po' Boy, you just let me hold that there shiny gun, and I'll plug both them dick suckers. Ain't got no respect, no decency."

Po' Boy hugged the paper bag tighter to his chest. "Ain't. This for me hooker."

"Po' Boy, you been yapping that smack for I don't know how long. That worm you got there, it ain't getting hard no more. Too many hard times. Ain't good for nothing but fish bait."

The two men shuffled up the crumbling steps of the basement and trudged up the alley toward Margaret Mitchell Square. They crossed the street in front of an EMT van that pulled away from the curb. The van slowed near them, then crept past. They slunk up to an idling MARTA bus and peeped through the open doors. The homeless men shrugged and climbed aboard the empty bus.

§

Daybreak. Shelley lay naked across the huge pillows in the sound-proof room of his house on Avenue B. The air ducts hadn't pulled in enough fresh air. He felt weak and disoriented. He struggled to open the gym bag and then fumbled out The Brain.

He flinched. He could wake up the sleeping beast. He shrugged. Whatever. But what better place to be if he did wake the beast.

He powered on the machine and tapped into the R file.

The To-Do file automatically popped up. He pressed "enter."

Shelley read the name: Jonah Jacoby.

He then fumbled The Brain back inside the gym bag. He took out his tape recorder and switched it on. He cued the tape. Again, he listened to the four-month-old conversation between him and seventy-five-year-old Jonah Jacoby. The old man had been Stacey's mother's closest friend.

Shelley: You never did see any strangers hanging around Katie Kane's house, did you, Mr. Jacoby?

Jacoby: No sir, never did. Strangers stick out round here like midgets at a dwarf convention.

Shelley: So Katie Kane didn't tell you about any strangers hanging around the county in the past few months. Is that what you're saying, Mr. Jacoby?

Jacoby: Sir, that ain't what I told ya. I told ya I didn't see no strangers. I didn't say Katie didn't see no strangers. Never said that. Never did.

Shelley: Did Katie Kane say she'd seen a stranger?

Jacoby: Sure, she saw a stranger. She said she saw a stranger. The damnedest thing. (Jacoby cackling)

Shelley: Who did she say she saw, Mr. Jacoby? Who was this stranger?

Jacoby: The fellow, he sold bibles for a living. He stopped by three time, she told me. In the evening every time. Said he was a New York fellow but that car had an Atlanta tag, she told me.

Shelley: Mr. Jacoby, why didn't you tell the police about this before?

Jacoby: Nobody asked me what Katie said. Ya asked me, didn't ya? Besides, I got to studying on it.

Shelley: Did Katie Kane say why the bible salesman dropped by so many times, Mr. Jacoby?

Jacoby: To convert her, why else, for Christ's sake. Don't ya know nothing, boy?

Shelley: (Long pause). So you, yourself, never saw the bible salesman, Mr. Jacoby?

Jacoby: Ya mind's bad? Ya crazy? I said I never seen him, didn't I tell ya that—Hey, don't I know ya?…Ain't ya Frank Lester's boy? Didn't ya kill all them gooks over across that pond and won that crackerjack prize? How about that, a crackerjack prize won by a guy from the Cracker State—hey, where's ya cute little baby sister? She was the cutest little thing. Ya baby sister, she was.

Shelley clicked off the tape recorder. What baby sister? He didn't have a baby sister. The old man was nuts.

The beast reared its head and looked. Shelley stiffened and put away the recorder. He waited. Nothing happened. He went back to thinking about all the legwork he'd done. For weeks, he'd driven up and down the dirt roads, knocking on doors, stopping farmers on tractors, and squatting beside old ladies at their fishing holes. No one had said anything about a bible salesman making the rounds.

Why would a bible salesman go back three times to convert an old witch like Katie Kane?

He rubbed his scratchy eyes, wrestling with a thought but not quite able to pin the thought down in his mind.

Suddenly, his mind lit up, bright. Here he was thinking about "the night that never happened," and the beast had yet to rear its ugly head. Now, maybe, after four wasted months, he could get on with finding the man who killed the wife and son of his best friend. Maybe he could.

He went back to thinking again. No time to waste.

A bible salesman and a bible.

The beast rose to its feet, turned its ugly head and locked hateful eyes with Shelley. Again, Shelley flinched.

Is that you, Frank?

30

SUNDAY, JUNE 5

JOCELYN SLADE READ the final news item off the TelePrompTer and kept smiling into the cameras.

"Thank you, Vern and Larry, for that helping hand you two gave me," she said. "Good evening to all, and good night from WTNT-TV News."

She sighed. The day was over. All debts paid.

"What was that all about, Jocelyn?" Stephen asked her.

She shrugged off her producer with a tired smile. "A dead horse. Let's not beat it, okay? I'm just too tired."

Behind the safety of her private dressing room, Jocelyn threw herself lengthwise the sofa, kicked off her shoes and stared up at the ceiling, wondering—no, worrying about what Bryce Boyd wanted to see her about. She'd invited Bryce over for dinner so he could unload whatever was on his mind this time. She nibbled her lower lip. It was becoming almost an everyday thing, her inviting Bryce over to dinner so he could unload his troubles.

She was not in a good mood but she owed Bryce an occasional ear. She squirmed. Her period was really ruining her day, and she didn't need Bryce around trying to get inside her bloody bloomers and—she bolted upright!

Blood! That's what she smelled inside that clothes closet in Stanford's cottage. Blood. A woman on the rag. Another woman in Stanford's closet! She'd kill the bitch.

She settled back down on the sofa, replaying events in her mind. Vern and Larry had caught her red-faced and muttering out of her

174

mind inside Stanford's closet. But the security guards, bless their good hearts, had let her off after she convinced them that she'd just wanted to surprise Stanford and to seduce him. When they gave her that "dah" look, she then explained that she'd come to give Stanford some. Their eyes lit up. That, they understood. Men.

Vern and Larry agreed not to turn her in to Sid. In return, she agreed to thank them at the end of her newscast. How about that? Another woman was in that closet with her. She'd kill the bitch.

Sighing, Jocelyn rolled over on her back. Pulling out her night-stand drawer she grabbed Mister by the balls, and she was set to put Mister to work when her private line rang out an emergency.

It was 11:39 p.m.

She snapped up the telephone.

§

At 11:57 p.m., Jocelyn Slade was almost running down the long cor-ridor leading to the broadcast studio. She was clutching the tiny pocketbook under her arm, compact mirror in one hand, powder-puff in the other hand. She was stretched out in full stride.

Stephen's call had lit a fire. She was motivated and motoring.

An anonymous caller had rang the station, warning that the fate of a thousand people rested in Jocelyn's hands. The caller gave her thirty minutes to beat it on down to the studio to save her viewers, and to become their everyday hero.

"Jocelyn, you okay?" Stephen Crane gushed as she blew past.

Her producer was hurrying beside her, wringing his hands and mopping his brow. Stephen was such a nervous wreck. She blew on down the corridor, pink silk scarf trailing long behind her neck. The tension was sky-high. They could all exhale now because the star was on the premises. The star had come. Not really. But hal-lelujah, anyway!

This was Jocelyn's neighborhood, and she was top dog (some say bitch) on the block. Even she had to admire how much like clay she was, molding herself into any shape: female on the run in one hot instant, and top-notch TV anchorwoman in the next cool one. She the employee stood on top of her world, and WTNT the boss loved the view. Her bosses loved everything about being the top TV station in the city. The suits drooled over the Gulfstream G200 she afforded those whackos in the executive suite to fly around in.

But all had not been so cozy between her and the WTNT-TV bosses. Once, they had scratched and clawed at each other's throat so viciously they were now bonded together only by contract and mistrust.

Back then maybe she'd pushed a little harder than she should have pushed, but those had been hard times in her life. Those days had demanded cutthroat action from her. Looking out for one's own ass was the hot flavor of the times. Everybody was doing it. It was the way of life at the station. Her personal life had been in upheaval. She didn't want AIDS or any other STD to cut short her career. So, she dumped Bryce Boyd, her live-in dipstick.

Bryce thought being faithful was an old geyser in a national park somewhere. Bryce just couldn't keep it in his pants. That she had been dealing with. But then he threatened her. A threat she would not deal with. The shithead had threatened to hang out their soggy linen for the hot gossip of Atlanta to dry.

The mere threat struck like a dagger to her heart.

Bryce had threatened her dreams. Her health went south on her fast, sending her life spiraling into a tailspin. First, her body went to seed, then her spirits broke down, and then her mind blinked out on her. The threat sent her tumbling down into a hellhole of despair, screaming her fool head off in the middle of the night. The screams jarred her awake at night.

Jocelyn nearly came unglued.

She ran away from Bryce Boyd to escape self-destruction, only to become even more tangled in the web she'd spun for herself. She hated Bryce's disloyalty and his betrayal, his drugs and his women, his nasty friends and his evil ways. She clung to her sanity by the thread of her wit. She hid out from the hectic days by working ungodly hours all through the lonely nights.

Slowly, begrudgingly slowly, she survived the lowest of the low points in her life. And the trauma made her better understand the woes faced by other people out there in the world.

Jocelyn understood what Stanford was going through now, and why he was avoiding her. Women were not high priorities in his life right now. She knew how hard it was to recover from an almost devastating blow.

She would never forget that night she collapsed in her anchor chair during a broadcast. Passed out on live TV.

Her doctors had been curt: take a long break or suffer a serious breakdown. She took a ninety-day leave of absence. In two weeks, the city's number-one station lost its top rating.

When the suits started pressuring her to return after only two weeks she not only fled the city and the state and the country, she fled the continent. She sought foreign medical help for her screaming headaches.

She swore right then on a stack of bibles that nobody would ever again know enough about her to blackmail her the way Bryce Boyd had done. So she'd paid double the money to confiscate and keep all her medical records and secrets to herself.

A month into her leave-of-absence, WTNT-TV New's audience share plummeted a third. The irony escaped no one. The night she collapsed on the set was also the night the station's ratings started falling. Key advertisers insisted on rate cuts, and got the cuts. Station management was horrified at the red ink gushing from the gaping hole she'd left in their cash flow. The station owners feared the worst. Other than their FCC license, they feared losing their most precious asset.

Jocelyn Slade was WTNT-TV News, and WTNT-TV News was Jocelyn Slade. Now she knew that. She decided a new pecking order was about to be established at WTNT-TV News.

The suits wanted her back to work after forty-five days. Again, she refused. Tempers flared, threats flew, and stinky stuff hit the fan—splat! When the suits accused her of violating her contract and threatened to sue, she threatened to quit the city for good.

The suits were shocked by her defiance. Not especially pleased with the way things were going at the TV station, the board of directors called a board meeting. They reeled in their fishy lawyers and told management to back off the threat to sue her. The fight jelled into a stalemate between two heavyweights now instead of one heavyweight and one lightweight.

Things had indeed changed.

The combatants eyeballed one another from opposite sides of the line drawn in the sand.

Other TV stations stoked the flames hotter between employer and disgruntled key employee. Soon a bidding war broke out for her services from Des Moines to Houston to New York City to Chicago to Los Angeles to Philadelphia to Honolulu to Tempe, Arizona.

While the lawyers huffed, puffed and played golf, Jocelyn slowly recovered. Her psyche healed with few scars, her spirits soaring enough for her to sometimes smile. Still she put her house on the chopping block and prepared to make a move.

No longer confident in the TV station's management, the board of directors were furious at both the stalemate and the bubbling red ink. They had to pick a side, and it was no contest, really. The board called another meeting and blinked.

The board fired the station's managers and their lawyers. They hired a new management team for the station. She signed a new $10.5 million, five-year contract which included a week's paid vacation every two months. She returned to work. Within a week, she was again the undisputed "darling of Atlanta's airwaves."

"Jocelyn, you okay, babe?" Stephen Crane asked her again, knowing she was always a wreck minutes before airtime. Five minutes past midnight she swiveled away from the profile camera and stewed in disappointment.

The producers gave her the bad news. A false alarm.

§

The next morning at 9 a.m, Jocelyn got a call from her secretary to call a Mr. Sweden, who said she had the number. Immediately, she dialed Dr. Grayson in Switzerland. The doctor told her someone was snooping around, asking about her illness and her treatment.

She thanked the doctor and hung up the telephone.

Who?

31

A MILLION-DOLLAR HIT.

A comforting thought to Candice, but not so satisfying now that she knew she had Little Bruce Wayne to worry about.

Candice Bergens leaned back against the smooth wall of the Jacuzzi, resting her arms along the top. The bubbles in the Jacuzzi massaged her muscles, but she had a mild headache.

How could she be so stupid?

Her legs churned the water. Even when she collected a $1-million bounty for offing the Miami Assassin, with Bruce on her butt she would have to hide in a deep hole under a big rock for a long time before she could enjoy the money. Still she made a mistake flying down to Miami. She should have tried another way.

But for $1 million she would run butt-naked through a nest of beer-sucking, sheet-wearing, cross-burning good ol' Georgia boys with red sweat rings around their collars, and brown tobacco-juice stain coloring their lips. That was an awful stereotype. She wanted to be a better person than that and not go blaming people for the culture they grew up in. No one got to pick the culture she would grow up in, because everyone was born weak and helpless.

Everyone had to be at the mercy of the people who raised them. For the most part, kids grew up to become like the people who raised them. But, thank God, some kids escaped that fate of becoming like the people who raised them.

Sometimes, a person's genes and the environment she grows up in, they both rebel against the status quo, the people who raised them—demanding to be different and, hopefully, better than the people who raised them.

She could not imagine a baby complaining about life: "Hey! I'm a steak person. I don't wanna be born in a poorhouse with three other kids living in it already—pass the neck bones!...Hey! You out there—yeah, you! I don't wanna be born black, you hear me; green's my favorite color, you twerp!...Hey, buster—yeah, you, you jerk! I don't wanna be circumcised; don't cut my thang off... Oh, no, no, I don't wanna be a girl; I wanna be gay, and I wanna be happy, too!"

She was a baby-sitter-for-hire for four years. She knew how babies learned good habits and bad habits. They learn by watching and hearing what other people do and say.

Until a kid reached the age of eleven or twelve, everything the kid learned, she learned from some other person. By the time the kid turned thirteen, she begins thinking for herself. And that thinking, too, is heavily influenced by what she already knows—which, of course, she learned from other people. It is a circle. A circle that only the strong survived long enough to be different and better.

That was her point. Nobody was born her own person. She only added on to the foundation other people out there had already laid down for her to build on. You are who you are because other people out there in the world made you that way. She vowed to be more understanding of other people and their fucked-up ways.

Oops! Oh, well, at least she was seriously thinking of changing herself and trying to become a better person. And thinking about changing yourself was always the first step in changing yourself for the good of yourself, and, often, changing yourself in spite of yourself (in the short run, anyway).

Meanwhile, she was going to shut down this Miami Assassin, and then open up her another Swiss bank account. That money would become her retirement account. With $1 million, she could earn 5% and clear $50,000 before taxes. She could live comfortably on a tropical island somewhere with that kind of income.

She'd already pinned down each date a drug lord was killed in Miami over the past five years. Soon, she'd have a list of Shelley-Frank's whereabouts on the dates those drug lords were killed.

Since Shelley-Frank ran a daily tab at the AICC; that would be easy enough to check out. She'd just get a copy of Shelley-Frank's bar tab. She would then compare the two sets of dates. She would either have proof that he was the Miami Assassin, or she would have proof that he was not the Miami Assassin. She sank beneath the surface of the water.

Soon, she would trigger the smart transmitter she had hidden under Shelley-Frank's Thunderbird and tail him to his nest.

She broke the surface of the water and giggled. Shelley-Frank was Mary, and she was Mary's little lamb. Role-reversal.

Again, Candice sank beneath the surface of the water.

§

After cruising the city for two hours, Candice had yet to find Shelley-Frank. She switched off the transmitter signal. No way Shelley-Frank had found her transmitter. The smart transmitter was the size of a button and stayed dead until she turned it on by remote control two hours ago.

She caressed the steering wheel, finally deciding not to put her back-up plan into motion yet. Give it more time. Be patient.

She switched on the transmitter signal again before turning onto Midfield Court. The receiver clicked. Her heart jumped. She slowed the car, her eyes locked on the needle. The strength meter peaked then dropped by half. She stopped in a strip mall parking lot to fine-tune the instrument. She opened the map. Her quarry was less than—no, the Thunderbird was less than a mile away.

She found Midfield Court on her map. She pulled back onto the street and raced east for Centennial Street. She felt a weakness in her stomach.

That was a gut check. Something was wrong. She shrugged it off and kept driving. The signal grew stronger three blocks past Centennial Street then peaked near the Royal Peacock Hotel. She crept into the parking garage and inspected each level.

She spotted the Thunderbird parked on the third level.

The hood was still hot.

She parked five cars down on the other side. She watched the car for half an hour before grabbing her overnight bag from the trunk. She hopped the elevator to the lobby. That was an old trick. Shelley-Frank parked the Thunderbird in one place, and he lived in another place. A fox, huh? Well, she still had the two .44 caliber bullets she'd taken from Shelley-Frank's gun holster.

Well, this vixen had one fine trick for his foxy behind.

The hotel night clerk, a youngster, was just what the doctor ordered for her on this night. A boy-toy for her sexual pleasure. She paid for one night, flashed the boy-toy a little cleavage and squeezed his hand when he gave her the key. She would have squeezed his thing for him, but it probably would have exploded in her hand. She could wait for that eruption. The boy-toy told her that he got off at six, so she invited him up for a nightcap at six-oh-nine.

She was going to mix a little business with a lot of pleasure. She needed the key, and the boy-toy was the key to getting the key she needed. While the boy-toy's mind fumbled the come-on, she slapped a container on the counter in front of him.

"Life Jackets," she said, "bring them when you come." She winked at the double meaning, licking her lips, and leaving them wet with her kissing juices.

"Stick out your tongue," she told him.

He did.

"Say, 'ahh,'" she told him.

He did.

She nodded her approval. "It'll do," she said, adding, "you can stick your tongue back in your mouth now."

He did.

§

Candice drank a delicious protein shake, showered and now lay spread-eagled on the big bed, still hot and bothered, and waiting. She wondered if Shelley-Frank rented a room there. She believed he did rent a room there.

An hour later, the boy-toy fell into her room.

She chewed up his young body and swallowed his mind whole. Three times she put the boy-toy's strong body through racetrack paces. She even went out her way to show him the imaginary noose she used to tie his young mind up into such neat little knots. She got off and spat him out. But she was confident the young man would one day make some hot-wired suburban wife an efficient suburban husband and an innocent suburban father to their darling two-and-a-half suburban kids.

Candice recited to the boy-toy her sob story. In fifteen minutes, she had a guest register in her room. In two minutes, she found what she was looking for. Ten minutes later, she stepped inside Shelley-Frank's hotel room. She spotted an almost invisible film of dust. It was another prop. No wonder Shelley-Frank was still alive with a $1-million bounty on his head.

Shelley-Frank was way too slick. Candice hustled down to the garage. The Thunderbird was long gone. She dragged back to her room. She needed to think of what to do next.

Later, Candice skimmed the photos, notes, and newspaper clippings she'd gotten from the library. She also had a copy of Shelley-Frank's bar tab at the AICC. Shelley-Frank had spent two days outside the city, and his bar tab on those days—zero. She read the newspapers for the nineteenth, one of the days Shelley-Frank had a zero bar tab and found a connection.

On that day, drug lord Jackie Pearson was killed in a hotel suite overlooking the Atlantic Ocean. Her eyes skipped over to the next column of newsprint. Art museum director Cicely Tyson was murdered the same day. Decapitated. Who did that broad piss off, big-time? Her watch chimed. Time for another stakeout.

Candice scooped up a newspaper photo of Stanford and slid it back inside the folder. She quickly slid it back out again.

She studied the man standing next to Stanford. She changed the angle of the photograph and pressed a finger across the top of the man's head. Dread tiptoed across her brow.

Mr. Stetson Hat.

§

That night, at 9:30, Candice parked her car on the first level of the Royal Peacock Hotel parking garage and waited.

The Thunderbird rolled past her half an hour later and parked. Instead of following Shelley-Frank, she hurried to the rear of the garage just in time to see him disappear inside the Cock and Bull Bar and Grill across the street.

She took up position where she had a clear view of anyone leaving through the front door or the back door.

She waited.

Fifteen minutes later, Shelley-Frank slipped out the back door. She followed a block behind him. Look out fox. For the vixen.

Shelley-Frank walked five blocks straight ahead. He circled dimly lit Micheal's Park then sat on a bench. She found a spot under an elm in the shadows and waited.

§

The next morning, Candice woke up still feeling the way raw sewage smelled. She rolled out of bed. Last night, Shelley-Frank had snookered her, but good. Made her look like a rank amateur.

Shelley-Frank had switched clothes in The Cock and Bull Bar and Grill with some clown, who then led her around by the nose in Micheal's Park like he was Mary and she was the fucking lamb. She'd followed the right clothes but the wrong man.

She was still confident she would find proof that Shelley-Frank was the Miami Assassin with a $1-million bounty on his head.

Candice slid the small case from under the bed, placed it on top of the bed, and flipped open the lid. She took out one of the two tiny transmitters she had custom-made from the two .44 caliber bullets. She would slip one bullet back in Shelley-Frank's gun belt and keep the second bullet for a spare. When Shelley-Frank left her bed this time, she would again be a lamb and make double-damn sure Shelley-Frank was really Mary, and not some john in a Mary suit.

§

The telephone rang once. She left the door open for him.

She heard him come in. Soon, the shower started up.

Minutes later, Shelley-Frank stepped into the bedroom.

She gave herself completely over to him to do with her as he wanted. And he did with her as he damn well pleased.

Two hours later, when Shelley-Frank left her bed she was less than a minute behind him. She was so sore in so many places and didn't care in so many ways.

The bullet transmitter chirped loud and clear on her receiver.

She tailed Shelley-Frank and kept well out of sight.

Shelley-Frank used all the tricks in the book to check his back trail every block or so without seeming to be checking his back trail. She crossed an obscure street, and the signal peaked.

She looked up and stepped back to read the green street sign: "Avenue *B*."

32

STANFORD ROME STARED down on Peachtree Street from his office window. Shelley had dropped off the face of the earth.

He hadn't heard from him since the bombing. He shut down his office for the night and drove to the Atlanta house he'd all but abandoned when Stacey and Christopher were killed.

He parked in the driveway and switched off the engine. He sat there, remembering all the good times.

A WTNT-TV News mobile unit crept past and broke his reverie. He got out the car and went inside the house. He stopped short in the foyer. The air did not breathe well. The flowers and plants were no longer there. Stacey had grown plants in every room with a view of sunlight. Their home had been a jungle. It took Stacey an hour to water and tend to all her pets. Living with plants and flowers had seemed such a natural thing for animals to do.

Inside Stacey's writing room, he stood by the roll-top desk and read a birthday poem she had written to him:

> To have known love with you is to have lived in the
> best of all possible worlds with you, snuggling in the
> warm glow of true bliss with you, sipping from the
> cup of love with you—a companion, a mate, a match
> with you—THE BEST OF TIMES with you!

He poured himself down into Stacey's chair. He had put it off for much too long. He reached under the ledge and peeled away the key Stacey kept taped there. He unlocked the drawer and took out the box of diaries. He stacked them on top of the desk by date. Maybe answers to who murdered Stacey and Christopher laid between the pages.

He found the one he wanted to read first and opened it to the first page—January 1, 1980. That was eight months after they met.

He began reading. Stacey burst alive in his mind, her voice as clear in his ears as the words on the pages were clear to his eyes.

Stanford first met Stacey Kane in the spring of 1979, at dusk, on a warm and windy South Georgia day.

He was only weeks away from relocating to Atlanta from Chicago, his home for the past five years. At the time, Stacey lived in Jacksonville, Florida, two hours away, but she was home nursing her mother, Katie Kane, who'd suffered a heart attack. They first met in a park near the Azalea State College campus. Stacey Kane had manipulated him from the start. He was walking across the parking lot of a strip mall. The same brisk wind scattering hats and uplifting skirt tails also carried a melody floating along on the breeze.

His body reacted in the strangest of ways. He felt as skittish as a quarter horse prancing at the starting gate of a big race.

It was not as if someone were calling out to him, or that the sound meant anything to him. The sound was an invitation.

That was what the sound was. An invitation.

Stanford spotted the young woman riding a swing in a park located across a dike twelve feet wide. The sight of her piqued his interest even more so than her song. Her legs went slicing through the air with the greatest of ease, and her bouncy black hair seemed suspended in the wind behind her.

She had the most beautiful calves.

He moved in on her.

But the swing quickly slowed before he got within ten yards.

"Somewhere," she said, slowly spinning the swing around until she was facing him, "somewhere, it is written down that the shortest distance between a man and a woman is a straight line."

She had been toying with him all the while.

She was not smiling. But her brown eyes grinned at him like she was a paying customer and he was a buffoon locked behind the bars of a cage. When in doubt, use her own words against her, he concluded and shrugged. It had always worked in the past.

He said, "don't you mean the distance between two points, and not the distance between a man and a woman?"

She laughed frivolously. "For there to be two of anything, there must first be distance between two things. Can you think of what's more distant than the misunderstanding between a man and a wo-man? Specifically, between black men and black women?"

Oops!

He didn't want to go there.

For that game she had to go find herself another player. She was so nice-looking. Her face expressed her personality, and it looked delicious. Her cheeks held a hint of jester in them, and her juicy lips highlighted her face the way color highlighted the horizon at dawn. But back to the "Oops!"

She just had to be putting him on.

He wouldn't play the gender game or the race game or the re-ligious game or the political game. His game was the sex game. If she wanted to play any other game, then later for her.

"Why do I feel like you're hustling me?" he said, deadpanned.

"I am hustling you—that's what girls do to boys, isn't it?"

He chuckled, not quite able to figure her out.

"It took you long enough to get over here," she said, "and you look like you've walked so far." She hitched an eyebrow. "Cat got your tongue?"

If she were a boxer, she would be standing over him now, glaring down at him, and daring him to get his sorry ass up off the canvas and fight like a man. Of course, he had to get up from the battering he was taking; after all, this was a mere woman, as far as he could see.

He studied her face intently before he spoke, trying for both ci-vility and manliness. "Those opal earrings and those tannin brown eyes are a perfect match for that sharp tongue of yours," he said.

"Better," she said, nodding. "I like a man with vinegar in him."

He knew it was lame but at least he was fighting back. "That's Flattery 101," he said. "Greasy kid stuff."

"Goody," she said and flapped her palms together like she was a performing seal. "Who are you? And what's your name?"

"My name's Rome," he said, almost reluctantly, as if she may one day use his name against him. "Stanford Rome. As to who I am—that's for you to decide. I don't have a clue as to who the hell I am. Who does have a clue as to who the hell he is?"

"Or she is," Stacey said, her eyebrow doing another St. Louis Arch. "Rome, Italy, or Rome, Georgia?" she demanded.

Her eyes were no longer liquid orbs of curiosity, they were now hard nuggets of malice. He could easily imagine himself spinning on his heels and running fast away from there, yanking at his hair and screaming his head off like a flaming lunatic. But he decided the male thing to do was to stand and fight—like a man.

"Rome, Stanford," he said with caution, sensing he was dealing with a feminist, a sensitive female, or a kook. Which was cool with him, as long as she didn't try to manhandle him. The opposite sex tended to do that and brag about it to her friends. Not good.

"And your name?"

"Kane, as in Stacey, not Abel, no kin. Call me, Stacey. Can I call you, Stanford? Good. I guess those folks in that ivory tower over there taught you how to abuse Flattery 101? You a professor or what?"

He studied her face another long moment.

"No, Stacey. Not a professor. An accountant. A CPA. You know the guy with the pocket protector, coke-bottle glasses, finger rammed up his nose. You know, the geek. That guy, that's me."

Her eyes danced with mischief.

"My Lord, you don't even say," Stacey said, gushing with another abrupt change of gears. "A Certified Public Accountant. Well, beat my billy goat, my Lord, till it cries for mercy then tell it to hush the fuss, please."

He stepped back. "Run that by me again," he said.

"What's so funny?" she said, flatly. "Do you find me funny?"

His sugary grin dissolved back into his mouth like salt, and he was getting a little pissed at her. Not a good sign. He could tell by her amused eyes that she saw how he felt.

"Stacey, if you're trying to make an ass of me, you succeeded. If you're trying to be an ass, you're two for two," he said, coldly.

Stacey smiled but it was the watered-down version.

"Oh, that," Stacey said, flippantly. "Well, that's just my mother's favorite saying. I tried it out on you for a reaction."

He thought on it and was appeased. "And your mother is...?"

"You've probably heard of her. Katie Kane's her name, but most folks call her the Doll Woman. You heard of her?"

He nodded. "The name, that's all." He saw no need to dignify the second name he heard people call her mother. He didn't believe in witches, and he certainly didn't believe Stacey's mother was a witch. But Shelley believed her mother was a witch. At least Shelley said he believed the Doll Woman was a witch.

Without warning, a man dropped from the branches overhead, landing behind him in a crouch. Stanford spun on the balls of his feet to meet the sneak attack.

"No!" Stacey shouted and shoved him enough to throw off his timing, and his foot whisked past the man's startled face.

Then came chaos. People were coming out of the woodwork. He was still down in his fighting stance, confused.

During all the commotion, more people came streaming toward them. The man lay stretched out on the ground as if the kick had landed. Everyone was talking at once. He stood out of his crouch. Stacey was trying to explain things to him. A photographer stepped out of a Port-a-John. A blond stepped from behind a tree, and more people crowded around, clapping, whistling, and hooting.

"We're a drama workshop," Stacey kept telling him. "We use bystanders, like you—smile, you were terrific!"

Applause exploded around him, as Stacey led her troupe into a rousing "Hip! Hip! Hooray!" Just for him.

He looked sheepishly at Stacey, and she stood on her toes and kissed his cheek. "You were great!" she said, beaming into his face.

§

Stanford set down the diary. He rubbed his forehead as if to erase the images. Yeah, Stacey, she had manipulated him from the start. He reread the entry he had read before the memories had taken over his thoughts.

Stacey wrote that Shelley had mistaken her for an old Denver girlfriend when he had first introduced the two. A thought zipped swiftly through his mind like a shooting star, and was gone before he could grasp the thinking inside it. That Shelley had mistaken Stacey for an old girlfriend should mean something to him, but he had no idea what it was supposed to mean to him.

He flipped the page.

Minutes later, his memories too heavy, he scooped up the diaries and left the house that had once been home. He had to shed all those memories from his thinking and, for the most part, he had done that.

He had to come back to the house to get the diaries, but that didn't mean he had to stay in the house to read them. The rooms held too many memories, memories he had to bury now. In the same way he had to bury their bodies in the ground, he had to bury his memories of them in the ground as well, in the ground of his mind—where they now belonged.

He took one last look at the room and turned for his escape.

He was very determined not to take the memories through that door with him.

33

WEDNESDAY, JUNE 8

SHELLEY PULLED THE Thunderbird over to the curb. He parked two blocks from the "Styles by Candy" beauty salon. Around midnight, Jud Judson squeezed in on the passenger side.

"Got some bad news," Jud Judson said. "Over at CapCity, there's a fairy giving top secrets to another fairy who works at RKL."

Shelley grunted.

The two men sat in silence, each watching his side of the street.

"What about the preacher man?" Shelley said.

"A mule from down Miami Beach way. His muscle, Mario, he came cruising through town, him and another guy. Interesting, this other guy."

Shelley grunted again.

"This here other guy," Jud continued, "well, he's Carlos Martinez's boy. Quinn Bucket is his handle."

"Mario and Carlos's man together?" Shelley said.

"Yeah. Next time you see the convict, ask about two NYC boys down looking for one of their own, oh—a few months ago. Seems he hitched a ride down South and got lost in all this southern hospitality."

§

Clayton Westwood scratched his head and watched his boss. He'd been edgy since yesterday when Thorpe had first told him about this meeting. Had Thorpe found out he had kept the Rome case opened when Thorpe had ordered him to shut it down? Boy, he was screwed. But damn if he was gonna bend over and spread his cheeks. Thorpe, the cocksucker, he would have to rape him first. Either way, he was screwed. Raped or no.

His boss meshed his fingers in front of his mouth.

"Clayton," Thorpe began, "Shelley knows more about the bombing and this butchery than Shelley says he knows."

Was this what the meeting was about? About Shelley? Clayton's face stayed stoic but his mind churned. He turned and glared at the other agent this time. "Can he leave?" he asked his boss.

"Listen, Clayton," Thorpe said, ignoring the question, "Shelley may know who the bomber is. Are you listening to me?"

"Then go arrest him," Clayton snarled, pointing at the third agent. "Does he have to be here?"

Thorpe's lips trembled as he stabbed a finger at Clayton's face. "That's your job, mister! Arresting people! I tell you who to arrest, and when and where to arrest them! You got that, hotshot!"

Yes, indeed. He was screwed. If he slugged Thorpe, he was really, really screwed. Slipping his hand into his pocket, he brought out his pocketknife, clicking the blade open and shut, and watching Thorpe turn a deeper shade of purple by the moment.

"I hear you," he finally said.

Thorpe's glare softened. "Remember the Miami Assassin?"

"Pure conjecture," he said.

Click-clack. Click-clack.

Thorpe massaged his temples. "Listen up, Clayton, I was in the loop from the get-go on this Miami-Assassin crap. I know the real deal. The bureau was as guilty as sin. Shelley, he operated pretty much as he damn pleased down there in the Bottoms. Hell, he was cleaning up the town, wiping out the criminal leadership. Just like he did in 'Nam. He tracked down and killed all those VC officers. He killed over a hundred, one crackshot at a time. Those mobsters didn't have a chance against the best sniper this country has ever seen. The new bossman was different. When he hit Lil' Havana, he told everybody in the office to get in fucking lockstep or get the fuck outta his town."

Thorpe Henry poked his hands deep into his pockets, and the gesture made his shoulders droop even more.

"You see, Clayton, Shelley, he got booted out of Miami when the new director heard about all that assassin crap—ha! The old boy blew his stack. I mean, careers were on the line. When word leaked out that the Miami drug lords had pooled their cash and ordered a $1-million hit on the Miami Assassin, shit really hit the fan then. The bossman went apeshit—and I do mean ballistic. He wanted to can Shelley, but who cans a Medal-of-Honor winner.

"Shelley, he had big-time friends all up and down the chain of command in both the House and the Senate. So the old man cut a deal with the powers-that-be on how best to keep Shelley out of harm's way, to keep him from being sniped. They all struck a deal. The old man shipped Shelley's ass out of Miami and off to Atlanta. The deal was to keep the fucking war hero alive."

Thorpe drew a weary breath.

"The bossman wanted to control Shelley," Thorpe said and snorted. "But, we both know that was bullshit thinking from the jump. I don't for a second believe even Shelley can control Shelley. So, four months after Shelley hit Atlanta, shit hit the fan in that town. It all started with the Chaserville Rebellion. You do remember the Chaserville Rebellion, right?"

Clayton nodded to keep the narrative going. He didn't believe what his boss was saying. The agency was just too damn good with its own smoke and mirrors.

"Thorpe," he said, "if Shelley was this Miami Assassin, he'd be dead by now. He's been a civilian for three years now. Why is he alive with a $1-million bounty on his head? Tell me that. Why?"

Thorpe went back to shaking his head with a pitying slowness, then his boss raised his arms in a helpless gesture.

"Listen, Clayton. I don't care for Shelley; that's true. But, Shelley, he's a bad boy—I never ever said Shelley wasn't a bad boy. And another thing, too. In Nam, Shelley killed a lot of people for this country, 'colored people,' he called them when he told the Congress to take that medal and shove it.

"But, still, the fact that he earned it—well, that means a lot, not only to the politicians, but that means a lot to all those VFW's and American Legion posts situated all across small-town America, believe it.

"Millions of diehard veterans wouldn't like the idea of anyone killing a Medal-of-Honor winner; there are only about 150 of them still alive today. The political pressure to track down such a killer would make our politicians cry more than crocodile tears. That medal is given by Congress for a reason. Any pro knows that, and Shelley would waste an amateur without breaking a sweat."

Thorpe sounded like a Shelley fan. His defenses shot back up.

Thorpe said, "Clayton, do you remember, about three weeks ago when Carlos Martinez's rival down in Miami got his head shot off his shoulders?"

"It crossed my desk," he said.

"Shelley was in the Bottoms that day. And yesterday, he visited Carlos in the Pen. Shelley and Carlos, those two, they can bomb with the best of them. See where I'm going with this, Clayton?"

"No, I don't," he said, shaking his head.

Thorpe shrugged and plucked his hat off the credenza. "Clayton, there's a connection between this bombing and Shelley. Find it, Clayton. And, by the way, FYI, I reopened the Rome case."

"Huh? You did? When?"

"But not this office," Thorpe said. "It's the Wild Bunch. They will contact you in the morning. The leader's name is Mike Thaylor. Clue him in, and bring him up to speed as quick as you can.

"Just know that jobs are on the line. Necks are being stretched, measured and fitted for a noose. A federal judge somewhere is pissed off because we pulled in our horns on this one. This federal judge, he's on the warpath."

"Why not this office, Thorpe?" he said. "Why the Wild Bunch?"

Thorpe looked at the third agent then looked back at Clayton.

"You got your orders, Clayton. The Rome Double-Murder case is off-limits to the Atlanta office." Thorpe again looked over at the third agent. "And those are my verbal orders to you."

He was too angry to answer. He opened the door. Pausing, he threw an icy glance back over his shoulder at the two men, then he turned and walked out, easing the door shut behind him.

§

A thick gray haze covered the capital city like a cloud.

For the second time in four days, Shelley drove under the arch and onto the grounds of the Atlanta Pen. If Carlos Martinez didn't tell him about Quinn Bucket without him asking, he was going to whack it off and drop it in the can on his way out of there.

Fifteen minutes later, Shelley was back inside Carlos Martinez's cell. Carlos looked up, snorted, and turned back to watching an old *Flip Wilson* rerun. Shelley stepped quickly up to Carlos and delivered two sharp karate chops to the sides of his neck. Carlos fell. He caught his former friend and Vietnam comrade and eased his bulk to the floor.

Carlos woke up spread-eagled on his back, bound, gagged and naked. Shelley held Carlos's limp dick in the palm of his left hand. In his right hand glittered a straight razor. The sharp blade was pressed against Carlos's glan penis just hard enough to draw a thin line of blood. The limp dick shriveled even smaller.

"Roscoe, you lied about those Hooch babies. Your man Quinn Bucket was canvassing town with a Miami thug. Tell me, Roscoe."

"Yeah, yeah, you right, you right. Him and Mario, they offed the Hooch babies. Or—orders from the preacher man. So—somebody offed his son. And it happened on their watch. I swear, th—that's the truth. Please don't do this thing to me, Cap'n."

Shelley suffered a flashback. The beast stirred. "Who was the son?" he said, dread slurring his words. Another flashback. And a grunt.

"Sturro. His name's Sturro, man. That's all I know. Sturro."

The beast reared its ugly head.

Shelley grimaced, his mind a blank, but the question Jud Judson told him to ask Carlos pierced that fog. "What about the two NYC dudes who came down here looking for one of their own." Another flashback. Another grunt.

Carlos made squealing noises.

The beast turned and looked.

"Th—These two dudes bounced down hunting a dude who drop-ped in and dropped out. Never said who they be tracking. I heard they be hound-dogging a fellow who owned a fancy NYC night-spot. Before the tax man got him. The two dudes, they came, the two dudes, they looked, the two dudes, they bounced back outta here empty-handed. Please don't do this thing to me, Cap'n."

"Names?" he said, the fog in his head clearing.

"No—Norman something. Don't do this thing to me, Cap'n."

He yanked Carlos's dick. The convict squealed and fainted.

Shelley dropped the shiny razor into the trash can.

The beast lay down its ugly head and sighed.

34

STANFORD WAS SPEEDING south down I-75, settling in for the three-hour drive to Twofer County. An 18-wheeler blew past the sedan, mud flaps sailing stiffly in the wind, and sucked along in the huge truck's draft was a WTNT-TV News van.

The sun shone like a beacon in the sky. The last drops of a spring shower dribbled from a sky bleached snow-white by the heat.

Twenty miles from Twofer County, Stanford clicked on the FM radio and pressed the "seek" button.

"Heyyy! Get that head outta that bed!"

He canceled the "seek" button. That voice belonged to Marion Monroe Sass, the son of his old classmate, Samuel Monroe Sass.

"Wake up out there y'all! It's me, again. Marion, the-loudest-mouth-of-the-South, Monroe Sass, some call me Quick Lips, but you can call me Motor-mouth, that's me, yeah man! Hey! This here good ol' South Georgia boy gonna be cooking here real soon, and we ain't talking no grits and eggs jive neither, baby; this kid's talking about some good ol' low-down South Georgia funk! This kid's about to blow your socks off, with your shoes on, Honey. Here it iiis, the biggest, the baddest, the best, and you know the rest; we ain't talking no U. S. Marine Corp neither, baby; we're talking, 'Coca-Baby,' the biggest hit in America today! Ah, shake it, shake it, baby, here's 'Coca-Baaabbby'!"

Stanford pressed the "seek" button again. The syrupy drawl of the farm reporter told the same old dismal tale. He cancelled the "seek" button again and listened.

"Hogs are down thirty cents to $39.25…pork bellies off sixty-five cents to $25.25…corn off a nickel to $2.19. Beans are off forty cents to $5.78 a bushel. Now, the bad news. Oranges squeezed up a nickel, and diesel shot up a dime…"

Stanford exited I-75 and drove east toward Twofer City. Creeping into the manicured town he remembered how bad things were before QueenBee brought Can-Can Textiles kicking and screaming into Twofer County.

The company, the county's biggest employer, hired 3,500 workers and paid them a $70-million payroll. All the new money introduced townsfolk to ulcers, property taxes, divorces, alimony, child support, "wife-in-laws," visitation rights, nursing homes, Prozac, ADD, Ritalin, juvenile delinquents, and many other middle-class diseases now afflicting folks and their once simple relationships.

Words like *fringe* and *benefit* became part of the local talk instead of being mistaken for two French words used to describe a nasty American disease with no cure in sight.

The one-man Twofer County police force of police chief Jake Keller was now a county-wide, fifteen-man trained army of law enforcement officers armed with radios, radar guns, breath analyzers, bulletproof vests, and armor-piercing bullets.

§

At the homeplace, QueenBee smiled when she saw him.

"I don't feel as bad as I look," QueenBee said. "And I do know how bad I look. I'll be glad when Stanley gets back. I hate he had to go to Paris with his mama. I wish he could have stayed here with us."

QueenBee squeezed his arm. "Stanley, he's such an excitable, bubbly boy. Sometimes I do get the urge to walk behind Stanley with a bucket and a wet mop. I just want to be there to sop him up in case he spilled himself all over himself. We do need him. We both need Stanley. He's our heir; he's our only heir."

QueenBee plopped a leather pouch on the table in front of him and settled back down in her rocking chair. She looked so tired.

"Where are the pups?" he said, not seeing Aretha and Franklin.

"Went to see the vet. Shots and a physical. Now, tell me what's making you so black under your eyes, besides our little monster?" QueenBee said.

When he told his grandmother about a rumor of James Kelsey's coming indictment, she said Justin would be stopping by to see her in a few days. Then she would ask Justin if it was true James would soon be indicted for racketeering. He had so misjudged James Kelsey, he told her.

QueenBee started rocking and studied his face, the sure sign that a history lesson was coming.

"Well, Stanford, you're not the first one to make a mistake, to misjudge a person. Even the almighty Albert Einstein made a mistake when he said God didn't get down on her knees to roll dice. Now we know that God shoots craps with our lives all the time. The whole world makes mistakes, Son. Enslaving black people was a big mistake that white people made. A shameful mistake we won't overcome for another 200 years, I tell you."

QueenBee sounded weary and depressed.

She continued to rock as she spoke. "We, black people, we are not the only people in the world to be so shamed; we're not the first; we're not the last. All people in the world, they all have had to carry their load of shame on their backs. They all have been both winners and losers. All people have won a few battles, and all people have lost a few battles.

"That's the history of people everywhere.

"Son, all people have a history. The Johnny Rebs were shamed, too, you see. We black folk, we are like Johnny Rebs, in a way, you know. We Africans, we let white folks buy us and sell us like we were livestock when we were not livestock—that's our shame. Johnny Rebs, they kicked a dog called the north, got bit pretty bad. They started a war then quit the fight—that's the shame of the Johnny Rebs, starting something they couldn't finish."

Rubbing her eyes, QueenBee sighed her weariness.

"And, today, Americans, black and white and yellow, men and women, boys and girls, the whole world, it seems, they all wonder the same thing:

"Why some black men act like they have no feelings at all, no compassion toward their families. Why can't people see? You damage the mind and the psyche when you breed men for strong backs and weak minds. Our men had no families to love. Why can't people see? Our men had no kids to raise. Our men, they had no women left untouched by the slaveowner to call their own. Why can't people see? Our men had no one to love. It was better for them not to love a woman than to love a woman and then the slaveowner sells his love from under him, or bed her down himself. Why can't people see? It was better for a man not to love a child than to love a child and then the slaveowner sells his child from under him. Why can't people see? It was better for the woman not to love a child or a husband than to love a child or a husband and then the slaveowner sells her child or husband from under her. When white folks accuse black men of not being good family men, they forget who first ripped apart the African family so they could control our black men."

QueenBee flinched and took a few calming breaths.

"We black folks had to build a new culture based on our slavery past. We had to build a positive future based on a negative past. That is not an easy thing to do. You do this hard thing while white folks are blocking your path at every turn."

Another deep breath, another long sigh.

"Son, hand me that pouch on the table before I talk myself down into a Twofer County dirt bed. We all make mistakes, Son, is what I'm saying to you. So a mistake is not a good yardstick for not liking someone. We all do wrong. It's human to do wrong. Being human is no crime, it's a struggle, Son. It's a struggle to do right for yourself and for other people out there in the world you love and care for."

QueenBee opened her arms like a gift. "Give me a big fat juicy hug before you leave me. You mean the world to me, Son."

He did.

"Any luck finding Katie Kane's sister?" QueenBee said.

He shook his head. "I ran ads in the *Denver Post*, and the *Rocky Mountain News*, and newspapers in Boulder, Colorado Springs, and Fort Collins. A nibble, no bites."

QueenBee sighed again. "It's a pity Katie Kane died the way she died. Without waking up from the stroke she had when she found out her daughter and grandson were dead. Well, at least now folks can forget all that foolishness about her being a witch and such."

QueenBee handed him a scroll tied with a blue ribbon. "Here's my last will and testament. Now, I have a few things to tell you."

35

STANFORD WAS THIRTY miles south of Atlanta when he heard a strange sound. It was his new cellular phone. He glared at it. His partners had insisted that he carry a cellular phone for emergency calls. He did but always turned it off once he left the city. He had forgotten to turn it off while he was in Twofer County.

He answered it and heard Consy Torrey's excited voice.

Hitting the high spots, Consy Torrey told him some disturbing news about CapCity Investments.

"See you in thirty minutes," he said and clicked off.

§

Half an hour later, Stanford stepped into Consy Torrey's office.

"Show me, Consy," he said and popped two ranitidine tablets. His stomach was already spewing a volcanic stew. He downed a glass of water.

The young RKL audit manager told him what Juanita must have stumbled on. Stanford realized, in effect, Consy was telling him why his partner was killed.

"I looked where you thought I should look. If Karon, he had—"

"Who's Karon?" he said, still scanning the papers in his hand.

Consy sat on the desktop, pumped with enthusiasm.

"He's my friend. Karon runs CapCity Investment's computers. Well, this morning, Karon emailed me this SOS. He had a hole in his software, and he needed a quick fix. So he kind of patched me into his machine, and I kind of—well, anyway, I started noticing some familiar names popping up on the screen. I had time on my

200

hand, so I did a few things here and a few things there. Bottom line, I dumped CapCity's borrowers into my data file, and kind of, you know, bumped them off our client list and—Bam! There it is. The results are in your hand there."

Stanford drank more water. He could tell by the loose language that Consy had done something that he shouldn't have done. But Consy had found out something Stanford should have known but hadn't known. The news was depressing.

"Don't worry about any repercussions about what you did, Consy. But thanks for leveling with me about everything. This will stay between you and me. Your method, that is. But, let's try to keep it clean from now on. Okay, Consy?"

"Okay," Consy said and smiled sheepishly. "I was counting on you saying that. Now, let me print something else out for you."

Stanford felt guilty. This was his fault. He hadn't been paying attention to what was going on around him. He hadn't been doing his job. He hadn't stayed on top of things the way he should have. He hadn't seen the firm caving in around him. This could turn out to be a nightmare. RKL was screwed.

"Stanford," Consy said, "half of our clients are either owned by CapCity Investments, or those clients owe CapCity some mighty big bucks; which, of course, is the same as being owned by them. And all CapCity Investment's borrowers are our clients except two. That's Taurus Industries and Southern Supplies."

"How many are in default?"

"None," Consy said.

"How many are cash-poor?"

"None," Consy repeated.

He nodded. "Are these mostly James's clients, Consy?"

Consy shrugged. "Yes. Some of our older clients, they owe Cap-City, but those clients are not James's clients. I'll say three-fourth are James's clients. Three out of four are his clients."

Stanford realized his mistake. He was a great Monday-morning quarterback. He had been too concerned about Lake Arrowhead when CapCity Investments was the problem. He surely should have been more suspicious when James had insisted that he take over the Lake Arrowhead account, their largest account, so James could concentrate on their new client, CapCity Investments.

What Consy found partially explained James Kelsey's supposed coming indictment. But, still, he just couldn't tie it all together.

Were Richard and Mark willing to pay him a million dollars to run Lake Arrowhead? Or were they willing to pay him a million dollars to keep quiet about something they thought he knew, something that could get them both jailed? But what did he know that could possibly send those two to jail? Lake Arrowhead's books had not been cooked, because he was the chef.

He gnawed his lip. Maybe Clayton could make sense of it all.

"Stanford," Consy said, interrupting his reverie, "Karon, he's the friend I was telling you about, he's getting me a copy of CapCity's proprietary information, a computer tape." Consy smiled a twisted conspiratorial smile. "And the tape, it's got everything, from who owns CapCity to who finances the company."

He frowned. "Consy, that's a bad idea."

"But, Stanford, don't you wanna know?"

"Sure I want to know. But I don't want you breaking the law to find out. There are other ways, legal ways, or less illegal ways."

Consy looked worried. "I see your point. But let's say, I get the information but I don't bring it in the office; how's that?"

"Consy, it's a bad idea all the way around. Don't do it that way."

"Are you telling me not to do it?"

Stanford groaned. Of course, he was not telling him not to do it. He wanted that information. He studied Consy's face. "Yes," he said, "I'm telling you not to do it."

He held Consy's gaze until Consy's worried face brightened.

"Okay, Stanford, I won't," Consy said. "I will not do it."

§

"The FBI is back on the Rome case," Clayton said.

"What?"

When Stanford dropped his bombshell on Clayton about what Consy had found, Clayton dropped a bombshell of his own.

"Then you guys must have screwed up big-time," he said.

"No," Clayton said, "in fact, we got a tip about a dead man. We're checking to see if it ties into the Rome case; that's it, Stanford."

"What's the dead man's name, Clayton?"

Clayton shook his head. "It will come out soon enough."

He handed Clayton a Vietnam snapshot of Shelley and the three men. "Is the dead man in this picture?"

Clayton studied the faces, pointing at the intruder. "Don't know him. This here's Markus Striker; runs MAPD's bomb squad. This here's a hot-rodder, Winston Horseshoe. And, of course, Shelley."

Clayton handed him the photo back. "The dead man's not there. Is this some kind of test?"

"No," he said, "not a test. Anything on that thumbprint yet?"

"Nothing. I'll let you know when I know." Clayton frowned at him now. "Stanford, Gregory, he asks about you. He asks about you a lot. We miss you not coming around anymore."

"Yeah," he said, feeling sheepish. "Me, too."

§

Henry Finch wore his long gray hair in a neat ponytail tied near the nape of his neck. Otherwise, Henry Finch fit the stereotype of a grown-up Beatnik: Bow tie. Vest. Bifocals. Penny loafers.

Stanford slid into the booth across from the IRS agent.

The Wood Stove Restaurant was nearly empty.

Henry Finch patted the back of his hand. "Hanging in there?"

"I am," he said.

The thirty-year IRS employee slid the brown envelope across the table. "We nailed the clerk who sold that information from the tax files," Henry said. "Thanks for the heads up."

He opened the envelope, took out the tax return and read it. "I thought you guys had stopped clerks from raiding taxpayers' files?"

"Impossible to police," Henry Finch said. "It's better; we're nailing more of the scumbags all the time."

The federal income tax returns in his hand had been filed by a Miami company called the LA Trust. Lake Arrowhead was listed as one of three subsidiaries. The second subsidiary was Prison City, Inc. The third one was Bottom Feeders, Inc., a deep-sea salvage operation. He whistled under his breath.

"LA Trust grossed over $100 million last year," he said, "and half was pure profit. Jesus." He looked up at Henry Finch. "What a cash cow."

Henry Finch merely nodded.

The return was signed by Alfred Warner.

"Warner; who is he?"

"A hotshot Miami lawyer," Henry Finch said. "He's the official signer for quite a few Florida corporations. You'll have to burst Warner's bubble to get a look at who really owns the LA Trust. But, of course, you know that."

He stared at the signature of the tax preparer: James Kelsey.

§

Stanford drove to David Harte's cottage. The psychiatrist was stuffing the trunk of his Mercedes. He didn't know how hard David would fight him on this. Would David tell him what he wanted to know? Or would David tell him to go fuck himself?

"What a nice surprise, Stanford," David said. "Get out. I've got a minute. What's on your mind?"

"Shelley, he's on my mind."

David gave him a sharp look. "Well, Stanford, we've reached a point where you must ask Shelley about his treatment. That's the way that works."

"Shelley won't talk to me about it, David."

"Nor I," David said, folding his arms like an exclamation point. "Ethics won't allow me, Stanford. You know the rules. You operate by similar rules."

"Shelley's in trouble," he said. "Deep trouble."

David's forehead wrinkled. "Stanford, I don't enjoy being an asshole. You convinced Shelley to see me. That was the second step in helping your friend. Recognizing that he had a problem was the first step. I can handle his problems from here. I won't violate my ethics, and I don't look kindly on those who insist I do."

He nodded sympathetically. "Ethics are fine, David. But Shelley has lived a very violent life, and Shelley is a very violent man."

"We're all violent to a degree," David said, tilting his chin. "What's that supposed to mean, exactly?"

"It means you can do more good for Shelley if you tell me what's twisting his mind so. Then I can play my role as a friend, a best friend. Is that asking too much, David?"

David propped a foot up on the car's bumper.

"Yes. It's asking too much, Stanford. Sometimes, not often, the last thing a person needs is a friend, as antisocial as that statement sounds. Sometimes, the last thing a person needs is a best friend, as crazy as that statement sounds, too. Stanford, a friend wears blinders. A best friend wears the widest blinders of all. There are times when a friend at a distance is the best friend of all. This is one of those times, I'm afraid."

David dropped his foot off the bumper.

"Stanford, look, I'm definitely not questioning the quality of your friendship. Your concern for your friend is as genuine and touching as any I've seen in all my years of practice. But, as you said, your friend's in deep trouble. He needs my professional help now. Trust me on this, Stanford. It's worse than you know."

He pressed on. "I disagree," he said, shaking his head. "In Shelley's case, I disagree. You've known Shelley all of five one-hour sessions. I've known Shelley thirty 365-day years, give or take four or five leap years. Shelley, he forgets and he needs me. I'm all Shelley's got. He has no next of kin, no family. Just me, David. Shelley has only me."

David twisted his body away from him like a defiant child. "So, this conversation is not about Shelley at all. This conversation is all about 'I.' This conversation is all about Stanford Rome."

The woods grew silent around them, almost eerie. Stanford lowered his eyes as if watching tiny parachutes floating down to the ground between him and David.

"Yes," he said. "Yes, this conversation is about me; isn't it?"

"Look, Stanford, you can't save your best friend's life by whacking off my patient's head. It's self-defeating."

He nodded again, then pressed the attack. David had to tell him what he wanted to know.

"Where's your best friend, David?" he said.

David cleared his throat, his torso appearing to sink into his hips. "Never had such a creature." David looked at his watch and shrank back from him. "Gotta run, Stanford. It's Wednesday; I have meetings on Wednesdays."

"David, please," he said, "please, David, tell me."

David studied his face as if searching for something missing.

"David," he said, "it's for me. I need to know for me. Shelley's the closest person to a brother I have. We need each other, Shelley and I. If anything happened to him I didn't know about, I could never forgive myself. You see, David. I'm carrying around enough guilt as it is. I should have been there that night they were killed. In fact, I was there. But I left them.

"So, tell me for me, David. Tell me for me."

"That's a low blow, Stanford," David said, looking irritated then angry. "Shit, Stanford, you're out-quacking the quack."

David kicked the tire. "Damn you!" He kicked the tire again.

"I'll say this much though, Stanford," David said, combing his fingers through his hair. "Hell—listen carefully to what I'm saying. Don't ask me to repeat it, and let's don't discuss Shelley again."

Sighing, David studied his face again.

"Can you at least agree to that one stipulation, not to discuss this with me again, Stanford?"

He thought about it. He could just lie. He would lie.

"Ah, hell," David said before he could lie. "Forget the stipulation. You're going to lie. So, just listen up, will you."

The psychiatrist turned his face up at the sky as if speaking to the stars.

"Shelley's problem escalated about five months ago. I mean, his problem really escalated about five months ago. You being a CPA and all, why don't you add up the numbers. Then you'll see what I'm saying, Stanford."

David lowered his eyes from the sky and turned them on him again. David smiled a smile that didn't quite seem to know whether it wanted to be a smile or not.

"Thanks, David," he said. "Thanks for me."

"You bet, Stanford," David said, adding with a shy grin. "Insofar as Shelley being dangerous, I hear you. I've already come face to face with the ugly end of that pretty gun."

36

ATLANTA/MIAMI

FRIDAY, JUNE 10

THE ATLANTA AIR was gray and unappealing when Shelley aimed the Thunderbird for the Kitty Kat Lounge on Telfair Street.

As he cruised the strip in downtown, he was besieged by a draconian tightness in his chest. He thought, for a moment, he was suffering a heart attack.

Carlos Martinez had pieced it all together for him.

Shelley not only knew who the bomber was, he now knew what motivated the bomber to torch the churches and butcher Atlanta citizens. Preacher once had a son named Sturro. Now Preacher didn't have a son named Sturro. That was the motivation. Shelley wondered if he had something to do with the missing Sturro. He wondered if the missing Sturro had anything to do with the trace of blood he found in his car trunk, just a trace. Hmm.

Sometimes, he had this insatiable appetite, this burning desire— a hard-on, really—to make gangsters disappear, the same way he made all those VC officers disappear during the big throw-down.

Suddenly he experienced a warm flush spreading out from his chest, and he had a strong urge to do violence to somebody. He felt his cock, and it was as hard as a railroad spike.

He felt like roaring.

Slowly, a calm washed over him.

But he still had a hard-on, and it was for the bomber and for the butcher man. Carlos had sworn on the head of his shrivelled-up dick that Sally Baby was the key to finding both gangsters. But he had to be quick about it because everyone and his mama would be trying to claim that $1-million reward the governor just posted for the bomber and the butcher.

Shelley parked the Thunderbird on Chesterfield Street and adjusted the tiny recorder in the small of his back before hustling the two blocks to Telfair Street. He had another hard-on that couldn't be knocked down with a jackhammer.

Shelley stepped inside the Kitty Kat Lounge and gave the room a quick once-over before stepping up to the bar.

"What it be Cap-tan?" Korea said with a nod and a smile.

Shelley leaned on the bar. "A she-male. Sally Baby. Seen him?"

The Kitty Kat owner nodded to a table. "Big man yonder."

"Thanks, Roscoe. Bag me a liter for the road." He leaned and whispered into Korea's ear, then he went to meet Sally Baby.

The big man ignored him when he sat down at his table.

"Mr. Sally Baby," he said to the 400-pound giant.

The big man rolled his eyes up, then rolled his eyes back down again like window shades. "Who be asking?" the big man said.

Shelley glimpsed movement near the front door and twisted the chair to see the door and Sally Baby at the same time. Sally Baby rolled his window-shade eyes up again.

Shelley saw a small man breach the doorway, looking like one of those life-sized sex dolls, except that his mouth was about one-half the right size for his face. The little mouth looked like a button on a shirt. The small man looked over at them for a long moment then turned and went back outside. Shelley stood.

"Where's your friend, the butcher, Roscoe?" Shelley said and slipped a hand into his pants pocket.

The beast reared its ugly head.

Sally Baby sneered and stood to his full six and a half feet. "Fuck you, and the horse you ro—"

Shelley was already slack in the knees, and was cocking his hips before the word "fuck" left Sally Baby's lips. He threw a straight right hand, jumping up into the punch, his powerful leg muscles driving the full weight of his 230 pounds of disgust into the sucker punch. He felt the big man's teeth and gums cave in from the chopping blow to his jawbone. Sally Baby fell over backwards, toppling tables and chairs on his way to the floor, and spraying a trail of blood and teeth. His unconscious body settled, quivering, like Jello on the floor. His breath escaped in a sigh of bloody bubbles.

Shelley stepped over Sally Baby, slipped the brass knuckles back into his pants pocket, and rubbed the back of his fingers. Nothing broken. He pulled out the syringe. He jammed the needle into the big man's buttock then pushed the plunger home.

The beast turned and looked.

He now had a hard-on for the butcher and for the bomber that couldn't be knocked down with *two* jackhammers.

Whap! The beast snapped its tail.

§

Clayton Westwood sat alone in his locked office. The Wild Bunch sat alone in the conference room, waiting to give him a preliminary report of what they found. Then he would write his response to what they found. They would include his response in their final report to Thorpe. He was acting the ass by making them wait. But he had to admit, today, he enjoyed very much acting the ass.

Click-clack. Click-clack. Click-clack.

Clayton hated Thorpe for bringing in the Wild Bunch to go over the murder case. To critique his work! And now Thorpe wanted him—him!—to spy on Shelley. He wouldn't do it. The backbone of any friendship between men was loyalty, and spying on Shelley was against much of what little in life he still halfway believed in. He just wouldn't do it. He had to first live with himself before he had to live with the rest of the world.

Meanwhile, back to the real world.

He had his family to support. That was the rub. His first loyalty was to his son and, to a lesser degree, his son's mother.

Clayton pinched the bridge of his nose. He thought it odd that Shelley hadn't given the faintest hint that he knew he'd been wearing a tail for the past two days. Two FBI trackers had finally nailed Shelley down to Avenue *B*, and yesterday he and a lab man dusted Shelley's house for fingerprints. He was still waiting for the results from the lab. He personally gave the lab man a hand because he was going to make sure Shelley got a square deal from Thorpe.

He pawed the back of his neck. What if Thorpe was right and there were links between Carlos Martinez, Edward Shaw, and Shelley today as there had been links between those three in Vietnam twenty years ago? And where were those three men today? Carlos was locked down in the Atlanta Pen. And Ed Shaw, he was locked down in a grave, and Shelley, he was locked down in life out there somewhere—doing God knows what to who knows whom.

Clayton had been taking shit all week from Thorpe, and now he was going to dish out some stinky stuff. When he finished kicking ass, his polished shoes would be splattered with a brown stain!

He went hell-bent for the conference room door, wearing a wood chip on his shoulders the size of a loblolly pine.

§

The Wild Bunch waited. Their file folders and coffee mugs sat in front of them on the conference table. Impatiently, they waited.

Clayton glared at all of them, then he steadied his glare on the leader. "So you guys have been bad-mouthing Atlanta, is that so?"

"Not at all. Who said Atlanta was a dump?" Mike Thaylor said, smiling. "Atlanta's not a dump; it's a cesspool."

"Yeah," Boz said, "your bomber, he just rearranged the garbage. Give me the Big Easy any day."

"Lack of culture," Goose said, "unless you guys wanna call driving fast a sign of civilization. This so-called city is just a collection of concrete and steel boxes surrounded by asphalt and tar."

"Yeah," Clifton said, "and who told these Atlanta folks that living fast is the same as living well?"

"What's an Atlanta Harlequin anyway?" Mike Thaylor wanted to know.

Clayton glowered and rocked forward in the chair. "Folks, this meeting could take us one hour, or this meeting could take us all day long, and I do mean a twenty-four-hour day, folks." He leaned back in his chair, smirking. "You guys really do like it here in Atlanta, now don't you, class?"

Thaylor, Goose, Boz and Clifton jeered at one another, then they all burst out laughing and started jeering him, pointing and jabbing their fingers at his face and really pouring on the ragging of Atlanta.

Three hours later, the hot coffee and the glazed donuts were two-hours gone. Clayton refused to order more. Nobody was laughing and jeering him now. Thaylor flipped another page of the ten-page report. It took him only forty minutes to read that page and question them about it. He was already on page three, with only seven more pages to go.

"Whoa, Thaylor," he said, holding up the folder, "what phone call you talking about in this report? There was no telephone call made from the house that night."

Without answering, Thaylor slid the open folder down the table to him. He read documents showing that a call had been made.

"What is this?" he demanded. He had taken all the shit he was going to take. "I asked you a question?" he said and rose to his feet, his body language in attack mode.

Thaylor threw up his hand. "Hold one," the leader said, "let's cut to the chase here. Clayton, Thorpe, he's out for your ass. We all know that. Thorpe hauled us up here because he knew we would find this call made from the murder scene at the time the murders went down. The upside is this is all bullshit. The downside is this is all bullshit missing from your case files. More worrisome, this is bullshit that will stick when Thorpe puts spin on it."

"The phone call," he said, "tell me about the fucking phone call."

Thaylor told him.

He sat slumped in the chair, rubbing the back of his neck.

Thaylor watched him a while before speaking. "We can't find a thing on that phone call in your files. Hell, you didn't find the phone call because the phone call was not there when you looked for it."

"No way," he argued. "It's impossible what you're saying."

"It happened," Thaylor said. "The phone call went to Jackie Pearson, who later got himself whacked down in the Bottoms."

"Who's Jackie Pearson?" he said.

"A drug pusher from down Miami way, Liberty City," Thorpe said. "A sniper blew out the back of his head three weeks ago. The streets say the word came from the Pen, right here in Atlanta—your turf."

Clayton shook his head. "No shooter makes a call after wasting two people. Somebody sabotaged the investigation; right, Mike?"

Mike Thaylor shrugged. "Probably."

"How will you handle this fuck-up, Thaylor?"

"Like always; however Roscoe tells me to handle it."

Clayton studied Thaylor with narrowed eyes. Then he laughed. "You're kidding me," he finally said. "There is no way I'm believing this. You are kidding me, right?"

"My point exactly," Thorpe said, and both men reared back in their chairs and roared with laughter.

§

When the conference room emptied of the Wild Bunch, Clayton stood alone. After failing again to get his son on the telephone, he shoved the useless device aside. He rubbed his eyes again, waiting on the call from Pencil Woods about those fingerprints taken from Shelley's house on Avenue *B*.

Who erased the telephone company's computer records?

When the telephone rang, Clayton snatched it up and plopped down on the table.

"Westwood...Give it to me, Pencil...Bruce Wayne? Like Batman's Bruce Wayne? Oh, that Bruce Wayne."

The telephone still pinned to his ear, Clayton slid off the conference table, rubber-kneed. "The prints on the 8x10 I gave you belonged to who—say again?"

§

Suspense oozed through the night like a snake in the grass, and drama pounded the moment like a drum. The tall man was on the move, forty miles south of Atlanta and speeding through the rain.

Three and a half hours later, the tall man stopped for gas at Exit 1 near the Georgia-Florida line. Another gas stop near St. Cloud, Florida, then nonstop to Lauderdale-by-the-Sea, Florida.

The tall man checked into the Starlight Motel and turned the wall heater on full blast. After a long cold shower, he stared at the face in the mirror, and the face in the mirror stared back at the tall man. Something vital inside him had broken down; something important inside him was melting away, and he was fast running out of time.

The tall man strapped the belt around his waist and dressed in black. He opened the gun case and took out a twenty-round 9-mm Luger. In its place he put the six-shot .44 Magnum. Picking up the telephone, he dialed the number Carlos Martinez had given him.

"Quinn Bucket," the voice said on the other end.

§

The tall man crept into the retirement city and drove straight for the mansion. He arrived early and waited. The weather was hot and muggy. His face swam in sweat. He was alive and riding high. He got such a thrill out of making gangsters disappear. The only thing he did that came even close to matching the intense pleasure he got was having sex with a sexy, strong-bodied woman. Nothing else came close. There was no third place in his pleasure dome.

At 2 a.m., the tall man shorted out the electric fence and scaled it. He was halfway across the lawn when the darkness spat out two pissed-off Rottweilers.

He dropped the charging guard dogs with two shots, then shot the two men running behind them. Tightening the cinch on the forty-pound backpack, he braced for the next wave of bodyguards. Four men armed with submachine guns charged from inside the mansion. He eluded the gunmen without firing a shot. Sprinting inside the house, he saw Mario the instant Mario saw him. He shot Mario dead.

Footsteps thundered toward him from behind. He swept up Mario's Uzi and mowed the four gunmen down as they ran into the room. In a crouch, he scooted across the room. When no more gunmen came, he met up with Quinn Bucket.

He and Quinn planted small explosives to trigger the larger ones Quinn had planted downstairs in every corner of the mansion.

Eighteen minutes later, he and Quinn were lying on the ground four hundred yards from the mansion. It was 2:47 a.m.

Three minutes later, Shelley pressed the detonator.

The inside of the mansion glowed in a brilliant red as if a supernova had ignited. The mansion erupted and shot a fireball spiraling up into the night, filling the sky with flaming debris. The bits and pieces of the building flew no farther than two hundred yards from the foundation, the blast so concentrated in its power.

"Got something for you, Quinn," Shelley said.

Shelley reached inside his shirt and shot Quinn a grin.

He peeled off the money belt and slapped it into Quinn's hand.

"Unemployment compensation," he told Quinn. "Lump sum."

37

FRIDAY, JUNE 10

"GOOD MORNING, Ms. Slade. And much obliged for that plug on TV you gave us the other Sunday night."

Larry, the Lake Arrowhead security guard, beamed at her. "You sure nuff looking good this morning, Ms. Slade."

"Seeing your smile brightens my own day," she said, beaming back, showing how it was really done. Larry was the security guard Stanford sent to wake her up the day she fell asleep outside his cottage while waiting on him to come back from jogging.

She had gone there under the pretense of interviewing him.

Stanford had come back from jogging and saw her asleep, but he conveniently forgot to wake her up. Instead, he had showered and left her there sleeping. But he did send Larry back to wake her up after he was long gone. A lesser woman would have been embarrassed, but the slight only made her more determined than ever. He was the one man she was going to fight for. He could try to embarrass her, he could try to make her jealous, he could try to make her angry, he could try to make her sad, and he could try to make her grieve, but all those emotions were lightweights compared to the heavy dose of love she carried around inside her heart for him. Plus she knew something about him that he had yet to admit to himself. She found out for sure the day she trapped him in the Twofer County Cemetery and saw that desperate look of confusion in his face. Sure, his eyes told her to go away, but his body language told her to wait. There was no doubt in her feminine mind that he loved her, too. And it was just a matter of time

214

before he let his guard down. That was when she would rush into his arms and press her face to his chest and listen to his heartbeat and squeeze him and claim him.

"Am I now persona non grata, Larry?" she said.

Larry reared his head back like a woodpecker in freeze-frame. "Break it down for me, Ms. Slade. What you asking me? I ain't got no college. Hell, my ex, she tells me I ain't got no brain neither."

Larry laughed a deep belly laugh. How could anyone not like him. He never put other people down. He just put himself down.

"Is Stanford in?" she asked. "At his cottage, I mean?"

"Sure is," Larry said, looking at his watch. "You might miss him though, this being a weekday and all. He's out running by now."

"Does Stanford run everyday?" she said.

"Everyday he's out there running." The telephone rang inside the guardhouse. Larry tipped his cap. "Good day to you, Ms. Slade. And have yourself a goodun, ya hear me now."

Driving away, Jocelyn still felt the eerie effects of loneliness, a heaviness in her entire abdomen. This morning when Stanford called his office to tell his secretary he was taking the day off, she had gotten a call from her trusted mole, who alerted her to Stanford's day off from the office. She then cancelled her day before it got started. Today was the day, she decided.

She drove slowly for Stanford's cottage, thinking how silly she had acted last week when she was at Lake Arrowhead. But that woman's face scared her half to death. And for nothing. Her mind had only been playing tricks on her. The woman just couldn't have been who she thought she was. And she hadn't been.

When she reached Stanford's cottage, she saw the sedan parked in the driveway. She switched off the engine and got out. Her feet hit the ground at the instant the cottage door opened.

Stanford stepped out in full running gear.

Her beating heart did a stutter-beat. *Uh-oh.*

Stanford glared at her. She felt herself getting pissed at his silent aggression. *Cool it.*

"Good morning," she said softly, cooling it and trying hard to keep cooling it. "Remember me, the chick you dissed the last time I was here? You really do know how to make a girl look bad. Much practice or am I the only chump?" *You're losing it.*

Stanford ignored her. He turned slowly around and pulled the door shut behind him. Then turning around to look at her, he jiggled the knob, then he jiggled it a second time, eyes still locked on her now scowling face. Stanford slowly stretched his neck before turning on his heels and jogging right past her without a word or a second glance. He passed close enough for her to smell coffee on his breath, and for her to see a smirk on his lips. Or was that an infant smile?

She watched him disappear around the bend, her eyes stinging, her throat burning. She didn't know whether to cry her eyes out or to scream her lungs out. So she did neither. Instead she sulked and clenched her fists until her nails dug down into her flesh. She was going to kill that bastard. Oh, yeah.

She choked back her tears. "Bastard!"

Crawling back in the Jeep Cherokee, she sat sniffling and fighting back more tears. Her heart was breaking. She had to endure and overcome. She had risked too much. She had come too far. And she was just too damn close to turn back now.

Minutes later, a movement in the distance caught her eye. She first thought it was Stanford. She focused and saw the thick broad shoulders of a big stag. He stood stark still beside a jittery doe. The proud antlered head swiveled, the black nose tilted up into the wind. The doe leaped away first, then the big buck popped from sight.

A male and a female. What was wrong with her? Was she nuts or what? She wanted to scream, now her crying spell was over. Her fingers curled, and she flexed them. She rubbed her palms warmly together, then she rubbed the tips of her fingernails together, sharpening them for battle.

Here she was—a horny angry woman. Out there was—a horny angry man. There in front of her—a nest. One man. One woman. One nest. No competition. Except Stanford's grief. She could overcome grief as competition. Damn right she could overcome grief as competition. Grief was an emotion and an attitude—not a woman; a feeling and an attitude—not a woman; a hurt and an attitude—not a woman!

She pondered her next move, shaking her head and chuckling at how stupid and sloppy her past moves had been. She thought about what to do now.

She thought about what she thought about some more. Satisfied with her new plan of attack, she grabbed her tote bag.

She strung on her sneakers and went jogging after her man.

At least Stanford hadn't chased her away from there. But there was no doubt in her mind, she would fight him if he tried. As more thoughts piled up in her mind, she kept clicking her fingertips together. At least he let her hang around. That was something. He had even taken the time to glare at her. He could have ignored her like last time, but he didn't. That was something. She was used to him ignoring her. If he started paying attention to her, she would get suspicious of his motive. Besides, how long could he keep this charade up?

That was the only real question. And it had to be a put-on. No man was as tenacious as she was. A woman like her on the make for a man like him had the sticking power of steak and potatoes.

Her big smile warmed the dried tear stains on her face. She was no longer crying. That was something.

§

Jocelyn staggered back to the cottage, sweating and gasping. Her thighs, her back, her neck ached so bad she wanted to puke. She felt as if she'd spent the past hour digging her own grave in a rock sauna, and now she was ready to die in it.

She rested her hand on the doorknob almost a full minute before she had strength enough to turn the heavy round thing. She leaned against the door, it opened, and she stumbled inside.

She heard the shower going full blast in the bathroom. Then she had the strangest thought. Where was his computer? She couldn't believe her stinking priorities. Here she was, dying from physical exhaustion, sexual negligence, and mental anguish, and she stood there thinking about a damn computer. She felt another crying spell coming on.

But she heard the shower stop, and the resulting quiet stopped the flow of tears to the outside.

The cottage was suddenly so quiet she was startled by her own shallow breathing. She swallowed to loosen her tight throat.

"I'll like a shower, too!" she shouted at the closed bathroom door, so Stanford would know she was inside. No answer.

"Fine," she muttered, "don't answer me."

She hurried back outside, snatched up her tote bag and beat it back inside the cottage before Stanford locked her out.

Stanford stepped from the bathroom and walked past her to the bedroom, unashamedly naked.

And he had a hard-on! After a cold shower. That was something! He was thinking of her. That hard-on was proof positive.

Who dat rode dat bull in here like dat! Who dat!

Her face flushed. Maybe he thought she was a damn nun! She felt ridiculous and had a thought to just get the hell outta there. It was just a thought. No running away, her. She laughed at herself again. Maybe Larry's self-deprecating style was rubbing off on her. That was a good thing.

Stanford came into the room wearing shorts, boat shoes, and a huge tee shirt. He handed her a plush towel set, and the gesture of kindness made her lightheaded. An act of love, she imagined. Boy, her emotions were all over the place. She could jump on his back, ride him down to the floor and have her way with him. Who would he tell? Who would believe she raped him even if he told someone? The more she thought about it, the more appealing the thought became. Not good.

"Breakfast in twenty minutes," he said, as if choking on every word. But he was speaking to her, and he could have gagged on his words for all she cared, as long as his lips kept spewing words out for her to hear. And if the man touched her, she would explode in a thirty-second spasmodic orgasm right there on the spot, and hopefully she'd live to dream about it.

In seven minutes flat she was out of the shower and back up in Stanford's face, smiling on the outside and grinning like hell on the inside. She had sunk beneath pitiful; she was wallowing down in the sewage of pathetic. But she was taking no chances Stanford might forget her so soon. She stuffed her wet clothes in a plastic bag and turned toward the kitchen.

Stanford whirled on her, angrily, stopping her in her tracks.

Whoa! The crazy man was gonna give her a frigging coronary.

Stanford aimed the fork at her nose. "Stay out of my kitchen." He turned back to cracking eggs into a bowl and ignoring her. She felt cowed. Stanford was scary. Maybe he was violent, too. But what the hell, if he beat the hell out of her, maybe that would do the trick. No doubt, she was losing his frigging mind.

Jocelyn stood at a safe distance, arms folded, watching Stanford cook *their* breakfast. The link sausages made her nostrils flare out, and she just loved the way he stirred a pot of grits. She would have never believed that toasting slices of wheat bread, buttering the slices and slapping apple jelly on the slices could be such a work of art. The way Stanford diced cheese into the eggs, whipped the eggs into a frothy lather, and tossed it all into the hot skillet made her proud to be standing there watching him do all those swell things with food she would soon be eating. The microwave sounded, and Stanford shook the sausages around in the container, punched in more time and acted as if he were the only person in the room.

Stanford was an asshole. He was such a frigging asshole.

She thought those ugly thoughts, but every time he happened to glance her way, she was smiling and on her best facial behavior.

Five minutes later, she was blowing on steaming hot grits and butter, and sitting across from the asshole she wanted to have babies with. Jesus. What a leap of faith. Having babies and hadn't even screwed him yet. What was she thinking? She wasn't thinking. She was feeling. Boy, was she feeling it—not it. Him. She was feeling him—not him. Stanford. She was feeling Stanford.

They ate breakfast under a no-nonsense truce of silence.

She drank the last of her juice and dabbed her lips dry. She thanked Stanford for breakfast and began taking up the dishes.

"Leave 'em alone," Stanford snapped, being mean to her again.

"Sure," she whimpered and backed away.

She sat on a barstool and watched Stanford clean the kitchen.

When Stanford finished the chore, the kitchen looked immaculate. He dried his hands on a towel and walked over to where she sat. "Let's sit here," he said.

They sat facing each other, one barstool between them. She felt goose bumps marching up her arms.

His eyes held hers so tightly her eyes had nowhere to run off to.

"Watch my lips," Stanford said. "Keep the hell away from me." His eyes screwed tighter into hers. "Are you with me on this? Keep the hell away from me."

Stanford's words were as cold and his words were as harsh as any words she had ever heard before, the menace unmistakable.

He hated her.

She could feel her heart flutter as if it wanted to shrivel, roll over, and die, but her mind quickly took over and spun an unreality, so she could live with the rejection. She quickly thought that it didn't really matter that he hated her guts.

Who cared if he hated her guts? She didn't care if he hated her guts. She loved the ingrate. She loved him. She just loved him. So there. Put that in your water pipe and smoke it.

She'd known all along that for her to nab this man, she had to give the performance of a lifetime. This was her moment to shine light on his darkness, or this was her moment to wither away into nothing in his mind. She had her audience, and that was all she'd ever wanted—a chance to present herself to the man she loved.

What better stage than here? What better time than now? Today was the day, she decided, and now was the time to act.

§

"I hear you, Stanford," she said and rose from the bar stool. "I'm leaving. But let me leave these few thoughts with you."

She slowly reached out and rested her palms on the back of his hands. He didn't move his hands away. He didn't even flinch at her touch as she expected him to do.

"Stanford, I have no control over my feelings for you. I don't even pretend anymore. I am obsessed with you. I wish I didn't feel this way. But I do. What can I do about it? Have you ever been so out of control like I'm so out of control, Stanford?"

Stanford watched her, but he didn't speak. She didn't expect him to. But he would listen. Even he knew when a woman would not be denied her say and that very important—last word.

She would insist on it, and she would dig ditches in his face if he resisted. He was a bastard, and if she sensed she had nothing else left to lose, she was going to jump him, draw blood, and claw his neck, right across the collar bone—bring some pain! Not really.

To make her emotional appeal to Stanford's heart as real as she could possibly make it, she thought about the saddest day of her life. She kept thinking about the saddest day of her life until she felt her body sort of close up on itself, sealing her inside a cocoon of past grief. When the sadness began to sting her eyes, she knew she was ready. She looked straight into Stanford's eyes—her own eyes filled with sadness and grief and pain.

"Me, I'm an orphan in this life, and I want you, Stanford."

She stepped closer until she stood directly between Stanford's knees, her thighs touching his. Her hands closed around his hands and squeezed ever so gently. Surprisingly, he kept looking at her, too, as if not daring to look away either.

She thought even harder about the saddest day of her life, the images driving her onwards.

"Wanting you, that's my problem," she said. "You have problems, too. I know. We all need to sometimes place our hearts into the caring hands of a lover. We need this if only for gentle safekeeping until we're strong again. I've been there, Stanford. It's not that you must love someone, Stanford. It's that someone must love you. It's a sexual thing, a sexual renewal. Maybe a one-nighter or a quickie romance is what it takes to get you back on track in life, I don't know for sure. But, Stanford, if you won't accept love from me, please, Stanford, accept love from someone else. I'll rather you accept love from another woman than for you not to accept love at all. If that ain't loving you, baby, I don't know what love is, Stanford."

She looked over his shoulder toward the padlocked bedroom. She thought even harder about the saddest day of her life, and the images became razor sharp in her mind. Emotions poured from her, coating each delicate word she spoke with true feelings.

"I don't know what you keep locked up in that room over there, Stanford. But whatever it is, I'm sure an exact duplicate is locked up in your heart. And that leaves no room in your life for an orphan like me. But, still, I love you, Stanford."

She removed one hand and stroked Stanford's cheek. Then with enormous will, she backed away from the man she loved. She stooped to pick up her tote bag without taking her eyes off Stanford's face.

She said, "If walking out that door ain't loving you, baby, then I don't know what love is, Stanford."

She swallowed a lump and turned for the door. She stopped and looked back over her shoulder at him.

"I'm lonely for you, Stanford. Are you lonely for me, baby?"

Then she was out of there. The walk to the Jeep was a mile long, and it took her forever to reach it.

§

Jocelyn Slade exited the taxi at 1710 Spring Street, and she walked two blocks to the seven-story building that was so inconspicuous it looked out of place even among so many similar buildings.

The first two things she noticed were the armed security guards and the metal detector. She told the guard who she was and who she came to see. The man knew who she was and snapped to it.

She pinned on the clearance badge for the top floor and was led to an elevator. The operator looked at her badge and spoke to her by name. She got off the elevator on the seventh floor and walked a half dozen steps to the office door. The nameplate taped to the door was a paper business card. She turned the handle, pushed the door open and stepped inside Kincaid Systems.

The male receptionist ushered her right in to see Curtis Kincaid.

The man who gave the business its name rose from his sofa and offered his hand. She shook it lightly. They sat on the sofa.

They spent the first minutes chitchatting, sizing each other up before she went immediately for the home run.

"Who hired you, Mr. Kincaid?" she said.

Curtis Kincaid studied her face about thirty seconds before he spoke softly, as if reminding himself to be careful with his big stick. Kincaid said, "My clients are confidential, Ms. Slade."

She smiled. "So are you, personally, confidential," she said. "I can tell by the size of the nameplate on your door. I can tell by how little information I can dig up on you."

"When you say 'dig up,' Ms. Slade, you make it sound so negative."

She leaned back, reconsidering her approach. "It doesn't have to be that way," she said, easing back on the throttle.

Kincaid smiled a wee smile. "You promise?" he said, sarcastically.

She leaned forward, menacingly.

Kincaid raised his hand. "Hold one," he said and leaned back as she leaned forward. He studied her again, reassessing her, as she had earlier reassessed him. Finally, he said, "What's in it for me?"

She gave him a dubious look. "I can forget I ever heard of Kincaid Systems and Curtis Kincaid," she said.

Kincaid thought on it for about thirty seconds. Then he slowly nodded. "Fair enough," he said. "Now ask me what you came here to ask me. When I answer your question. I want you to just get up and leave; fair enough?"

"Sounds like a plan," she said.

"Is it a deal?" Kincaid said.

She studied his no-nonsense face a long moment. "It's a deal," she said. "Now, who hired you?"

Curtis Kincaid spun around to the computer screen. He hit a few keystrokes, and pressed the print icon. The printer hummed then rolled out a sheet of paper. Kincaid folded the paper in half and handed it to her.

"Good day, ma'am," Curtis Kincaid said.

§

The telephone woke Jocelyn from a deep sleep. Her private line again. She snapped up the receiver. Not another false alarm.

An hour later, she was motioning to her producer. She kept her fingers crossed. It was 3:15 a.m. The TV studio had the atmosphere of a morgue. Was it all true this time, or was it just another hoax? She wanted so badly for the bulletin in her hands to be true. She crossed the fingers on her other hand and watched the executive producer, his senior producers, and his editors huddle together like the team they were. An aide passed a headset to the editor, who passed it along like a hot potato to a senior producer, who nodded to the executive producer, who swiveled and held up both thumbs.

"Yeah!" someone cried out.

The few people in the newsroom cheered. The station's stringer in Miami Beach had nailed down a crucial part of the fax the station had gotten from an anonymous source a couple of hours ago.

"Three, two, one, you're on, Jocelyn."

She was beaming a special smile tonight. "Good morning to you, Atlanta," she said, exuberance replaced by professional cool.

"I'm Jocelyn Slade. Ladies and gentlemen, this bulletin just in. The mastermind behind Atlanta's terror, a man called Preacher, is no more…"

38

SATURDAY, JUNE 11

TWENTY-FOUR HOURS had passed since Candice found out where Shelley-Frank lived on Avenue *B*. She had been watching the place for more than an hour. And now she was going inside to take a good look around.

She leaped the fence surrounding the house and landed in the backyard. Giving the kudzu-covered house a quick once-over, she quickly spotted the wires connecting the alarm to the monitoring station down at the Electronic Eye Surveillance firm. It was 2 p.m.

To be safe, she waited a few minutes longer.

At 2:05 p.m., she slipped on her rubber gloves and went inside Shelley-Frank's domain. For her to spend one hour inside the house, the cost was five large. She made a quick sweep of the small rooms; nothing there interested her. When she opened the door leading downstairs to the basement, her skin prickled.

She felt as if some enslaved spirit had brushed past her in a rush to escape the basement and its prison.

She beat back her apprehension and slowly, cautiously descended the stairs. She stopped abruptly on the bottom step when fear as sharp as a paper cut sliced across her brow. She could almost feel the trickle of blood there. Candice took one careful step backwards, then another backwards step. She was halfway back up the staircase before her unwilling legs finally obeyed her orders and stopped retreating.

She stood still for several minutes, listening, and fighting down the dread ballooning in her chest. Then she started back down the stairs, one slow step at a time until she reached the basement floor.

Candice stood erect with a foot of height to spare. The finished basement was dimly lit by small shadow lamps in three corners. The dark fourth corner was sealed off from the rest of the vast space by a portable partition. There was a room with a narrow plate-glass window taking up one half of a wall.

Pressing her nose to the cool glass, she saw huge fluffy pillows tossed over the floor. The door didn't have a handle on it, but she found a hidden floor switch recessed three feet to the right of the door. She stepped down lightly on it. Nothing. She pressed her weight down on it.

The thick heavy door swung inwards. She hesitated a second before stepping boldly inside. The door slowly closed and sealed with a sucking sound. She was surrounded in a cocoon of silence. She rubbed her hand over the thick plush carpet and even thicker padded walls.

Looking up, she saw an overhead camera with a wide-angled lens covering the entire room. She found the inside floor switch and pressed it. The door opened, she stepped outside, and the door resealed. A soundproof room. Why is that?

When she looked toward the dark area of the basement, another paper cut slid across her brow, and she felt another trickle of blood.

She held the .380 out in front of her like an extension of her arm. She edged within two feet of the portable partition and stopped. Someone was on the other side. Not only did she smell him, every other sense told her he was there The odor was outrageous. Why did he let her get so close, and he hadn't made his move yet? And why was she waiting for him to make his move? She had to look. She might lose her head, but she had to risk it and look. She tightened her grip on the butt of the .380 and poked her head around the partition.

What she saw didn't immediately register, but her brain saw no immediate danger. In scant moments, the scene crystallized into hard reality. The big man was strapped down tight on top of a gurney. Her mind accepted that the man presented no danger to her, so her eyes made a quick sweep of the space before again coming to rest on the man tied to the gurney. He was a huge man. Had to weigh at least 400 or 500 pounds. He was gagged and blindfolded, which explained why he hadn't reacted to her presence.

Candice stepped in front of the man to look down at his face. She looked and nearly pissed her pants.

She shrieked and fell back, gasping. Shrieking again, she fought back a weakness in her muscles. She tried hard not to pass out—finally, strength surged back into her muscles, her legs started moving again, churning, moving.

Backpedaling away from the gurney as fast as her legs could carry her, she stumbled, falling flat on her ass, but her legs, they never stopped churning. In a panic like she'd never felt before, she flew up the stairs like her legs were propellers, and she all but dove back through the window. Her legs never stopped churning, not even as she leaped the fence surrounding Shelley-Frank's house on Avenue *B*, her legs never stopped churning.

Twenty minutes later at 2:35 p.m., Candice sat in the dark corner of a bar nursing a scotch on the rocks and sweating military bullets by the bucket full. Her legs were no longer pumping but her legs, like the rest of her body, her legs, they kept twitching, anxious and ready to take off running again at the slightly noise. She fumbled the liquor glass up to her lips, and she drank.

She had to pee, but no way she was going inside a room as confining as a toilet. She dabbed her dry lips with a paper napkin, and she drank. How could that be possible? It didn't make sense to her. It didn't add up. Shelley-Frank had nabbed the Surgeon!

The Surgeon was in Atlanta. That meant his sidekick, that sneaky little killer, was somewhere close by. How did Shelley-Frank get past that nightmare and nab the Surgeon? She fumbled the glass to her lips again, teeth clanging against the rim, and she drank.

But now she saw the whole big picture. Little Bruce Wayne, the Surgeon, and Preacher were the three faces behind the bombing and the butchery in Atlanta.

A three-headed terror was loose in the city of Peachtree streets.

She thought about the money.

That trio could be worth $1 million to her. Was it possible for her to make $2 million before she got the hell out of Atlanta for good? Was it at all possible for her to become a millionaire two times over and have big money again? What had started out as a freebie for mother dearest had escalated into what could become her biggest payday ever. She tried to smile but there was no mirth left inside her brain. She was skittish and in full panic mode.

She gulped down the last of the drink. Only one. She had to think. Little Bruce Wayne was on the loose in Atlanta somewhere. She'd better hit the road, and fast would not be quick enough to leave town. But how could she even think of walking away from another million dollars? The first million would soon be in the bag. If Shelley-Frank left the Surgeon in that house alone tonight, she would go back and swipe the big man right from under his nose.

But what about Bruce?

She had to think this thing through. Now, where was Bruce? Shelley-Frank could—no, Bruce had to be dead, or else the Surgeon wouldn't be tied up down there in that basement. She really, really had to think this thing through. Shelley-Frank couldn't possibly kill Little Bruce Wayne.

Could he?

Bruce could walk up to Shelley-Frank and cut out his heart before he even knew he was cut. Bruce could get just that close to Shelley-Frank. Bruce's biggest asset was also his biggest negative— his small size. He looked like a harmless choirboy, a teenager. That made him dangerous. His foes underestimated who they were dealing with. Shelley-Frank wouldn't give Bruce a second look on the street. That would be his undoing, and he would be dead.

Since the Surgeon was all tied up, that meant Bruce didn't know where he was. But she did know. Okay, that made sense. She could do it and get out of there before Bruce showed up. No doubt, Bruce would show up. But how could she steal an unconscious 400- or 500-pound man by herself? Think.

An idea started taking shape in her mind. It was a crazy idea.

But these were crazy times. How much could his head weigh?

Twenty pounds? Thirty at the most? Maybe forty. She could handle forty pounds of head. She thought about the time she saw her cousins saw off a deer's head. It was a little on the messy side, and bloody. She had to pee.

She pressed her thighs tighter together. No doubt about it, she had to go back to Avenue *B* and swipe the Surgeon's head right off his shoulders. She just had to do it. It wasn't as if the Surgeon had anything to live for. He'd bombed a red-blooded American city, and the people of Georgia, the people of Atlanta, they were going to fry the Surgeon's ass in due course. So no big deal. Dead was dead. And a head was a head. She really had to pee this time. She checked the .380, got up and squirmed her way to the restroom.

§

Candice kept Shelley-Frank's house under tight surveillance. She followed when he left. She tailed the Thunderbird to the Atlanta International Country Club, then she raced back to Avenue *B*. She had one hour to swipe the Surgeon's head off his shoulders, stuff it inside the thick plastic bag, and then inside the bowling bag.

She called in and got the go-ahead from the Electronic Eye Surveillance supervisor. Another five large it cost her. But this time she had a key. Slipping on her gloves, she opened the door and went inside, carrying her tool sack and bowling bag. When she opened the basement door she felt the same dread flush her brow as that first time. But now she knew what to expect and steeled herself before descending the stairs. Standing there on the bottom step, her nerves hummed with energy.

Suddenly, bells rang out on both sides of her head.

She spun around on her heels.

"Candy Girl."

The small voice spooked her.

A warm moistness gathered at her crotch.

"Drop the .380, Candy Girl."

Candice couldn't move a muscle.

"Drop the gun and don't turn around," the small voice said. "I'm partial to blowing out your spine on GP. And you could never ever again wipe your own ass."

She dropped the gun, and she did turn around.

Little Bruce Wayne was all teeth and glee. He was such a handsome man.

The runt knew damn well she was going to turn around. She had never taken orders from him, and she never would take orders from him. She feared him. God, he terrified her. But damn if she was going to grovel. She knew the little squirt was going to torture her to the limit of human endurance and the height of his bizarre imagination.

Once, the sadistic little runt threatened to ram a cherry-bomb firecracker up her "cute lil' ass," light a ten-minute fuse around her "pretty lil' neck," then watch her suffer ten minutes of hell before her "asshole blew inside out"—his exact words.

"Candy Girl, I find you in the goddamnedest places. Now what am I to do with the best cunt east of the Rockies besides slice her ass off an ounce at a time, good pussy or no?"

"The big little man," she said with a brashness she didn't feel.

"My—my, still think you kin to Phyllis Diller and Moms Mabley, huh, Candy Girl? Still throwing around that pussy like nickels and dimes, huh? That cunt's got too many miles on it. Now, how much to take out this here boy? What ya getting for the hit? What makes Roscoe worth enough to get Miss Fancy Pants on his black ass? Tell me, Candy Girl. What's up with this shit? You don't do your own kind. Now, give it up. Who's paying you?"

"I won't be sharing with you, Bruce; why do you need to know?"

Bruce grinned. "Ah, just listen to you, Candy Girl. You misread the cards completely, dear child. You're busted. Out the game. But you, I know you. You don't case a nobody for three months and not cop enough cash for a Lamborghini. Don't you lie to me now, Candy Girl. Don't you go pissing me off. I'll take you apart. I'm your old pal; remember, Candy Girl? Don't you fuck with me. I'll mess you up."

Sure, she remembered.

Her old pal wanted her to remember. Then he was going to take her apart the way Muhammad Ali took Floyd Patterson apart for calling him "Cassius Clay." Bruce wanted her to remember that, for several months anyway, they had been almost perfect lovers. But when she demanded more from Little Bruce than just being poked enough to moan and groan and come, he couldn't produce on such a high level from such a low start.

Bruce was the roughest little big-stick man she'd ever met—he was a freak, he was. Little Bruce just went on and on in a big man's way, using his big stick on her the way men used their big fists on one another.

It was good—God, yes. But Bruce started breaking down her body and smothering her spirit. It was good—God, yes, it was good. But sometimes, not often, good was bad.

She reached a point in her relationship with Bruce where she wanted to be stroked, hugged, and listened to. But Bruce was not that type of man and was grossly stunted that way, a dwarf, if that tall. It was Bruce's way or the highway. So when she replaced Bruce's stuff with a toy, then Bruce packed up his shitty attitude and hauled his ass on down the highway, dragging a grudge against her. Now, he would filet her behind one thin slice at a time.

Bruce was so cruel.

"So, Candy Girl, how much you getting?" Bruce said. "I'm asking for the last time."

"Said the little big man," she mocked. She knew that was a mistake the instant she saw that choirboy look get sucked back into Bruce's razor face.

Bruce Wayne snapped out a six-inch stiletto. Hungrily, he stepped toward her with blood in his devilish eyes.

She took a step back. "Okay, Bruce," she said, "I'll tell you what you wanna know." She threw up her hands. "Come on, Bruce; for old time sakes."

"Fat chance, Candy Girl. I'm sticking you. I'm sticking you."

Bruce Wayne stutter-stepped, then he stopped in his tracks, whiffing the air like a coon dog reeling in the scent of a treed coon. Turning almost lazily, Bruce glanced around the room, bewildered, searching for an unseen enemy.

What Bruce didn't see, Candice did see. She held her breath.

Holding her breath, she slowly turned her head away from gas seeping down from the ceiling ducts, hoping she didn't cough. She could hold her breath for well over a minute, but with all the stress she was under, a minute was probably the best she could do. Ten seconds.

Cough, you little runt. Cough, you bastard! She caught instant religion, praying for Bruce to cough, and praying she didn't cough. Dear God, make the basta—excuse my language, dear God, but make him cough. Twenty seconds.

Bruce's eyes slashed around the room in a panic, and he gasped. And then her curses and her prayers were answered.

Little Bruce Wayne coughed and dropped the stiletto.

Again, Bruce coughed then he fell gagging to the floor, clawing at his throat and gagging to breathe. Thirty seconds.

She sank to the floor, keeping her nose low and swam over to the floor switch and pressed it. Nothing happened. Forty seconds.

She banged the floor switch with her fist. Nothing happened!

Fumes squeezed water from her eyes, her throat scratched and burned. Don't cough! She struggled to her knees, then to her feet, her head pounding for relief, and her lungs fighting for a breath. Fifty seconds.

She stomped down on the floor switch with both feet. The door crept slowly open. Stumbling through the opening, she collapsed inside. Sixty seconds.

The door closed, sealing with a sucking sound.

Candice coughed and burst into tears. Seventy seconds.

39

TWOFER COUNTY

SATURDAY, JUNE 11

QUEENBEE ROCKED BACK and forth, the rhythm of the rocking chair keeping tune with the rhythm of her thoughts.

She squeezed the dice in her hand.

She felt uneasy. Justin was coming to visit for a minute on his way back home to Atlanta from the University of Florida in Gainesville. She glanced at the clock. Jake Keller had driven Justin from the airport to the homeplace. She watched the door. Any second now.

Then, Bertha appeared in the doorway with Justin.

The tall man's arms hung long at his sides, and his shoulders sagged at the corners as if each hand held half the world in it.

She was so happy. "Welcome home, Son."

Justin strode into the room. They hugged each other like they meant for the feeling to last a lifetime. "I'm so happy to see you."

"Me, too, QueenBee. Me, too."

Justin unwound to his full height, head and shoulders above her, and she beamed up into his eyes. She was so proud of him.

The U. S. Senate Judiciary Committee would soon vote on Justin Grimes' nomination to the U. S. Court of Appeals. Another Twofer County boy makes damn good.

Bertha served tea and cakes then left them alone.

Justin's eyes told her he still hadn't opened that safe-deposit box. She had given him the key the day he graduated from law school. So, he still didn't know the truth. Good for her.

"How's Faye?" She loved teasing him. "You proposed yet?"

Justin cut his eyes at her. "QueenBee, Faye's got the same attitude Faye had when you first dumped Faye in my lap ages ago."

Justin was forever blaming her for his good fortune with Faye. She had only suggested that he hire Faye as his legal assistant. It just so happened she suggested it when she was cleaning her twelve-gauge shotgun. But if he got the wrong impression about a shotgun relationship, then who was she to judge if he was right or wrong. But she had accepted that Justin Grimes was destined to head for the hills any time a woman tried to get close to him. The man ran from love like a rabbit ran from a fox.

"Justin, you're going to keep right on dallying until some joker's gonna snatch Faye right out from under your nose."

Justin's smile flamed out. She knew it would.

"QueenBee, I've sent murderers to prison by the hundreds, some for the rest of their lives. To condemn Faye to a lifetime of me would be cruel and unusual punishment in any court of law."

Justin squeezed her hand.

"QueenBee, there was not that much love floating around that orphanage where I grew up, just unmet needs. The little love there was—well, it was spread kind of thin among forty love-starved boys. Marrying Faye won't work for me, and it won't work for Faye. I've been lonely too long for marriage to work for me, QueenBee."

Justin stroked her hand as if trying to rub some life back into her dull eyes.

"QueenBee, many boys in that orphanage, they grew up bitter and mean. Not me. I escaped that empty life because of you, QueenBee. I never felt unwanted. I never felt as if nobody cared if I lived or died. You loved me, QueenBee. You loved me when it meant something to me to be loved. You loved me when I was a child. There's no greater love anywhere than the love of a caring adult for a motherless child. I may never taste the sweet juices from the fruits of the tree of love with a woman like Faye. If that's my destiny, then it is because I was a boy without a mother. But I do have a heart, thanks to you, QueenBee. I'm warm-blooded and kind, thanks to you, QueenBee. And I can never repay you for loving me when I was a boy, QueenBee."

Her small smile was a dim reflection of how she beamed inside.

"QueenBee, when I was a boy, I remember, you and Bertha drove from Twofer County to Atlanta, 250 miles, to spend one day with me…every other week you came. Sometimes three times a month you came to see me, you came to mother me. I spent many weeks and months, holidays and summers, in your home right here in Twofer County, South Georgia, QueenBee. Happy days I've spent here, at the homeplace with you and Stanford and Shelley, with Jud and Jake and Fred Junior, with Bertha and, of course, the irrepressible Thomas Jefferson Lee, my pal, Colt."

The judge's eyes telescoped out. "You anchored my life to the ground here in Twofer County, and I thank you again for that."

She smiled. "You have such a way with words, Justin."

"And you have such a way with boys, QueenBee."

Justin was gonna make her cry.

"Now, QueenBee, I want something more from you. I've never asked before. Now, I'm asking for something more from you."

Justin's eyes hooked her eyes like a fisherman hooked a fish. She saw pain in a face where she'd rarely seen pain before.

"Go on," she said with wary misgivings, "ask me your question."

"Tell me about me, QueenBee. Where did I come from? What's my history? Tell me about me, QueenBee. Who am I, really?"

She wiggled off the hooks that were his eyes and looked away. The plea in his voice made her suspicious of where he was coming from to get where he wanted to go. She slowly raised the teacup to her lips and sipped, her mind grinding away at the question. Justin Grimes had played her like a fiddle. And she deserved no less than she got. An old goat like her tangling with a young fellow like that, a trained judge, no less. An old fool, she was.

She couldn't outsmart the judge, but she could sure out-bully him. The judge in him had set her up with the speech. She watched Justin withdraw inside himself, his eyes narrowing into slits.

Justin turned his slitted eyes on her.

"QueenBee, a woman told my law clerk she saw me at Lake Arrowhead, a resort in the mountains of North Georgia. But I've never been to Lake Arrowhead. I ignored a friend at Brown-Abernathy Airport, I'm told by my friend. But I haven't been to that airport in months. QueenBee, I'm seen in too many places by too many people for these misidentifications to be coincidental."

Justin paused, tugging his chin. "QueenBee, someone in Atlanta looks like me. I intend to find out who it is. I can't think of a better place to start my search than to start with you, QueenBee. You know more about me than I know about myself. That's what I came to hear you tell me. Tell me about me, QueenBee. I have a double in Atlanta. How is this possible, QueenBee?"

Justin glanced at his watch and frowned; she knew she had him. Then he smiled. "Way to go, QueenBee? You simply outwaited me again. But I'll be back. I'll be back asking the same question."

When she asked Justin about James Kelsey's possible indictment, the judge gave her a real look of concern. He said he didn't know anything about it but would get back with her on it.

§

An hour later, QueenBee was looking over the rim of her teacup at Curtis Kincaid of Kincaid Systems, a highbrow Atlanta private detective firm who'd done work for her for nearly twenty years.

"You can see the position I'm in, can't you, QueenBee?"

QueenBee said, "Mr. Kincaid, say again why you think the work you do for me got your men hurt, work you've done for me, off and on, for nearly twenty years. I was your first client, I believe."

Curtis Kincaid nodded graciously. "You were, QueenBee."

She studied Kincaid's drawn face. "Mr. Kincaid, why quit me after all these years we've done business together, me and you?"

Kincaid fished an envelope from his pocket, removed a folded sheet of paper, unfolded it and handed it to her.

"Just this one job, QueenBee. It's too dangerous for my men and me. Kincaid Systems will never quit doing work for you, Queen-Bee. This one job…well, it's just too dangerous for my men."

She read it and handed it back to Kincaid with a grunt.

"How did it happen?" she said.

"They were ambushed in their hotel room. Two men busted their kneecaps and threatened to kill them next time."

She thought absentmindedly, rubbing her breast bone. "Police?"

"Like always, QueenBee. No police. As you wanted it."

She rattled the dice softly. "Okay, Mr. Kincaid. Send me a bill. I'll pay those men until they're working again."

"That's kind of you, QueenBee. But we have workmen's comp, and the firm makes up the difference in pay."

She waved off the objection. "I can't stop you from quitting this job. And you can't stop me from paying these men, Mr. Kincaid."

"As you wish, QueenBee," Kincaid said.

"Then, it's settled. One last thing, Mr. Kincaid. Before you leave me, any last advice on this matter."

Kincaid thought a second. "Yes, QueenBee, I do. That office on Lake Shore Drive, in the Chicago Landings, shut it down. Whoever crippled my men, they've got a bead on the place. Shut it down."

"Will do," she said. "Now about that other matter you're looking into. Any news?"

"Oh, I almost forgot. She paid me a surprised visit yesterday just like you said she would."

"You give her the name she wanted?"

"I sure did. I gave her the name you gave me."

"Good. Thank you, Mr. Kincaid."

"Anything for you, QueenBee."

She grunted, and the dice made an agitated noise. "You say that, Mr. Kincaid. But you run when you're needed," she said.

Kincaid looked around the room then lowered his eyes.

"Speak your mind, Mr. Kincaid. The mutts are locked out."

Kincaid looked up and finally said, "QueenBee, you're a big-time player; you've always been a big-time player. Me, I'm minor league; I'll always be minor league. I said that to say this. You be careful, QueenBee. You're butting heads with the Chicago mob."

§

"Who's going to replace Kincaid?" Fred Junior said later that day when QueenBee told her lawyer about Kincaid quitting.

"You are," she said, holding up a hand. "You won't get killed. You are just going to shut down that office for Kincaid's man and—"

"QueenBee, I—"

"Ah, hush up, Fred Junior," she said. "Have you ever dealt with the Nation of Islam before?"

"Bigots," Fred Junior mumbled. "No, I haven't. Lucky me."

"Well, Fred Junior. A bigot's a bigot when the bigot's the other fellow's bigot. When the bigot's my bigot, the bigot goes by another name. Wanna guess the name, up Chicago way, Fred Junior?"

Fred Junior groaned. "Not Malcolm Xavier."

"You betcha," she said. "He'll look after you while you're there."

40

TWOFER COUNTY

MONDAY, JUNE 13

STANFORD PULLED DOWN the visor to block the setting sun. A South Georgia springtime mist gave shape and body to the air.

He and Stanley drove west on Interstate 10. They were leaving West Jacksonville, Florida and speeding back to Twofer County. He still hadn't decided what he would do differently to find the killer this time. He still didn't have a plan. But his desire was sky-high

He punched in the cruise control and glanced over at Stanley looking over the whatnots and gadgets he'd bought at the Jacksonville Flea Market. He made a fist and nudged his son's shoulder. Stanley gave him the quickest glance, smiled and was again lost in inspecting what he'd bought.

He turned the attention of his mind elsewhere.

He felt bad for the RKL staff.

He glanced over at his son again. Stanley was unwrapping newspapers from the figurine of a Florida panther.

"Stanford," Stanley said, not taking his eyes off his work, "don't you need a full-time woman in your life, and not a part-time kid?"

The question, surprisingly, surprised him. "Say again," he said.

Stanley stopped turning the figurine and looked at him. "I said, 'you need a full-time woman in your life, not a part-time kid.'"

"Now that's a thought," he said. "But, how do you know I don't already have a woman. And this kid, I don't know any such part-time kid."

"Me, I'm the kid," he said, flippantly.

What had that woman done to his son over there in Paris? Hell, where was his son? That boy over there was an imposter to him. Wait a minute. He glanced over at Stanley again. Nope, he was dead wrong about that. That was his kid, his son. Oh, yeah.

Stanley reached over and clicked on the radio.

"No rap," he said. "No boom-boom."

"Old folks," Stanley grumbled and tuned in a station, keeping the volume low. Curtis Mayfield's "Superfly" became the soft background music. "Old school for old folks," Stanley grumbled.

"Thank you," he said, "my headache is a pain-in-the-ass masquerading as my son. Although I don't own such a creature."

"Heyyy," Stanley said, leaning away from him, hugging the door and pointing his finger like a gun. "That's a good one. You're witty."

The kid had definitely been watching too much TV.

Stanley unwrapped a piece of chewing gum.

"Well, I guess that ends the monologue," he said.

Stanley squinted at him, popping the gum into his mouth. "Are you saying I can't talk and chew gum at the same time? You dissing me? Your own son, your own flesh and blood; you dissing me?"

He sighed. "No, just trying to get along with my own flesh and blood."

"You don't have to get along with me, you know. I'm just your son. Just feed me, shelter me, and burp me."

"Burp you, huh? Burp as in b-u-r-p, *burp*?"

"Just checking to see if you're hearing me," Stanley said. "Now, since we'll be spending so much time together, we need some ground rules around here." Stanley deepened his voice. "We are having a TV this summer; right?"

"Having as in 'having a baby,' or having as in 'gazing into the boob tube'?"

"Hmm, the latter," Stanley said.

"No," he said. "No TV for us this summer."

"Can I play my rap and listen to V-103, twenty-four, seven?"

"Please say, 'may I' instead of 'can I.' And yes, you may, except not twenty-four, seven. Maybe three-seven. Or two-seven. Or maybe even one-seven."

Stanley cut his eyes at him. "Then, may I play my rap music as loud as I can and listen to V-103 all night long this summer?"

"N-o, no," he said.

"N-o, no," Stanley mimicked.

Michael Jackson's "Man in the Mirror" became the background music. They rode in silence. He reached over and tugged Stanley's earlobe.

Stanley jerked his head away. "N-o, no," Stanley said and grinned. "We're gonna get along just fine this summer, Stanford. As long as I give the orders and you take 'em."

They laughed and rode in silence awhile.

"Stanford," Stanley said, "why's QueenBee paying for our Paris loft?"

He looked over at Stanley as the question settled into his mind. "Because she has lots of money; that's why."

"You didn't know about that, did you?" Stanley said.

"No," he said, "I didn't know."

Stanley looked away from him and held the Florida panther up to his face before setting it down in the seat between them. Then, Stanley folded his arms hard across his chest, turned away from him and pressed himself against the passenger door as if he wanted to hide or to just simply disappear.

He drove in silence for a few minutes, wondering what to do. His son was obviously in some kind of pain. He had just gone through a jumble of emotions that made him want to vanish right before his eyes. Not good. He saw a sign announcing an upcoming rest area—one mile.

He exited the expressway and parked in the spill-over parking area for cars. He switched off the engine.

"Let's stretch our leg," he said.

"I don't want to," Stanley said, still hiding his face.

"Why not?" he said.

"Because I lied to you. Before I left for Paris with Chris. I said some mean things, but they were all lies."

Still hiding his face, his son continued. "QueenBee, she didn't tell me this. But I heard her tell Chris. I eavesdropped on her and Chris. QueenBee told Chris to make an excuse, any excuse, and leave the country and take me with her. She gave Chris a lot of money, a whole lot of money. I saw her checking account. It had over $50,000 in it. QueenBee told Chris she was scared someone might try and hurt me next. Chris panicked like she do under pressure. Later, when I asked QueenBee, she set me down and talked to me like I was a man. She told me she expected me to be like you and granddaddy, and Papa. She expected me to act like a man when things got hard. I—I…"

Stanley started crying again, his shoulder shaking. "I can't help crying," he said between sobs. "I just can't help it."

"I know," he said. "It will pass. Tell me the rest."

After a few more sniffles, his son continued. "I told QueenBee things were hard for you, and you were not acting strong. You were acting mean. You just wanted to find the men who killed them. QueenBee told me to tell you how I felt. And I did tell you. But I was just angry that I had to go away, to go away and leave you…when you needed me."

Stanley unwound himself from the door and looked at him with tears in his eyes.

"I'm sorry. I never meant what I said. I lied to you. I won't ever lie to you again, I promise. I should have told you about Queen-Bee and Chris." Stanley sniffled and dragged a sleeve across his nose. "We men, we have to stick together, don't we?"

He opened his arms, and his son fell into his embrace, squeezing him hard and sobbing.

"You damn right we do," he said. "We men, we do have to stick together."

§

Stanford sped back onto the expressway, an half hour from Twofer County. He felt warm and fuzzy inside.

"Hey, that's my song," Stanley shrieked, shoulders bouncing up and down like he was slip-jointed. Stanley turned up the volume, dancing on the seat of his pants. His mother's son, no doubt.

His son was physically bigger and cockier than ever. His attitude was that he was indestructible, and that he could do anything. He wore his hair shorter, almost a military issue. The haircut gave him a juvenile look. A long neck, a plump body, and two big bright eyes as black as baby doll eyes. Stanley's face had shed another layer of round lines to give him the sharp adult face he would wear for the rest of his days, or until he turned forty, whichever came first. His son wore a watch that had all the bells and whistles, but he wore no other jewelry.

His little person was being beaten into shape by those insane teen years he himself could easily remember. His little boy, his son, was being gobbled up by the mind, the body and the soul of a man.

He and Stanley, and Stanley's mother, Chris, had been a family three years before the divorce, which wasn't really a divorce because they hadn't been legally married. But they split, sharing joint custody of a confused young Stanley. Then he moved to Atlanta to start his life up again without the aggravation of having to see Chris everyday. Stanley commuted every other weekend from Chicago to Atlanta and spent every holiday and every summer with him.

After he and Stacey married and went on a week's honeymoon they returned to find Stanley and Chris waiting for them. Stanley had insisted on coming to live with his father and new bride. He had been on a two-day hunger strike and refused to go to school. His then eight-year-old had come to Atlanta to stay with them for good. He was ecstatic, and Stacey was happy.

"Listen to this," Stanley said, curling a leg under his buttock.

> Florida State Trooper Struck and Killed by Hit-and-Run Driver. Florida state trooper Donnell Strickland was struck and killed late Tuesday night or early Wednesday morning. The trooper's body was discovered by a Columbia County deputy sheriff. Investigators say they are looking for the driver of a Ford Thunderbird with Dade County license tag number MMF 1728. The FHP dispatcher said Trooper Strickland was back on patrol for thirty minutes after he'd stopped the Thunderbird, so the driver is not a suspect in the death of the trooper. The Thunderbird's license plate had been stolen in Miami the same night. Anyone with information about this homicide, please call the FHP: 904-222-1313.

"End of item," Stanley said and looked at him. "This was January sixteenth. The same night—"

He nodded. "Yeah. Which newspaper is that?"

"The *Florida Times-Union*. Jacksonville."

Columbia County was only thirty minutes from Twofer County.

James Brown's "Papa's Got A Brand New Bag" became their background music, as he exited I-10 west onto I-75 north. They sped for the Georgia line, the clouds low, dark, and everywhere.

They rode in silence for a few miles.

He said, "I'm glad you're back, Son. I kind of missed you.

"Kind of?"

"Yes," he said, smiling, "kind of."

"Me, too," Stanley said. "I kind of missed you, too. But I'm getting on your nerves already, I know."

"That's your job. You're good at it. That's why the IRS gives parents a special deduction for kids. Each kid decreases a parent's life span by 3.2 years, at least."

Stanley looked at him, frowning. "Does that mean I'm better at getting under your skin than Chris was?"

He laughed at that. "Only half as good as your mother. Now, she's the expert at yanking my chain."

They laughed, and Stanley turned down the radio volume. "Stanford, can I have Mother Kane's gun when I get grown?"

"Gun? Mother Kane didn't own a gun. She hated guns."

"Wrong answer," Stanley said, as The Temptations now sang about a runaway child running wild. "She kept a gun in the doll room, in the Shaka Zulu doll. She always moved it when we visited, me and Christopher—"

Stanley broke off his words. "Anyway, Christopher and I—" Stanley stumbled again. "We were over there that day, and Mother Kane, she forgot to take the gun out her nightstand by the bed, and I looked in and saw it. I picked it up. Mother Kane walked in, and she had a conniption right there on the spot. She made me promise not to mention it to you and Stacey."

He thought it over. "Well, that's news to me. But no gun for you. Did Mother Kane say where she got the gun from?"

"Mr. Jacoby, he bought the gun. He taught her to shoot, too. And he taught—" Stanley gulped. "Well, it was a shiny gun. It was a .38. Stanford, when are we going to marry Jocelyn Slade?"

"Jocelyn Slade?"

The kid's mind was jumping all over the place.

Stanley smirked. "You bad. Jumping Jocelyn Slade. That's fat."

"Stanley—Jesus."

"Ha!" Stanley said and jabbed a forefinger at his face. "Taking the Lord's name in vain, taking the Lord's name in vain!"

He groaned as the first raindrops splattered the windshield. He would be a babbling idiot before the week was out. He was rusty at this. He had to get back into the groove of hanging around a teenager and being a father again. He cut his eyes over at Stanley and grinned, shaking his head.

"Not good, over there talking to yourself," Stanley said without looking up at him. "My airhead friends, as you call them, they say their parents talk to themselves all the time. If I was a parent to some of my friends, I'd be talking to myself, too. Anyway, this one kid, his name's Zacharene, he said he asked his mom why she talked to herself so much, and Zacharene said his mom told him she wasn't talking to herself, that she was, like, you know, talking to his brother. Then Zacharene, he told his mom he didn't have no brother. And Zacharene's mom then told him that she had aborted his brother. So Zacharene says, 'then, why do you talk to him more than you talk to me?' And his mom says something weird, like, 'cause your brother, he's the oldest.'"

Stanley gawked at him. "Don't you find that just a little strange? Anyway, Simonette, she says Michelle says…"

He kept glancing over at his son while his thoughts went else-where. So Mother Kane had owned a gun. Where was this gun, this shiny .38? Why hadn't anyone else mentioned a gun? Why hadn't he found cartridges in the house somewhere for a gun, for a shiny .38? And that dead Florida state trooper, was his death connected to the death of his wife and son?

The hit-and-run was only thirty miles away. An hour after they were killed. The mystery Thunderbird, how was it connected?

The rain was a steady downpour now, soothing background to the cadence of Stanley's voice. It may have been raining outside, But inside the car with him, his son was shining.

He smiled as he realized that he finally had a plan.

He knew now what it was that he would do different this time around in hunting the man who killed Stacey and Christopher.

Now he knew.

Hallelujah.

41

MONDAY, JUNE 13

SHELLEY, THE GOVERNOR, and an aide were speeding down I-75 in the governor's limousine, hogging the left lane and cruising at ninety miles per hour. They were an hour north of Twofer County and the homeplace.

Shelley was at an uneasy peace with himself.

Preacher had given his last sermon. The butcher was on ice, and soon enough he'd have the bomber defused. And that ugly chapter in the city's history will be closed. Now where was that little runt who'd looked inside the Kitty Kat Lounge that day he nabbed Sally Baby. If only he knew then what he knew now. But it was only later the butcher had told him the whole story.

Shelley wheeled the stretch limousine onto the homeplace. The governor used his personal wheels to conduct the state's business. The naysayers said he was crazy for riding around among common folks in a stretch limousine. The governor reminded them he had campaigned in a limousine while his opponent had walked the state pleading poverty, and he whipped the gumshoe two to one.

Besides, QueenBee was not common folks. She was South Georgia royalty, and everybody who was anybody knew that.

The governor told his critics he wasn't about to turn his back on money he'd bust his balls to get his hands on in the first place. He was in no way ashamed of being filthy rich, and the only reason he didn't have his own private air force was because he was a big chicken about flying around in a metal tube without a parachute. And if he wore a parachute, folks would know he was a big chicken

244

about flying. That wouldn't do. The governor. A chicken.

Shelley thought the governor was mad like a fox and was glad the governor wouldn't be governor next term when Stanford became lieutenant governor. The new governor would just keep that mansion warm and cozy for Stanford to live in. A pity he had to keep even Stanford in the dark about his own political future.

But, hey, that was one thing he hadn't forgotten. When they were boys, in matters of politics, Stanford simply did what Shelley told him he needed to do.

Shelley knew getting Stanford to run for lieutenant governor was just a matter of finding the killer, then Stanford could get on with his life. Since the beast was no longer stomping around inside his brain, he would bag the killer soon enough. Of that he was certain. He had gathered all the little pieces over the past five months. It was just a matter of churning the little pieces into the big picture. Then he would know who killed the wife and son of his best friend.

While the governor was visiting QueenBee, he would go to the crime scene to get that bible. His memory was returning bit by bit. A bible was out of place there. Katie Kane hated bibles, preachers, and guns. She had been an equal-opportunity hater.

Shelley slowed the land yacht at the guardhouse. He motored the window down and nodded. Bubba nodded back and raised the gate. Where were those two mutts, he wondered. His friends, he corrected. The limousine sped for the big house on the hill. He was home again. He dreaded seeing QueenBee like nothing else. But all he had to do was to make certain he was never alone with her. That was easy enough to do with the governor hanging around.

After a five-month, self-imposed exile from Twofer County, he was back. And for the first time since Vietnam he'd been pain-free for longer than a few hours. For two days now the beast hadn't stirred in his head; not once had that monster showed its ugly face. Today, maybe he would make things right with QueenBee.

David Harte had really fixed him up.

Wheeling the long car along the driveway, he parked in front of the farmhouse. He hated Big Flossie was dead, but she died a good death, too. Just like Eddie died a good death. He missed Eddie. That was a good sign for his memory—missing Eddie.

He slid the panel back. The governor was stretched out on his back, his head buried in the assistant's lap.

"Homeplace," he told the governor and slid the panel shut.

Several minutes later, the governor stepped to the ground and stretched before walking around to the driver's side.

"Lord, Jesus, it's hot—and sticky," the governor complained.

Shelley powered the window down.

The governor said, "you're supposed to open the door."

He slid the sunglasses down on his nose and looked up at the governor. "Who died and made you king, Roscoe?" He pushed the sunglasses back up on his nose.

"You getting out, right?" the governor said.

He pushed the sunglasses down on his nose again. "Busy-Busy," he said. "A worker bee, I am."

"QueenBee wants you, too," the governor said. "Orders."

He eased off the brake pedal. "You go, first, my faithless leader." He nodded at the blond. "Your lil' lady there, she's gotta go motoring with me. That tightens your jowls or what?"

"Keep your paws to yourself and that thing in your pants."

§

Shelley was wheeling the limousine onto Katie Kane's property when it hit him. He already had the lil' runt who had looked into the Kitty Kat Lounge the day he nabbed Sally Baby. He nabbed him in the basement—him and the big fellow. He had them both. One on the inside. One on the outside. How about that.

The first warning sign greeted him:

No Guns or Bibles Allowed

He parked in the shade under a tree, slid the partition back and looked into the rearview mirror. "I'm gonna lock you in. You can control the music and the air from back there. Keep your motor running," he told the governor's companion.

"How long?" The blond said.

"Nine inches," he said. "How deep?"

The blond flashed him a finger and grinned at him.

Shelley switched on the hidden recorder before stepping out into the soggy South Georgia heat.

Inside, he searched the bookcase. No bible. He searched the room. No bible. He stared at the spot where he saw the boy's body that night. The beast reared its ugly head. That froze him stiff. He willed himself to relax. His muscles went slack, and he waited.

When nothing else happened, he moved down the hallway and past the doll room. The beast turned its ugly head and looked. He stopped. He waited. He moved forward, cautiously, mindful of the beast lurking just beneath the surface of his next thought.

He kept moving and suffered the dread. From the doorway, he looked inside Katie Kane's bedroom.

That's when he first smelled them. But it was too late. By the time he smelled them it was way too late to do anything but wait for them to make the first move and show themselves. Any move he made would be a stupid move. He had no idea where they were. And they knew exactly where he was.

But the beast would not be intimidated. The beast reared up on its haunches. Shelley dropped in a defensive crouch and slapped the butt of the .44, but stopped himself. He didn't clear leather.

"Don't, Roscoe," the voice said. "Speak up, mutts."

The air vibrated with guttural growls.

The deep throaty snarl of a wolf pack filled the room. The bull mastiffs were descendants of the wolf. Now, the genes of the fierce wolf came to the forefront. Aretha's jaws started snapping in overdrive. The snarls and growls and snapping jaws riled the beast in Shelley's head.

He could kill both dogs easily, but why kill them when QueenBee was a crackshot and would kill him. She taught him to shoot a pistol. So why kill the mutts—his friends, he corrected. If he got QueenBee—he perished the thought and felt guilty and ashamed. QueenBee was the only mother he and Stanford ever had.

"Closer, mutts," QueenBee ordered.

The monstrous bull mastiffs growled in aggressive stereo, their guttural sounds both hair-raising and blood-curdling. The dogs crept to within one mighty leap of his throat, growling, snarling, displaying their large and gap-toothed canines.

"Closer, mutts," QueenBee ordered again.

Aretha halved the distance with such a powerful lunge forward that her hindquarters nearly didn't stop in time to keep her from sprawling out of control in her aggression. Loops of drool twisted through the air. Her huge jaws were snapping at such a fierce rate that it sounded like the thunk-thunk-thunk of a guillotine falling continuously on a neck.

Suddenly, Aretha got so agitated she seemed ready to lunge.

"Stay Aretha. Stay, I say! Back off, mutt."

Aretha dropped into a crouch, belly dragging the floor, inching backward, snapping, yapping, and snarling.

"Don't, Shelley," QueenBee said. "Stay, mutts. I mean it, Aretha, stay your behind. In the corner or I'll shoot you."

Aretha rose from her crouch and backed away into the corner, still snarling, yapping, and snapping.

Whap! The beast snapped his tail, and Shelley was moving. And so was Aretha. And so was Franklin.

"I am she who is, come for me."

The words dropped Shelley instantly, and Franklin slammed into Aretha, knocking her snapping jaws away from Shelley's throat. Aretha hit the floor, sprawling, but she sprang up mightily and attacked Franklin. But the big male reared on its haunches and met her fierce attack with his own ferocity. They stood jaw to jaw on their rear legs like two heavyweight boxers.

"Heel!"

The big dogs dropped to the floor and raced to her side.

"Shameful," she said. "Shameful."

"Guard, Franklin," she said.

The big male trotted over to where Shelley lay unconscious and took up his post. Franklin licked Shelley's hand and whined.

"I know," QueenBee said. "I know, Franklin; he's family. But we're at loggerheads, now; Shelley and me."

"Fetch, Aretha."

Aretha retrieved Shelley's gun and, whining, brought it to her.

"Ah, hush your whining. You wanted to rip out his throat. Hussy."

§

Click-clack. Click-clack. Click-clack.

Clayton Westwood, FBI Atlanta chief, leaned back in his executive chair and propped his feet up on the desktop. He sipped more water to waylay his nausea. His entire career was on the line.

That crime lab report made him haul out the old antacids. The lab had matched the thumbprint Stanford had given him. It was a perfect match to prints taken from Shelley's house on Avenue *B*. Shelley had sabotaged his investigation right under his nose. It was his own fault. One hell of a fix he was in. And Shelley had stepped off the face of the earth; nowhere to be found.

Click-clack.

Shelley had made that telephone call to Jackie Pearson. But why in God's heaven would Shelley kill them? He didn't believe it. Not even God Almighty could make him believe that nightmare.

Click-clack.

But didn't someone raise the possibility two killers were there that night, not one? Didn't the medical examiner say Christopher's eyelids were closed after the body had cooled? Didn't Stanford say his son's eyes were closed when he got there that night? There had been too many muddy footprints to tell how many killers were there, but the consensus was one. The cops had found two slugs.

Click-clack.

One slug could have been fired from inside the bedroom, but that theory hadn't been pursued either. Clayton dropped his feet to the floor. Damn. He was screwed. He lifted the telephone and punched in a number. He told the man who answered what he wanted and hung up. He called his son again. No answer.

He slammed the phone down. That son of his was one great big ol' pain in the crack of his ass. Wouldn't conform and refused to fit in. Reminded him too much of that old block from which the chip came from. Damn kids. If he didn't love 'em, he'd hate 'em.

His private line buzzed.

Clayton snapped up the telephone. The analysis of the second slug dug out of Katie Kane's wall made his eyes tear up. "Thanks," he said and hung up the phone. "For nothing."

They had assumed the two slugs were fired from the same gun. They were wrong, and he was screwed. Some maniac had bombed an American city, had plucked Atlantans off the city's streets and butchered them, and the fingerprints of the sociopath suspected of committing those crimes were found in Shelley's house.

And Shelley was missing. Boy, he was screwed.

Bring on the petroleum jelly.

42

A WEEK AWAY from its summer solstice, the sun was a blazing white disk. The ninety-three-degree heat had vaporized the morning clouds and dusted the blue sky a chalky white.

The relative humidity was ninety-two percent, the wind speed, zero. Stanford sat behind the desk in his office. He picked up the telephone for the fifth time within the last hour to call Jocelyn Slade. For the fifth time within the last hour, he hung up the telephone. He was a coward. There was no doubt. That was a fact.

He dug the envelope from his inside coat pocket. Into his palm, he poured the three slugs fired from Katie Kane's .38. He poured the slugs back into the envelope and stuck it back into his pocket.

§

Two hours later, Stanford poured the same three slugs out on top of Clayton Westwood's uncluttered desk.

"Clayton, these were fired from Katie Kane's .38," he said. "The one the killer stole from her nightstand that night."

Clayton leaned back and squinted at him. "First I've heard of a gun, Stanford. Besides, correct me if I'm wrong, it was my understanding Katie Kane hated guns."

"Clayton, she had a gun. Her friend Jonah Jacoby, he bought it for her, and he taught her to shoot it. These slugs came from the tree they used for target practice. Slugs from Katie Kane's .38."

Clayton, studying him, cleared his throat and took out his pocket-knife. "That's quite a leap, Stanford. From Katie Kane owning a gun, all the way to the killer stealing the gun Katie Kane owned. Even

250

Carl Lewis has problems with that big of a jump." Clayton leaned back. "Why don't you tell me the whole story. No BS."

Click-clack.

He told Clayton everything. Clayton was frowning long before he finished telling it. The click-clack of Clayton's pocketknife rose and fell with the pitch of his voice as he told it.

The click-clack stopped. Clayton sighed and leaned slowly forward as if to better evaluate Stanford's sanity.

"This story is thinner than gnat's shit, Stanford. I don't see a killer stealing a .38 that ties him to a double homicide. If he was that stupid, even Maxwell Smart and Agent 99 would have him locked up behind bars by now; don't you think?"

He shrugged off Clayton's logic. "Clayton, at least it's something new to hang your hat on. It's something to look into. You did say for me to call on you if I needed your help. Right?"

Clayton gave him a pitying look. "Stanford, you've been one busy fellow, I tell you. You running a CPA firm and two murder investigations. Not much time for a life on the side, I suppose?"

His lips parted but he closed them again. Instead, he thought a moment and said, "You're so right, Clayton. I don't have much time for a life on the side. Not much time for a life on the side at all." He shrugged. "But, whatever. Now about that gun, Clayton."

§

Back at Lake Arrowhead, Stanford fretted some more over RKL's too-close ties to CapCity Investments. Lake Arrowhead and CapCity together made up 75 percent of RKL's business. CapCity was not only an excellent Atlanta citizen but a big-time player in the community. CapCity had donated 2,200 hours and over $500,000 to Atlanta's Big Sisters/Big Brothers programs—the mayor's pet project. The company also fully funded a shelter for abused women with children—a favorite of the city council president.

CapCity was well-connected in Atlanta politics.

He heard tires crunching across his gravel driveway. He was standing in the door when the Jeep Cherokee came to a rolling stop. He was very surprised to see Richard Stoole climb from behind the wheel with a white envelope in his hand.

He welcomed Richard inside.

They sat down at the dining table across from each other. They

251

sipped Scotch and the talk dwindled down to silence. He was letting Richard take his own time getting to the reason for his visit. Richard kept toying with the envelope in his hand, and he kept waiting Richard out.

Richard leaned forward tentatively. "Stanford, I'm leaving Lake Arrowhead. I'm calling it quits."

What Richard said didn't register until after he had replayed the words in his mind twice.

"Richard, what do you mean, you're leaving Lake Arrowhead?"

Richard got up, walked to the bar, straddled a stool and sat scanning the labels on the whiskey bottles.

"Richard," he said, "who owns Lake Arrowhead?"

"A rich man," Richard said, "a man who wants anonymity."

He joined Richard at the bar. "Richard, what's Prison City?"

Richard cringed. "Actually, Stanford, it's easier to tell you the setup. You know everything else. Then it will all make sense, you being who you are and all. So here's the setup. Lake Arrowhead is one part of a two-part holding company called the LA Trust.

"There's Lake Arrowhead, and there's Prison City. You don't know about Prison City; it's the operating division. There's nothing yet to operate, so Prison City, it's inactive. Mark and I, we're not involved in Prison City. So, to that end, neither are you. We're involved only with Lake Arrowhead. Lake Arrowhead owns all the property. That's me and Mark. Lake Arrowhead's the money arm. Soon enough, Lake Arrowhead will lease all its property to Prison City. That property includes about 100 square miles of land down in one South Georgia county, and—"

"A hundred square miles, Richard? One hundred square miles?"

He knew Lake Arrowhead had bought a lot of real estate, but he didn't know all of it was located in South Georgia, and certainly didn't know all that land was in one South Georgia county.

"Yes, Stanford. Land for a huge private prison."

"In Georgia?" He chortled. "You better lay off the Prozac, my friend. You try privatizing Georgia prisons, and you'll be stepping on some mighty big toes in this state. Prisons are big business in Georgia. The DOC won't let you put them out of business. Those bureaucrats would give Uzis to the inmates first."

Richard placed the envelope on the table. "Not when you go and tell the same taxpayers how it costs them $20,000 a year to lock up one prisoner. Money talks and you know that, Stanford, more than I know it. You know numbers. But what I'm saying to you is that my job's over. Mark's job's over, too. Lake Arrowhead has done its job. Now Prison City takes over. Prison City will be run by the new guy. But, here's why I dropped by. To show you this."

Richard pulled two snapshots from the envelope. He laid them out on the bar, side by side, in front of him.

He looked at the snapshots, instantly recognizing both faces.

He said, "so that's why you want me to become the president of Lake Arrowhead, to run this Prison City for you?"

"You're not getting it," Richard said, pointing to one of the snapshots. "This guy here, he'll be running Prison City."

He looked closer at the first snapshot Richard pointed to.

He said, "Justin Grimes, the judge; he's the new guy?"

Richard pointed to the second snapshot. "This is the judge."

Richard pointed back to the first snapshot. "This here's the new guy. He's my replacement. He's from Paris. Paris, France. These are two different guys, Stanford. They are not the same guy."

"Bullshit, Richard. This here's Justin."

He studied both snapshots again, eyes darting from one snapshot to the other one.

"And this one's Justin, too," he said. "Don't play me."

"Not so, Stanford; I'm playing you not."

Richard pointed to the first snapshot again. "This guy, I'm telling you, Stanford, he's been holed up here at Lake Arrowhead for the past two and a half weeks."

"No!" he said, defiantly.

"Stanford, I see this here guy everyday. This is the new guy."

"Damnit, Richard, you've got to be kidding me.

Richard crossed himself. "Stanford, I swear, I kid you not."

43

TARTUFFE JITT WAS a new man. He was pruning his speech.

After three solid weeks of peaceful solitary confinement at Lake Arrowhead, he had fallen in love with country living. He had never known such a calm life. His worst fear was the serenity would suddenly blow away in the next breeze and be lost to him forever. He had at last found purpose in life and was now like his father.

Jocko wanted to make society work better, and now so did he want to make society work better. Prison City would be his contribution to lift society up to a safer level.

He poked out his chest and sucked in a deep lungful of fresh mountain air. Didn't the Rockefellers, the Carnegies, and all the old-monied rich, didn't they wash away guilt that way? Didn't they wash away the blood from their millions and millions and millions by giving away a large portion of the interest earned on their blood money to the multitudes? Didn't they set up tax-free foundations to do good to try and offset all that evil they had done to make so much money in the first place?

You bet.

Well, he was going to offset Jocko's evil by locking up society's criminals, on the one hand, and by then giving society's criminals the real opportunity to better their lot in life, on the other hand. Prison City would lock up career criminals forever, and was nearly ready to go public and make its intentions known. So, now he could finally get to Atlanta to see this Judge Grimes with his own eyes, to see what all the fuss was about him looking so much like some federal judge in Atlanta.

He would also get a second chance to get a personal feel for the city. He had watched Atlanta on television for three weeks and had reached several opinions about the town. The city-too-busy-to-hate continued to amuse him. The city was a take on itself, a caricature. The seriousness of the city was a mockery in both words and deeds. The city-too-busy-to-hate was just an apt a slogan as the city-too-busy-to-love. A more fitting slogan was the city-too-busy-to-care. But the ultimate slogan would be: love you and yours and hate everyone and theirs, but let's all smile and keep it a secret—don't ask; don't tell.

Atlanta was a two-faced town brimming with happy talk.

The most righteous among them could also be the most corrupt among them. The city was a flirtatious place where one local tribe was hell-bent on destroying any other local tribe for no other reason than group conflict seemed a way of life in Atlanta. The city also prostituted itself, luring victims as a beautiful slut in a red miniskirt on a street corner early in the morning lured Johns. Then Atlanta turned mean, falling on her victims, not as a thug in the dark shadows late at night, but as businessmen selling their goods in broad daylight.

And religion was a joke—a showcase their kids would grow up to become. What a waste of time, talent and money.

Tartuffe flexed his biceps. Enough about a city to pity. He knew his way back to the City of Lights.

But, right now, he had a hard-on for a woman, and the maid was looking less and less like a frog each morning he saw her. Maybe tomorrow. Maybe not. Maybe the next day. Maybe not. It had to happen soon. But now back to the speech.

He had shorten his Prison City speech to five minutes. He had another hour before Mr. Timbutu was supposed to show up. He switched on the tape recorder. He had to cut another forty-five seconds. Five minutes was the attention span of any politician.

Tartuffe adjusted the microphone and started speaking.

After four minutes, he paused five seconds, then continued.

"Prison City's 200 square miles will be enclosed by a mile-deep buffer zone to isolate it from contact with civilians. Prisoners will work eight-hour days, six days a week to pay restitution to victims and to repay the state its expenses. Any remaining cash would be sent to inmate's families or saved for inmates' release. School attendance will be compulsory six days a week, six hours a day.

"So, ladies and gentlemen, fourteen hours of each inmate's day will be spent earning cash to pay his debts or learning skills to become a better citizen."

He stopped the watch: five minutes, ten seconds. Not bad.

He heard the maid and his cock got instantly hard. Ah, man. He shunted his thoughts to other things. Another thing about Atlanta, no one seemed to be looking out for the teat that fed them all. They treated the capital city like a whore that everyone can have his way with, but no one wants to be nice to. The city acted the whore and the people acted the johns.

That did it. His cock was soft, and the maid was gone.

§

"Good morning, Mr. Timbutu," Tartuffe said, his once-pale skin now soaked in pigmentation of a darker hue.

The air was muggy after an early morning rain.

Timbutu stuffed the suitcase down in the gaping mouth of the Checker cab's huge trunk. Tartuffe stretched out in the roomy backseat and pondered the next part of his plan to recruit the Nigerian to his cause.

Tartuffe stroked the beard that smoothed his sharp chin to the point of dullness. Once in Atlanta, he would do the practical and cut an extremely tall man like himself down to half a man's normal size.

The princely Nigerian slid behind the wheel. They drove away from the hotel's canopy, speeding for the Lake Arrowhead exit.

Tartuffe had accomplished much in three weeks. He was now imagining what his mother looked like. Tall and slim? Brown-eyed and dark-skinned? How would he greet her? Hello, mommy dearest. Or what's happening, you undeserving, deserting bitch!

He turned his attention to Timbutu as the taxi put Lake Arrowhead behind them. Leaning forward, he said, "Mr. Timbutu, would you like to have a new job?"

"I like this old job," the Nigerian said. "The boss say you asked that I pick you up. The boss like that. I like that."

Was he being talked down to? Probably not.

"A yes or a no, Mr. Timbutu." He had expected a "yes" from him.

But Timbutu's dark eyes shifted back and forth from the road to the rearview mirror. "What I do? What you pay?"

He suppressed a smile. "You drive a luxury car of your choice, at triple your pay." Chew on that, Mr. Timbutu.

"I say I make four large a week, and I love a Mercedes Benz?"

"I say I pay you twelve large a week, and you drive a 560SEL."

Timbutu slowed the car, his dark eyes locked steady in the rearview mirror now. "Am I that lucky and you that rich?"

"When can you start, Mr. Timbutu?"

"How do I know you won't hire me for one week for the new job then you fire me and I have no old job?"

Were these negotiations or what?

"How do I know you won't work one week, you quit, I have no driver?" This man was used to getting his way, his mind too quick for who he hired himself out to be.

"We make contract," Timbutu said.

His own cleverness had led him right into Timbutu's trap.

"A six-month contract," Timbutu said.

"Three months," he said.

"Five months," Timbutu said.

"Three months," he repeated.

The taxi sped up the entrance ramp to I-75, and merged cleanly into the southbound traffic.

"We split the difference. We do contract four months," Timbutu said. "Where to, boss?"

Now he was being talked down to. But what the hell. Right on, Mr. Timbutu. "Downtown Atlanta, Mr. Timbutu," he said.

§

An hour later, Timbutu parked a rented Ford Aerostar van at the twenty-six-story Richard B. Russell Federal Building in downtown Atlanta, next to a WTNT-TV News mobile unit. Vans and campers littered the parking lot, and a crowd gathered near the steps of the highrise office building.

Tartuffe settled down in the wheelchair, his legs covered under a blanket. He locked the wheelchair in place and powered the hydraulic lift down to the ground. Tartuffe unlocked the wheelchair and rolled off the lift. They gawked at the hundreds of wheelchairs scuttling around the pavilion like water bugs on a pond.

Tartuffe steered the wheelchair across a wide field of red, white, and blue protest signs. He said, "Mr. Timbutu, you couldn't have planned this better."

Minutes later, they had deftly maneuvered through the crowd.

The full beard, dark sunglasses, and wig obscured Tartuffe's hard features. The wheelchair did indeed cut a tall man down to half-normal size. From down in his wheelchair, Tartuffe noticed something he had not noticed before riding in a wheelchair. People went out of their way not to notice him sitting down in the wheelchair. Tartuffe swore never again to not notice a person sitting down in a wheelchair.

He entered the courtroom alone. Timbutu hung back.

Tartuffe positioned the wheelchair between the rear wall and the last bench with an unobstructed view of the judge's bench. Then, Tartuffe felt a stare burn his neck like a branding iron.

His first sweeping glance told him the woman eyeing him was very pretty. His second sweeping glance told him the very pretty woman was from television. His third sweeping glance told him the very pretty woman from television was walking his way. And she was the same very pretty woman he had barely escaped at the airport over three weeks ago. The disaster coming his way was the darling of Atlanta's airwaves—Jocelyn Slade.

Wow! She looked stunning. Even red-headed Francine was a pig compared to this gorgeous woman. Where had his head been the first time he saw her? No wonder the Nigerian thought he was crazy for leaving her behind at the airport. He now agreed with Mr. Timbutu's assessment of his sanity.

But why was a news anchor doing courthouse duty reserved for cub reporters, and why was that same news anchor now looking at him like he was cherry topping for the six o'clock news?

The newswoman smiled then leaned down to whisper into his ear, but Timbutu wedged his face between their faces. The Nigerian turned his face toward the newswoman as if he were about to kiss her. The interference stopped her words in mid-sentence.

"Let's talk," the Nigerian spoke in a harsh demanding voice Tartuffe hadn't heard Timbutu use before. The news anchor took notice of the cold eyes boring into her face like drill bits.

She shrugged and obediently followed Timbutu while casting a hungry backwards and almost suspicious glance over her shoulder at him sitting down in that wheelchair.

Tartuffe turned his attention back to the front of the courtroom, the bailiff saying bailifflike things, people rising. Then into the courtroom strode the very tall Honorable Judge Justin Grimes.

Tartuffe's penetrating stare grabbed the tall man's face, latching on like radar, his fingertips digging down into the leather arms of the wheelchair as he tried calming himself.

An eerie feeling swayed his vision. He felt weak, disoriented.

Watching the judge's loping strides to the bench gave Tartuffe an out-of-body experience. He felt as if that were him up there looking out across the courtroom, but this was him sitting down here in a wheelchair looking up there at himself.

That was him up there! Goddamnit.

Hidden inside that man up there was a baby he knew well. They shared an egg together, they did. By God, they were "eggmates"!

Deep in the core of his prenatal brain, there burned an emotion, the memory of him and his brother together. Broooother!

His eyes stung and seemed to be spinning around in his head.

The judge was six-seven or eight. Same as him. The judge's body language was controlled. Same as him.

Tartuffe eased the small binoculars from under the blanket and up to his eyes. He stared straight into a mirror. Same as him.

Someone had betrayed him. Someone had betrayed his brother. That long, angular face triggered such a hunger in his gut that he nearly came unglued. Same as him.

The judge spoke, the voice sending shivers bunny-hopping up and down his spine. That voice? Same as him. What happened next stunned him. He felt betrayed. The judge looked out over the courtroom and stroked his chin with his left hand.

Brooooother!

§

At Lake Arrowhead, Tartuffe was exhausted. High, one minute; low the next. He had now dropped into a deep, deep funk.

Why had Jocko kept them apart?

Why had Jocko kept them ignorant of each other?

Was that why he hated Jocko so? Had he subconsciously known

he had a twin out there somewhere? Had that gut feeling of betrayal driven his hatred for Jocko so right, his hatred so true? Who else knew about his twin besides Timbutu?

Maybe that newswoman had guessed, but she couldn't be sure. But Timbutu pulled such a fast one over on her that she may not even raise a fuss since she had been so bamboozled by the fast-thinking Nigerian.

Timbutu had gotten the anchorwoman alone and sold her on a story. Tartuffe was enrolled in the government's witness protection program, and the wheelchair protesters outside were part of a protection scheme. Timbutu promised her an exclusive interview for later. So when Jocelyn left, her gofer stayed behind to keep an eye on them. But they got away from the gofer and abandoned the empty wheelchair in the handicap stall in the men's restroom.

Later, Timbutu told him who he really was.

He was a political refugee from Lagos, Nigeria, an Igbo hiding from a Hausa-Fulani noose waiting for him back home. The professor was now at the Atlanta library researching Judge Grimes's background. He didn't mention the Nigerian rock prison to Timbutu nor his belief that Nigerian soldiers were the worst kind of madmen.

Tartuffe sipped cognac.

Could he find his mother by first finding the judge's mother? He thumped the pen on the writing pad. No, he could not. The judge was raised in an orphanage: The Atlanta Stanhope School for Boys.

He sipped more cognac, tugged his chin then put pen to paper. Tartuffe wrote two separate lines on the paper.

He wrote: Judge, would you like to meet—your father?

He wrote: Judge, would you like to meet—your wombmate?

44

STANFORD WATCHED THE Jeep disappear around the bend.

Richard's words seeped deeper into his psyche. Richard said the new guy wanted RKL to stay on as CPAs for Lake Arrowhead.

The threat of losing Lake Arrowhead as a client was gone. And Mark Davis was gone. And Richard Stoole was gone. But what did it all mean? He tugged his chin. He thought of Justin and shook his head. Justin Grimes had a twin.

Justin didn't know he had a twin. How the hell could that be? He and Justin grew up together in Twofer County, even though Justin went to school in Atlanta. No way Justin knew he had a twin. It was so farfetched. QueenBee would have told Justin if he had a twin. Wouldn't she?

QueenBee couldn't have known. That was why she never told Justin about a twin. Even if QueenBee hadn't told Justin about his twin brother when he was a boy, she surely would have told Justin about his twin once Justin became a man. So, QueenBee's not knowing was the only reason she never told Justin. He poured a glass of Pinot Grigio and gulped it down.

Sanford gulped another glass of wine. After he gulped down the third glass, he stumbled into the bedroom and fell on the bed.

§

Seventeen restful hours later, Stanford sat bright-eyed and bushy-tailed across from Jud Judson.

"Shelley, he's got a house over on Avenue *B*," Jud said. "Clayton and the Feds, they dusted it for prints."

261

Stanford frowned. "Clayton and the Feds? What house on Avenue *B*? What are you talking about, Jud? I didn't know Shelley had a house on Avenue *B*."

He had slept fifteen hours straight and woke up with a sail full of second wind. He had arrived back in Atlanta by noon. He took another day off from the office. Jud Judson was his first stop. He needed to talk to someone he trusted, and the only people he trusted and could depend on were the boys he grew up with.

Jud threw off the right head nods and made the necessary throat noises to let him know he was not only listening to what he was saying, but he was also hearing what he was saying.

But Jud's ears didn't really perk up until he mentioned Clayton had called Shelley a cold-blooded killer.

"Jud, have you seen Shelley or heard from him?"

Jud shook his head. "Nothing. You neither?"

He shook his head. "Hadn't heard from him in three weeks. He and the governor, they went down to see QueenBee two days ago, Monday. No one has seen Shelley since they left there."

"Shelley, he'll turn up," Jud said. "He always does. And Clayton's right about Shelley. But let me let you read it for yourself."

The chair squeaked when the private detective rose and took a manila envelope from his safe. Jud handed it to him. "This is all Shelley's doings. You read while I go bleed the ol' lizard valve."

THE CHASERVILLE REBELLION OF 1983
by
Donald Lee Burton

In the summer of 1983, a sniper killed Atlanta drug lord Franklin Douglas in a part of Atlanta called Chaserville. Allegedly, Franklin Douglas was killed by Ted Waterman, a dairy worker, who was then gunned down by Douglas's bodyguards. But who REALLY fired that fatal bullet into Douglas's head? The Franklin Douglas killing opened a floodgate of terror, and killings became the new Atlanta rage.

Blood bled into the gutters.

Two days after Douglas's demise, Richard B. Woods, Atlanta's biggest cocaine dealer was blown to smithereens. Woods and his lieutenants were pulverized by what the MAPD bomb squad esti-mated as two 750-pound bombs, a thousand pounds of dynamite, and dozens of incendiary devices.

To count the number of dead from the blast, the coroner sub-tracted the number of drug peddlers after the explosion from the number of drug peddlers before the explosion. Twelve dead. The death of the notorious Richard B. Woods made it an even baker's dozen.

The bloodshed baffled the experts.

The horrendously high death toll shook up an already shaky underworld in the capital city. An entire subfamily of Atlanta gang-sters had been wiped out in one thunderous blast. Three days ear-lier, a federal judge had thrown out a ninety-three-count racketeer-ing indictment against Richard Woods because the police work had been so sloppy. The judge sent Woods laughing back out into the streets, the crime boss deaf to the persistent beat of distant jungle drummers.

The Atlanta blood bath continued.

Five days later, six members of the Smiths, a mobster subfamily dealing in prostitution, drugs, and gambling were all gunned down in four separate killings around the city. Each man shot behind his right ear with a Glock 9mm. Blood now gushed and flowed.

Thirty-three more gangster-styled killings were tallied before the bloodletting stopped. But not one big-time Atlanta mobster was left in business when the survivors quit the city for safer grounds elsewhere.

Unlike other metropolises, Atlanta was mob free. Forty-two gang-sters died in the Chaserville Rebellion of 1983.

§

The chair squeaked when Jud sat back down in it.

"Shelley, he killed Douglas and the rest of them," Jud said as he tilted his noisy chair. "Remember that butchered cop, Garcia?"

He nodded. "Yeah," he said.

"Him, another cop named Gerald, and Shelley, they raided Crazy Ed's Liquors one night—"

"Ed Berserk? We did some work for him."

"I hope you got paid. Berserk, he's a morgue baby now. MAPD just ID'ed him. Anyway, Shelley's raid on Crazy Ed's triggered the

Atlanta bombing and the butchery. Now, Shelley's missing, Garcia and Gerald are crippled, and Berserk's dead. All four were at Crazy Ed's that night. Two other men there that night were fished from the river. Those 'Hooch babies' were up from the Bottoms. Down Miami way. Shelley, he made like Houdini with the son of a Miami drug lord, the one responsible for the bombing and the butchery.

"When Shelley killed the mobster's son and made the body disappear, the old man buried a damn empty coffin. Then he took his grief out on Atlanta. Bombed those churches and mutilated those folks, including that husband and wife, the Smallmon, I believe were their names, and that MARTA bus driver. Well, that same Miami drug lord got himself blown to hell and back five days ago down Miami Beach way. So, I see it like this. We may not know where Shelley is now, but we sure as hell know where he was five days ago."

§

Back at Lake Arrowhead, Stanford fretted about Shelley. He knew Shelley had killed people, but he never saw Shelley as a killer. The widest blinders of all, David had told him. He had been wearing the widest blinders of all. His best friend was a killer. He picked up the glass swan and palmed it in his fist.

Then he threw it smashing against the wall. He muscled up a smile but it was a painful effort. Later, when he was sweeping up the broken glass, he saw the copper-tipped audio plug that he'd placed inside the swan. The same audio plug he had found under the big oak outside. Fingering the plug, he wondered about it.

He picked up his binoculars and went outside.

Standing under the oak tree, he searched the branches with the binoculars. In about a minute, he spotted the tree stand. He hung the binoculars around his neck and climbed up to take a look. He found the amplifiers.

He left the amplifiers in place and climbed down. He went inside and searched the cottage. He found the transmitters. He left them in place and went back outside. He dug up the duffel bag and dragged it inside the cottage. He could feel the difference.

He turned the duffel bag upside down on the floor.

Out tumbled pine cones and rocks.

45

WEDNESDAY, JUNE 15

STANFORD GOT OFF I-75 at International Boulevard and turned onto Peachtree Way. He thought about Jocelyn for a moment then he tried not to think of her again. He had to stay focused on what was happening now, and he had to keep away from that woman.

She was nothing but trouble, and he knew that.

He thought about the stash, wondering how long the cash and cocaine had been missing. He'd reburied the duffel bag and the pine cones and rocks. He thought about what David had said about Shelley and sank into despair. How could he help his best friend?

He thought about Stanley being down in Twofer County with QueenBee, who angrily nixed the idea of an Atlanta loft.

"Not my last great grandson, you won't!"

After what Stanley had told him in the car, Monday, he offered no protest to his grandmother's grave concerns. Now he would have to get on down to Twofer County to raise his son and find the killer. That was all he wanted on his plate right now. Not cash and cocaine. Not Lake Arrowhead. Not RKL. Not Jocelyn Slade. He only wanted to find the killer, raise his son, and help Shelley.

Stanford cruised along Peachtree Street as if looking for some-place to be. The pedestrians were mostly couples leaning together like lovers and walking close like friends. He thought of her again. He just couldn't stop thinking about that woman.

§

Stanford pulled into Jocelyn's driveway and parked his sedan between a shiny red Ferrari and Jocelyn's Jaguar. He hesitated only a moment before getting out.

He brushed almost angrily past the Ferrari and strode up to the front door of the house. He was not in a bad mood—just moody. His shirt hugged him like the proverbial monkey he was about to get off his back. He poked the lighted doorbell and watched the penlight of the peephole. Footsteps. Silence. The light went out of the peephole. The doorknob turned. The door opened.

The cool air from inside the house washed Stanford's face, and Tony Bennett's crooning voice pushed past the head of the hazel-eyed woman standing there. She was smiling at him as if he were a fine diamond she wanted very much to buy. The catch of breath in Jocelyn's throat was as much music to his ears as were the daring highs and lows of Bennett's powerful voice.

"Hi, Jocelyn," he said.

His voice sounded as strong and as sure as his voice had ever sounded. A jolt of adrenaline kicked in, and the smell of Jocelyn drove Bennett's music into his lonely heart like a stake.

"Hello, Stanford," Jocelyn said. "Please come in."

She stepped aside. He walked past her and turned facing her. Still smiling, her eyes as alive as her lips, Jocelyn closed the door gently and leaned back against it for a moment before she almost propelled herself toward him. She melted into his chest. He covered her, wrapping his arms around her soft body like a cloak.

Jocelyn was so right on both counts. He did need somebody, and that somebody just as well be Jocelyn Slade. At the instant he remembered the Ferrari, a man stepped into his line of sight.

He tensed and half-turned even before the man spoke.

"Excuse me!"

The angry voice was packed with menace. He felt awkward and couldn't quite judge the threat of the Ferrari owner fast enough. The man was giving off conflicting signals. He locked eyes with the man after a quick scan showed no signs of a weapon, but anything could be hidden under that sports coat. The man was thick with muscles and that was a weapon in the hands of a man who knew how to use them. The man looked like he knew how to use them, and he looked like he was not shy about using those muscles. He watched the man's hands. The threat was a bruiser, two inches taller and forty pounds heavier than he was, and he looked like he'd just stepped from the cover of Muscle Mag International. But a little flab showed about the face.

He'd stepped in it. Now what was he going to do?

He felt Jocelyn curl her arms around his arm, hindering any move he could possibly launch against the bruiser. Her armlock also prevented him from protecting himself if the bruiser made a move on him. He worried his arm free from her armlock, only to have her quickly and smoothly reattach herself to his arm, clutching it with even more force.

"You better go," the man demanded. "You better go now."

Talk. But no movement. Then the big man did move. But it was so subtle that if he hadn't known what to watch for, he wouldn't have seen it. The big man was also swift, he could tell. This could get ugly real quick. He had made his two dumb moves by showing up unannounced and then ignoring the presence of another man in the form of that Ferrari. He was becoming annoyed at Jocelyn. Why didn't she just step in and handle matters before things got out of hand? If she wanted him to leave. So be it. Good night. But she would have to be the one to show him the door, and not the competition. He still hadn't said a word. Still waiting for the talk to end, and for the big man to make his move. Then he realized he was kind of hoping the big man would make a move. He was rusty, but the big fellow looked a little hung over, and he looked a little pudgy around the face. Maybe he couldn't take the big fellow, but he knew he could put up a good showing. And right now, the way his week had gone, a good showing would do him just fine.

But Jocelyn didn't handle matters, so he instigated.

"Your house, Jocelyn," he said, "should I pack it in and—go?"

"No," Jocelyn said, "you stay. Bryce is leaving. See you, Bryce."

Jocelyn, still attached to his arm, was now glaring at the competition, who now seemed so at ease he looked sleepy-eyed. Not good. That was bad. The bruiser was definitely in attack mode.

Jocelyn tensed, her tension traveling through the arm she was attached to. She saw it, too. She knew the guy. She knew him well.

Jocelyn said, "cool it, Bryce. Call me tomorrow. We'll talk."

Bryce smirked and shook his head, no.

He stayed loose. He wondered how Jocelyn was going to handle her sticky situation. This confrontation was no longer between him and the bruiser. It was now between the bruiser and Jocelyn.

Jocelyn said, "Bye, Bryce; call me tomorrow. We'll talk then."

Bryce shook his head again. "I'm staying. Slick, he's leaving."

Slick. Cute. He smiled, sort of.

"Stanford," Jocelyn said, "do you mind if Bryce stays? For one drink, at least? If you don't mind, I don't mind."

Cop out. It was her house, but she was making it his decision. He smiled, sort of, and kept watching the bruiser.

"It's settled then," Jocelyn said, not missing a beat. "Bryce, take off your attitude and sit down in a chair. I'm fixing drinks." Jocelyn stepped closer to them. "Let's introduce ourselves. Bryce Boyd, meet Stanford Rome."

They moved hesitantly toward each other. Their palms slapped together. They squeezed. Bryce's grip was firm. He flexed the hand Bryce tried to break, as Jocelyn almost skipped away for drinks.

"So, Bryce," he said, smiling, "tell me all about yourself."

"I'm a salesman," Bryce said. "I sell pain to assholes like you. You saw that Ferrari, you blind or stupid? I was here first." Bryce stepped toward him. "Go." They stood four feet apart. "Go now."

"Easy, fellow," he said, "any closer and bang goes the ol' hanging thang. And Bryce Boyd is Bryce Ann."

If the guy was good enough and launched a sneak attack, he wouldn't really see the punch until it was too late. He would have to depend on the more reliable sense of movement, and that required peripheral vision. So he angled his head for a peripheral look and sank in his knees about two inches without seeming to move at all. But he was certain Bryce saw the slight drop in height by the way the man tensed up.

Bryce lost a few inches of height as well and went loose-limbed while sliding back two steps, leaving his space but watching him. Yes, indeed, Bryce was going to be a handful.

"You good with those hands?" Bryce said, coldly. "We could do some real damage to each other; if you're good, I mean."

Jocelyn returned with a serving tray. Bryce didn't seem to notice. He shot Jocelyn a glance, and saw shock in her face.

"Bryce!" Jocelyn shrieked.

But he was moving even before the shout came, spinning left, bending backwards at the waist, away from Bryce. A roundhouse kick went whisking past his head. Spinning back right, he barely avoided another vicious kick that whistled past his head from the other side. He leaped in the air, elevated, but Bryce Boyd was already in the air, higher than he was—and waiting. Not good.

"Bryce Boyd!"

They both landed on their feet like dropped cats. Bryce deflated like a kicked dog. He danced away a few steps, still up on his toes. Bryce hadn't tried very hard to hit him. That was just a little demonstration of how good he was. Bryce was good. No, that was bullshit thinking. Bryce was damn good, and Bryce was in much better shape that he looked. He was impressed. Maybe he should force Bryce to execute him with his damn feet. Boy, can he pick 'em.

Jocelyn glared at Bryce with a lean and angry look he'd seen before on the face of only one other human being. His best friend.

Bryce grinned at Jocelyn, then scowled at him.

"I'm out of here," Bryce said, with a knowing smile. "Not as soft as I look, am I, Fred Sanford? You're full of junk, man."

He smiled, sort of, and gave Bryce his due—a thumbs up.

Bryce was gone, and he got the girl without throwing a punch. Not bad for a guy who started out making two dumb moves.

§

Hours later, lying on the bed, facing each other, Stanford and Jocelyn nibbled each other's lips.

"Why don't you do wild and sexy things to me again," she said.

"You think I should?" he said, between her nibbles and bites.

"If you must ask, then you surely aren't a prime-time player."

"Sounds reasonable to me," he said.

Jocelyn's wandering hands crawled over his hips to find his butt. "Let's play grab-ass again. Want to?"

"I'll rather play doctor," he said.

"Hmm," Jocelyn crooned. "Like gynecology, maybe?"

"That will do. But, first, you're the urologist; I'm the patient."

"You the gynecologist, and I'm the patient," Jocelyn said.

"I've got a better idea. Let's play CPA. I ask you a math question and you give me the answer. What's twenty-three times three?"

§

Later, they lay sprawled across the waterbed. Jocelyn rubbed his nose with hers. "You have a whopper of a nose," she said.

"Mean kids reminded me of that very fact everyday of my young life. My least favorite taunt was Harley Four-Barrel. I believe most African males have sizable snouts. Symptomatic of the race."

A fingernail made little circles on the tip of his nose. "I believe you're a little dated about races in the world," Jocelyn said. "There is no African race. There are only three races running around on the planet, according to archaeologists and people who decide things like that. And, for your information, Mr. CPA, African is not one of the big three. Race is more than skin color and continents and big noses and small noses, you know."

"Oh, yeah? How's that?"

"Well," Jocelyn said, "according to the same experts, Caucasians, so-called white folks, they make up 49% of the human condition; Mongolians, so-called yellow folks, they make up 33%; Negroids, so-called black folks, we make up 18% of the human condition."

Not wanting to talk shop, he didn't respond.

Jocelyn snuggled up closer to him. "No shop talk, huh? Well, we can put that mouth of yours to better use, you know."

"Do I have to open my mouth to do what you want done?"

"Not if you can lie like Pinnochio and somehow make this thing here grow a few inches longer," Jocelyn said and pulled his nose.

"So, size does matter, huh?"

She kissed his lips lightly. "It could matter, but only at the end, but by then, it's too late for size to matter?"

"Oh?" he said. "Why's that?"

"Because, silly man, by then, things are tightening up so much down there, size doesn't really matter at all. You see, something else is shrinking down so fast and furious that as long as it's bigger than a pinkie, things will turn out just fine."

"Oh yeah?"

"Oh yeah," she said. "And speaking of bigger," she added, wide-eyed and stroking him even bigger.

They fell on the bed and were soon joined at the hip. Deep down inside of him he pulled her, deep down inside of an empty hole that Jocelyn Slade completely filled.

46

LAKE ARROWHEAD

WEDNESDAY, JUNE 15

SHELLEY KNEW HE was running out of time. It had been over forty-eight hours since QueenBee and those mutts bushwhacked him in Katie Kane's house. He had no time to lose, but Francine was being difficult. She was sassing him about what she had to do to help him get from under QueenBee's spell.

"Be mean," he told Francine. "Just be yourself."

Shelley drove the borrowed Lincoln Town Car around Lake Arrowhead and raced for David Harte's cottage. He glanced at the clock. He hated being late. He was already five minutes late.

He turned his attention back to Francine.

"One more time," he told the redhead.

"I got it the first time," Francine snapped. She crossed her arms across her chest. "I'm no airhead." Her pouty lips parted, and she smiled at him. "That's not a complaint, so no shit about what I said, later, okay? I just want you to know I can be mean and tough. I just don't want to carry this stupid gun. I hate guns. Guns kill people, and I don't care about politicians talking about guns don't kill people. How do I know when this shrink is doing something to you he's not supposed to be doing? Tell me that. How am I supposed to know that? How am I supposed to know when the shrink ain't shrinking right, tell me that, huh?"

He smiled and waited a three-count to make sure she was finished, then he said, "one more time, Francine. Here's the way it's going down." He told her again.

"Are you with me so far on this, Francine?"

"Go ahead," Francine said, "I'm with you."

"Okay. The quack explains this to you, and I'm listening, you see, making sure he tells it straight. If he don't do things the exact way he says he will do things, then you point the gun at his head—no, at his chest; point the gun at his chest. It's a bigger target—"

"I can shoot him in the head," Francine snapped. "I know how to shoot. I didn't say I couldn't shoot a gun. I was on my high school shooting team. I can shoot. I just hate guns. That's all. I can shoot him in the head."

"Good. Shoot him in the head."

Finally, he could undo what QueenBee did to him inside Katie Kane's house. The old woman was so damn sneaky. He was just glad he had already switched on the recorder before she jumped him. He never expected her to anticipate he'd go to Katie Kane's house first instead of first going inside the homeplace with the governor. But QueenBee had only anticipated his habit. And going to Katie Kane's house first had been his habit since the murders.

She spoke those words, and he lost consciousness.

It was like she had switched him off. But the tiny recorder had taped everything QueenBee had said to him. She had hypnotized him. That was how she'd cured his headaches. She had been hypnotizing him all his life, and he never knew that.

That was also how David made the migraines go away. Hypnosis. David told him that post-hypnotic suggestions could be erased. He had already edited out what he didn't want David to hear on the tape. QueenBee had asked him about the Miami Assassin and about his secret agenda, but David didn't need to know all that. When QueenBee found out where he was on "the night that never happened," he heard her crying on the tape.

Then QueenBee gave him a post-hypnotic suggestion to return to the homeplace in a fortnight. That was what he wanted David to erase from his mind. QueenBee had her one chance. She would never get a second chance to mess with his head.

§

Thursday, 7 p.m. The sweltering eighty-degree warmth was down from the day's high of ninety-three, but the wet, heavy air was still simmering on medium heat.

As soon as Consy Torrey saw the white Pony Express delivery

step van park near the curb in front of his duplex, he scratched the Dachshund's head and put the dog on the floor.

A misty rain fluttered along outside, saturating the air.

The uniformed driver balanced the notebook computer upside down on top of the square box and hurried to the door through the misting rain. She rested the box on top of her steel-toed boot, rang the doorbell, then heaved the box back up into her arms, her moves robotic, precise, all wound up.

Consy unlatched the screen and signed for the package.

The driver hurried back to the delivery van under an increasingly heavy rain. Consy relatched the screen door and stood watching the raindrops pounding the concrete with such a driving force the drops exploded like water bombs. Then he turned away.

Consy set the box on the table, thinking what a heavy cake.

Someone from the office had remembered that tomorrow was his birthday. He snipped the string with scissors and tore off the paper with a forefinger. He slid a box cutter along the top to lift the lid. A red satin ribbon poked up. He untied the ribbon from the black plastic bag. A ripe stench smothered his face and sent him reeling backwards, gasping.

The stench rushed down into his lungs and gut. He dry-heaved, clutching his lurching stomach and suffering.

The box thudded to the floor and burst open, pouring out the horror inside. Consy shrieked, staggered back and screamed. The CPA spun on his heels, stumbled to his knees, but he shot back up on his feet and fled. He ripped the latched screen door off its hinges. He tore down the street with the screen door looped around his neck like a guillotine,

His pitiful wails trailed behind him like smoke.

The Dachshund licked caked blood from Karon's cold brow.

PART FOUR

QUEENBEE

47

Saturday, June 18

The Boeing 737 cut through the rough turbulence like a snow-plow, and the cabin vibrated like a cheap car.

Candice was flying back to Atlanta after spending a week hiding out in Denver. She'd gotten away from Little Bruce Wayne—the little runt—plus she needed time to recover her psychic strength that had been so drained by that sociopathic killer.

A week ago, she nearly died. But that was all behind her now. She'd gotten the hell out of the Peach State for good, and she had money enough now to live the good life in another country until the day she died an old rich woman. She had big money again, and she was back flying first-class again.

From her shoulder bag, she took out the newspaper clipping of Stanford Rome standing next to Mr. Stetson Hat.

She studied the clipping for a moment, then ripped it apart. She stuffed the pieces inside the magazine pocket attached to the back of the seat in front of her. Not even Stanford Rome and Mr. Stetson Hat bothered her now.

When the flight attendants passed around drinks, Candice simply smiled and waved her off.

Candice settled back, sighing, trying to burrow her butt deeper down into the cushions. Life was grand again. She hadn't found out who killed Stacey and Stanley as she'd promised her mother she would. She had failed mother dearest as mother dearest had failed her when she'd been young and helpless. They were even now. The jet shook and she shuddered, her thoughts jolting back to Atlanta and that midget killer again.

She'd escaped death because Shelley-Frank's knockout gas saved her. But it was her own quick thinking that had sent her stumbling inside that soundproof room and diving under those pillows before she coughed. When she came up for air later, the basement was empty. Everyone was gone. Shelley-Frank, the Surgeon, and Little Bruce Wayne, all gone. She found the motion detectors that alerted Shelley-Frank to someone moving around down in his basement. Shelley-Frank had then released the gas.

Shelley-Frank had been so surprised to find two unconscious people down there instead of one person that he hadn't bothered to look for a third person. She'd stopped trembling long enough to get away unseen. She completely abandoned Atlanta. It took two days of hiding out in her Lake Arrowhead suite to get her nerves back.

She'd seen on CNN where another friend of hers, Miss Poetic Justice, had blown Preacher's ass to smithereens and change. That mansion had been flattened like a pancake. Now Preacher had to explain to Saint Pete why his ass arrived at the pearly gates in bits and pieces instead of two chunks, a right cheek and a left one.

In her room those two days of hiding out, she'd pulled out week-old recordings taken inside Stanford's cottage and listened to them for the first time. That was when another old girlfriend of hers, Lady Luck, smiled—no, grinned on her. On the recordings, she heard Stanford dumping the duffel bag and counting the content. He'd sounded angry to have found it. She heard him go bury it.

She found the duffel bag Sid and the security guards had been in the woods hunting last month. She found it buried behind the cottage. She dug it up, emptied its precious cargo, refilled it with rocks and pine cones, and reburied the duffel bag.

She stashed all the cocaine and most of the money, and flew to her safe haven in Denver. Back home, she'd looked her mother straight in the face and told her that Stanford had nothing to do with the death of his wife and son. But she hadn't looked into her mother's eyes. Her mother didn't allow such familiarity between mother and daughter, the locking of eyes.

Her mother had finally told her about Katie Kane. They were identical twins. They were born in Seldon, Louisiana. The two sisters got separated a year later when their mother died and their father was lost at sea. Katie Kane was adopted by a Georgia family, and her mother was adopted by a Denver couple.

In January, Katie Kane recovered from her heart attack only to be told her daughter and her grandson had been murdered.

Katie Kane lapsed into a coma. Days later, she died without regaining consciousness. Weeks later, her mother read an ad in the *Denver Post* of her sister's death, and of Stanford's search for his dead mother-in-law's twin. Instead of contacting Stanford directly, her mother had hired an Atlanta private detective who stiffed her for a few grand.

Then her mother sent her to Atlanta to find out if Stanford had had anything to do with the murders.

And now almost two months after she first set foot in Atlanta, she was heading back to Atlanta for only the second time in her life. This time she was stroking her stomach each hour on the hour. She leaned back and thought of her last hours in Denver.

She'd met her lawyer at his Cherry Creek office across from the Tattered Cover Bookstore and made final preparations to leave the city and never have to come back. Her mother was a mother to her no more, just a pain in the ass that could only become an even bigger pain in the ass, the older she got. But no more. She would never return to the Mile-High city of her birth, not even to bury the woman she feared she would one day become.

She had already made her mother's funeral arrangements, all the way down to the obituary and the cremation. But there was really no need for her mother to know about all that—since she was so terrified of fire.

At the Denver airport, she'd dropped the lawyer's check in the mail, as she said she would. And, won't he be surprised to receive a check in the mail, as promised. Well, she'd learned one thing when she came home this last time.

Now, she knew precisely why she felt so cold and distant and, sometimes, so hateful toward her mother.

Her mother never once said she loved her—not once in her entire life did her mother ever say, "I love you, Candy."

She rubbed her stomach and felt herself becoming teary with emotion, but she easily fought back the feeling of that emotion.

She was her own mother now, and she was flying back to Atlanta to fetch her baby's daddy—on the fly.

§

Six hours later, Candice Bergens was back at Lake Arrowhead. She would stay away from her Atlanta digs a while longer. She was so glad to be back home. She was hungry and wanted to see her baby's daddy. Her body was such a beehive of urgency and high energy, her pulse thumping even faster in only her fourth week of impregnation. At the rate she was going, she would be a speed freak before the end of her first trimester. She had to find Shelley-Frank to tell him he'd be a daddy in thirty-two weeks or less. She palmed her stomach for signs of growth, but her belly was as flat now as when she last checked her stomach ten minutes ago.

She felt safe back inside her old suite at the hotel. She hadn't checked out when she left a week ago. She hadn't wanted anyone to know she was gone, and she didn't want anyone to know she was back. She flopped on the bed and took a ten-minute breather, then she headed back down to get her vanity kit from the car trunk.

That was when she spotted her baby's daddy at a distance.

Shelley-Frank, he and another man…Sid, they were loading…a crate—no, a coffin into a hearse. She eased back farther into the shadows and watched them work.

Sid got behind the wheel of the hearse and drove off.

Shelley-Frank followed the hearse in the Thunderbird, and she tailed the Thunderbird. Where were they going? Who'd died? She stopped and turned around when she saw both the hearse and the Thunderbird leaving Lake Arrowhead. David would know what was going on. Besides, she wanted to get wasted just one more time before preparing her body to live a clean life for two people instead of living a wild and carefree life for one person.

§

Candice parked behind David Harte's Mercedes.

She rang the doorbell three times before she opened the door with her key. Inside, she had a bad feeling and slid out the .380. Walking quietly through the house she worked her way toward the back door leading to the gazebo. She heard a noise and stopped. Leading with the .380 in front of her, she crept out the back door.

Squirrels scattered and birds squawked. She eyeballed the surroundings and saw David sprawled across a chaise lounge under the gazebo. Near David's hand was a fifth bottle of Rum, more empty than full, and two thick half-smoked marijuana joints. She covered the sleeping man with a blanket.

Then she surveyed the mess.

Papers were strewed all about the chaise lounge, and a tape recorder laid near David's feet. She scooped up the papers and used the rum bottle as a paperweight. Shelley's name grabbed her eye; she picked up the sheet of paper and read what David had written about her baby's daddy.

Then she listened to the recorded tapes. Her eyes stung by the time she switched off the machine, and her sniffles dragged along tears until she was weeping out of control.

§

Back in her Lake Arrowhead suite, Candice reached her painful decision. She called Alfred Warner in Miami and told the lawyer about her meeting with the now dead Preacher. She asked if the bounty was still good since Preacher was now explaining his missing ass to ol' Saint Pete. She agreed to pay him $250,000, and the lawyer assured her the $1 million bounty for the Miami Assassin was still available to be claimed.

Candice palmed her stomach again and vowed to track this animal down and to whack him. Tonight. Then off to Miami to collect her bounty, and then she was getting the hell out of this damn country for good. She should have stayed away from Georgia. That was a mistake. Coming back had been another big blunder. It was her own damn fault that she now had to whack her baby's daddy.

At the AICC, she was going to corner Shelley-Frank and whack him on sight. She owed that much to her cousin of the first kind. She would repay Stacey for stopping Mr. Stetson Hat from blowing off her face.

She would repay Stacey by killing the man who had sent her and her son to such an early grave.

Sure, there was some justice in the world.

And her dead father was right: all justice was man-made.

48

IN CHICAGO, BLISTERING thunderstorms had raged all day long, transforming the Windy City into the rainy city. Fat raindrops jumped dancing off the asphalt like liquid drumsticks.

The beat was both steady and rhythmic.

Jones turned off Lake Shore Drive and drove for the Chicago Landings office building. There was a thin line of difference between Jones driving up and down Lake Shore Drive, and a Great White cruising the warm waters of the Atlantic.

He was going coon-hunting.

Jones was a block away from the Chicago Landings. He had already crippled two men hunting for Johan. He never told Johan about that, and he wouldn't tell Johan about this lawyer either. If the lawyer didn't talk to him, then he was going to put that motherfucker down for the count, too. Jones disappeared down into the underground garage. He parked the van in a parking space near the elevators for handicapped drivers. He strapped himself into the motorized wheelchair in the cargo bay.

After double-checking the stun gun, the syringe, and the pistol, Jones lowered the ramp and the wheelchair to the garage floor. He unstrapped himself and drove the wheelchair off the ramp.

Jones called the elevator and watched the numbers decrease as the elevator fell down the tube to collect him.

The elevator doors sprang open—Jesus!

Jones stared up, way up into the hateful faces of four big black motherfuckers, and each one of the sons-of-bitches was toting some heavy iron on his person. Jones willed himself not to go for his pistol, gripping the arms of the wheelchair to make sure he didn't get stupid and get dead. They looked like mountains from down where he sat. The mountains slid on past Jones as if he didn't even exist sitting down in that wheelchair. Jones rolled aboard the empty elevator, pressed the floor he wanted, the urge to puke not so strong now.

Jones got off the elevator on the twenty-first floor; his heart was still thumping along like a hummingbird's. He rolled down the hallway to suite 2100. He rapped on the door. No answer. He waited. Seconds later, Jones rapped again, a little harder this time.

The room door slowly opened.

The first man Jones saw was not the door opener but a man standing behind a lectern at the far end of the room.

A preacherman.

"Welcome to the black house," the preacherman said as if they had been waiting for him to show up. "I'm Malcolm Xavier. My father's father's father was your slave, and now you're our slave. Come, come, enter the doom room. Please."

Suddenly, the wheelchair flew inside the room like it had been shot from a cannon. The suddenness nearly gave him whiplash. A stiff foot to the sternum abruptly stopped his forward movement, and the boot nearly crushed his heart. He knew he was going to die. His heart stuttered a few times before regaining its rhythm. It took him well over a minute to stop gasping and to recover his breath. But he was still a little dizzy from the blow to his chest. When he could lift his head, he saw nothing but black faces, all glaring down at him like he was the only slaveowner at a slave convention.

He squinted under the hateful glare of about fifty Nation of Islam foot soldiers.

Malcolm Xavier stared at the huge window then glared back at him. "I hope you be wearing your wings, massum, because you're going back down those twenty-one stories the hard way."

Jones did a quick nervous calculation. He could pop at least six of them black motherfuckers before one of them shot him dead. That thought calmed him somewhat. Hell, Jones wasn't scared of dying. He'd killed too many motherfuckers to be scared to join them all in the lockdown. The preacherman would be the second motherfucker to die. Numbers three and four stood to the immediate left and right of the preacherman. Jones knew now he had less than two seconds to snatch out the pistol and get off the first shot. No more than two seconds.

Jones waited for a foot soldier to make the first move. That unlucky motherfucker would be the first to die.

The moments flew by on the soft wings of a dove, and not a sound was heard. Jones was still waiting for a foot soldier to make his fatal last move when the preacherman finally turned his head and spoke to a man behind him, a man Jones couldn't see.

"Well, Half Brother," Malcolm Xavier spoke louder to the still unseen man as if the man were deaf, "you seen enough already?"

That motherfucker Half Brother would be number five to die, Jones calculated, and he'd get off one more shot before the foot soldiers blew him away and threw his corpse out the window.

Jones sensed movement behind him and tried to lift his pistol. His arms were wrenched violently behind his back then snatched up over his head by strong, brutal hands. Other searching hands stripped away all his goodies. But Jones' eyes never once left the face of the preacherman. Again Malcolm Xavier turned his head to speak to the unseen man. "Half Brother, massum here, he was gonna do some mighty nasty things to you with his toys, you see."

Malcolm Xavier turned his obscene eyes back to Jones. "Well, massum, here's the plan. You can either get up outta that creeper and walk outta here, or you can spread your wings like a buzzard and fly your stank ass outta here. Your choice, white boy.

"Now, get up outta that chair and walk!"

The voice boomed around the crowded room. "And walk! You are healed, my brother, get up outta that chair and walk!"

Jones stood, almost defiantly since he knew he was a dead man. The only thing that kept him from spitting in the motherfucker's face was his mouth was as tight as a constipated asshole and all dried up. He was surprised no one was surprised he could walk.

Malcolm Xavier pointed Jones to the door held open by a foot soldier. Jones walked toward the door, knowing the foot soldiers would shoot him in the back. He wouldn't reach the door alive.

But Jones did reach the door alive.

The elevator car was held open by another foot soldier standing well over six feet tall. The elevator car wouldn't have a bottom in it. Jones knew that. But he stepped on anyway.

But the elevator car did have a bottom in it.

The elevator fell for nearly twenty seconds. Down in the garage Jones would be shot when he stepped out the elevator. He knew that. He would never make it behind the wheel of his van.

But he did make it behind the wheel of his van.

Those motherfuckers had booby-trapped the van. He would be blown to pieces. He knew it but turned the ignition key anyway.

The van didn't explode.

Then, real fear set in, a cold, biting fear that caused his hands to tremble. If those black motherfuckers didn't kill him soon, he would die of anticipation. Jones moved the shifter into reverse and expected the van to be riddled with bullets before he reached the exit. He lifted his foot easily off the brake pedal. The van crept backwards out the parking spot, then he headed for the exit.

The suspense was just too much for Jones. He wanted to stop the van, jump out in the middle of the expressway, rip open his shirt, poke out his chest, and yell for the motherfuckers to just do it and get it the fuck over with!

But no bullets came.

Jones drove a half mile from Chicago Landings before he stopped and parked. He felt weak enough to melt into a puddle on the ground. There wasn't a dry spot on his body. Raindrops pounded the van as he sat there. He was pissed. He flicked off the wipers and wiped his brow. He was going back one day soon to kill every one of those black motherfuckers. No doubt.

No doubt about that. Starting with the preacherman and ending with that Half Brother motherfucker.

§

The sun beamed hot and punishing in Twofer County. Typical.

Humming, QueenBee rocked, helping the last painful thought to set and jell in her mind. A dunce, she'd acted like an old fart.

That day she nabbed Shelley in Katie Kane's house, she had learned all she needed to know from Shelley. She gave him a post-hypnotic suggestion to return to the homeplace. But Shelley had never come back. Now, she knew why. She no longer controlled him. Shelley was out of her control. That was both heartbreaking and frightening. She'd controlled Shelley at Katie Kane's house, else he would have shot her dead before Aretha and Franklin could take him out.

She had seen two of Aretha and Franklin's great, great kinfolks take out a 250-pound black bear protecting her cubs. They didn't live to strut around the homeplace about it; they didn't live at all. But neither did the bear. It had been a twofer—two for one. Take Shelley out, those two mutts would have.

Shelley was still as quick as a backdoor lover. She didn't want to hurt Shelley. He was a grandson to her. She wanted to help him live with his demons. But if she had to she would not hesitate to dust him.

But her post-hypnotic suggestion hadn't worked on him at all.

Now the monster she'd controlled all these many years was now out of her control. Her creation was loose out there, somewhere, doing God knows what to who knows whom.

At Katie Kane's house, she hypnotized Shelley to learn things she needed to know. She learned much more than she ever wanted to know, but all were things she needed to know.

She learned about Shelley's scheme to get Stanford into politics and the governor's chair. First, he planned to get Stanford elected lieutenant governor, and the new governor would suddenly die in office, making Stanford the new governor—such a hare-brained scheme. She erased the scheme from his mind completely. She learned about Shelley's resurrection of the Miami Assassin, and she erased the resurrection as well. When she learned that Shelley had been at Katie Kane's house the night they were killed, she fell apart. Now she felt every one of her eighty-three odd years, knowing she must destroy the monster she'd created in Shelley's mind when he had only been a boy.

She had to stop him, and her best hope was Thomas Jefferson Lee. Colt was a fine example of the freaky way nature fine-tuned and upgraded the human brain. By making weird exceptions of everyday rules, Nature anointed weird people and their weird minds to haul human thinking up to the next higher level.

That was her thinking anyway. In the end, the freak will inherit the earth, not the meek.

At twenty, Colt graduated from Georgia Tech in Atlanta with a physics degree. But Colt had always wanted to become a Twofer County deputy sheriff, so QueenBee told Jake to entice Colt back to Twofer County with a job. Six months after Jake hired Colt, Jake promoted him to chief jailer; three months later, to deputy sheriff; and one month after that, Jake promoted Colt to detective.

Long before the word *superhighway* was coined, Colt and his gadgets were surfing that blacktop, trying to find Rooster for her. Colt searched tall men's shops and custom-tailors; huge construction projects, charities, foundations, private jets, private clubs, private yachts; passenger lists for the *Queen Elizabeth II* and the Concorde; debutante balls, opera houses and ballets, visas, passports.

Colt had snooped in so many other places in his futile search for Rooster. But Colt never found the man she'd been looking for.

Now she had another task for the man whose nickname everyone misunderstood from the start.

§

In Chicago, Fred Junior held the newspaper advertisement and the three-color flier at arm's length. He nodded approval at the results. The layout was just what QueenBee wanted.

Over on the sofa, Malcolm Xavier set aside the thick lease agreement like it was a full diaper and got to his feet.

"Two months left on this here lease; is that right, Fred Junior?" Malcolm walked around, eyeballing the suite.

Fred Junior set the flier aside and studied the ad some more.

Malcolm said, "Fred Junior, who are you trying to find?"

He looked up at Malcolm. "I'm just looking for a man."

Malcolm cackled. "You better be mighty careful about who you say that to. Other men are out here looking for a man, too."

"Yeah," he said, kneeing the suitcase shut to latch it. "Malcolm, thanks for the assist. That guy could have killed me. I wonder why QueenBee told you to look out for me, but she didn't tell me I was being looked after."

"Because I'm black, and you're white," the Twofer-County bigot said. "That means I'm smarter than you are."

"Probably," the lawyer said. "Anyway, Malcolm, as payback, this place is yours for two whole months. I'm outta here. Oh, by the way, I've got a $12,000 damage deposit. I'll like to get it all back, if you don't mind. It's QueenBee's money."

"Bet, Fred Junior." Malcolm grinned. "You know, Fred Junior, you was one dumb white boy in school. Why you so smart now?"

Fred Junior thought about it and shrugged. He was a C student in high school at best, and he would have failed a grade or two if QueenBee hadn't pushed him just enough and not too much.

"Mistakes made me smart," Fred Junior finally admitted. And it was so true. He had screwed up so many times and in so many ways that now all he had to do was not to make the same mistake twice. Any new mistakes would be few.

He turned for the door. "See you, Malcolm."

"Hey, wait a minute, hold one, Fred Junior." Malcolm held up one of the fliers. "Answer me this then. Why is it you got a picture of you, and a drawing of Justin on this flyer here?"

"That's not Justin. Looks like Justin, but that's not Justin."

"Okay, okay," Malcolm said, "then tell me this, if you be looking for the man in the drawing, why is it your picture is the one on the flier? Makes me think you don't wanna find this here man. Makes me think you want this here man here to find you. Now, ain't that right, Fred Junior, what I'm thinking?"

"Now, Malcolm, you're thinking way too much," he said. "Just setting yourself up for a lobotomy is what you're doing."

Smoke billowed in Malcolm's eyes for a moment before those same eyes flared up. Fred Junior realized his mistake the instant he made it, and he groaned. He tensed for the blowup.

"You're over 200 years too late for that, Fred Junior." Malcolm spoke in his hate voice. "Your white ancestors done beat you to it; they already done lobotomized my people. Your white ancestors wouldn't let 'em learn and wouldn't let 'em love and wouldn't let 'em take off the chains. Your white ancestors stole our humanity. What do black men like me know about romancing a woman when our daddies and our daddies's daddies had to fuck on the run or fuck under the gun as breeder stock? And a small man like me didn't wet his wick any at all—"

"Hey!" Fred Junior threw up both hands, glaring at his tormentor. "Can the speech, Malcolm Xavier. You can just can the speech. I grew up with you. And I grew up with that same ol' tired damn speech. Spare me the grief already. I'm sorry for what I said, and you have no idea how fucking sorry I am. Let me tell you how sorry I am, then I'll tell you how sorry I am that my sorry-ass white ancestors—"

"Hey!" Malcolm threw up both hands. "Spare me the grief."

"My point exactly," Fred Junior said, mimicking Shelley and grinning along with the man QueenBee called Twofer County's most outrageous bigot, the man she'd exiled from the county because of his bigotry. "Thanks, Malcolm Xavier. We're square."

They kept laughing at their inside joke.

"No, Fred Junior," Malcolm grinned, "you're square. Me, I'm hip."

"Okay, you're hip. Now, help me take these things downstairs, then you and I, we're taking a ride to The Print Shop over in Lincolnwood. You got a key, right?"

§

Jones pulled out of the Chicago Landings parking garage four-car lengths behind the blue Lexus. The Lexus turned left onto Lake Shore Drive. The van fell in twenty yards back, in the middle lane, ready for whichever way the Lexus turned.

The Lexus sped through Grant Park and hit I-94, threading traffic all the way to Lincolnwood. The driver parked in a strip center where dusk hung like drapes over the neighborhood.

Jones recognized the two men who got out the Lexus, and they used a key to go inside The Print Shop. Jones glanced at his watch. A minute later, he got out the van and stole inside The Print Shop behind the two men. He saw a light on in a back room and hugged the wall. Then he heard angry voices.

Edging along the wall, Jones got close enough to peep around the doorjamb. The same two men from the Lexus were up in each other's face like two dogs and one bone. He watched and smiled.

Jones backtracked along the wall, eased back to the front door and locked it. Then he whipped out the silenced twenty-two and tiptoed to the back room. The men were still arguing.

Jones stepped through the opening.

The Nation of Islam preacher went for his gun. Jones shot the lanky man once in the chest. Then he turned the silenced muzzle on the lawyer and scowled.

"Well, Half Brother," Jones said, "you seen enough already?"

49

TWOFER COUNTY/MIAMI/ATLANTA

TUESDAY, JUNE 21

STANFORD ARRIVED IN Twofer County at 4 a.m. The bread trucks and milk trucks were already racing up and down the two-lane black top under a quarter moon.

He was no longer anxious to ask QueenBee about Justin's twin. He was thinking of Jocelyn Slade, and he kept thinking about that woman.

When he arrived at the homeplace, he couldn't sleep right away, so he read Colt's report. Colt and Stanley had gone to Florida to look into the death of the Florida state trooper who was killed the same night Stacey and Christopher were killed. Thoughts of Justin and of Jocelyn were squeezed out of his mind by the report.

The report said two telephone numbers were scribbled on the margin of the dead trooper's new ticket book. Those two numbers belonged to Jud Judson. A document expert said the dead trooper had written the numbers down on his new ticket book only hours before he was killed. A Florida investigator confirmed Jud's alibi on the night of the murder, but Stanford noticed something about one of the two telephone numbers was missing from Colt's report.

One of the two numbers was Jud's unlisted private line, and only a handful of people had that private number. So if Jud hadn't given the trooper his private number then only eight other people could have possibly given the number to the trooper that night.

He filed that tidbit away and flipped the page of the report.

The report said an Ohio motorist had reported seeing the then-alive trooper and the Thunderbird, both, parked along the interstate. But the Florida Highway Patrol investigators dismissed the motorist's information because the motorist said the trooper's patrol car had a bubble on top. Not true. The trooper's patrol car had been a slick top. Stanford jotted down the motorist's telephone number and flipped the page of the report.

The trooper's license plate check didn't report the car tag MMF 1728 as stolen in Miami, 300 miles away, eight hours earlier because the owner had yet to discover it stolen. After the traffic stop, the trooper radioed his dispatcher that he was back on the road again. The dispatcher's log said the traffic stop took seven minutes. Half an hour later, a hit-and-run 18-wheeler killed the trooper at the same spot where the trooper had stopped the mystery T-bird.

Stanford rubbed sleep from his eyes and read on.

The Dade County tag on the mystery T-bird had been stolen off an identical car, down to the same black color. Stanford thought about that for a moment. Was that a coincidence or did the driver know that much about traffic stops? Was the driver a cop or an ex-cop? The key to connecting the trooper's death to Stacey's and Christopher's deaths was the driver of the mysterious T-bird.

Since the license plate was stolen in Miami, Stanford assumed the car was stolen in Miami as well. He closed the pages of the report. Interesting stuff. His gut gurgled as if in agreement.

Six hours later, Stanford had arranged for Jennifer Stanley to fly him and Stanley down to Miami, so they could search for the driver of the Thunderbird.

§

It was raining hurricanes and dolphins, cats and dogs when Jennifer touched the plane down at Miami International Airport at three in the afternoon.

Stanford and Stanley started their search at the airport rental agencies that rented T-birds. They came up empty.

The next morning, he and Stanley inspected Miami and Dade County stolen-car reports. That afternoon they pored over Miami and Dade County car registrations.

The next day, they canvassed car rental agencies that rented T-birds and were also located away from the airport. They got their first lead when Stanford greased the hands of eager rental agents with $100 bills. In return, they received copies of T-bird contracts written on January 15 and 16 by Sunshine Car Rental Agency. Sunshine rented twice as many T-birds than all the other car rental agencies combined.

He and Stanley examined each of the thirty-eight contracts and found that only four of those thirty-eight T-birds had been driven more than 500 miles. They verified the destination of all but one of the four cars. That one T-bird had been driven 678 miles in the twenty-four hours it was rented.

Round-trip from Miami to Twofer County was 650 miles.

Stanford's hopes went up, but Stanley's excitement bordered on maniacal. They went to find the woman who'd rented the T-bird.

§

Stanford pulled into the driveway at 20332 Shamrock Place at one in the afternoon. A black Mercedes Benz Diesel, a canary yellow Porsche 928, and a bright red Shelby Mustang GT were parked in front of the $2-million split-level home.

Loud music throbbed from around back. Stanford followed the sounds to a closed gate. He lifted the latch. He and Stanley walked through. Stanley's hand flew to his mouth. His son guffawed.

Stanford spun Stanley around and marched him back through the gate. "Stay put," he told him. He went back through the gate and latched it behind him. He went up to a nude couple.

"My name's Stanford Rome. I'm looking for Mrs. Cicely Webb."

A hefty man stopped his caresses and stabbed Stanford's face with ice-pick eyes, and his left hand fell from sight.

"You passed her on your way in," said the silver-haired Adonis. "She's under that new dirt you saw. She's been laying on her back now for five whole weeks. A natural position for a slut, I suppose."

Adonis went back to kissing the naked woman's polished toes.

Stanford tore his unwilling eyes away from the woman's outrageous breasts. He cleared his throat. "Mr. Webb, I need to speak with you privately for a moment, if I may."

"You may not! Get outta here before I call the cops."

"Mr. Webb, I'm looking into a scandal involving you—"

"Don't even try it!" Webb stood wobbly to his feet, gripping an iron rod in his left hand like a blackjack.

Stanford didn't move. The man was obviously drunk and moving much too sluggish to be a danger with the pipe. But he relaxed and stayed focused on a counterattack just in case.

The man said, "I know she was fucking that Atlanta cop, and I don't give a shit. The bimbo's where she belongs, dead and fucking buried, and don't you go digging up her whorish ass in front of all my friends." The man tapped the poker in his palm once and got the smacking sound. He tried again, missed, and the pipe clanged to the patio. The man looked dumbly down at it then picked it up.

"Got any more questions," the man said, "go ask the buck she was sucking. Go ask that fucking Frank. End of fucking story. Now get your nigger ass off my property—you goddamn redneck spic!"

Stanford obeyed. Adonis had a hard-on for somebody, but was confused about which group he was really pissed at—the asshole.

It was again raining in Miami when Jennifer lifted off from Miami International Airport.

§

Back at the Twofer County Airport, Stanford dialed Jud Judson in Atlanta. He told the private detective about Cicely Webb, who was decapitated a month ago, on the twentieth. She rented a T-bird for her boyfriend, Frank, an Atlanta cop on January fifteenth, the day before Stacey and Christopher were killed.

Next, he called the Ohio motorist, a comrade, a CPA. She convinced him she saw a bubble on top of the trooper's car, partly by reminding him women saw better at night than men did. He hung up the telephone, and the airport's loudspeakers blared his name.

Ten minutes later, Stanford was merging fast into I-75 southbound traffic, racing for the Florida state line. Minutes after crossing into Florida, he saw flashing blue lights whirling in his rearview mirror. He stopped on the shoulder of the road .

The police officer approached with his ticket book in hand.

"Will you please step to the rear of the car, Mr. Rome, with your license, insurance and registration."

The young Columbia County deputy sheriff looked over the license and registration then studied his face. Interestingly enough, the deputy's hands shook in the ninety-degree heat.

"Mr. Rome, I'm Virgil Highland," the deputy said. "I talked with your son, Stanley, a couple of days ago, him and Tom Lee. I gave them the official version of what happened the night your wife and son were killed. Now, I'm here to tell you the truth, if you promise the truth is between me, you and that fence post over yonder." Virgil's eyes slid away from his. "Promise me, Mr. Rome?"

The pulsating blue light haunted Virgil's concrete face.

He shook his head. "Can't promise that, Virgil."

Virgil's eyes squinted. "Why not, Mr. Rome?"

"Simple. I may have to break that promise. To get what I want I may have to break that promise, and to get what I want, I would break that promise in a heartbeat, Virgil."

Virgil handed his papers back. "Do drive safely back to Georgia, Mr. Rome." Virgil stomped back toward the spinning blue light.

"Virgil!"

The deputy stopped.

"Virgil, if I can use the truth without revealing who told me, will you still hold me to the promise?"

The deputy shook his head. "Mr. Rome, I've been married three years, yesterday, a week ago. Got me two fine boys, and a church-going wife. Can't risk my family to help you—a stranger."

"Then, why are you here?" he shot back. Damn if he could let this opportunity just walk away from him without poking the man carrying it away from him at least once in his ribs.

Virgil studied the ground then looked up, his back not as erect.

"When I was a lil' boy, Mr. Rome, QueenBee, she saved my life. That's why I'm here. We were dirt-poor white trash back then, and probably still is. We couldn't pay her nothing for the good she did us all. But QueenBee, she never stepped on our pride like lots of folks did back then. QueenBee, she expected us to pay up. She hired my oldest brother to work at the pecan house so we could pay our own way. That made it so I could stay in school and be the first one in my family to finish high school. QueenBee, she gave us a little more than an equal opportunity to save ourselves. Now my brother, he runs that big pecan operation QueenBee's got up in Twofer County. I owe QueenBee. I owe QueenBee a lot. This family owes QueenBee a lot. But I won't sacrifice my boys to repay that big debt to QueenBee, no sir."

Virgil walked toward the blue light flashing into his eyes.

That was when all the bits and pieces finally came together to form a complete picture in his mind. He could now see clearly what happened that night. He knew the truth.

The Chicago CPA was right.

"Virgil!" he shouted after the deputy sheriff.

A huge hawk squawked and took to the sky, a rabbit squirming in its talons and drops of blood trailing in the air like purple rain.

The deputy sheriff kept walking.

Stanford's eyes lit up with understanding. "Virgil! Your bubble! You were there. It was your bubble. You were there that night!"

Virgil opened the patrol-car door.

He stepped toward the departing deputy sheriff, talking as fast as he could talk and still be understood by Virgil.

"The trooper was there, wasn't he, Virgil? He was driving a slick top. There were three cars there, not two cars. That Ohio motorist just didn't see the third car, the trooper's car; that Ohio motorist just didn't see the slick top. There were three cars there; you, the trooper, and the T-bird; right Virgil!"

Virgil's tires squalled an angry reply.

Stanford punched the air. "Yeah," he said. "Yeahhh."

§

The next morning, in Atlanta, before his meeting with James Kelsey, Stanford called Jud Judson, who hadn't located an ex-Atlanta cop named Frank.

Also, Jud said nine people knew his unlisted home telephone number: Fred Junior, Jake Keller, Justin, four of Jud's investigators, Shelley, and Stanford. Almost as an afterthought, Jud told him that Shelley was probably hiding out at Lake Arrowhead.

Jud said Sid Nelson, the security chief, and the other guards all owed their jobs if not their lives to Shelley, who had rescued each of them from some unpleasantness in life if not outright disasters.

Stanford was scared for Shelley, who had some of the worst felons on earth for his enemies. For Shelley to lose his memory was the worst thing that could possibly happen to his best friend.

It was three o'clock in the afternoon when James Kelsey strode into Stanford's office and closed the door behind him, six hours late for their 9 a.m. meeting. James' smirk set him off.

When James sat down he went straight for James' jugular.

"James, why are the Feds indicting you for racketeering?"

James' face was empty, expressionless.

"Stanford," James said, shaking his head, "those white boys, they are playing you like a fiddle again, I see. And here you go, fronting me like they want you to do. So I can do the white boys' dirty work for them, so I can dump the sad facts of life on you like I'm gonna do right now this minute. You need an old-fashioned talking to."

The condescending tone irked him. "James, are you a crook?"

James' temples flared as if horns were trying to break through the sides of his head. James bent forward, snarling. "Don't you two-step with me, fellow." James hurtled the words at him like verbal pitchforks. "Talk to me straight or don't talk to me none at all."

Elbows planted on his desk, he bent forward, nearer to James. "I wanna break your face is what I want, you bastard."

James stiffened and half-stood, crouched.

But Stanford broke off the stare-down. He got up from behind the desk and walked over to stand by the window, the farthest he could get away from James Kelsey without abandoning his own office. He was afraid he would hit the older man and hurt him really bad. Every fiber in his body wanted to lash out at James but his will held tight reins on his emotions.

"James," he said, "you had no right bringing Richard and Mark into this firm to destroy us. We employ a hundred people, and you have no right to jeopardize our livelihoods because you resent my character—just because you resent who the hell I am."

"Bullshit, Stanford. You're just way too soft. That's the whole problem, your softness. You're a lamb among wolves out here. So, don't you dare go around knocking down my way, knocking down my small contribution. Your way is not the only way, my friend."

"What contribution can you make by getting indicted?"

James waved a dismissive hand. "The rich people in this country, they didn't get rich doing it your way. The rich in this country, they got rich doing it their way. And the rich, they stay rich by making people like you believe they got rich by doing it your way."

James snorted. "Take off your blinders, Stanford. Forget what's going on in front of your big nose. It's a movie; a fiction disguised as a nonfiction. It's all fake is what I'm telling you."

"Is your indictment fiction?" he said.

James shrugged off the question.

"I don't know about any indictment. But I do know that I was to Richard and Mark back in Kansas City, what you're to Richard and Mark now at Lake Arrowhead. There's no difference between what I did for them in Kansas City, and what you're doing for them now. So if that's an indictable offense what I did in KC, then what you do at Lake Arrowhead is an indictable offense as well."

"Bullshit, James." He was still determined not to let James know how much he knew.

"Besides, those white boys, they ain't all bad," James continued, ignoring the interruption. "They've got a lot of good in them. They used me for their purpose, and I used them to make my small contribution to the cause. We used one another, Richard and Mark, and me. Here in Atlanta, so many black kids need jobs. CapCity makes investment loans to ghetto businesses who are now our RKL clients. These are the same black businesses that couldn't borrow a thin dime from any Atlanta bank. These black RKL clients employ 2,800 people, mostly black teenagers, who've got 50% unemployment across the country, and 60% unemployment in this so-called black mecca, you suckers call Atlanta. This town is all about image and PR. There is no substance here. Right here in this black mecca, you cats can't even provide jobs for your own black kids."

James snorted. "Atlanta is a plantation town where black people now eat the whole hog instead of just the chitlings—get real."

"James, who owns CapCity Investments? Richard and Mark?"

"Not those two. They only pump $2 million a year into CapCity. But," James said, raising his hand, "those white boys, they don't know CapCity lends $6 million a year. That extra $4 million CapCity lends to black businesses, that is my contribution to the cause. So, Mr. High-and-Mighty Stanford Rome, don't go knocking what I do until you can do better."

He said, "So you're the one piggybacking $4 million through CapCity? You've got that kind of money? Where—"

He knew the answer before the question left his mouth. Damn.

"What's it to you?" James said. "Richard and Mark, they offered you half a mil for a year of your time, offered to make you filthy rich with stock options, and you blew them off. What do you want? To help the cause, or to help yourself? That seems to be all you Atlantans are interested in, helping your damn selves. Flashy houses, flashy cars, flashy threads, flashy toys, and lost, flashy dumb-ass kids. You can't grow a good corn crop from bad seed corn. You chumps don't know that. It seems all you Atlantans worry about is 'who's trying to pass.' Man, get a life. Trying to pass was a Civil War problem—Jesus, it's damn near the twenty-first century.

"So if it's not money, Stanford. And it's not a big CPA firm that you want, then what is it that you want? These guys, Richard and Mark, no matter what color their skin is, these guys offered you a legitimate chance, a legal chance, to get rich. They offered you a chance to make this firm a real force in this town, and you blew them off like they were winos begging down on Peachtree Street somewhere. What do you want from this life, brother-man—goodness for goodness sake?"

Stanford stared out the window and down on Peachtree Street. He knew what he wanted. He knew exactly what he wanted. He wanted to find the man who killed his wife and son. That was what he wanted. He turned back to James.

"James, who's piggybacking $4 million through CapCity?"

James smirked at him. "Ask your friend Shelley about that. Now, Stanford, let me answer your next question before you even ask it. I turned on Richard and Mark, and told you everything because Mark Davis, he's the one who had Juanita Robeson killed."

§

"Stanford, pick up on three," a staff accountant yelled from down the hall where he was studying for the three-day CPA exam.

Stanford, still reeling from what James told him, picked up the telephone. He recognized Virgil Highland's voice at once.

"Mr. Rome," Virgil said, "Donnell, he lied about sending that Thunderbird on the way that night. He and the driver, they talked thirty minutes longer than the dispatcher's records showed they talked. The driver, he was an old classmate, Donnell told me. That Ohio witness was right, too. She saw a patrol car with a bubble on top. And you were right, Mr. Rome. The car with the bubble, it was me."

50

WEDNESDAY, JUNE 22

QUEENBEE SUFFERED A sinking feeling. She closed her fist around the dice and squeezed.

Justin Grimes was back only forty-eight hours after he'd last left the homeplace. His quick return could only mean one thing. He had opened that bank deposit box she'd given him the key to when he first finished law school.

Now he knew the truth. She fought back hurtful emotions.

The judge's deep-set eyes and his gaunt face triggered memories she would rather forget, things gone past long ago. The judge's demeanor told her he knew it all. She steeled herself for the worse when she saw that Justin held a piece of paper in his hand.

Justin crossed his legs, and he asked an unexpected question.

"QueenBee, who's my father, and why haven't I met him?"

The question puzzled her. He'd asked the wrong question. So he still didn't know the truth. That other truth. Her brow smoothed over as she stared at the paper in Justin's hand.

"Justin, your father, he never knew you existed." Her heart was breaking. "Your father, he never even met you, Justin."

"Is my mother alive?" Justin said.

"Ask your father that question," she said. "He knows."

"I'm asking you, QueenBee. I've never asked you that before."

She rattled the dice once before the bones fell silent in her fist.

"I haven't seen your father, I haven't spoken to him, and I haven't heard from him since you were knee-high to a duck, Justin. I never knew how to contact him. Your father just recently contacted me."

"But did you know my father was alive?" Justin said.

"I believed your father was alive, Justin. I never knew that as a fact. It was just something I believed."

Justin's face bloomed into one great big question mark. She rattled the dice three times then squeezed the bones into silence.

"I see," Justin said, sighing the sigh of the damned. "I've always wanted your son to have been my father, and you—but you're not my grandmother. I know that now, QueenBee."

"Justin," she said, "Stanford, he's my only grandson."

Justin looked dazed as he handed her the paper in his hand.

She read it. "This is your handwriting," she said somberly.

Justin shook his head. "No, it's not my handwriting, QueenBee. I received that letter yesterday by courier." Then Justin's eyes turned steely hard. "QueenBee, who's my twin?"

Her hands noticeably shook. "Ask your father that question, Justin." Before he could respond, she rose to her feet.

"Strange," Justin said, "I have a living father and a living twin."

Justin cupped his fist in his hand and studied her like she was an accused being judged in his court. His face weakening into the pale color of smoke, Justin let his arms sag heavily to his sides.

"QueenBee, was my twin, was he raised in an orphanage?"

"Son," she said, "I know nothing about your brother. I know nothing at all about where your brother was raised. I know nothing about who raised your brother."

Justin opened his mouth to speak then closed his mouth with the words unspoken. He stroked his chin with his left hand. "Then is there any doubt about who my father is, QueenBee?"

"Son, there's no doubt, none, about who your father is."

"QueenBee, is there a connection between Stanford's father and my father?"

"I—," she stuttered. The question forced a reflex. "I—," she stuttered again, this time, clutching her chest.

Justin jumped to his feet, and the bull mastiffs rose off their haunches, growling. Justin froze. Bertha burst through the door, black bag in one hand, telephone in the other one.

"Go to work," QueenBee told the bull mastiffs. Franklin bolted through the doggie door. Aretha turned her glare from Justin to the floor, then she sulked away toward the doggie door, throwing a final hateful glare back over her shoulder at Justin before she too bolted through the doggie door.

"I'm fine," QueenBee said. "Justin, he just surprised me. He just surprised me, that's all. I'm just fine. Thanks, Bertha."

When Justin left an hour later, QueenBee sent for Colt.

The fake shortness of breath had worked. Justin forgot to ask that question again, or he knew the answer and let her off the hook. No, only three people knew the answer and he was not one of them. Yet. But she had just gotten some exciting news.

Fred Junior had found Rooster. She was sending Colt and the boys down to Miami Beach to fetch Rooster and bring him here to the homeplace. The bones sang such a joyous song in her fist.

§

Charles Jones gazed down on the clouds from three miles up.

The Lear 31 was a hundred miles south of Chicago when the pilot cut power by a third. The Lear 31 banked hard left, bypassing the congested skies of Chicago's O'Hare, and flew on for Rooster's Pointe. Jones' cheeks glittered like glazed porcelain in the glare of the overhead reading lamp.

Jones reread the fax that printed out minutes before the Lear 31 scrambled from Atlanta, only two hours after they'd left Miami Beach. Johan, his boss, had sent Jones to find Johan's brother Jocko, and Jones had come back empty-handed. Not good. Not good at all.

Jones was glad he didn't have to kill anybody else. The lawyer would now stop looking for Johan Bonnell. He had escorted the lawyer down to Miami Beach and driven him to where he could find the man he was hunting. Shooting that black Muslim motherfucker had been the right thing to do. The lawyer turned into some talker after seeing him dispose of the preacherman that way.

The lawyer was looking for the same man the other two men had been looking for when he blew out their kneecaps. So it occurred to Jones that no matter how many men he crippled and killed, bounty hunters would keep coming to find his boss. So to end the hunt forever, Jones gave the lawyer the man pictured on all those damn flyers. By now the lawyer had nabbed his man and was on the way back home to Twofer County with his prisoner.

Jones plopped the attaché case onto his lap and opened it. He aligned the magnifying mirror framed by tiny spotlights and went to work. Piece by piece, he peeled away his latest disguise. Jones carefully inserted the green contact lens into the slots between the broad nose and the forehead with the unruly cowlick.

He switched on the finger warmer. He inserted a finger in each slot for a minute, slid the finger out and easily peeled off the fake fingerprint. He placed them beside the deep-tan cream and the skin-lightening cream. Jones dipped a finger into a jar of artificial heat, rubbed the compound on his chin, and peeled off the cleft. He peeled away tissue-thin butterfly pads that widened his nose.

The copilot brought him another fax.

Jones was down to his suntan. Back under the seat went the attache case. He read the fax, as the Lear 31 circled the Rooster's Pointe landing strip once then broke down through the clouds.

§

Down in Dade County, Florida, Colt watched three men climb into a limousine and head south on U. S. 1 toward Miami Beach. The tall man was the one they came to grab. From the rear seat of the rental car, Colt studied Fred Junior's profile. The lawyer looked as if he'd spent the past two weeks digging graves.

Colt had never seen Fred Junior so unkempt. He felt outdone by the lawyer, who had done for QueenBee what he hadn't been able to do for her in all the years he'd been looking for Rooster.

Six hours ago, Fred Junior notified QueenBee that he'd found the man called Rooster. Jennifer Stanley then flew him, Willie Butts, and three off-duty deputies down to Miami to nab Rooster and to haul him back to Twofer County for trial. But at least Fred Junior hadn't lost both knees like those two Atlanta private detectives had lost. And poor but lucky Malcolm Xavier would be recuperating at the homeplace for at least another month.

Fred Junior had told him and QueenBee one hell of a tale about what all happened to him in Chicago.

Willie Butts pulled away from the curb and trailed the car trailing the limousine. Colt stole a glance over at Willie Butts. He held nothing against Willie Butts. But he has just never trusted people he thought were a little bent in the mind, and Willie Butts was a bent-minded person. He would never let Willie Butts within twenty feet of him with a weapon. But this time he did allow Willie Butts to bring along a few tools of his perverted trade—just in case.

A Buick LeSabre with two thugs inside tailed close behind the limousine. Willie Butts hung farther back. The limo hung a left on McShiver Drive. Fifty yards later, it swung into the parking garage of a swank apartment house.

They parked and waited. Willie Butts slumped in the front seat and gnawed on his lip. The part of his lip stuck in his mouth was a whole shade lighter than the part of his lip not stuck in his mouth. Willie Butta was a lip sucker when they were snotty-nosed kids.

Colt sat in the backseat and pinched the bridge of his nose. He had time to think, so he thought of that little problem he found two weeks ago when he tapped into the FBI's computer files. The name Jackie Pearson had jumped out at him, the same Jackie Pearson the killer had called from the murder scene that night.

He never knew what Shelley had been up to. And he couldn't find Shelley to ask him. So he just undid what he had done. He reversed it. He'd put back into the telephone company's computer the call that had been made that night from Katie Kane's house to Miami. He had deleted the call from the telephone company's computer because Shelley had asked him to. Replacing that call had put the FBI back to investigating the murder case as he knew it would. Why Shelley had him erase the call didn't make sense to him, and Shelley wasn't around to make it make sense to him.

He sighed and looked over at Willie Butts, who looked ready to do what they came to do. He and Willie Butts waited until the off-duty deputies took care of the bodyguards. Then they forced the limousine driver upstairs to fetch the mark.

The driver knocked on the door.

The mark opened the door.

Willie Butts rushed inside and laid the naked mark out on the floor like a bear rug. Colt saw right away the mark looked like Justin Grimes. When the mark woke up, Willie Butts was leaning on the wall, watching him stir, and rocking to some imaginary tune blaring away inside his long narrow hatchet-shaped head.

His childhood nickname was *Tomahawk*.

§

"Listen mutts," QueenBee said, as she walked through her greenhouse, Aretha and Franklin rousing about her feet like a foot patrol. She had to talk to somebody, just so she could hear herself think. "This is my story, and I'm telling it to you two mutts."

She fingered the droopy leaves of a spider plant.

"It was June 24, 1953. I went walking. I walked all the way to the backwoods of the South Georgia Deep."

She sniffed a reddish purple petunia.

"I walked all the way to our shanty shack, our castle, Stan Rome's and mine. That dreadful day changed my life for the worse."

§

The forty-eight-year-old QueenBee walked deeper into the backwoods of the South Georgia Deep. The sun had just squeezed itself between earth and sky, and was now busy burning away the thick fog, leaving the heavy air dripping wet.

Ribbet! Ribbet! Giant bullfrogs sang out their sexual intentions, their rustic croaks haunting the pervasive body of fog as she waded through the mist. Ribbet! Ribbet!

The fog thinned, but the heavy dew clung tenaciously to all it touched. She and Stan Rome had often walked miles into the deep backwoods. Thirty years her senior, Stan Rome had been a vibrant, vigorous man. Then in 1949, her seventy-four-year-old lover hit the sack as lively as ever, got sick in the wee hours, had a turn for the worse before dawn, and died at daybreak—with his boots on.

That was what she told everybody. But if the truth be told, they'd been doing the horizontal bunny hop when he croaked. At the edge of the fog, she could smell the fumes of the stream long before she heard water lapping and gurgling over rocks strewn about the bed.

Kneeling, she splashed the cool water all over her face, then she stared down at the woman staring up out of the water at her.

She raked her fingers through a thick mane of short black hair covering her head like sod. A "six-footer," she weighed about 160 pounds, had big bones, big breasts, and she still had thirty-two pearly whites enamored with only the wee hint of a liar's gap.

She walked deeper and deeper into the backwoods of the South Georgia Deep.

The thick mist churned away from her body heat then swirled back around her like a wake. She moved steadily through the fog like the passing of a mighty battleship.

51

STANFORD STOOD AT his office window, staring out to where the horizon should have been.

The rain was pounding down. The downpour had started before dawn and continued unabated all morning long. So much water made for such a dreary day. He cradled the telephone to his ear and listened to Heidi, Clayton's secretary, tell him that Clayton had left the office for the day. But she gave him a name and a number at the FBI crime lab to call about the thumbprint.

He hung up and dialed the FBI lab. Corey Adams, the lab chief, had left for the day as well.

Five minutes later, he called the FBI lab again.

"Mr. Rome, it's me, Pencil Woods," the man said after he'd identified himself but before he could say what he'd called for. "Oh, you probably don't remember me," Pencil Woods said. "I ain't much to remember. You did some work for my wife and kept them IRS fools from trying to take everything she ever had."

He dove through that big opening. "Did we help her?"

"Ahh, man, shoot yeah. You even went back three more years; them jokers ended up owing her four thousand pepperonis. After paying you, she still had two fists full of dollars left over, and she didn't owe them fools a plug nickel." Pencil Woods laughed. "Well, anyway, what can I help you with today? What's that you needed from Corey? Maybe I can help you out since Corey's not here."

"I called about a thumbprint Clayton sent you, a glossy 8x10."

"Oh, shoot yeah, what do you wanna know about it? I know all about that. The darnest thing, too. Not enough points there to make a clean I. D. But Corey, he had just matched some prints he and Clayton took from a house over on Avenue *B*. I remember that cause Clayton, he went over there with Corey, you see. So I say to myself, I say, 'something's up, Pencil, when the chief go along with a tech just to lift some prints.'"

"Pencil," he said, "you got a match on that thumbprint?"

"Sure, Mr. Rome. The same print from Avenue *B*. It was the same print. It was a good guy's print, not a bad guy's print. So that was a dead end for folks over there."

"Oh?" he said. Clayton had lied to him about the thumbprint. "Whose prints were those, Pencil?"

"Your boy's. Both of 'em belonged to the war hero."

§

Stanford rang the doorbell to Clayton Westwood's home. The thinning clouds had stopped sprinkling rain, and the sun was peeking out almost cowardly through holes in the cloud cover. When Gregory Westwood opened the door and saw him, the strapping six-footer's face lit up like a street lamp.

"Mr. Rome!"

The boy exclaimed and poked out a huge hand that engulfed his as Clayton's always did. Gregory led him down into his father's office, talking a mile a minute. When Gregory left him and his father alone and closed the door, Clayton's face grew gaunt.

"I'm sorry about that, Stanford." Clayton slumped in the chair. "Pencil Woods, he called me. Said he told you about the prints."

"What's going on, Clayton? You lied to me. Why was that?"

"Shelley, he was there." Clayton slumped in the chair even farther and pulled out his pocketknife. Click.

"Shelley was there. At Katie Kane's house that night."

He sat down. He could feel a part of his brain adding that new information to what he already knew about that night. His brain was rearranging the old information based on the new information, and he looked at Clayton, almost at a loss about what to think.

Nothing clicked. The new information changed nothing.

"But Shelley, he didn't kill them," Clayton quickly added. "That I know. He was just there; that's all. He was just fucking there."

"No, Clayton. Shelley was in Miami that night. I know he was in

Miami that night. I checked. Shelley was in Miami that night."

"That day, Stanford. Shelley, he was in Miami that day."

His throat tightened. "I checked," he said. "I checked."

"Stanford, Pencil Woods has told you about the thumbprint. I'm sorry I misled you. But you weren't too forthcoming on the print yourself. I had to go through the trouble of figuring out for myself the print matched up with the piece of rubber glove you gave me a month ago to analyze. And since you gave me that thumbprint, I've learned the second bullet, the one dug out the wall, was fired from a different .44 Magnum. There were two .44 Magnums there that night—Shelley's .44 Magnum, and the killer's .44 Magnum."

"Run that by me again, Clayton. What second bullet?"

"Stanford, the bullet that killed your son was fired from a different .44 than the slug we dug out of Katie Kane's wall. The bullet we dug from the wall, that one bullet came from Shelley's .44. The bullet that killed Christopher, it came from a different .44. That's what I'm saying, Stanford. Shelley had nothing to do with the murders. But Shelley was there that night."

Then it dawned on him what Clayton was saying. "Oh, I see," he said. "The two bullets found at the—"

"We screwed up on that," Clayton said. "We assumed both bullets came from the same gun." Clayton sighed. "We just recently found out they were fired from different guns. We screwed up."

"Well," he said, "I'm sure confused now."

"Stanford," Clayton said, sighing, "the coroner, he said your son's eyes were closed at least an hour after he died. Shelley, he was the one who closed his eyes, of that, I'm sure. That puts Shelley there an hour later, after the murders had been committed. Somehow, it seems to me that Shelley had been on the killer's trail in Miami and then Shelley had followed the killer to Katie Kane's house.

"But Shelley got there an hour later, after the killer had struck and gone. In a nutshell, I believe that's how it went down. I believe that's why Shelley was there that night, Stanford."

The Thunderbird. The thought popped up in his mind like a jack-in-the-box. Clayton was right about some things, but wrong about other things. He hadn't told Clayton about the Thunderbird and the hit-and-run death of that Florida state trooper. He had to say something, even if it was something he already knew.

"Why didn't Shelley just say he was there, Clayton?"

"The migraines," Clayton said, as if he'd expected the question. "Shelley has memory problems; you know that, Stanford."

Yes, he knew that. More thoughts formed in his mind. David Harte said the murders happened around the same time Shelley's full-blown migraines started.

"Clayton, where's Shelley now?"

Clayton shook his head. "I don't have a clue. I haven't heard from him in—since I told you we were pulling off the case."

His mind was trying to conjure up a reason for Shelley to have gone there that night. He hadn't been following a killer.

It was more probable that a stranger passing through the county that night had been the killer. But the killer came and left on foot when a car was parked there just for the taking. That had always bothered him. The killer had to have already had transportation. But no tire tracks were found. Rain or no rain, they would have found tire tracks if they had been there to be seen. And nothing was stolen, but the gun. That didn't make much sense either.

But Stanford didn't believe either scenario.

The only scenario that made sense was that Shelley went there that night to kill his mother-in-law. Shelley feared Katie Kane's heart problems would sooner or later entice Stacey back to South Georgia to take care of her, and Stanford would return to South Georgia with her. That was no reason to kill her. But who said Shelley had been acting with reason. Shelley had gone there to kill her. He knew Shelley, and that scenario felt right to him. Instead, Shelley had killed Stacey by mistake and then killed Christopher to hide his terrible mistake. He believed that. Shelley then killed the trooper, who could place him within thirty miles of the scene.

Emotions swelled up inside him like a mushroom cloud. In the next few seconds, he was gasping and gawking down at the carpet in Clayton's office. He sensed Clayton standing next to him and looked up. He took the proffered towel and slowly wiped his mouth to clean away the vomit.

§

Stanford was in a very foul mood when Mark Davis slumped down beside him on the couch. He had to find out for himself if Mark had Juanita killed. His stomach was still a little tender from the retching but damn if he had time to feel sorry for himself. He had problems to solve and, of course, asses to kick.

"Stanford," Mark began, "your clients, they are beneath you. No matter how much it hurts you to hear a white man say that about a black company, it's true. You know it's true. RKL can be ten times as large. RKL can hire ten times as many AU graduates—yes, ten times as many, Stanford. Believe me, I know why you do what you do. You have this thing in your heart for your people. I commend you for that. It's really great. You're committed to those students, but let's face it, Stanford, RKL is just a feeder CPA firm for the Big-Six, those big white CPA firms. You train these rookies fresh out of college, and they leave you for greener pastures as soon as they pass the CPA exam. They all run off to the Big-Six CPA firms to suck up the big salaries, the big expense accounts, the big prestige, and to get the big heads. And you, you lose all that time and money you spent training them. So, what I'm saying, Stanford, is why not run with the big dogs for a while. That's all I'm saying. You've paid your dues to your people; now, it's time to look out for self."

Stanford glanced at the clock again, then returned his attention to Mark Davis.

"Mark, why did you have Juanita killed?" he said.

Mark's eyes slitted and turned reptilian. The lawyer slowly rose to his feet like a man who'd just been ambushed.

"Repeat that, mister, and I'll sue you till hell freezes over."

Mark left his office in a huff.

Stanford picked up the telephone.

Mark stepped on the elevator alone and pressed *Garage*. The elevator car plunged nonstop. In the garage, the doors sprang open. Mark Davis stepped out.

The first kidney punch took away Mark Davis's legs, and the attorney sank to his knees, groaning. A kick to the face broke Mark's jaw. A downward thrust popped the first kneecap. But Mark had already passed out before the second kneecap snapped.

Rain pounded the pavement outside.

§

It was ten that night when Stanford cornered David Harte in the gazebo behind David's house. David looked three sheets to the wind and wasn't at all thrilled to see him standing there.

"You again," the psychiatrist said without preamble.

"Shelley's missing," he said. "You've got to help me, David."

"All I've got to do is stay white and die," David said. "Isn't that how it goes, 'stay black and die'?"

"I suppose," he said. "David, I need your help."

"You're sure getting under my thick skin, Stanford." Then David chuckled and pointed an unsteady finger. "Be careful of what you wish for."

"David, help me."

David looked at him awhile, then looked away. "You're a good man, Stanford. And you're a damn good friend to Shelley."

David closed his eyes and combed his fingers through his hair, then he turned and looked at him again.

"Stanford, I'm going to tell you all you think you want to know about Shelley. I'll dump all this misery on your back as you want it; if that's what you want. Is that what you want, Stanford, more misery? More suffering?"

David's voice was terse. "Say it. If you want it, ask for it."

"I do want it," he said. "It's what I want. Dump it on me."

David snorted and shook his head. "Stanford, Shelley, he has the worst case of psychosis I've ever seen in all my born days. Stanford, Shelley, he's going to kill me for what I know."

He stared dumbly at David. "Ahh, David, please."

David Harte continued. "Shelley, he's going to kill me because I know too much, and that's reason enough for him. Besides, you need a conscience to justify what you do. Unfortunately though, Shelley doesn't have a conscience like you and me, Stanford. Your friend has been feeding on himself too long to have anything resembling a conscience. Shelley, he only has notches on a gun. Not a conscience. And he doesn't know the difference between the two."

David paused and rubbed his eyes.

"Here's an analogy about your friend. Shelley is not only driving that souped-up race car he's speeding around in; Shelley, he's also sitting in the backseat of that souped-up race car he's now speeding around in. In fact, Shelley may believe he IS the damn souped-up race car he's speeding around in. In the language of the street, my friend, Shelley, 'he's all fucked up in the head.'"

David's eyes were desolate, like a vacant and trashy corner lot.

"Stanford, inside Shelley there's an evil buried so deep—"

David paused then sighed heavily.

"Stanford, the only patients I've ever given up on, the people I couldn't help, have been the truly mad. I call them the 'bye-bye insane.' There's just no help for people who have no sense of space and time. Those people are hopelessly zombies. And Shelley, he's hanging onto his space and time, his sanity, by sheer willpower alone. That's what makes Shelley so damn scary. When Shelley blows up, it will be ugly. I suspect a lot of people are going to get caught up in the explosion. Including me, for sure."

David's shoulders slumped even lower.

"Stanford, did you know Shelley's foster father molested him; his foster mother knew about it. But she did nothing to stop him?"

Stanford leaned away from David. Stunned.

"What, David?" He forced a dry chuckle. "Isn't that a dangerous game, David; I mean, prying into a forty-year-old man's past to dig up childhood trauma? How can you use a child's fantasy to crucify a forty-year-old man? We all fantasized so much back then when we were kids that we couldn't tell reality if reality bit us up the crack of our butts. Hell, back then, my fantasy was my reality, for crying out loud. My dreams were even real. Frank Lester molesting Shelley, ahh, David, come on; be real. Shelley would have killed the bastard. And, I would have known about it."

David smiled like a cat with a mouthful of feathers. "You're right for the most part, Stanford. Mostly, a child's fantasy is a child's reality. But, in Shelley's case, you're wrong. I have other proof—the best proof that it happened."

"And that is?" he said. "What's this 'best proof' you have, David?"

"Shelley himself is all the proof I need. He is a predator. Not your typical natural-born-killer type, but he's someone who was conditioned as a boy to kill as a man. Severely abused as a child, even traumatized, Shelley's humanness, it never fully developed like our own humanness developed, yours and mine. Shelley is as stunted psychologically as a dwarf is stunted physically; that's what I'm saying, Stanford. Shelley's a psychological dwarf, a warped mind, a predator raging through life like a bull tearing ass through a china shop is what I'm saying to you."

He shook his head. "David, Shelley never lived with the Lesters;

I told you that. When did this alleged molesting take place?"

David studied him and sighed. "Frank Lester, how did he die, Stanford? Tell me that. How did Shelley's foster father die?"

"He fell and broke his neck; that's how. He was a drunk."

"Where was Frank when he fell and broke his neck, Stanford?"

"On his front porch. His wife found him dead that morning."

"It was the back porch," David said, lifting his eyebrows.

"No, it—you're right. Back porch. So what?"

"Where was Shelley when his foster father just happen to fall and break his neck, Stanford?"

"Shelley was home," he said.

"He was at your house, right?"

"Yes. That's what I mean, David. Shelley never spent the night at the Lesters. He slept at the homeplace, and no kid left the homeplace after dark set in. Besides, Aretha and Franklin—two 120-pound bull mastiffs—they patrolled the homeplace from sundown to sunup when we were boys.

David rubbed his eyes, sighing again.

"Stanford, Frank so traumatized Shelley that he didn't just pretend the sexual molestation wasn't happening to him. No, Shelley, he didn't just create a fantasy world to hide in while Frank was molesting him. Shelley, he didn't just become your usual schizophrenic with split personalities and all that other crap. No, Stanford, Shelley, he became much more than that."

"Yeah," he said, "he became a war hero, and the best damn FBI agent to wear a badge. That's what Shelley became. But, what Shelley is and what Shelley always will be is my best friend, and my brother."

David fidgeted. "Stanford, this may sound like it's right out of science fiction, but I'm telling you what I believe. I believe your friend, Shelley, is under someone's hypnotic control. As unbelievable as that may sound. That's what I believe."

"Ahh, David, you know hypnosis can't force a person to commit a crime against his will. There's no individual mind control. Group mind control, yes, but not one-on-one mind control."

David rubbed the back of his neck. "Okay, listen to this. I talked to the people over there in Birmingham, the ones who are raising the money to build that Medal-of-Honor Museum in Alabama.

Personally, Stanford, I've always believed Medal-of-Honor winners were either borderline psychotics before they became soldiers, or they flipped out the first time they saw blood and guts in a war and became psychotic that way. I bet, to a man, the childhoods of those brave soldiers were screaming mirrors of horror.

"The people in Birmingham told me that what Shelley did over there in Vietnam makes Audie Murphy and those other Medal-of-Honor holders look like Vienna Choirboys. The director, himself, said Shelley was the baddest of the bad when it came to killing people over there. You see, Stanford, Shelley, he can easily be hypnotized to kill. You're right. Shelley was this country's best at killing during the war. As they say in the street, 'are you up with me on this?'"

David was right, but he was defending Shelley from years of habit.

He sighed. "But who hypnotized Shelley to kill you, David? It doesn't make sense. It just doesn't add up."

"I don't know that, Stanford. But I do know that Shelley will kill under hypnosis. I do know I've never seen anyone so susceptible to hypnosis as Shelley is. It's as if someone has been hypnotizing Shelley since he was a boy. His trance is so peaceful, and so deep, and so unbelievably real to him that it just blows my mind."

"QueenBee," he said softly.

David raked his hand across his head. "I'm afraid so," the psychiatrist said.

"Well, David, I can see what you're saying has some truth in it. I can see QueenBee making Shelley easy to hypnotize. But that doesn't mean she's hypnotized him since he's been a man, and it sure doesn't mean she hypnotized him to go around killing people. Hell, David, QueenBee doesn't even know you.

"Besides, if QueenBee would have been hypnotizing Shelley as an adult, then when his migraines started up again, he would have gone back to her for treatment, don't you think?"

David stroked his chin. "Look, Stanford, let me put it to you this way. If you mistreat a boy in childhood, that boy gets even with you when he becomes a man. The man the boy becomes eventually gets back at you. The man the boy becomes, he may seem to love you, he may seem to forgive you for mistreating him when he was a boy. But it's all a trick. The man the boy becomes may not even know it's a trick. The man the boy becomes may even fool himself into believing that he's forgiven and forgotten. But it's all a trick, a mind game. Revenge is always lurking there, a chance to get even. Payback. Especially between parents and kids. You can tell how much your kids hated you as a kid by what those kids do to you, or not do for you, when you get old."

David smiled sheepishly. "It amazes me still that so many parents die and bust hell wide open, and they are shocked their adult children treated them so badly when the parents got old."

David shook his head.

"But those parents' conscious minds conveniently forgot what terrors they were when the child was young. But the child's unconscious memory stays razor sharp, never forgetting, and just waiting for the day he'd cut that parent's throat. Those cruel parents, now reaping the pain they themselves sowed, they act so hurt and innocent. And outsiders look in, and they say, 'my, what terrible children; they don't care nothing about their old parents.' But, payback's a mother between a parent and a child. Take that to the bank."

"But, David, who hypnotized Shelley to kill you?" he persisted.

David held up a trembling hand. "Wait, Stanford, let me finish. I—I know three more things you should know. One, Shelley tried to kill QueenBee with some kind of Trojan Horse. Two, Shelley sent someone a head on a silver platter. Three, Shelley knows more than he's saying about who killed your wife and son."

He started to speak, but David raised a hand, silencing him.

"Stanford, Shelley couldn't get his pound of flesh from the people who turned his early childhood into a horror show. But he's gotten a ton of flesh from other people—especially the Viet Cong. Eventually, Shelley will turn against the people who loved him and helped him, and he won't know the difference. What I'm saying is watch yourself, Stanford. No one had done more for him than you and your grandmother.

"And Shelley has already gone after her."

52

THE FIRST DAYS of summer scorched the capital city.

The sizzling ninety-five-degree heat was only occasionally eased by the early-morning or the late-evening scattered rain showers and thunderstorms.

Jocelyn had again escaped the heat of the city.

She glimpsed the Thunderbird as she neared Lake Arrowhead, and did a double-take, but she kept driving. Judge Grimes was quickly back on her mind. She had called the judge's office.

The judge's law clerk assured her the judge did not in the past nor did he now own property at Lake Arrowhead. The law clerk said the day she'd seen the judge at Lake Arrowhead, the judge had been speaking at a conference in South Rivers, New Jersey.

It all checked out, what the law clerk said. She was confused, but her "snoop" antenna said she was onto something. Her confusion motivated her to dig deeper. What a story this could be.

She neared the Lake Arrowhead guardhouse, powered the window down and crossed her fingers. She signed in, then propped an arm on the window ledge. "Larry, I just missed Shelley, and I do need to get to his place. I've only been there at night. I forgot how to get there. I'm meeting Stanford there. Can you direct me?"

"Just a sec." Larry got a map from inside the guardhouse. He opened it, pointed out the way then handed her the map.

§

Jocelyn found Shelley's cabin, but it was a struggle. The log cabin was located two miles down a dirt road in an undeveloped, some would call it rugged, portion of Lake Arrowhead.

The cabin looked spooky and uninhabited.

She had an hour's daylight left to search the place. Maybe she could find something to clear up her confusion. She took the .38 from the glove box and placed it on the seat beside her. She parked the Cherokee pointing back the way she came.

What she came looking for was a mystery to her.

Her instincts said there was a connection between what she didn't know and Shelley. She had been secretly investigating Shelley, trying to find a weakness in Stanford's armor, anything to help win him over to her way of thinking. But she got a shock.

She uncovered so many whispered rumors in law enforcement about Shelley: he was the vigilante the Miami newspapers called the Miami Assassin; he triggered Atlanta's Chaserville Massacre; he triggered the Atlanta bombing and mutilations.

Rumor after rumor after rumor.

Enough of rumors. She came to see for herself. This one could make her career—proving that Shelley did all those crazy things.

She left the key in the ignition when she got out. From the moment her left foot touched the ground she had grave second thoughts. But she dismissed her doubts and kept going. The door to the cabin was unlocked. She pushed it open, looked back over her shoulder for just a moment and slipped inside.

She flicked on a wall switch. An overhead light fixture lit up the place. She kept her hand on the switch and scanned the room. It was mostly bare: the usual appliances sat in a corner. In another quarter of the room rested a table, four chairs, three lamps, sofa, sofa chair. Gun cabinet. Weight set. A computer.

She went straight for the computer.

She saw stacks of pocket notebooks laying next to the keyboard. She picked up one, fanning the pages. It was a day diary. She put it back on the stack and opened a storage box. It was jammed with more pocket notebooks. She picked up a pocket notebook for May and perused the pages. She stopped scanning and started reading. By the time she'd read three pages, her heart was pounding ninety beats a minute. She had to pee.

Jocelyn squirmed, the words tumbling, the images spinning through her mind like a horror flick. Bible salesman…spinning…

Norman...spinning...NYC nightclub...spinning. Her mind just kept on spinning...Bryce Boyd...spinning...boardinghouse...spinning...telephone calls...spinning...IRS...spinning, spinning.

Jocelyn hugged her stomach to calm herself. Where did he get this from? Bryce? It had to be Bryce. But where did Bryce get it?

She heard a loud ruckus behind the cabin. She heard growls and angry banging. It sounded like some wild animal rattling a cage and trying to break out. She nearly pissed her pants. She hopped up and down on her toes. Each part of her anatomy wanted to escape in a different direction. The gun? On the seat. She left the damn gun on the seat! She heard something running behind the cabin, and she hurled herself at the door. The gun. She had to get to the gun. She flung the door open and lunged through the opening for the Cherokee, running, expecting, any moment, to be grabbed from behind and slammed to the ground and eaten alive.

She grabbed the door handle, jerked the door open to leap inside. Her lunge was halted in midair.

Strong hands clamped her arms from behind.

She screamed.

As soon as both feet touched the ground, she felt herself being spun around like a top. She started fighting, kicking, clawing and peeing. The strong hands released her. But the momentum of her struggle sent her falling back against the seat. Her head bounced up off the seat and locked in place. Resting back on her elbows, she found herself staring then gawking into the oldest eyes she'd ever seen on a human face.

His face was a mask of contradictions. The old black eyes glared down at her like a wild animal—no, like an alien. She knew he was going to kill her. But his face was different than his eyes. He had the fresh look of a boy in the face, an eagerness to believe something—anything—an innocence. He was studying her. She was too terrified to speak, scared all the way down to her wet panties. It was his eyes; it was as if he knew something she didn't know, or did she know something he didn't know? Something in his old eyes had changed just that quickly. From understanding to confusion? From hate to...to—what? Sorrow? Sadness? Regret?

Something in the mountain air between them connected, as if they had traded places—No, it was not that real. It was a fiction.

317

They hadn't traded places. Their ghosts had traded places, or was it their memories trading places? She was dumbfounded by the crazy images floating around inside her head. Either he would kill her or he wouldn't.

Her heart was beating up into her throat.

He backed away from the open door. She felt as if he were sucking light from her with those cold black eyes of his, searching and staring almost aimlessly—like that 1,000-yard stare she had heard so much about, but had never before seen.

Those old eyes leaped from her eyes to the whole of her face as if he'd just taken a snapshot of her ghost. The way his eyes sucked in her face was almost motherly. The heat of his glare diminished her mounting fear he was going to rip her apart. She now knew he wouldn't hurt her. He pointed at her. His lips moved but no words came out. So, he gestured with his head for her to just leave.

Her relief was so totally overwhelming that it took all her will-power to keep from throwing her arms around his neck and kissing him—in spite of those cold black eyes.

She scooted behind the wheel without taking her eyes off his face. She found the ignition switch and eased her foot over to the gas pedal. He was staring even more intently at her face. She turned the ignition key. The engine sprang to life. She pulled the door shut, her eyes still on his face.

She pulled the shifter into "drive" and pressed the gas pedal. The truck moved. In seconds, his image appeared in her rearview mirror, still watching her. She felt so at ease the calm scared her.

She had been afraid until they had looked at each other—face-to-face—for the first time in their lives that she knew of.

She was not afraid now. But her stomach felt hot, sour and boiling, and bile trickled up into her throat. She nearly gagged on the bitterness—the acidity. She pulled over to the side of the road.

She opened the door, dropped to the ground and vomited.

When she heaved on empty, she stood, wiping her mouth with the back of her hand and looking back the way she'd come.

A half mile back, she could see the Thunderbird pulled over to the side of the road. Shelley was standing in front of it, binoculars pinned to his face, watching her.

53

HIS SAD EYES stared back down at the printout as if his gaze could somehow make the ink soak back up into the paper, and make the words vanish from his mind completely.

"This will kill him," he muttered.

"Kill who?" QueenBee said from the doorway, key in her hand.

QueenBee listened as Colt told what spewed off the printer.

"There's no doubt about it, huh, Colt; I mean about Shelley?"

"None," Colt said. "Shelley, he was there that night."

"How did the blood get there, on the bible, I mean?"

"Shelley, he tore a hole in his glove when he was in Katie Kane's bedroom. When Shelley closed Christopher's eyes he got blood on his thumb, and then he'd picked up the bible and stuck it up on the bookshelf. That's where Stanford found it, and that's how Christopher's blood got on Shelley's thumb. Stanford, he gave the thumbprint to the FBI. It's Shelley's thumbprint."

Her chest tightened, and breath became a burden. "That's a lot of dumb things for Shelley to do, you reckon?"

"Shelley's not Shelley anymore, QueenBee."

"Sure, you're right, Colt. Sure, you're right. Shelley, he's for sure not Shelley anymore."

She rattled the dice with the singsong cadence of a timber rattler. Her mind retreated into the past.

They sat in silence.

She finally focused her eyes back on the Twofer County detective. She cleared her throat and spoke easily.

"Colt, as a child before Shelley came to the homeplace, Shelley, he'd been so beaten and so mistreated by his folks and by people not his folks. His poor crazy mama, Emma Whitfield, she tried to kill Shelley as soon as he was born, as soon as she laid eyes on her son that first time; she tried to be rid of him. I got that from the midwife who delivered Shelley into the world. For that breach of motherly love, the state locked his mother away for four years.

"The thing to know is that Emma rejected Shelley from day one. That's the worst thing that can happen to a new baby. Colt, a rejected child spends the rest of its born days getting even with the rest of the world. Punishing the world for what its own mother had done to it from jump street. That's the pity."

She swallowed and rattled the dice to the cadence of cicadas.

"Colt, when I first laid eyes on Shelley, he was nine years old. Shelley, he was so unloved. Shelley was born into a family of crazy folks, and I mean, bouncing-off-the-wall crazy folks. I don't know if that craziness came from inbreeding or what. His daddy, Isaiah Whitfield, he was the biggest of the crazies, but he had an excuse for how crazy he was. You see, Isaiah, he got shell shocked in the Second Great War, you know. The government sent Isaiah a check for a while, then the government locked Isaiah up and lost the key. And for good reason, the government lost the key. Isaiah, he did a Charles Manson on two people for no other reason than Isaiah was bent crooked beyond straightening out. As twisted and brittle as a pretzel, Isaiah was."

She sucked in more slow breaths, saw the furrows digging into Colt's brow. She smiled and said, "I'm okay. I'm just feeling Shelley's pain, that's all. Just feeling my boy's pain.

"Now, as I was saying. Emma Whitfield, she got sent away for four years for trying to smother Shelley. But the state let her out, and she got pregnant all over again. She had a girl that time, and that's when Isaiah did that Charles Manson on those folks I told you about. The state locked Isaiah away for good that time. Poor Emma, with Isaiah gone, she nutted up big time. The government hauled her back to the crazy house and locked her up for good."

She rattled the dice, slowly, softly, the sound mimicking a somber New Orleans funeral march down Bourbon Street.

"Shelley's mother's sister, she took Shelley in after that. She was a nut case, herself, but the sister, she was blood family. That aunt, she just beat Shelley so black and blue the government snatched Shelley away before the aunt got around to killing Shelley, chopping him up, and feeding Shelley to her hogs as slop. That's how nutty she was. Damn crazies, they all were, I'm telling you. Next came another relative and another whacko, and a snake charmer, to boot. Same thing, same result, things didn't work out. So then the government got smart and stuck Shelley in an orphanage.

"Now, we're getting close to when our paths crossed, Shelley's and mine. Frank and Gaylene Lester, they took Shelley from that orphanage when he was nine years old. But in some ways when we met, Shelley, he was like a newborn—in a world of people who loved him, who really loved him.

"Two nights after the adoption, I woke up to find Gaylene whining at my doorstep. The poor woman's hair stood on her head like weeds. She told me that Shelley was waking up all through the night, screaming his fool head off.

"Gaylene, she was not one for putting up with foolishness like that. She had been gnawed down to her last nerve. She was hauling Shelley back to the orphanage at first light. When that child heard the word 'orphanage' he put a clamp on my leg I couldn't shake loose. That's when a strange thing happened."

QueenBee paused and the beat of the dice fell silent in her fist.

"Frank, he changed his mind. He said they would keep the boy, if I agreed to keep trying to get rid of his screaming fits. Frank's behavior didn't make sense to me until five years later when Shelley was fourteen. I'll get to that later.

"So, Colt, the next day, Gaylene, Frank and I, we made a deal. The Lesters stayed the adopted parents. But Shelley, he lived with me and Stanford. As Shelley got older, I saw more and more of his demons, and I buried his demons deeper and deeper down inside Shelley's tortured soul. I did it just so Shelley, he could grow up somewhat normal, you see. Normal, like the rest of you boys.

"Colt, one night, Shelley got bad sick. You boys had gone night swimming and Shelley, he swallowed something that griped him up bad inside. That's when I found where Frank had been loving the boy too much for too long. I decided right then to horsewhip Frank Lester to within an inch of his sorry life."

She snorted. "Lucky for Frank, he got drunk and broke his neck before I got my hands on him. But I took care of that demon for Shelley, too. I gazed even deeper into Shelley's eyes, and I buried that devil deep down there with the rest of those sorry experiences Shelley had lived through as a child. And now Shelley is suffering through them all again as a man."

QueenBee rattled the dice in her fist and kept up the cadence.

"Colt, I may have pushed so many horrible deeds, so deep down inside the boy Shelley, that maybe I ruptured the man Shelley's soul. Maybe I tore life right out of Shelley, as surely as if I'd gutted him with a butcher knife."

She rattled the dice continuously, sorrowfully, a whining clatter.

"Those demons, Colt, they stayed buried deep down inside Shelley until that Vietnam War set those demons free."

QueenBee studied Colt's face, the dice dancing and clacking together in a rhythm, the bones singing their sad and sorry song.

"That devilish Vietnam War undid all I had done since Shelley had been nine years old. The army, in all its wisdom, shipped Shelley overseas, him and his demons. Those demons that I had buried six minds deep, they all broke free of the shackles I'd slapped on them years earlier. Those demons, Colt, they were the ones who killed all those colored people over there across that pond.

"Those demons, they were the ones who won for Shelley that Medal of Honor that he dished into the Timseesee River. When Shelley dragged back home from that horrible war, I couldn't bury those demons back down in the cavern of his mind anymore. The demons, now they were one Medal of Honor too strong for me to ferret out of there. So I did the next best thing to putting a bullet in Shelley's head myself. I let those demons be. Shelley's hunger to kill another man was inside him to stay until he died."

The bones sang, and kept on singing their sorrowful song.

"When Shelley came home with those medals and ribbons and citations and such, he was already loaded, cocked, and locked.

"All I did was aim that killing machine at a real target. And aim Shelley at a target, I did, Colt. Aim Shelley at a target, I did."

She shivered from the memories, echoed by the bones, moaning. She kept right on telling it, and the bones kept right on singing it.

"But inside Shelley there's a good man buried beneath all that pain. Shelley, he was a good boy. Shelley, he would rather Frank do what Frank did, as long as Frank didn't send him back to that orphanage. Shelley, he figured that if Frank loved him that way, so be it as long as Frank loved him."

She sighed and the dice lost their voice. She set the dice aside and picked up an envelope, tapping it softly into her palm.

"Since that war, Colt, Shelley, he'd always come to the home-place for relief I gave him. Then Shelley, one day, he stopped coming, as you know. Now, Shelley, he's back killing again, and Shelley, he's forgetful, not knowing enemies from friends anymore."

She gave Colt the envelope. "Stanford sent this. Read it."

Colt opened the envelope. He read the note inside, and for the second time that day, disgust crunched up the face of the Twofer County detective. Now Colt knew what she knew.

Shelley sent that Trojan Horse that killed Big Flossie.

A psychiatrist had removed that post-hypnotic suggestion she had given for Shelley to return to the homeplace. The psychiatrist had undone what she had done. That made matters worse. Shelley would now self-destruct. She knew that.

"Colt, I unshackled Shelley's demons. I sent him to take out certain gangsters. But now things have gone terribly wrong. Shelley, he's is out of my control. I've got to do something about that. Any question about what I've said so far?"

"Yes," said the Twofer County detective, "whatever happened to Shelley's baby sister?"

§

Bertha ushered Josh into the library where the motorcyclist gave QueenBee an envelope embossed with the logo of Imperial Funeral Home. She read the note inside and studied on it.

When QueenBee scratched Aretha's ear, Aretha licked her hand, and Franklin yawned. When she scratched Franklin's ear, Franklin licked her hand, and Aretha yawned.

Why would Shelley obey her now and deliver this man to Twofer County when he ignored her other suggestions? Was Shelley still under her control or wasn't he? Had the psychiatrist undone what she'd done or hadn't he? Stanford's note said that he had. But no matter. She turned to Josh.

"Josh, go tell Jennifer I need her; tell her to bring her airplane when she comes; tell her to leave Top Cat home when she comes.

"And, Josh, when you fetch Jennifer, go tell Colt that Jennifer's flying him to the mountains."

"Mutts," she said. Aretha and Franklin rose off their haunches. "Go to work."

The bull mastiffs came alive, energy surging through them, and they bolted through the doggie door.

Now alone, QueenBee prepared herself to meet Rooster for the first time in over thirty-five years. Jake Keller was bringing Rooster over to the homeplace.

The sheriff had kept Rooster locked down in the Twofer County jail for two weeks now. He was held down in that special cell few people knew about. She slumped in her rocking chair and started a slow rock, her mind rocking along as well. Soon she was rocking away the years, remembering vividly that first time she laid eyes on the man she named Rooster.

She went rocking back into time, the images she saw sharp enough to draw blood, rocking and rocking back into time.

§

QueenBee heard footsteps rising and falling behind her.

The forty-eight-year-old QueenBee had walked six miles into the backwoods of the South Georgia Deep. The sun was a mere head above the treetops. A twig snapped to the right and to the rear of her, and she stopped walking and listened.

She walked on.

Twenty minutes later, the shack popped into view.

The living woods had all but gobbled up her getaway place.

Stan Rome had called the shack their castle, but she saw the shack as a gingerbread house sweetened by the molasses of their undying love and everlasting devotion to each other. Today was the fourth anniversary of the day her man died—with his boots on.

Auld lang syne swept over her like a gush of wind. She longed for times gone past long ago. There was a time when those woods throbbed like a heartbeat. The skinners cursed and grunted and drove stubborn mules deeper into the thick forest of pine trees.

The skinners and their beasts of burden, slaved to harvest the precious crops of timber. The cantankerous men waged hand-to-hand combat with pine trees, mules, timber rattlers, and the stifling heat in the backwoods of the mighty South Georgia Deep.

QueenBee glanced around.

She saw nothing but absolute proof of what time can do to all things, especially to all things man-made. Stan Rome's castle had been of shifting sand and would soon be blown away. Greedy time had nibbled away all but the crumbs of her gingerbread house.

When she stepped inside the shack, a hot stench smacked her face. The smell of blood was strong. A click to her left, and she snapped out her gun, pointing, looking, turning, searching out who to shoot. She saw two click beetles scuttle from a corner and eased her grip on the gun.

"A bit jittery today, old girl," she muttered and put away the pistol Stan Rome had bought her the same day he found three strangers on their land hanging from a tree by their necks. The bodies had been mutilated and torched.

She stepped closer to a crumbling wall, saw the unexpected and again snapped out her .38. Those tiny legs had left behind a faint trail of red. She peeped around the corner, saw a shoe and drew her head back.

"Roscoe," she said. "You over there. You trespassing. You gotta skedaddle from here. This is private property you squatting on."

The shoe didn't move.

She peeped farther around the corner and saw the man. He lay on the floor. His back was propped against the wall at an awkward angle, a gun stuck under his shirt, the muzzle aimed her way. The boyish face showed a massive will to live, but his gut was bloated like a melon. The man could have been a dinosaur lizard, the way his long legs curled up under him like a tail.

"I—I—," the creature muttered.

"I know, Roscoe, I know. You gonna shoot me down like a dog, you are. One fancy trick to pull on an old fart like me, if you can. Roscoe, you look worse than some dead folks I done seen. You look fit enough for a South Georgia dirt bed, I say."

She stuck her gun in her hip holster and stepped closer to the man. "Look at you, holding a gun on a woman old enough to be your mama. Oughta make your own mama real proud, I bet."

She squatted in front of the man's desiccated face. His pale gray rubbery skin was stretched tight across a gaunt face stamped with the unmistakable stress of death. He was ripe for the graveyard. What had this man been like before meeting this end?

His hair was thin and stringy like every other strand was dead and gone. She imagined his hair once hung long and bronze and thick. He looked forty by the pain in his face, but she imagined him to be no more than twenty-five years old. His long elephant ears dangled like glad hands all ready to clap.

For the man to laugh, she imagined he would have just reared back that big head and bellowed. His belly laugh would make fluttering hearts skip entire beats, and she bet his world just had to have been one great big barrel of fun, she just knew.

She whiffed gangrene and scooted away from the stench.

"My, my, Roscoe, you got yourself more troubles than the Okie got water snakes, let me tell you."

The man's brow was slick. Hot sweat mingling with the cool dew on his skin left a sheen on his handsome face. She touched his brow. Hot. She pushed up an eyelid. Nothing. The flesh had a sponginess to it as if cotton balls lay under the skin. How he'd fought off shock for so long was a mystery to her.

"Does your mama still draw breath somewhere?" she said to the unconscious man. "Your papa, is he walking around upright?" She stroked his brow. "Who cries for you when you're no longer here to cry for yourself?"

The man's head toppled over into her lap.

"My, my, what's inside this big head of yours—lighter stumps?"

She lifted the man's shirt and jerked her head back, gawking. "Jesus Christ! Sneak a peek, take a look."

She roared with laughter.

Standing as straight, if not as tall, as a South Georgia longleaf pine was the longest, skinniest dick she'd ever seen. She stopped guffawing and pushed up the man's other eyelid. The smoky veil over that eyeball too lacked that three-dimensional gaze so indicative of a welcome mat, that was so telling of when someone was at home or not at home—nobody home. Still she couldn't just sit by and let this dying man die.

How could she let death walk away with this man after all Carrie Rome had taught her about compassion? How could she not use her healing talents and still live with herself? She'd saved dying folks before, even some already up to their necks inside a South Georgia dirt bed.

But this fellow stretched out in front of her now was already up to his eyeballs in death. Her hands were as busy as her mind, and before she realized it, she'd stripped the man naked. She chewed oak leaves to keep from vomiting and kept patching up the man's holes the best she could. She poked intestines back inside from where they leaked, muscles quivering like quality horseflesh. That was when she spied the puncture marks on his right side. Her stomach resisted; and she scooted away from the man again.

"My, my, Roscoe."

She tugged on an ear lobe. "You couldn't quite figure out which way to die this fine South Georgia morning, I see. Didn't you know snakes had fangs and could bite you? Sure snakes bite. Snakes bite all the time. That's what fangs are for, didn't you know that?"

She slumped back against the crumbling doorway and gazed out across the thick stand of loblolly pines. The dying man's chances had been slim, at best. Now all bets were off. If he'd been up to his eyeballs in a dirt bed, he was now up to the top of his brow. Nothing she could do—unless—What if?

What if—what about the mushrooms? She glanced back at the man struggling to draw breath. He had nothing left to lose that he wasn't already losing. He was dying just as surely as she sat watching him leave this world.

But what if he had a reaction to those mushrooms? Easy enough to answer. He'll be dead before she could apologize for feeding them to him. Or he could have a delayed reaction like some folks had, and he could go mad and become a danger to himself and a danger to everybody around him. But since he was already dead up to his brow anyway, so why not the mushrooms?

If he still kicked the bucket, so what? He was kicking it anyway.

She hurried down to the great oak.

Embedded in the rich black soil, under the oak's wide canopy of leaves, grew her precious mushrooms.

She picked one, held it lovingly in her hand, and whiffed it. In her hands, the deadly mushrooms were a tonic that started healing on contact and a powerful stimulant that sparked a demonic zest to live. They will get rid of that old gangrene and heal his torn organs and muscles. The snakebite was a cinch to fix.

The man gasped. She worked quicker.

§

The sheriff stood the tall man in the middle of QueenBee's library. Rooster was blindfolded and gagged, shirtless and pale. His collar was an electronic model.

Aretha and Franklin sat on their haunches between QueenBee and the tall man, their black piercing eyes aimed like lasers on the tall man's face.

QueenBee studied Rooster's face. Her memory shot back thirty-five years into the past.

Rooster's hair was thinner, but those ears, they still stuck out like two glad hands ready to clap. This was Rooster.

Rooster's head wasn't as big but neither was her own head as big as it used to be. She stepped back and took in a face that could still make fluttering hearts skip whole beats.

She stepped closer to Rooster. The two bull mastiffs crowded in, keeping their heft between QueenBee and the tall man. When she reached out to touch Rooster, Aretha let go a deep snarling warning. She dropped her hand and looked at Aretha.

"Aretha, I do believe this man understands he's not to move. So go drop your rump in a corner."

Aretha slunk away and drop her heavy body in the corner.

She looked down at Franklin. "What about you?"

Franklin yawned.

She turned back to Rooster. She touched Rooster's left side just below his ribs. The man recoiled from her touch. When she traced her fingertips over Rooster's stomach, she frowned. She felt along Rooster's right side just below his ribs and got another shock.

She shot Jake an incredible look.

"This is the wrong Rooster."

54

TWOFER COUNTY

FRIDAY, JUNE 24

JOHAN BONNELL FELT woozy. He was suffering major stress from a severe lack of sleep. He'd been awake for forty-nine hours. The reclusive real-estate tycoon felt weak and irritable, and he was sick to his stomach with dread and despair.

Jones was right.

She couldn't be trusted. He gulped another cognac and burped. That old woman was going to kill him, for sure. He clutched the empty glass like a baseball, cursed like a sailor and hurled the glass smashing into the wall like a maniac.

He grunted satisfaction then pressed his palms to his temples, suffering his agony wordlessly and mute. Rashad bounded into the room, quickly sized up the situation, and melted back out of sight.

Johan clenched his fists. Who did she think she was, ordering him around like he was a servant and a slave? But who was he kidding? His fist unfolded. He had to go, and he knew he had to go. Poor Barbra and the kids. The shame of his gangster past would be a big burden for his family to bear.

He had lived a full life. She wanted him. Not his family. She wanted to kill him. Not his family. She just wanted to shame and humiliate him in front of his family. Then she would kill him. So if he went and took his medicine, Barbra and the kids would be safe. Then so be it. He could always kill himself.

But she warned him about that, too.

Johan knocked down one more drink before stretching his long frame out on the sofa. Drowsiness puddled like water around his ankles. His shallow breathing grew deeper. Johan's thirty-five-year nightmare continued to roll inside his mind like a slasher movie.

§

RELIEF HEADED SOUTH, the headlines promised.

A high-pressure area kept shoving a cold front toward suffering Twofer County. Left in its wake were thunderstorms and a simmering warmth. Gone was the 100-degree heat of the past three days. Meanwhile, more hot, humid days lay ahead for South Georgia and Twofer County.

Standing by the hangar housing Jennifer Stanley's eight-passenger Bell helicopter, Colt watched the Lear 31 break down through the clouds and streak for touchdown at the Twofer County Airport. Thunderclaps roared faraway like cannon fire. Over the past hour, the temperature had dropped twenty degrees, and the humidity had soared twenty points.

The sleek jet whooshed in over the treetops, wobbling like an albatross. The rubber wheels skirted the runway, and white smoke puffed up from the tires of the aerodynamic jewel shaped like a rocket ship. The swift-looking jet roared to the hangar and stopped a few hundred feet from Jennifer's idling helicopter. The steps of the jet unfolded smoothly to the ground. A tall man appeared in the doorway like a messiah and stared out over the tarmac.

Johan Bonnell turned and glanced back inside the Lear 31 at his children one more time. Johan saw the confusion and dread in their faces. Their distress saddened him. So here they were. He'd done as QueenBee ordered him to do. He'd gathered his brood and beat it on down to Twofer County, posthaste.

Johan Bonnell tugged at the lapel of his jacket and turned away from the eyes of his children. He stared out at the waiting helicopter, rotors spinning. That time machine was going to fly him thirty-five years back into his goddamn past. He gnawed the inside of his lip. Dear God, have mercy on me and mine, he prayed. Then he descended like a man walking up the steps to the gallows.

For the third time in his life, and for the first time in thirty-three years, Johan Bonnell stepped down onto Twofer County soil.

§

Colt rubbed the back of his neck as the parade of people walked past him. Where were all those people coming from? Two hours ago, another Lear Jet had landed. He just couldn't make sense of all the people. Jennifer had already made three flights into the deep backwoods. What was all the commotion about? He hated that QueenBee was keeping him in the dark and out the loop.

She said he had more important things to do.

Colt studied the airplane that was flying him to Lake Arrowhead and back, and he worried about Top Cat. He had hoped Jennifer was going to be pushing that stick instead of that empty-minded brother of hers. Top Cat scared the hell out of him last time, and he almost shot the fool while they were still up in the air—just the two of them. Colt saw Top Cat bouncing toward him like a kid let out to play for the first time in a week.

The Twofer County detective groaned.

"Whaddaya say, Colt .45. Hope you ready to get on up there and play grab-ass with the Almighty Lord God?"

Without any hesitation at all, Colt pulled out the long-barreled .38 Police Special and flipped out the cylinder. He made a scene of checking the cylinder and a bigger scene of clicking the cylinder back in place with a snap. Colt glanced at Top Cat.

"A nice day for dying—Oops, I mean flying," he said.

Top Cat's grin went south of the border.

§

The Honorable U. S. District Judge Justin Grimes appeared in the doorway of the Lear 31. He too paused in the doorway. He stared up at the clouds tumbling in over the pine trees before he too descended the steps like a man venturing off into the vast unknown.

Johan Bonnell, his family, and Justin Grimes piled into the helicopter for the last leg of their two-legged journey from North Chicago. With a heavy load, the whirlybird lifted off the ground and rose high into the sky. The copter spun on a dime then scooted for the backwoods of the South Georgia Deep.

Back into time, when, and back to a place, where, fate changed QueenBee's life forever.

Back to a time.

Back to a place.

Justin Grimes closed his eyes. He remembered the tale QueenBee had told him. How incredible a tale it was for him to hear. He had lived his whole life without knowing his mother, but he would be seeing his mother soon. QueenBee hadn't told him that. But his mother, she waited at the end of this helicopter ride. He felt his mother would be there as strongly as he felt his intestines tighten like coiled springs, his mother would be there.

For the first time in his lonely life, Justin Grimes surrendered himself into the arms of self-pity.

He felt so sorry for himself.

§

QueenBee sat calm in the eye of a gathering storm. She'd nabbed the wrong Rooster but no matter. When the man saw Willie Butts laying out the tools of his trade, the impostor spilled his guts about the real Rooster. And now here they were—all of them.

The impostor's name was Jocko Jitt, the identical twin of Johan Bonnell—her Rooster. His man Charles Jones had intentionally taken Fred Junior down to Miami Beach to nab the wrong man.

For over thirty years she'd hunted Rooster. Each time she'd gone to Atlanta to visit Justin at the Stanhope School for Boys when he was a boy, she'd met with private investigators. She'd hired them to hunt down Rooster, the man she now knew to be Johan Bonnell.

When Jocko Jitt told her where the real Rooster lived in North Chicago, she sent Justin to fetch Rooster for her. So now she had the real Rooster. She would try him before the eyes of his family, find him guilty of his crimes, then shoot him dead in front of the entire courtroom. And damn the consequences.

Those were her intentions. Her intentions were just.

§

In the deep backwoods of the South Georgia Deep, U. S. District Court Judge Justin Grimes sat behind the raised bench of Queen-Bee's custom-built courtroom. He was handsomely robed.

QueenBee listened to Justin explain the procedures of her kangaroo court. The paneled courtroom was genuine all the way down to the cameras overhead recording the proceedings. Six TV monitors ringed the room. For now, the screens were dark.

Justin's law clerk, Faye Boatman, was the court reporter.

The five spectators were Barbra Bonnell, Rooster's wife; Theodore Bonnell and Joetta Bonnell, Rooster's teenaged children. Jocko Jitt, Rooster's brother. Gerald Schwartz, Rooster's's physician.

The defense attorney was George Bonnell, Rooster's son. The

prosecutor was Fred Wainwright Junior. QueenBee and Bertha McConico were the witnesses who would testify against Rooster.

Justin banged the gavel again.

"Let's let the trial begin. This is a case of Queen Beatrice Rome aka QueenBee of Twofer County, Georgia versus Johan Bonnell of North Chicago, Illinois aka Rooster."

Justin turned to Faye Boatman. "The reporter will now read the charges QueenBee brought before this court by accusation."

Justin then turned his attention to Johan Bonnell. "The defendant will rise to hear reading of the charges against him."

Johan Bonnell stood beside his defense attorney son, George Bonnell, and Faye Boatman read the charges.

"The good people of Twofer County charge Johan Bonnell, aka Rooster, with malicious rape and first-degree murder."

Johan pleaded not guilty. The proceedings continued.

Fred Junior rose and made his opening statement.

"Ladies and gentlemen, we will prove that on the night of 15 September 1953, the defendant did maliciously rape a Twofer County citizen, and the defendant did indeed kill in cold blood one of our citizens. Thank you."

George Bonnell gave the defense's opening argument.

"Ladies and gentlemen, we the defense will refute each charge most vigorously. There was no rape. Rather, the accuser victimized the accused. There was no murder. It was an open-and-shut case of self-defense. The defendant was, himself, violently attacked in the dead of night. And in the heat of the fight, the passion of the battle, the defendant did find a gun on the ground.

"The defendant did, indeed, pick up said gun, and the defendant would have used said gun to defend his life, except the attacker charged into the gun held by the defendant. It was that charge into the defendant that caused the gun to fire prematurely. That gun, ladies and gentlemen, did not belong to the accused; no, that gun, ladies and gentlemen, that gun did, in fact, belong to the accuser. The defendant never knew a wild shot killed a man. That is just one more unproven charge in a long list of unproven..."

§

Justin watched the scenario unfolding in the courtroom, and he stroked his chin. These people here were his family. At the tender age of thirty-four, he'd found his family. But his mother? Where was she? Was Barbra Bonnell his mother? Justin sighed, shifting his thoughts onto the people in the courtroom.

What QueenBee was doing was wrong. He had no choice but to stop her from killing Johan Bonnell, the man she called Rooster. In QueenBee's mind, her kangaroo court was lawful, and killing Johan Bonnell was justice. He knew better. Killing Johan Bonnell would be cold-blooded murder.

He had to stop QueenBee from killing the man he now knew to be his father.

Fred Junior rose to his feet. "Your Honor, I call my first witness, Miss Bertha McConico, to the witness stand."

Justin pursed his lips. He knew all along Bertha was involved in this thirty-five-year-old mystery. She and QueenBee were connected at the hip. When QueenBee took the witness stand later on, then he would really learn things he knew nothing about.

Bertha took the stand, was given the preliminaries. Fred Junior paced in front of the witness stand before he spoke.

"Miss McConico, when and where did you first see the defendant?"

"August 26, 1953, in the deep backwoods," Bertha said.

"Miss McConico," Fred Junior said, "please tell this court about meeting the defendant on August 26, 1953."

"Well, Rooster—that's the name QueenBee gave him back then, he was back-shot twice. He was snake-bit by that ol' timber rattler. Rooster, he was ate up with that ol' gangrene. QueenBee, she snatched that dead man up out of a South Georgia dirt bed, for sure, and QueenBee, she put Rooster back up on his feet like he was superman. I was a witness to this miracle."

"Miss McConico," Fred Junior said, "please tell this court some things QueenBee did to save the defendant's life."

Bertha cleared her throat and continued.

"QueenBee, she sewed Rooster up where his gut was split open by that gun, and QueenBee, she dressed Rooster down where he was bit by that timber rattler. QueenBee, she flushed Rooster out because he was sick from that gangrene, and QueenBee, she fed Rooster mushroom brew and roots and herbs, and QueenBee, she kept Rooster's wounds clean. QueenBee, she made Rooster's bowels move, and QueenBee, she made Rooster go, so Rooster would live. It was like QueenBee, herself, was God and she made Rooster from her own ribs, and then QueenBee, she blew breath back into Rooster when Rooster had no breath."

"Excuse me, Miss McConico," Fred Junior said, "but how could you and QueenBee do all these things if the defendant was unconscious all this time. He'd been unconscious, right?"

Bertha leaned forward. "QueenBee, she chewed Rooster's food up in her own mouth. Then QueenBee, she shoved that same food down Rooster's throat and down into his gullet. QueenBee, she shoved enemas up Rooster's own rump to make Rooster dump. That's how QueenBee did it all while Rooster, he slept the sleep of dead folks."

Bertha was telling about the first time they met up with Rooster. But she would tell about that second time she met the murdering, raping kidnapper.

After that second meeting with Rooster, she became very wary of strangers in Twofer County. That was when she got her first set of bull mastiffs. Breeding a bulldog with one of the biggest dogs in the world was a great idea. The bull mastiff was fearless, powerful, loyal, tenacious, intelligent, and, most of all—big. And they were one of the most stubborn and bullheaded, for obvious reasons, dogs to manage and control. They only lived about eight or nine years. She would soon be getting her fifth set of Arethas and Franklins.

Bertha rose from the witness stand and drew her attention.

Fred Junior spoke up. "Your Honor, I call Miss Queen Beatrice Rome to the witness stand."

55

STANFORD DROVE FROM Atlanta under low black clouds. He arrived at Lake Arrowhead numb of body, mind, and soul.

The only experience that came close to the agony he now felt after confronting Clayton yesterday was the agony of finding the lifeless bodies of his wife and son.

Much of what people did in life he understood.

That Jocelyn Slade was not Alice Cooper, he understood burying the bad past for the sake of having a better future. That Mark Davis had Juanita Robeson killed, he even understood greed, the motive for what Mark did. That James Kelsey was a crook, he had no problem understanding James wanting to help the cause of black people his way. That Shelley sent QueenBee that car bomb, he halfway understood that QueenBee and Shelley were on the outs and were after each other. That Shelley killed Consy's friend Karon, he understood that Shelley was an unconscionable killer who didn't want Karon to give CapCity computer disks to Consy and expose CapCity as a money-laundering outfit. That Shelley went there that night to kill Katie Kane, he understood that Shelley saw her as an enemy to his plan. That Shelley never said he had been at Katie Kane's house that night, he understood the connection between the brain's migraines and the mind's forgetfulness.

He could understand almost anything a person did in life.

But for Shelley to know what happened that night and to keep that knowledge from him. That he did not, would not, understand.

No way Shelley knew who the killer was. If Shelley knew that, then the killer was already dead. There was no doubt in his mind about that. But where was Shelley? If Shelley was hiding out at Lake Arrowhead as Jud said, then why couldn't he find him? He'd checked every building on the compound, but still no Shelley.

Since Shelley and the guards were close, he couldn't ask them for the obvious reason the guards would warn him. Then Shelley would crawl under a bigger rock. He sent word to QueenBee telling her what David Harte had told him about Shelley.

He had second thoughts about doing that. QueenBee might send someone after Shelley. He hoped his grandmother knew Shelley would kill whomever she sent for sure.

He stopped at the Lake Arrowhead guardhouse. "Hi, Larry."

"You got company, Stanford," Larry said. "Ms. Slade. If she's not at your place, she's over at Cap'n place."

The shock registered on his face before he had time to mask his surprise. He winged it anyway. "Where did she head first, to my place or Shelley's place?"

Larry told him, adding, "And I'm afraid I've got some bad news. Hot off the wire. Mr. Davis, he died from that beating them thugs gave him yesterday. Died in the hospital, ten minutes ago. Just got the word. Didn't know the man at all, just seen him around. I'm just passing along what I heard."

Mark Davis was dead.

Stanford followed the paved road until it became a dirt road.

Mark Davis was dead.

He drove the rutted path, his rifle and knives in the backseat now. His mouth was dry. Harsh images of prison cells, prison walls, prison showers, prison guards haunted his thinking.

Mark Davis was dead.

He drove faster, running away from what he'd done. He hit the brakes, swerved into a ninety-degree turn and drove even faster.

Mark Davis was dead!

He slammed on the brakes, the sedan swerving, and he fought the wheel, the rear end of the car fishtailing dangerously, the car thumping to a stop six inches from the trunk of a fifty-foot pine.

Mark Davis was dead. He stared through the underbrush at the small cabin standing fifty yards off the road. He forced prison and Mark Davis from his thoughts and cut the engine. He got out with his rifle and looked up. Lightning zipped across the sky through the clouds and left thunder roaring in its wake.

Mark Davis was dead.

Again he forced prison and Mark Davis from his thoughts and went inside the cabin. He turned on the lights.

The overhead light fixture shone bright. Stanford noticed the computer gear in the corner. He didn't know Shelley was so involved with computers. He had to pressure Shelley to carry a small pocket computer to help him remember things. He took a quick tour of the cabin.

Half the cabin was one great room; a fourth of the space went to the tiny kitchen and eating area, and another part of the room consisted of a table, chairs, and small living area with music and weights. Storage boxes were lined up against one wall alongside a red toolbox and three canvas bags.

Small notebooks littered the space around the computer, and a storage box was filled with notebooks. Shelley had carried those notebooks around to help him remember things before he started carrying the pocket computer. The Brain, Shelley called it.

Mark Davis was dead.

Stanford found the first bedroom locked, and the second one filled with boxes. He heard rustling behind the locked door of the first bedroom. He lifted the rifle muzzle, listening.

"Who's in there?" he called out and cupped an ear to the door. He thought he heard a baby shaking a rattle and cooing.

He leaned the rifle against the wall, took a pry bar from the toolbox and popped the lock on the door. He nudged the door open with the muzzle of the rifle. He saw where the cooing was coming from. But that was no baby. The man sitting on the floor in the center of the empty bedroom wore a dog collar on his neck. His feet were shackled to a chain bolted to the floor, and one hand was handcuffed to a waist chain that was also attached to the shackles on the man's legs. Then he heard the real noisemakers—three huge timber rattlers. They sure grew them big in North Georgia.

The snakes made his skin quiver. Two snakes were five-footers. A third looked like a six-footer. The little man was almost insane with fear and lack of sleep. He was small enough for the six-footer to swallow him whole and make a meal of him. And he had a tiny mouth. His mouth looked as small as a hole in a donut.

The little man gripped a tiny stick in his fist. The large number of splinters on the floor meant the stick had once been at least five feet long. Now it looked like a pencil in his hand. The timber rattlers grew agitated, the rattles singing their nauseous song. When the two five-footers started crawling around, the little man started falling apart before his eyes.

"Calm down," he said, but the man just kept right on crumbling. He leaned the rifle against the wall and carried the toolbox inside the bedroom. The snakes crawled away in a corner and huddled, flicking their tongues and making lots of racket shaking their rattles. He knocked the chain loose from the bolt set into the floor. The instant the little man saw he was free, he squirted from the room and snatched up the rifle before Stanford could stop him.

The little man had been just that fast.

The little man sneered, the long gun unsteady in his small hands. The face that was once filled with fear and terror was now jam-packed full of unadulterated hatred. Stanford charged him. The little man pulled the trigger. Nothing happened.

Stanford kicked him in the kidney so hard he thought his foot went clean through the little man. After wiping the runt off his leg, he tied him up. He gagged him by trying to shove an oily rag down his throat and out his asshole.

"The safety was on, you lil' fuck," he said and kicked him again.

He bagged one of the five-foot rattlers in a canvas bag, tied the top of the bag and stuffed the bagged snake into a second canvas bag and tied that one, too. Then he hauled the runt outside by the nape of his neck and threw him in the car trunk. Then he hurled the bagged snake in on top of him and slammed the lid.

The lightning, the thunder, and the wind muffled the little man's big screams. He got in the sedan and sped off, throwing gravel. He could still hear the screams. He switched on the radio.

At his cottage, he saw no signs Shelley had been there. He went over to the dummy and pulled out the two throwing knives. He removed the bulletproof vest and could hear the screaming.

Back outside, he slapped down on the car trunk. "Another peep out of you, and I'm going to take the snake out the bag and let you two go at it." He repeated what he said. The screaming stopped.

Halfway back to Shelley's cabin, Stanford saw bright headlights dancing through the trees, racing his way. He slowed down and stopped. The Jeep Cherokee slowed down and stopped.

Larry said, "Stanford, we got us a man missing out here, and we out looking for him. His name's Tartuffe Jitt. Hadn't seen anyone come this way, have you?"

"No, Larry, I haven't. What happened?"

"Don't know yet. He just disappeared. Vanished—"

The radio squawked. Larry spoke into the mike then turned back to him. "Gotta go. Say, you ain't seen David Harte, have you? Nobody answered the door, but his car was there."

"No. I didn't see Jocelyn either. You said she was up here."

"Oh, dang, Stanford, you missed her. She left ten minutes after you came in. She was in some big hurry, too, like a boogie man was at her. Did you find that shack okay?"

He nodded. "Yes, it was empty."

"Good. I don't have to go check. Boy, that's one spooky place, if you ask me. Got a bear cage in back; you know that?—Hey, I was wrong about Mr. Davis. He didn't die from that beating he took. Somebody poisoned the man right there in the hospital. Poisoned him right there in the hospital."

When Larry sped off, Stanford drove slowly, relieved he hadn't gotten Mark Davis killed. He was no murderer. Yet. That was a good thing. He drove half a mile before the paved road ended and the dirt road began. Fat raindrops splattered the windshield. He turned on the wipers. The rain was pounding down. He couldn't see the first shack through the sheets of rain but still reached the second one in spite of the deluge. He parked the car as far into the underbrush as he could but the rear bumper still poked out a little. He sat in the dark, listening to the rain crashing down all around him, torrents of water pouring from the sky like a waterfall.

After twenty minutes of nonstop rain, the water deluge slackened then abruptly stopped as if a hand turned off a tap.

Back inside Shelley's cottage, he nosed around some more. He tinkered with the computer but couldn't log on, so he browsed through the journals and waited for Shelley to show up to check on his prisoner.

Half an hour later, he tried again to sign-on to Shelley's computer notebook but couldn't guess the correct password. Plugging the notebook into the docking station, he made a few more stabs at the password. He threw up his hands and quit.

He went back to reading the journals, finding many references to "Frank." Back at the computer he typed: F-R-A-N-K.

The computer whined, and the screen lit up.

Stanford popped in floppy disk number one. He scanned the directory and called up a file. He saw Shelley had computerized his day journals at the beginning of the year. He scrolled back to January 16: blank. January 15: Shelley was in Miami. January 17: Shelley was back in Atlanta. Scrolling back to New Year's Day, He found an entry that kept him reading for several more minutes.

James Kelsey's words echoed in his head. "Ask Shelley."

He didn't have to ask Shelley. It was right there in front of him.

Shelley, Ed Shaw, and the Lake Arrowhead guards had been hijacking cocaine mules for years. That also explained why the intruder hadn't shot him the night the plane crashed. Jesus. Shelley was robbing drug dealers and pumping the cash through CapCity Investments as loans to Atlanta black businesses. They were pumping $4 million a year through CapCity Investments. That was how James Kelsey was doing his part for the cause—his way. His thoughts were clear enough, but his emotions were mixed.

Who got hurt but the drug peddlers?

He rationalized. In his mind, there were two types of drug peddlers: the illegal kind, dealing in heroin, coke, speed, and grass; and the legal kind, dealing in Prozac, Valium, and other legal feel-good drugs. Chemically speaking, when it came to feel-good drugs, there was little, if any, differences between drug dealers on the corner, and drugstores on the corner. He left the computer and turned his attention to the VCR tapes.

He switched on the VCR and punched in a tape.

He stared at the screen, wide-eyed, and disbelieving.

Shelley lay sprawled across huge pillows in a padded room, naked and wild-eyed. He couldn't tear his eyes away from the spectacle unfolding on the screen in front of him.

The scene was insane—absolute madness.

His eyes stung.

56

QUEENBEE SETTLED DOWN in the witness chair.

Aretha and Franklin sat on their haunches on either side of her. The bull mastiffs' alert black eyes stared out into the courtroom, expectantly.

After the promise to tell the truth and the preliminaries, Fred Junior studied her eyes before he continued speaking.

"QueenBee, would you please tell this court what happened to you on that night of September 1953."

She milked the moment. After thirty-five years of silence, now she could finally tell what happened to her that night.

"That night," she began, "that night was September 15, 1953. I was here in the deep backwoods. Right here, at this spot. At what was then a shanty shack. Me and him." She pointed at Johan Bonnell. "Me and Rooster over there.

"Bertha, she'd gone back to the homeplace for the night to see after little Stanford, my grandson; he was just four years old back then. His father, my son, was away on a business trip. Bertha and I, we switched places every night so one of us was always there to tend to Rooster's wounds, and one of us was always there to take care of little Stanford. Rooster was deathly sick.

"That night, I stayed with Rooster. He was up and about. The young buck healed quicker than anyone I'd seen before."

Justin leaned forward, straining to hear.

"When it came time for Rooster to take his tonic that night, I had to go fetch him. When I saw Rooster, I got a little concerned. Not much. I found Rooster squatting on a stump like a frog on a log. He was staring up at the moon like it was a bug he wanted to flick his tongue out and eat. And the moon, that night, the moon was as big, and the moon, that night, the moon was as bright as I'd ever seen the moon to be. Under that bright moon, Rooster, he turned, and he gave me a shifty-eyed look. The moonlight struck his face just right, and it was a sight to see, let me tell you. I—"

She paused, remembering that face, reliving that night.

"I knew right then I was facing me a whole heap of troubles from that man. There was something in his eyes that just wasn't right."

She paused and took in another long slow breath.

"Rooster, he jumped me then, moving quicker than I'd ever seen a man move before, lightning quick, Rooster was that night. And Rooster's eyes…my, my, Rooster's eyes, his eyes were yellow like daisies were yellow, and his eyes, his eyes were slitted like a wolf's eyes were slitted. I saw that yellow-eyed, slit-eyed look and I went for my gun, but Rooster, he was a mite quicker than me that night. Rooster, he punched my lights out, he did. The gun flew outta my hand like I threw it, but I didn't throw it. Rooster, he hit me just that hard. When the gun hit the ground, it went off. Boom! Like I'd pulled the trigger when I hadn't pulled the trigger at all. Me, I went right off my feet. I hit the ground like a potato sack, I did, sure did, hit the ground like a potato sack. But I jumped up fighting like something I'm sure Rooster had never seen before either."

She stopped her telling for a moment, remembering.

"But my fight, it was just a fuss. All for naught. Much ado about nothing. I've been kicked by a mule before and butted by a billy goat. But I'd never before been punched in the face by a man. And let me tell you, folks, ain't much difference between the mule and the man. But when I did get my hands on Rooster, I didn't let go until I had me some satisfaction. I started biting Rooster as hard and as fast as my thirty-twos would let me bite that man. Rooster, he didn't like my biting him one bit. I could tell by the way Rooster was wailing and carrying on. But those big bites didn't faze Rooster much, let me tell you. Rooster, he just kept right on keeping on."

She rubbed her temples, dizzy from telling it so fast.

"Rooster, he knocked me out cold. When I came to, Rooster, he was having his way with me like an animal would have its way with another animal. But I kept my cool, groping around on the ground until I got my hand on my gun. I tried to stick the ugly end in Rooster's ear, but he hit me again. He was the punchingest man.

"Rooster, he punched me like I was the shooter who put the bullets in his back; like I was the snake that sank the fangs in his flesh; like I was the gangrene that poisoned the blood in his veins; like I was the devil when I was the saint. His punches, they tore me up inside. I saved Rooster's life, and he tried to take my life, he did."

Fred Junior cleared his throat. "QueenBee, tell this court what happened after the defendant used you for his punching bag."

The thought brought back more anguish than she wanted to believe, the memories one with the pain in her chest.

"Rooster," she said, "Rooster, he killed a man that night."

Fred Junior let the answer linger a moment.

"And, QueenBee," Fred Junior said softly, "what was this man doing when the defendant shot and killed him?"

"This man was beating Rooster off me when Rooster shot him."

Fred Junior stepped closer as if to comfort her. "QueenBee, tell this court what happened next, after the defendant shot this man?"

"Rooster, he took off like a yellow streak through the woods."

"QueenBee, when did you see the defendant again?"

"May 24, 1955," she said, curtly.

"QueenBee, would you please tell this court about that second encounter with the defendant on May 24, 1955."

She turned her stare on Johan. "Rooster, he returned to Twofer County looking for a money satchel he said I stole from him."

"Did you steal a satchel from the defendant, QueenBee?"

"No," she said.

"Did you see this money satchel?" Fred Junior said.

"Yes," she said.

"Did you ever possess this money satchel, QueenBee?"

"Yes," she said.

"Tell the court about the money satchel, QueenBee."

QueenBee kept her eyes locked on Johan's face. "A man named Fang, he found the satchel near the swamp. Rooster, he never said he'd lost a satchel, and I never said to him I found a satchel. Rooster and I, we trusted each other like that."

Her words dripped with sarcasm.

"QueenBee," Fred Junior said, "when the defendant returned on May 24, 1955, did you then tell him that you'd found the money satchel?"

"No. The yellow belly, he threatened to kill me and my kin. I kept my tongue, I did. Until this day, I kept my tongue."

When Fred Junior cleared his throat, the sound washed over the quiet courtroom like a rattle then a roar.

"QueenBee," Fred Junior said, "how did you keep the defendant from finding out you'd found the money satchel?"

She cleared her throat.

"I never owned land in my name in thirty years. I still don't."

"How much money was in the money satchel, QueenBee?"

"Forty thousand dollars," she said.

"Thank you, QueenBee. No further questions, Your Honor."

Fred Junior sat down.

Justin said, "ready for your cross-examination, Mr. Bonnell?"

"Yes, Your Honor," George Bonnell said.

The defense attorney took up position in front of the witness stand. "QueenBee, until the night of 15 September 1953, when was the last time you'd had a man?"

A murmur rose in the courtroom. The air trembled.

"Objection!" Fred Junior leaped to his feet and charged George Bonnell. "I object—"

Justin jumped up, slamming the gavel down hard. "Overruled!"

Aretha rose off her haunches growling, her hackles raised.

"Hush," QueenBee hissed.

Franklin rose off his haunches and moved to stand in front of the chair, crowding QueenBee. Aretha moved in closer as well. The bull mastiffs' hackles were raised, their fierce eyes locked on the two attorneys, who stood toe-to-toe, pointing and jawboning.

Justin slammed the gavel again.

The two lawyers kept shouting, pointing, and snorting, both gasping to be heard, and Justin kept banging the gavel up and down like a madman pounding nails.

"Overruled! Overruled! Overruled!"

When the gavel snapped, the noise fell apart like a trinket.

Justin was leaning over the bench so far he looked fit to pounce down on George Bonnell's head and peck out his little brain.

"Mister," Justin said, snarling and jabbing the broken handle at George Bonnell's red-streaked face, "Mister, you better damn well know what you're saying, or I'll punch your lights out myself."

George Bonnell slipped a finger under his collar to loosen it.

"I hadn't had a man in four years," QueenBee said.

All eyes turned on the witness stand like spotlights.

Justin sank back down into his chair.

"You have your answer, Counselor," Justin said. "Carry on."

"Thank you, Your Honor."

Defense attorney George Bonnell turned back to face the witness stand. "QueenBee, isn't it also fair to say that, in your own, subtle though it may have been, feminine way, you led the defendant on? Isn't that fair to say, QueenBee? That you asked for it, so to speak?"

Fred Junior popped to his feet again. But Justin pounded him down with a loud slap of his palm against the bench.

"Sit! Let's let the truth be told here today."

A pin dropped.

"No," she answered, "that's unfair to say."

"Why is that unfair to say, QueenBee?" George Bonnell said.

"I'd just had sex the night before," she said, staring directly at her inquisitor.

A feather dropped.

First, George Bonnell frowned. Then his jaw slackened. Then his eyes brightened, and then his face lit up like stadium lights.

"Your honor! Your honor! This witness has perjured herself! She told this court she hadn't had sex in four years!"

Justin waved off George Bonnell and looked at her.

"That's not what I said," QueenBee said. She glanced up at Justin and saw that his eyebrows had shot up, too.

She turned her hot glare back on George Bonnell.

Aretha rose off her haunches, snarling at George Bonnell, her hackles raised.

"I said," she said, "I hadn't had sex with a man in four years. That is what I said, Mr. Defense Attorney."

57

QUEENBEE REPEATED WHAT she'd said, still staring into George Bonnell's face. "I said I hadn't had sex with a man in four years. That's what I said, Mr. Defense Attorney."

She dropped her bombshell on the witness stand and now sat among the pieces in the courtroom.

"No more questions for this witness, Your Honor," the defense attorney said, and slumped down in the chair next to his father.

Fred Junior, crimson red in the face, dropped down in his chair and didn't move a muscle. Justin tugged his chin and kept watching Fred Junior turn even more crimson in the face.

"Mr. Wainwright," Justin said, "take two long breaths then tell this court if you have any redirect for this witness."

Fred Junior rolled his eyes up at Justin, took one deep breath instead of two and stood, facing the witness stand.

"QueenBee," Fred Junior said, "please tell this court the name of your rescuer, the name of the man the defendant shot and killed, that most tragic night in your life."

"Odis Rome," she said. "Rooster, he shot and killed my only son. Rooster, he shot and killed Stanford's father."

Justin gawked down at QueenBee in shocked disbelief.

"No more questions for this witness," Fred Junior said.

George Bonnell said he had no more redirect.

"The witness may step down," Justin said, rubbing his temples.

When QueenBee stepped down from the witness stand, she felt thirty-five years lighter than when she'd first stepped up to testify.

Sighing, Justin spoke with little energy, "Mr. Wainwright, please call your next witness."

"The prosecution rests, Your Honor," Fred Junior said.

Justin said, "Mr. Bonnell, please present your defense."

The defense attorney rose wearily, raking a hand through his hair. "Your Honor, I call Johan Bonnell to the witness stand."

Johan Bonnell took the stand and was given the preliminaries.

"Mr. Johan Bonnell," George Bonnell said, "please tell this court what really happened that night, September 15, 1953."

Johan squirmed and then he started talking.

"She came on to me," Johan said. "And I came on to her. A man saw us come on to each other and didn't like it. The man attacked me. I just defended myself. I acted in self-defense."

George Bonnell spoke softly. "Mr. Bonnell, did you force yourself on a then forty-eight-year-old woman, who was old enough to be your mother, a woman, at the time, already a grandmother?"

"No, I did not force myself on a grandmother."

George Bonnell said, "Mr. Bonnell, please tell this court about the alleged, the so-called, murder, if you will."

"Murder?" Johan said, almost sheepishly.

"It's claimed you shot and killed a man," George Bonnell said. "Please tell the court what happened that night, Mr. Bonnell."

Johan squirmed some more, digging in.

"Well," Johan began, "this man, he jumped me from behind and hit me on the head. He knocked me to the ground. He hit me, I don't know how many times. He nearly took my head off. When I realized he had knocked me on top of the gun, I picked it up and pointed it at him to make him stop whacking me on my head. That's all. To stop him from whacking me on my head. That's when he ran into my arm. The gun, it went off. I just wanted him to stop beating my brains out. That's all. That's the God's truth, so help me."

"So, Mr. Bonnell," George Bonnell said, "what you're saying to this court is that you feared for your life that night?"

"Scared me to death," Johan said. "They tried to kill me. Her and her son. It was two on one. And I was the one. They tried to kill me, not the other way around. And that's the God's truth.

"So help me."

58

JUSTIN GRIMES'S MIND was deeply troubled.

He was trying to figure out what really happened that dreadful night in '53, while at the same time dealing with the horrible fact that his own father had killed QueenBee's son. His own father had killed Stanford's father. He was sick with shame and disgust.

That was the root cause of his deeply troubled mind.

He wondered how QueenBee could think of murdering a man? Now he understood. It was plain old revenge. But why had Queen-Bee mothered the son of the man who killed her own son? Did she mother the son of the murderer as one part of some skewed or twisted logic of using the son to get her hands on the father?

No matter, he still had to convince QueenBee that Johan Bonnell, his father, was innocent despite overwhelming evidence to his guilt. But if his father was not guilty, then what ignited those violent events that night in 1953? What triggered it all?

Suddenly, all that troubled thinking he'd done nudged a brand-new thought into his still troubled mind. Could they both be telling the truth? Did Johan attack QueenBee as QueenBee claimed, and as Johan denied? Did QueenBee seduce Johan as Johan claimed, and as QueenBee denied? What if they had attacked each other that night? What if the truth was deep enough and wide enough for both versions to fit inside the truth?

If Johan's sickness didn't cause the violence, then maybe Johan's cure caused the violence. And what was the cure? The roots, the herbs, and the mushrooms were the cure, plus the constant nursing QueenBee and Bertha gave him. Did QueenBee take the same roots and the same herbs she fed to his father?

"Your Honor."

George Bonnell broke Justin's reverie. "Your Honor, I have no more questions for this witness."

Fred Junior then waived cross-examination.

"Mr. Bonnell," Justin said, "you may step down."

"Your Honor," George Bonnell said, "I'll like to recall an earlier witness to ask one more question of that witness."

The prosecuting attorney merely nodded his okay.

"Call the witness, Mr. Bonnell," Justin said.

"I recall QueenBee to the stand," the defense attorney said.

Back on the stand, QueenBee kept staring at the double doors at the rear of the courtroom.

"QueenBee," George Bonnell said, "in 1953, your husband had been dead four years, did you have a boyfriend during that time?"

"No, I did not have a boyfriend during that time, Mr. Defense Attorney."

"Thanks, QueenBee. No further questions, Your Honor."

Justin looked at Fred Junior. "Mr. Wainwright?"

"Yes, I have one question as well," Fred Junior said and stood.

"QueenBee," Fred Junior said, "tell the court what else happened when the defendant returned to Twofer County in 1955."

"Objection! I—"

"Shut up!" Justin snapped. "I want to hear this."

QueenBee kept her gaze on the double doors.

"QueenBee," Fred Junior said, "what else happened when the defendant returned to Twofer County on September 15, 1955?"

She turned her attention back to Fred Junior. "When Rooster returned to Twofer County on September 15, 1955, he kidnapped a year-old baby from the arms of his Twofer County mother. The mother, she never saw her child again."

"Objection! I—"

Suddenly, the heavy double doors to the courtroom opened like stiff wings, the ebony doors seeming to strain with effort.

The courtroom fell as silent as a bitterly cold winter night.

In the doorway stood a tall man.

Both bull mastiffs leaped forward two feet, snarling at the tall

350

man. Aretha leapt forward another two feet, snapping her jaws and slinging drool at the tall man.

"Hush," QueenBee said. "Sit."

Franklin instantly retreated and dropped back on his haunches. Aretha hesitated, throwing one more snapping snarl at the tall man before she too went back to her position alongside QueenBee.

QueenBee tensed, her eyes now solidly glued on Justin's face.

The tall man's arms dangled loosely and naturally at his side as if he carried the burden of the world on his strong back. The tall man stared in at all of them in one long searching glance.

A low murmur in the courtroom rose higher in pitch.

First, one head, then two heads, then as a wave all heads turned from the face of the tall man standing in the doorway to gawk up at the face of Judge Justin Grimes sitting on the bench. Then all those eyes fell back down to gawk at the face of the tall man standing in the doorway of the courtroom.

All eyes moved, first up, then down like that except for the eyes of QueenBee, and the two bull mastiffs.

The tall man's head slowly turned, eyes searching the room and settling on the face of Judge Justin Grime with an almost audible jolt. The tall man stepped inside the courtroom. He moved like a wooden toy pulled jerkily along by a string. He moved like a man walking across hot coals.

The tall man stopped in front of the witness stand, but his eyes were still locked up on Justin's face.

Justin leaned over the bench to gawk down more intently on the face of the tall man.

As the two men gawked at each other, Fred Junior cleared his throat three or four times, and then he spoke.

"QueenBee, I ask you, is this the man who grew from the baby the defendant, thirty-three years ago, snatched from the arms of a Twofer County mother?"

"Yes," she said, "this is he."

§

The recess was half an hour old.

QueenBee listened as Justin and Tartuffe talked to each other. The three of them sat alone in a consultation room. The brothers had all too quickly run out of conversation for each other. They both turned their attention to QueenBee.

Justin said, "QueenBee, why did our father take one of us and not both of us when he returned to Twofer County in '55?"

She swallowed one lump and up popped another lump.

"Your father," she said, "he never knew about you, Justin. You and Bertha were away. Your father never knew there were two babies who looked like him instead of one who looked like him."

"I don't understand." Justin's expression was pained. "If my mother is alive, why was I raised in an orphanage?"

She rattled the dice.

"To keep me from my father?" Justin said.

She rattled the dice. "Ask your father that question."

They returned to the courtroom, and the trial resumed.

§

Tartuffe sat apart from the others, watching them as if they were all confined in a zoo. Tartuffe couldn't believe these people were his folks. He singled out the faces in his mind now as QueenBee had singled out the faces to him during the recess.

Jocko Jitt was his uncle, not his father as Jocko had led him to believe. And Jocko had hired the Nigerian madmen to kidnap him, so he could save him. All because Jocko wanted him to feel obligated to go to Atlanta to run Lake Arrowhead and Prison City for him. The near-death experience in that Nigerian rock prison that drastically changed his life for the better had been a charade.

Johan Bonnell, the man on trial, a man he'd never seen before, was his father. George Bonnell, the lawyer, was a half brother. The two teenagers were half siblings. He even had a stepmother.

Jocko became his father because his real father Johan had married Barbra Bonnell before Johan learned he had a son. Johan gave his son to his brother Jocko to raise, so Barbra would not know her husband had another son. That made his stepmother his anti-mother. His life was a charade. Sickos, all of them. Sickos.

Tartuffe shook his head to keep from laughing out loud at this, his outrageous family. He kept shaking his head and cursing the day he was born into such a crazy life. What a family.

But it would do. Any family would do.

Finally, he laughed. He'd never before felt so safe.

What a fucking family.

PART FIVE

SOUTH GEORGIA
DIRT BEDS

59

ARETHA WAS ALERT to every move Johan Bonnell made. The bull mastiff's piercing black eyes were riveted to his face.

QueenBee watched the new defense attorney Justin Grimes and defendant Johan Bonnell as if they were two sitting hens, and she, a chicken hawk circling the henhouse they sat cackling in.

The recess was over. The trial participants piled back inside the courtroom. She intended to shoot Rooster with the same gun he used to kill her son thirty-five years ago.

Justin sat like a tower of power beside his father, ready to fight her, the only mother he'd ever known, to save him, a murdering rapist who killed her son. So be it. Justin had insisted. Then so be it. Not even God Almighty could save Rooster. She would get even with the man who turned her life into a thirty-five-year nightmare of waiting for this day to arrive.

George Bonnell, the new judge, tapped the broken gavel and called her kangaroo court back to order.

The trial resumed.

"Mr. Wainwright," the new judge said, "the prosecution may continue cross-examining the witness."

Johan Bonnell sat low in the witness chair.

"No more questions for this witness," Fred Junior said.

"Any redirect, Mr. Defense Attorney?"

"Yes, Your Honor," said Justin, the new defense attorney. "First, I recall QueenBee to the stand for more questions of redirect."

"So be it," the judge said.

Again back up on the witness stand, QueenBee waited for Justin Grimes to question her for the first time.

"QueenBee," Justin said, "you're an herbalist. You believe herbs can heal the sick body. You believe herbs can sometimes prevent or retard certain illnesses of the body, is that correct?"

"That is correct," she said.

"QueenBee, during the weeks in question, were you, yourself, taking huge doses of ginseng to boost your stamina so you could give Mr. Bonnell the round-the-clock care he needed to live?"

She studied Justin's face closely. She needed to know where he was going with his questions, so she could cut him off at the pass.

"Yes," she said, "it's true."

Justin studied her a moment. "QueenBee, isn't it true that ginseng drives the libido, and...it makes one—well, horny?"

She hesitated. Smart rascal. She studied Justin's face.

Justin said, "My question to you, QueenBee, is this: did all that ginseng turn you on, so to speak?"

The words touched her. Deep inside, she felt the light touch of reality. She felt as if a key had slipped easily into a lock on a door hiding secrets in a room tied to her long-ago past.

The key turned.

Justin backed away from the witness chair as if she had already answered his question when she'd done no such thing.

"No more questions for this witness, Your Honor," Justin said.

"The witness may step down," Judge George Bonnell said.

But she did not step down. She sat there, waiting...waiting...for the click of the lock and when it came—there it is, the click.

The bolt shot back on the door hiding secrets in a room.

Her flesh shuddered from the impact. Huge flakes of rust fell to the floor like dandruff scratched off the scalp of Old Man Time. Slowly, deliberately, a thick oak door gaped open like a mouth. And QueenBee stepped through the portal hole to disappear back into her past. Her long-ago distant past. QueenBee, she went walking back the same way she'd come, walking back to where she'd lived long before she was born, she went walking back down the long lonely road of memory, a place where her past and her present clashed like magnificent armies, walking back to when the big lie of her life had been born into the world of reality.

She felt as if a part of her soul were locked down in a basement, banging on the trapdoor and crying to be let out of the cellar.

"The witness may step down," Judge George Bonnell repeated. The words drew her back inside the courthouse.

QueenBee stood. Aretha and Franklin rose off their haunches.

QueenBee stepped down from the witness stand. The bull mastiffs escorted her back to her seat.

The defense attorney called his father back to the witness stand.

Justin studied his father's face a moment before he spoke.

"Mr. Bonnell," Justin said, "earlier, you told this court that when QueenBee found you in her shack, you were near death. Yet, you attacked QueenBee a mere twenty-two days later. In about three weeks, Mr. Bonnell, you had recovered from gunshot wounds, a snakebite, and gangrene; is that correct, Mr. Bonnell?"

"Yes," Johan said. "That is correct."

"Now, Mr. Bonnell, you being a reasonable person, and we're all reasonable people in this courtroom, so correct me if I'm wrong. But, are you, being a reasonable person, telling this courtroom full of reasonable people that you had regained enough strength from three life-threatening conditions to beat the living daylights out of a strong woman like QueenBee had been back in 1953? Are you asking this courtroom full of reasonable people to believe this fairy tale, Mr. Bonnell, this fabrication of reality?"

Justin stepped closer. "Aren't you lying to this courtroom full of reasonable people, Mr. Bonnell, to save your own skin?"

Johan spoke in a strong voice. "I told you the truth."

Justin rocked back on his heels, studying his father's face with a sternness. Then he rocked forward off his heels and started pacing the floor, his head now rocking up and down as if agreeing with some conspiratorial voice whispering up inside his head.

"I believe you did tell this court the truth, Mr. Bonnell," Justin said, planting himself once again in front of the witness chair.

"The truth is that you were more than healed by QueenBee. The truth is QueenBee made you better and quicker than you were before your close brush with death. The truth is QueenBee healed you beyond your old health."

Justin stepped back closer to the witness chair.

"Mr. Bonnell, isn't it true that what happened that night is as much a mystery to you now, as that awful night was a mystery to QueenBee back then, and as that awful night is a mystery to us today—isn't all that the God-loving truth, Mr. Johan Bonnell?"

The question hung like the *Mona Lisa* on a wall for all to see.

Johan wore the look of a desperate man down on his knees digging like crazy to uncover those things gone past long, long ago.

"Mr. Bonnell, have you considered that the same mushrooms, the same ginseng, the same roots and herbs that healed you, that these same remedies also turned you into a rapist and a killer?"

When Justin Grimes placed his face to within two feet of Johan Bonnell's face, the eyes of the father and the eyes of the son locked across thirty-three years of separation between them.

Justin spoke soothingly to his father.

"Mr. Bonnell, tell this court the whole truth, and nothing but the truth. Tell this court the truth, Mr. Bonnell."

Johan spoke with iron. "I have told you the truth. I have told you the whole truth. I have told you nothing but the truth."

§

"Liar!"

Aretha leaped up, growling low in her throat, her eyes pinned on Johan Bonnell's face.

QueenBee gripped the arms of the chair so hard the wood bit into her skin like teeth. She pushed up on her feet.

Franklin rose off his haunches, his hackles raised, growling low in his throat, eyes locked on Johan's face.

The bull mastiffs' growls deepened.

She turned to the bull mastiffs. "Stay," she said and made her way toward the front of the courtroom, eyes locked on Johan Bonnell. Franklin stayed put. But Aretha padded silently behind her, hackles raised, eyes fierce and alert.

QueenBee said, "I'll get the truth from his lying mouth."

She stopped in front of the witness stand, her eyes locked on the eyes of Johan Bonnell. "You're a dead man," she hissed.

"I am she who is, come for me," she whispered to him.

§

The past spilled from Johan's mouth. The year was 1953. The Korean War had ground to a stalemate.

Four weeks ago, Johan Jadestone had been young, tall, and hot-

358

blooded. But a mere three weeks ago, Johan Jadestone had been more dead than alive. And now today, Johan was again young, tall, and hot-blooded, plus more, much, much more than any of that.

Johan squatted on a stump.

His muscles hummed with strength.

In every direction he looked he saw pine trees as tall as any trees he'd ever seen before, some looked taller than Chicago sky-scrapers. Johan flexed his muscles. He'd never felt so strong be-fore, never felt so horny before. He stroked his crotch and whined. His meat poked out like an iron pipe. Those two women saved his life, but what else did those damn women do to him?

Johan launched himself off the tree stump like his pants were on fire and went stumbling off into the woods to do what he'd done four times a day since he'd been up running around under his own power. More often than not, he fought back the urge to beat his meat into submission until he wept from the need to whack off.

The urge again satisfied for now, Johan perched back on the tree stump like a bullfrog on a log, and was hard again as soon as he smelled their scent. They were 100 yards upwind but still he could smell them. God, what was happening to him?

Were those two women witches? Were they? His crotch throb-bed, and he shuddered from self-restraint. The women wouldn't answer any of his questions.

They wouldn't tell him where in the hell he was, not even which of the forty-eight states he was in. The older one talked a lot when she thought he was sleeping. She called him Rooster. He felt her knocking his hard-on around like his dick meant no more to her than a play toy. The vixen. That's what she was—a fucking vixen.

Johan squeezed his eyes shut. But he was alive. That was good. What about his brother? Did his brother escape the death ride from Cleveland down to Miami? He tugged his chin with his left hand, groped his crotch with his right, gritted his teeth and groaned from the ecstasy of it.

He was deep enough in the backwoods to stay out of harm's way. He hadn't seen another soul except for those two women—two vixens. And he'd walked two miles in all four directions and nothing but pine trees everywhere he looked. Fucking pine trees. He still had nightmares. The two men who shot him; where were they now? Were they out there in the boonies searching for him? And Jones? Jones! Where was Jones? Was Jones alive? Dead? The money! Oh, God, the money. The $40,000 in the money satchel. Did Jones escape with the money satchel? Or did those women get their hands on the money—those vixens? Where was his money?

He was heated. He swung around and saw her, his blood bubbling. The vixen was walking his way, her body silhouetted against the moonlight, hips swaying like the motion of the ocean. Sweat bullets shot up from his pores like missiles from a silo.

He was trapped. Nowhere to go. Nowhere to run. He smelled the vixen. She had an aged-wine quality about her.

Before she could speak, Johan turned, lunged and attacked her with a ferocity that stunned even him. His huge hands engulfed her small wrists like shackles. He drove her to the ground with a strength he'd never known before. The woman squirmed, kicked, screamed, and tried to bite him, her resistance sending his anger surging into a hot rage. He smacked her with his fist.

The vixen grunted and staggered back, shaking her head.

Then the vixen spat and charged him. She rammed her head up into his chin, and pounded him with her fists. Blood squirted from Johan's mouth. He clamped the woman's wrists again, but she jerked one wrist free and gave him a nasty bite. Pain shot through the back of his hand. The woman whipped out the .38, and Johan hit her again, this time the blow sent her sprawling backwards. The pistol flew from her hand, hit the ground and fired.

The gunshot echoed through the stand of loblolly pine trees.

Johan towered over the dazed woman sprawled on the ground at his feet. Then he bent down to claim his prize. The woman's fist crashed into his groin, and he lost his legs. Another fist smashed into his face, but he brushed the punch aside and jumped to his feet. He sidestepped another charge, and they squared off under the moonlight, circling each other. He swung at the woman's head and missed. She charged him again, her fists flying. Again, he sidestepped her; again, he swung at her head; and, again, he missed. But this time when the vixen ducked under his wild swing, she lunged in and sank her teeth into the flesh of his back.

Johan yowled and flung her away from him. His back was on fire from the vicious bite. The woman bounced to her feet, turned and charged him again. But this time Johan was more than ready—he was cocked and locked. The punch he threw was short, crisp, on target, and thrown from the hip. His fist hit her flush on her chin. The concussion of her brain bouncing off the back of her skull put her to sleep.

Johan sank down beside her, salivating and wiping his mouth, his loins lurching and his spine rolling in some sort of animalistic dance of swaying and bucking.

Johan, hurrying, mounted her body with an animal strength that consumed him in its mad fury. Beneath him, the woman stirred, and his imagination ran wild and fanciful, the woman blooming beneath him like a flower, opening herself to him as a goddess to a god, the woman's passion driving him to a height he'd never before known, her lips whispering encouraging words into his ear, as he spilled himself into her again and again in a sea of love.

Suddenly, a man appeared out the dark like a spirit and attacked Johan, smashing his face, kicking him. Johan tried to roll away, only to be met by another vicious kick. He rolled, he was kicked; he rolled, he was kicked.

Johan struggled up on his knees. He scrambled away from the man's punishing blows but another powerful kick cracked into his ribs and dropped him gagging on his back. Johan landed on top of the woman's gun. He rolled and snatched it up, finger searching for the trigger when again his attacker plowed into him. The gun exploded in noise, and both men slammed to the ground.

Johan crawled from under the dead weight of the groaning man and stood over him still holding the gun in his hand. Johan gawked down at the man writhing on the ground then looked down at the gun clutched in his hand.

The naked woman leaned on an elbow, rubbing her swollen jaw with her left hand. She squinted up at him standing there in the bright moonlight, smoking gun in his hand. She looked over at the groaning man squirming on the ground and pushed up on her feet, stumbling over to the man now lying motionless on his back.

She stared down into the man's face, gawked at the dark spot in the center of his chest then reached down and touched the blood.

Her head snapped around, eyes full of the moon.

"You're a dead man," she hissed.

60

FRIDAY, JUNE 24

A THROWAWAY MAN, Jud Judson thought as he gnawed on a hang nail like a mutt gnawing on a bone.

He replaced the telephone on the cradle, shrugged and waited, eyes fixed on his office door. He watched the doorway as if he expected an alien to turn the knob and slither across his office floor on its belly. However, events didn't quite happen that way.

The door opened, and a street bum shuffled into Jud's office.

The man stood before him looking like last week's coffee without cream, and smelling like street garbage during a week-long garbage strike in the summertime. The veteran street bum shot him a shifty-eyed appraising gaze while expertly easing the door shut with the sole of a shower shoe patched with strands of fishing line.

The street bum squinted his eyes, hugging a rumpled brown paper bag even tighter to his chest as if shielding himself from love.

After sizing up his visitor, Jud uprooted his elbows and settled his hands palms down on the desktop and pushed up on his feet to tower a foot and a half over the stooped little man.

"I'm Jud Judson," he said, walking from behind the desk and poking out a hand.

The street bum squinted at the hand then ignored it.

"I knows who you be," the snaggletoothed man drawled, narrowing his tight, reptilian eyes. "You knows who I is, too, huh?"

"No," Jud said, "why don't you school me on who you be."

"Folks, they call me, Po' Boy. You can call me, Po' Boy, too, if you take a mind to. Don't have to if you don't wanna."

"Okay, Po' Boy. What's in the bag you be hugging?"

Po' Boy's raggedy-mouthed grin polluted the room. "You wanna know, do you?" Po' Boy's eyes popped open as wide as dimes.

"And I's gots me this good eye up in my ol' head, too, sure do. This good eye, it watches out for folkies—cause folkies, they sneaky, you know. This here dead eye here, it ain't no account, no sir."

Po' Boy cackled once, twice, then fell eerily silent. He seemed momentarily confused about where he was and why he was there.

"I's used to be an African prince," Po' Boy puffed up and said. "Wanna hear me tell it, do you?" Po' Boy stretched his neck like a turtle would do. "You wanna hear me tell it or don't you?"

Jud was street smart enough to know when he had to give street bums time to sneak up on the point. Having the upper hand was a serious game to street people with nothing left to lose but their next meal. Once a street bum knew he had something you wanted, he forced you to listen to all that static hissing inside his head. He ranted about once being a prince, a king and a queen, but never about being a bum, a child molester, or a retard. Why was that?

Po' Boy frowned at his attitude and cut the noise short, his pimple of a head jutting forward like a snapping turtle would do.

"I's come to collect. What you pay to hear me say what this good eye here done seen, huh?" Po' Boy cupped an ear. "Word's out." He poked out a hand. "And I's come to collect what's due me."

Jud leaned forward. Now it was his turn to kick ass—bum or not. "I don't buy information, Po' Boy."

Po' Boy jerked his hand back, recoiling away from him in horror. "What you talking 'bout? Sure you do! Sure you do! You gotta!"

He shook his head. "Po' Boy, no duckies. We barter but no paper."

Po' Boy twisted back around, hope kneeling in his eyes. "Noo, I's gots me habits that gotta eat three squares like a man eats. I needs me some duckies, some paper, so I can bury my root in a hooker like I wants to do, and I's need me some paper to plant my root."

Po' Boy rubbed forefinger and thumb together in the universal language of the dollar bill.

"We barter is what we do," Jud said. "Booze, drugs, no duckies."

Po' Boy shook his head like a cheap washing machine. "Duckies. I's wants me a woman. I's wants me a hooker all to myself. I's ain't talking 'bout no mule-faced whore uglier than me. I's wants me a high-class hooker like the big shots. Hookers take duckies."

Jud stared into Po' Boy's one good eye. "Po' Boy, if that brown paper bag has a silver-plated .38 inside—"

"Yeah?" Po' Boy stretched his neck longer. "And if this good eye done seen who toast this man who had this peashooter, huh?"

Po' Boy's neck was straining so it seemed as if his head were set to pop right off his shoulders like a cork popping from a bottle.

"Whacha gonna do for me then, huh, Mr. Private De-tec-tive?"

Jud pressed the bum's crusty old face between his big hands. "Po' Boy, I's gonna set you up with a Bahamas Mama until that root of yours has been nibbled down to a stump."

Jud then planted a wet kiss in the middle of the bum's forehead.

§

Thunderclouds were circling the capital city when Sid exited I-75 North onto Moreland Avenue in East Atlanta. The 250-mile drive from Twofer County took a mere three hours driving time. Not even Georgia state troopers fucked with a hearse flying down the road like a bat out of hell.

Sid parked the smoking hearse next door to the Pridgen housing projects. He left the driver's side door unlocked, keys dangling in the ignition, and rap music blaring from the radio.

Sid hunched over, turned up his collar and walked off splashing down the street in the driving rain.

A teen jumped up inside the empty, music-filled hearse and bounced behind the wheel. "Cool!" The teen fired up the engine.

In jumped another teen. "A meat wagon!"

And a third teen. "Whoopee!"

When the coffin lid bumped up a half foot, the teens merely turned and stared at it. But when the coffin lid creaked all the way open, the teens screamed and ran away fast.

§

Clayton Westwood was wolfing down peach pie and chocolate ice cream when his front doorbell chimed. The FBI chief stopped the videotape of the WTNT-TV Evening News he'd recorded earlier. Grumbling, he set the dessert down and picked up his pocketknife to ease his frustrations. Click-clack!

He dropped the pocketknife in his pocket. He loved watching that sexy Jocelyn Slade. Gorgeous face and a very nice behind on her. Stanford, the lucky dog!

Clayton stuck an eye to the peephole, then flung the door open. "Shelley, where in the—"

Shelley's fist drilled Clayton right between his eyes.

The stunning blow knocked Clayton stumbling backwards and sprawling on his butt. Shelley was on him. Another heavy punch smacked into Clayton's face, sending pinpoints of colors dancing the Watusi behind his eyeballs. Spittle looped under his chin. Clayton groaned from the jarring pain and rolled over on his side. He knew his collar bone was broken. The heavy pain behind his ear meant his jaw was broken again. Tears leaked from his eyes.

He heard feet padding across the floor behind him. Gritting his teeth, he twisted his shoulder around, more pain slashing across his back like a whip. But he held the position, snaking his hand into his pocket for his pocketknife. Bright red blood leaked from the corner of his mouth.

He saw Shelley moving toward him as if he had a large wind-up key poking out his back. Crippled with pain, he trembled and tears shot from his eyes as he withdrew the pocketknife. He farted and yelped, a hot searing pain burning through his chest like fire.

Click.

Shelley stopped near his tear-stained face and crouched like a predator about to feed. He lashed out with the pocketknife.

He imagined driving the blade deep into Shelley's neck, all the way up to the hilt. Blood, warm and thick, spurted from the hole, drenching his fist with its stickiness. Shelley yowled and jerked his head away, pulling the knife from Clayton's bloody hand. Reeling and staggering and stumbling, Shelley gripped the knife handle, yanking the blade from his neck. He yowled and thrashed about. The deep stab wound sent a rope of blood spewing and twisting in the air like a hangman's noose searching for a neck.

Clayton squinted to see. He saw Shelley's back turned to him. Shelley was bent over, hands on his knees like he was huddling with ten more of himself. And then came the reality check.

To Clayton's surprise and horror, he saw that all that blood had been one big illusion, a trick his mind played on him, so he would not know he had only seconds to live. The mind was sneaky that way. No blade had been driven deep into Shelley's neck, all the way up to the hilt. No blood, warm and thick, had spurted from the hole, drenching his fist with its stickiness. No rope of blood had whipped through the air. Just loops of sweat and fear. The knife blade had missed Shelley's carotid artery and hit nothing but muscle.

Clayton slumped, accepting the reality check and his fate.

Shelley's head swiveled around, grinning, blood leaking from under Shelley's chin like the tears of a clown.

Whap! The beast snapped its tail.

§

Shelley slithered through the night like a snake in the grass, and drama pounded the moment like a drum.

Shelley rang David Harte's doorbell once then kicked the door down to the floor with a loud crack. He stepped inside, heart pumping pure adrenaline, lungs sucking air by the gallon.

David Harte lay sprawled across the pit group like a bug pinned to a specimen board. Shelley threw back his head and bellowed, the territorial roar bouncing down from the cathedral ceiling.

Shelley was lost deep inside his own mind, stumbling around in a maze of confusion. Trapped inside himself, he was now ticking like a celestial clock. Again, he bellowed, now a raging bull crashing around in a house of mirrors that was now his mind.

The psychiatrist rose from the depth of the huge pillows, rubbing his eyes, and squinted up into Shelley's mask of terror.

David smirked. "It's about time, you crazy bastard. What am I supposed to do now, Roscoe, piss my pants?"

The psychiatrist snorted and lay back down. "Go to hell."

Whap! The beast snapped its tail.

Shelley pounced and when he straightened to his full height, he had his big thick hands locked around the psychiatrist's neck.

Heaving David high over his head, with great ceremony, Shelley stared gleefully up into David's face and squeezed life from him.

When the flailing arms and legs finally fell loose and still, Shelley dropped the corpse in a heap on the floor. Then he walked away as if a ravenous hunger had been completely sated.

Shelley stepped over the destroyed door and trampled out into the night as if he hadn't just killed his therapist.

In his freaky mind—whap! The beast snapped its tail.

61

STANFORD WAITED. INSIDE Shelley's cabin, he pressed his finger-tips to his temples; they throbbed with blood as he thought about Shelley. He'd always had tunnel vision about Shelley.

His blind spot for his best friend was thirty years wide and was as deep as their blood was thick. He'd just finished taking Shelley's cabin apart.

He now sat surrounded by the spoils of his search as if he were a baboon licking his coat clean among the bones of his kill. He'd been so blind to Shelley's pedigree.

Shelley's daddy, Isaiah Whitfield, was a shell-shocked World War II veteran and a certified nut case who killed two innocent people for no apparent reason at all. His mama, Emma Whitfield, was so insane she tried to kill Shelley before he could enjoy his first meal outside the womb. Shelley's foster father, Frank Lester, was a sexual predator and a pedophile who molested Shelley for years. His foster mother, Gaylene Lester, was a loony bird with the maternal warmth of a snake. Stanford could only shake his head at his naiveté and his blind spot. It was impossible for Shelley to be any more or for Shelley to be any less than who Shelley was.

A person—for the most part—can be no more or no less than the character traits he's born with and the environment he's raised in. However, a person is always greater than the sum of his genes and his environment—only because he has a conscious mind.

Everybody had used Shelley for their own selfish reasons. Frank Lester used Shelley to satisfy his sexuality. Gaylene Lester used Shelley to satisfy a husband she obviously couldn't please. The Army used Shelley to slaughter little men in black pajamas on another continent. The FBI used Shelley to kill gangsters down in Miami. QueenBee used Shelley for only God knows what. He used Shelley for his own alter ego and for someone to care about and love.

They had all used Shelley until they had used him up. None of that justified what Shelley had done, but all of it contributed to what he did. As David said, a person needed a conscience to justify what he did, and Shelley didn't have one of those.

David had warned him.

Stanford tightened the leather cinch about his waist, becoming more weighed down and more burdened. He continued to hurt.

For his best friend and for himself.

§

Thomas Jefferson Lee, from the lowlands of Twofer County, South Georgia, felt surprisingly at ease while sitting in the Lake Arrowhead Hotel lobby in the mountains of North Georgia. He always felt so uncomfortable around strangers, but this time, he enjoyed watching the people come and go.

Back home, he always spent the better part of his day working under a ceiling he could reach up and touch standing on his toes. But now sitting beneath a ceiling four stories high made him feel like a bottom feeder and a little dizzy whenever he looked up and saw the ceiling so far beyond his reach.

Colt thought about what Shelley had done, his blood boiling over. QueenBee was South Georgia royalty. She practically raised all six of them from hell-raising boys to halfway decent men.

The more he thought about what Shelley had done, the madder he got. It was time for him to get a move on. He stood, stretched, and headed outside to his rental car.

Colt had driven the rented Ford Taurus to within two miles of Stanford's cottage when he spotted a car parked on the side of the road. He cut his speed from forty to twenty so he could get a good look at the car. But that was no car; it was a hearse. Then he had to swerve to miss running down a man—no, a boy. Stanley!

Colt's heart jumped a beat. He jammed the brakes and ordered Stanley inside the car. He peppered Stanley with questions.

Stanley told how he'd left Twofer County hiding inside the coffin.

When Sid parked the hearse in Atlanta, he climbed out the coffin and drove the hearse from Atlanta to Lake Arrowhead where it just now ran out of gas on the side of the road.

All Colt could think about was the pain and the grief QueenBee would suffer when she found Stanley missing from the homeplace. He had to get Stanley back to the airplane where Top Cat was waiting. But they still couldn't leave until he'd tracked Shelley down like QueenBee sent him to do.

Swerving the rental car into a screeching U-turn, Colt went racing back toward the hotel. Stanley begged him to turn around, but he drove faster. Stanley screamed at him. Colt kept ignoring him. When he glimpsed the pistol in Stanley's hand, he grabbed for the gun while fighting to keep the car on the road and out the ditch. He missed when he tried to grab the gun. Stanley made him pay, sinking teeth into the back of Colt's hand. The car swerved.

Colt cursed, fighting the wheel. The back of his hand was burning. Stanley yanked open the door and leaped out into the night.

§

Stanford flipped through another notebook. Each one had a To-Do List written on the last three pages. He was reading the notebook dated Saturday, February 6—three weeks after the murders—when he heard a noise. He went outside to check. He opened the car trunk to check on the killer with the mouth like an asshole.

The little killer was still there. He slammed the lid down and went back inside. He picked up the notebook dated Saturday, January 23, a week after the murders. He read a few pages, his hard feelings about Shelley softening the more he read.

On first glance, that night seemed to have happened the exact way Clayton said it happened. Shelley somehow had anticipated the killer's plans and had followed the killer to Katie Kane's house. But the killer couldn't have known Stacey and Christopher would be in Katie Kane's house that night. Unless the killer knew ahead of time that Katie Kane would suffer a heart attack.

Stanford pinched the bridge of his nose and caressed his eyes. He again tried to think things through. It couldn't have happened that way; it was just too far-fetched. He felt tired and thirsty.

The killer had to have known Katie Kane would have a heart attack, or else the killer had to have known Stacey and Christopher were going to be there that night. It was one or the other. It could be neither or it could be both.

He decided to work under the premise the killer knew his wife and son would be there that night. If any evidence didn't fit that premise, he would throw out that evidence and keep the premise. He had to think differently than the cops because the cop's thinking had gone nowhere. That was the premise. Next question.

How did the killer know they would be in Katie Kane's house that night? And how did the killer know he would not be there but at Lake Arrowhead flirting with Jocelyn Slade? He felt sad. But he had to keep focused. He fought off the lump of sadness and kept concentrating on thinking things through and finding the killer.

He stuffed the notebook dated January 23 in his pocket, and picked up one dated Saturday, February 20. He flipped to the last three pages to the To-Do List. Shelley was checking boarding-houses for new renters around the time of the murders. The cops had checked the hotels, motels, trailer parks, and campgrounds.

Stanford read the notebook dated Saturday, February 27. Shelley had checked on the boardinghouses. He found two boarding-houses that he was going back later to double-check.

Stanford read the To-Do List in the back of the notebook. Shelley planned to find out who owned a defunct NYC nightclub the IRS had shut down for not sending in withheld payroll taxes.

New York City nightclub? He wondered about that connection.

He frowned at the words on the page. Why would a defunct NYC nightclub interest Shelley? What would such a place have to do with the killer? He paced the floor but couldn't easily walk the jitters away. He dragged a stool to the middle of the room and sat on it. He sat tapping the throwing knife in his hand and turning things over in his mind. He flipped the knife in the air, caught it and flipped it in the air again. Over and over, he flipped the knife up in the air and caught it, thinking of how the killer knew they were going to be there that night.

Then he saw headlights.

The headlights danced through the trees. It was a Jeep Chero-kee, but his gut said Shelley was driving. The headlights went out. The heavy engine shut down. The door slammed. Through the window, he saw the figure of a tall man cut through the gloom.

He rose from the stool, turned on the balls of his feet and threw the knife into the doorjamb, inches to the side of the door. The handle quivered and sang. He picked up the rifle and leaned back against the edge of the stool, waiting for Shelley to walk through the door. He felt a wave of sadness build up inside his stomach.

He heard footsteps approach the door and stop.

Then the door came alive in front of him, exploding from the doorjamb and sailing past his face like paper debris, and cartwheeling across the room like a fool. Stanford had dove to the side to keep the door from smacking him. The rifle flew from his hands. He hit the floor and rolled, coming to rest on his back. He had the wind knocked out of him, and he gasped to breathe. He rose up on his elbows and gawked at the terrible menace glaring at him.

Blind rage filled the empty space where the door used to be.

As did Shelley's dark quivering bulk.

Shelley's face glistened like slick acrylic. Blood caked his neck like a crimson collar. His red eyes looked like hot flames flickering in his head, or a candle waving inside a Halloween pumpkin. The big .44 gripped in Shelley's fist looked like an extension of the rage blazing in his twisted and contorted face of madness.

Stanford was terrified. How could he possibly deal with this? He couldn't tear his eyes away from the bore of the big .44 aimed at his face. He felt dizzy. He swallowed. "Shelley, wha—"

The muzzle of the .44 Magnum flashed. He heard no sound.

The bullet slammed into his chest like a battering ram with a big fist on the end of it. But he didn't feel the pain that went with a bullet ripping into and through your chest like that. Neither did he feel the force that lifted him off the floor and from under the thumb of gravity. He felt—nothing. He felt nothing.

He hit the floor on his butt and skidded.

He lay on his back, gasping, his lower jaw opening and closing like a blowfish out of water. He could only see psychedelic flashes of Shelley moving toward him. Then he sensed a force coming alive inside him, and moving around inside him.

At first Stanford felt nothing. He was without a body to feel with. But a fire was lit inside him, a strong, undeniable, burning will to live had just taken control of the rest of his life, as if he, himself, had been doing such a poor job of staying alive. He now sat in the back seat with nothing to say. His will to live was indeed taking him along for the ride.

He could see Shelley straddling him. He could see Shelley leveling the muzzle at his face. He wanted to close his eyes. He willed his eyelids to shut down, but his eyelids not only stayed open, they stayed locked wide open, because he was no longer in control. He kicked Shelley in the crotch without even knowing he had kicked Shelley in the crotch. The sudden blow dropped Shelley to his knees. He rolled out of Shelley's reach and stifled a scream. The bulletproof vest felt like an iron lung.

His fear overrode his paralyzing pain. But the wheezing behind him sent his fear ratcheting up another whole notch. He cut his eyes sharply to see Shelley on his feet and coming for him. Again.

§

Colt cursed and kept stuffing tree limbs and pine cones and leaves under the left rear tire stuck in the ditch. Then he jumped back behind the wheel, pressed the gas pedal lightly and drove the car slowly forward. He then shifted to reverse and drove the car slowly backwards, rocking the car forward and backward for about two frustrating minutes. He finally worried the car out of the deep rut the left spinning tire had made.

With all four tires now back on solid ground, Colt swerved the car around in the middle of the road and raced back toward Stanford's cottage, the car fishtailing down the road. Stanley now had a ten-minute head start, but he had short legs and was hoofing it.

A quarter mile later, Colt slowed the car to a fast-walking speed to keep from driving past Stanley. Creeping along the dark road, Colt stuck his head out the window to listen and to see better. He heard a rustling and tapped the brakes, bringing the car almost to a standstill. The blackness bled red in the glow of the brake lights.

The car rocked to a stop. He kept his foot on the brake, and the night continued to bleed. Then the chill of cold steel touched Colt's neck like a sloppy kiss.

§

Stanford lay pinned to the floor on his stomach. But, at least, he was back behind the wheel of his own life, back in control again.

He rolled his eyes upward to peer into Shelley's face and into his eyes. There was no there there anymore. He wanted to hug

Shelley. But there was no Shelley there to hug anymore—either.

His eyes darted from Shelley's face and swept around the room for an escape, for a weapon, anything. He spotted the rifle. Too far away but he had to go for it. He was dead if he didn't reach the rifle in time. He broke into a frantic dash across the floor on his knees and elbows. Shelley cut him off from the rifle in two easy steps and threw a slashing kick that struck him on the hipbone. He fell to the floor. His body shook in spasms, and his legs flailed.

Shelley reached down and hooked him under the armpits, and swept him off the floor like he was a child and up into his powerful arms. Shelley was crushing him in a bear hug. He flexed his back muscles and poked out his chest to keep Shelley from crushing his ribs. His lungs couldn't expand to take in air.

He looped his arms around Shelley's thick neck, but didn't have strength to choke him. His head flopped down on Shelley's face as if he wanted to sleep. The pain barely registered anymore; it had sapped his strength. Only when he tasted blood in his mouth did he know he'd ripped into Shelley's neck with his canines. The force did it! His strong will to live had saved him. Again.

Shelley yowled and loosened his grip for an instant.

Air exploded down into his lungs with such force that he got a rush from the inhalation. But Shelley kept his strong arms locked around his back and his feet off the floor. Without the floor for leverage, he couldn't muscle himself free from Shelley's grip. So he started wiggling, swaying his shoulders. To keep from falling, Shelley moved his feet in cadence to his wiggling and swaying. He and Shelley went twirling around the room in a lovers' embrace; pathetic dancers lost in the movement of music.

He bit Shelley again, sinking his canines into his thick neck. He jerked his head around, ripping flesh from bone. He kept biting Shelley's face, incisors ripping his flesh like knives. Blood flowed from the wounds. But, still, Shelley held tight to his death grip.

Again he slashed Shelley's face with his teeth as they danced. He bit Shelley's nose and his lips as they waltzed around the room in a rhythm of sadness and madness and death.

He bit Shelley's eye socket as they danced. He head-butted him again and again as they danced until his head felt woozy. Shelley almost stumbled, but recovered his balance and squeezed.

With the last of his small strength, he drew his arms back and slapped Shelley across both ears. The blow sent pain jolting up his arms. Shelley's grip loosened. The blow shook Shelley's equilibrium. He'd rocked the big man for the first time. Again he drew back his arms and slapped his palms against Shelley's ears. Again the blow staggered Shelley and, again, the smothering grip across his chest slackened. Again he slapped Shelley across his ears, this time with a viciousness that fed on itself.

Shelley's mouth popped open.

Shelley dropped him.

Shelley sank to his knees.

Gasping to breathe, his feet hit the floor, and his knees buckled. Air exploded down into his lungs. He sucked in huge gulps of air.

He watched as Shelley pried himself back on his feet. But he didn't try to move. He didn't care to move. Shelley stood in a half-crouch clawing blood from his half-closed left eye; the right eye was swollen shut. Shelley couldn't see.

The thought gave him a second wind. He rolled on his stomach, grunting, drawing his knees up so he could stand. He dragged over to where Shelley was trying to wipe blood from his half-closed eye. He stopped two feet away from Shelley and threw a kick to Shelley's knee to cripple him. The kick never landed.

Shelley wasn't where he should have been. Stanford knew Shelley had suckered him even before the punishing blow struck him behind his left shoulder blade. A big bone popped, and it felt like someone had driven a stake through his neck. He hit the floor and bounced, and he lay there, groaning, fighting to stay conscious.

He couldn't tell if his collar bone or his neck snapped. Either way he was down for the count, and this time he was done.

Pass the fork.

Shelley bent down and rested the warm muzzle of the .44 on his forehead. He heard a click. Then again, he felt a force come alive inside him; this time, speaking words only vaguely familiar to him, words bubbling up from the deep confines of his childhood.

"I am she who is. Come for me."

62

QUEENBEE SAT IN the sunroom. Her rocking chair was still, and the dice in her hand were silent. She felt as if she held happiness in one hand, sadness in the other hand, and she was stuck right smack in the middle.

Aretha and Franklin were out working.

They didn't like her being alone with strangers. But when she explained that Justin was their brother. They both went off to work satisfied. She studied Justin's face with a passion.

The past few hours had drained both of them, the trial and the trial's outcome. The deceptions, the half-truths, the outright lies, they had all come home to roost in her henhouse. All came to pass because she found a dying man on her property thirty-five years ago, and she nursed him back to health.

They were gone now. It ended so suddenly. They left as quickly as they came. No good-bye; no 'see you later,' except for one; no hugging—just quick distance between them, the Bonnells and the Romes. Lives were started. Lives were ended. Lives were lived. All because she did a good deed and saved a man's life. She turned away from watching Justin's face to watching the hummingbirds feasting on her sugar-water feeders.

"Justin," she said, "Rooster, he may not be guilty of rape; he may not be guilty of murder. But, your father, he sure is guilty of kidnapping your brother from Twofer County."

QueenBee turned away from watching the hummingbirds and back to watching Justin's face.

375

"But if I can survive thirty-five long years living with a lie, then I suppose I can survive a few more years living with the truth."

Justin started a slow rock in the rocking chair he sat in.

"You did the right thing, Queen—pardon me, I mean Mother. You acted wise—as always."

"Say that word again for me; won't you, Justin."

"Mother," Justin said.

"One more time for the road," she said.

"Mother," Justin said.

"Good. Now, say what you started to say to me before I got to feeling and acting—well…motherly."

"Well, Mother, my father didn't rape you—that sounds weird. Saying it makes me feel—well, foolish, to be honest."

"The middle name for this family is *weird*. If you talk a minute about this family without saying something weird about it, then you aren't really talking about this here family—believe it."

They both chuckled through the hurt they were both feeling, the hurt of all those missing years.

"Mother," Justin said, still shaking his head, "my father didn't rape you—still sounds weird. Anyway, your creation raped you. Johan—my father did not murder your—my brother. This is too weird to talk about."

"I get your point," she said. "If you'd rather cut it short."

"Nooo, let me get it said. I need to hear myself say it. That's therapeutic." Justin continued. "Your creation murdered your son and my brother. The bottom line, Qu—Mother, is that letting my father live was the right thing to do." He sighed. "Now, there, I've said it, and I've heard myself say it."

"And you feel better," she said.

"Absolutely," Justin said.

She rattled the dice, keeping the singsong going awhile. This kinship was weird to Justin. But the kinship was not weird to her one bit. She had known the truth all the while, except she hadn't known why Rooster went berserk on her after all she'd done to save his life. The roots and herbs and poison mushrooms explained the rape and the killing well enough. That, she should have known.

That she did know, but that knowledge got lost in the hatred she had for Rooster after he killed her son. She knew those mushrooms could drive a person loony, but she didn't want to remember. She didn't want to know she had caused Rooster's murderous, raping rampage. Shame on her and pass the amnesia tablets, please.

Still, the roots and herbs and poison mushrooms did not explain the kidnapping, not at all.

"I didn't let Rooster go, Son," she said. "You got Rooster off the hook with me is what you did. It happened just the way you said it happened. I believed what I wanted to believe. I deceived me."

She made a weak smile. "I have learned something new under the sun. Just because something never crosses your mind doesn't mean it's not the truth. It means you have small knowledge; you're narrow-minded, and you're not very wise."

"True," Justin said.

"Son, do you think Tartuffe will return to Twofer County to see me like he said he would?"

"Of course, he will. I got the sense he was bored with the life he's living. And, that's one thing this family is not, and that's boring. From what he told me, he may be the perfect guy to spearhead your campaign—you know, the one to build a university right here in Twofer County.

Her heart nearly skipped a beat. "What?"

"I cheated. I read your so-called Last Will and Testament. You wanted me to read it. How's that for obeying your mother."

She stood and threw open her arms.

"Son."

Justin stood and bent nearly double to hug her.

"Mother."

He curled his long body around her old bones. The feeling was so comforting to her that she got swept away on mighty clouds of joy.

63

OUTSIDE THE CABIN, the sedan's trunk lid creaked up six inches and stopped. The huge timber rattler tightened its coil, rattling its annoyance, the agitation reaching the high pitch of a beehive.

The trunk lid creaked all the way up and locked in place.

§

Candice Bergens kept the bore hole of the .380 screwed to Colt's neck while slapping handcuffs on his wrists. She forced the Twofer County detective in the car trunk and jumped behind the wheel.

She raced toward Stanford's cottage.

Candice parked in Stanford's gravel driveway and jumped out, running, the .380 leading the way.

The outdoor lights were on. The door was ajar a foot.

She pressed an ear to the opening then peeped in. It was dark except for the outdoor lights and the car lights spilling inside.

She gripped the .380 tighter, stood to the side of the doorjamb and pushed the door open wider with her left hand.

"Stanley?" she said. "Stanley, are you in there?"

She nudged the door wider with her left hand, letting the outdoor light spill deeper inside the dark room. She edged inside and felt along the wall for the light switch. She clicked it on.

Stanley sat slumped on a stool at the bar, staring at her like she was a ghost. The cop said the kid had a gun. She didn't see a gun, and then she did see the gun. On the bar. She lowered the .380.

"You okay, Stanley?"

She walked toward him.

"Oh, Stacey," the boy muttered, "Sta—"

The name startled Candice. The boy, reaching for her, melted off the stool, crumbling; she lunged, catching his head in her hands. They hit the floor together, his head hugged tightly to her bosom.

§

Stanford couldn't think. The pain was unbearable. The rage in Shelley's face was gone. Shelley sat on the floor, stupidly, staring at the open doorway. He followed Shelley's line of sight and squinted. He could barely see two forms swimming in the opening. Then, he recognized the runt with the asshole for a mouth, and he was swimming alongside a very big man.

They both had guns in their hands.

The two men disappeared from his line of sight. He couldn't turn his head; his neck was locked in one position. His neck had to be broken, or sprung, if there were such a thing as a sprung neck.

He heard them moving behind him, circling him.

Then he felt a bee sting on the back of his neck.

When Stanford finally regained consciousness, he was stretched spread-eagled across a tabletop in the middle of the floor on his stomach. His arms were looped under the table and tied together at his wrists, and each ankle was tied to a separate table leg. Drool pooled around his mouth.

"I popped that shoulder back in for you," the man behind him said. "And I gave you a shot of juice for that pain."

Suddenly, all hell broke out behind him in one of the bedrooms. Someone wailed. As soon as he heard the man leave to investigate, he went to work freeing his hands and feet.

He started squirreling his body over the tabletop down toward his feet until he looked like a diver frozen in a jackknife dive. Twisting his body like a contortionist, he managed to reach his left leg and untied the rope. Twisting his torso back hard the other way, he reached his right leg and untied that rope. He then scooted over the edge of the table and slid on down to the floor. His arms were still wrapped around the two table legs his feet had been tied to.

The ruckus behind him grew even more rowdy and maddening.

Using his head, he lifted the table legs off the floor, struggling and straining until he could slip his arms under the table legs to free himself. From one of the bedrooms came a scream that curdled Stanford's blood. The runt flew past his face like a human cannonball and smashed into the far wall—headfirst.

The delicate bones in the little man's necks snapped like kindling. His body lay twisted on the floor like a child's toy, his head resting at an ugly angle on his shoulders, and his popped eyeballs bulging out their sockets like light bulbs.

The pursed lips looked even more like an asshole.

A gunshot exploded, his heart jumped, and the giant appeared.

He muscled the rifle off the floor and up into his arms. Bracing his back tight against the doorjamb, he rested, willing his body to stop trembling. He rested the stock of the rifle on his left forearm, and found the trigger. He slowly, painfully lifted his forearm, pointing the muzzle straight at the giant.

The giant kept the gun down by his side and grinned.

Stanford pulled the trigger and nothing happened.

The giant raised the .44 and grinned at him.

Stanford dropped the rifle and leaned back against the wall, his head two feet from the throwing knife stuck in the wall near the doorjamb. He raised both hands over his head. The giant looked over at his broken partner. His fist closed around the handle, his eyes pinned on the giant. The sharp blade was buried deep into the wood, so he wormed it loose. Then with a last desperate tug, the knife broke free, and he pushed off the wall with his hipbone, and fell away from the door in the same motion.

The giant fired the .44 and missed by a mile.

He threw the knife and hit the floor hard. The steel flew arrow true. His shoulder popped out again, and he yowled from the pain.

He lay there, his muscles in spasms.

The steel blade bit deep into the giant's chest, up to the hilt. The big man stood gawking down at the steel handle protruding from his chest. Then the big man stiffened and nose-dived, driving the steel blade all the way through his chest cavity.

Almost a minute passed before he recovered enough to think clearly. He thought of Shelley and wormed his way into the bedroom. Shelley sat crumbled on the floor, his back braced against the wall. Shelley stared dumbly at the open doorway, his chin on his sternum. His knees bowed outward.

His legs folded under him like an accordion when he had dripped down the wall to the floor on his butt.

Shelley's face was a picture of horrors. He wormed his way over to where Shelley sat in a daze. He melted down next to Shelley's side. Each time Shelley's chest rose and fell, a gurgling sound rushed from the hole in his stomach. He brushed at the blood in Shelley's eye. But more blood seeped in from gashes in his brow.

Shelley opened his mouth to speak. Blood poured out instead of words.

"Shelley, why?" he besieged his friend. "Why did you kill them? How could you? You are my best friend. How could you?"

Shelley tried sucking in a deep breath, his throat rattling from the effort. Blood bubbles grew on Shelley's lips. "See-see."

"What do you mean?" he said, angry at the circumstances.

Shelley kept lolling his head from side to side.

He kept trying to focus but his emotions kept getting in the way. "You are my best friend, aren't you, Shelley?"

Shelley's head jacked up once, jacked down once, jacked up once.

"You are my best friend, too." He cradled Shelley's bloody, swollen, disfigured head. "You are my best friend, too, Shelley."

Shelley shuddered and his chin sank back down on his sternum.

"You killed Stacey and Christopher, didn't you, Shelley?"

Shelley lolled his head left then back right.

The fog of emotions blew away, and he was finally able to focus on what Shelley was telling him.

He felt alert. "Then who? Do you know who? Who, Shelley? Tell me who did it, Shelley. Who?"

The bubble on Shelley's lip swelled. Shelley shuddered. The bubble burst, spewing out Shelley's last breath.

"See-see."

Shelley's head rocked still, and he grunted once. Shelley's head sagged. Then his big body inhaled a gasp, exhaled and went loose.

Stanford cradled the head of his dead best friend.

"See-see," he repeated over and over, "See-see...See-see..."

64

SHELLEY WAS DEAD. Clayton was dead. David Harte was dead. Justin was his uncle and one of QueenBee's two living identical twins. Justin's father killed Stanford's father, QueenBee's other son.

He thought of Stanley and all the crazy things he did and lived—and lived. He laughed as more tears filled his eyes—and lived. Inside the second bedroom, the one he always kept locked, Stanford sat watching the laser printer churning out copy.

He thought about Shelley every day, and he dreamed about his best friend a lot at night. He was battered and bruised, but his best friend was dead and, for the most part, buried. He was so full of bitterness and hate he had little room for grief. And if not grieving was wrong, then wrong was right for him. He may be bitter toward his best friend, but he made certain Shelley's funeral plans were carried out as he instructed.

He had the body cremated and held no services. And yesterday, Colt carried out the last of Shelley's three wishes when he rowed a bass boat up the Timseesee River and fed his ashes to the fishes.

As a kid, that had always been Shelley's wish, to feed himself to the fishes in the Timseesee River. He was beginning to squirm to ease the pressure of the confining body armor protecting his ribs and collar bone. His neck hadn't been broken but it sure felt that way. The feeling reminded him of the old-fashioned crook-in-the-neck, only five times stiffer.

He lifted more sheets from the receiving tray, all information about the Jasmine Club, that New York City nightclub Shelley had been looking into. The Jasmine Club had been open for only three years. For the first two years, the nightclub was owned by Jocelyn's old boyfriend, Bryce Boyd. A year before the IRS shut down the Jasmine Club for not sending in payroll taxes the company withheld from employees' paychecks, Bryce Boyd sold the Jasmine Club to Norman Gene Bates.

He lifted more pages from the printer tray, including a photo of Norman Gene Bates. The handsome face didn't ring a bell. He set the photo aside. He did recognize Bryce Boyd's photo right away when he lifted it off the printer. He set that photo aside.

He spread out the telephone records for the boardinghouse where Norman Gene Bates lived for three weeks. Bates had gotten a telephone call at ten p.m. every evening. Except the day of the murders when Bates got a call at five p.m.

After receiving that five p.m. call, Bates left the boardinghouse for good, leaving behind a box of bibles. Bibles? Now that rang a bell. He kept reading more bits and pieces but nothing adding up to the whole story.

He sat down and went over the telephone calls again.

Each telephone call to Norman Gene Bates came from a different pay phone in downtown Atlanta. Except for the last call. That last call had come from a pay phone at Brown-Abernathy Airport in north Fulton County, about twenty minutes from downtown Atlanta. Stanford tried to think and focus on that last call, but his mind kept squirming back to the Jasmine Club.

He gave up thinking about the telephone calls and went back to thinking about the Jasmine Club. He reread Colt's report. The Jasmine Club was important to him only because Shelley had thought it was important. Still, he couldn't figure out a connection between Shelley's investigation and the Jasmine Club. He needed to know more about the nightclub. But who could he ask? Norman Gene Bates? He didn't know Bates and didn't know where to find him. Bryce Boyd? Now that was a thought. He knew Bryce, and he knew where to find the dapper Bryce.

§

The sedan crept past Bryce Boyd's split-level house. Lights were on inside and the garage door was closed. Stanford rested before getting out. The air was warm, still, damp, and heavy.

He inched his way to the front door. He rang the doorbell, got no answer after three rings and turned away, inching his way along the sidewalk around to the back of the house. He made his way along a ten-foot-high privacy fence. The gate was open. He took two steps through the gate and looked out past the volleyball pit and the patio. He didn't see anyone so he made his way toward the back area. It was well lit with two banks of tennis lights blazing over clay tennis courts. No one was playing, so he sidled over to the rear door of the house and pushed the lighted doorbell.

The announcement chimed pleasantly inside.

He waited, rang once more then rested his hand on the doorknob. He thought about it, shrugged off the thought and turned it. The knob rotated, the bolt clicked back, then he nudged the door open a crack. He called out Bryce Boyd's name. The exertion sent pain knifing through his side. He gasped, leaning against the doorjamb until the pain eased. That was dumb. He shuffled inside the house, gasping with each small step, and nudged the door shut behind him.

Resting one hand on top of the banister, he stared up at the formidable stairs, He took the first awkward step leading up to the second-floor level. One careful step at a time, stopping to rest after each step, he slowly made his way up the stairs. Four steps from the top, the stench stopped him in his tracks. He nearly gagged and that reflex sent more jolts of pain searing down his neck and spine. He groaned, leaning on the railing almost a minute before he could force himself to take another step.

At the top, he rested another minute, keeping his face turned from the nauseating smell from his childhood. The first whiff of rotting flesh, human or animal, always reminded him of roasted Brazil nuts. The only stench worse than what he was now trying not to smell was the stench of a skunk. He didn't need to go farther. The stench didn't lie—that was the stench of human flesh.

Using the wall for leverage, he edged his way down the hallway to check each room. It took him more excruciating minutes to look inside the first two bedrooms and the bathroom; all three were empty. At the door of the third bedroom, he retched and nearly vomited. He smothered his nose and mouth with both hands and took slow shallow breaths. The reflex sent bolts of hot, punishing pain searing across his neck, shoulders, and back. He quivered as another groan seeped through his clenched lips. When the muscle spasms eased, he slowly, carefully dabbed his temples.

Smothering his nose and mouth again, he pushed open the third bedroom door and edged inside.

Stanford stared down at the dead man.

The bloated body was the size of a sumo wrestler, and it was surrounded by a pool of dried black blood that looked like splotches of tar. Blow flies swarmed the head. Maggots swam in the soup of the neck. A reflex caused his stomach to lurch. He turned to leave, glimpsing letters scribbled in the blood but not taking time to read them. He shuffled from the room hugging his stomach.

He got a towel from the bathroom and wiped his fingerprints off everything he touched. That took nearly half an hour. He would call the cops later.

Finding a jar of vapor rub in the medicine cabinet, he shoved a glob up each nostril. Then he soaked a towel with rubbing alcohol. He tied the towel over his mouth just beneath his nose. The alcohol stung his eyes and nearly gagged him, but it was a lesser evil than the stench of a ripe dead man. Back inside the bedroom, he read the three letters scrawled in the blood then he left.

He dialed 911 from a convenience store and gave them Bryce Boyd's address. Then he drove for Jud Judson's office.

§

Two cars were parked in Jud's parking spaces: a Corvette convertible and Jud's own rattletrap Ford sedan.

Inside, a gorgeous redheaded woman was sitting in Jud's office sopping tears when he walked in. She was clutching a briefcase in her lap as if it had the Theory of Everything mapped out inside.

Jud introduced her to him as Francine, Shelley's friend.

Francine sniffled a hello and then held the briefcase out to him without preamble. "Shelley, he loved you like a brother, Mr. Stanford," she said.

Francine patted the back of his hand as he took the offering. Then, as if to complete the transaction and distance herself from the briefcase, she took a pair of dark sunglasses from her purse and hid her eyes behind them.

He tried to wait for Jud to return from escorting Francine to her car, but when Jud got back he was already elbow-deep in the briefcase. His enthusiasm for the contents inside soon cooled. Jud watched him sort pieces of papers into different stacks on the small table.

"None of this surprises you?" Jud said.

Stanford stopped shuffling papers and thought on the question. "Mark Davis may have ordered Juanita killed," he said, "but James Kelsey was the one who beat her to death with a damn poker."

"True," Jud said.

"Maybe I'm surprised James Kelsey brutalized her," he said. "I knew they didn't get along. I never knew he hated her so much."

"He did," Jud said. "You not surprised he iced the white boys?"

"Richard and Mark?" He shook his head. "No surprise there."

He returned to sorting papers from the briefcase. Trying to decipher Shelley's handwriting was like trying to read hieroglyphics.

"Trying to read Shelley's handwriting is like trying to read Egyptian writing," Jud said.

"No shit," he said.

"No shit," Jud said. "Stanford, James Kelsey, he had his own reason for wanting Juanita dead, you know."

He looked up. "What do you mean by that, Jud?"

"Remember that trio I pointed out to you at James' memorial?"

"James' girlfriend, Dorothy," he said. "And the couple they hung out with."

"Well, the other man's girlfriend, her name was Wanda. Except that Wanda, she ain't no man's girlfriend because Wanda, you see, is actually a Warren; if you see what I mean. Wanda, she's a girl's girl. The three people and James, the four of them, they shared a triplex together in Clayton County."

Jud eyed him. "Did you know that about James?"

"Know what?" he said. "Know what about James?"

"Those autopsy boys over there tell me you could have driven a MARTA bus up James Kelsey's behind."

"No shit." He thought about it, then chuckled.

"No shit," Jud said.

He thought about it some more. That was why James hated having Juanita so close to him. A woman could probably more easily see any feminine traits that unintentionally popped up from time to time. He was dumb to the fact. Never crossed his mind.

"Yes, I can see it now," he said. "James kept Juanita away from him by making it pure hell for her whenever she came too close."

Jud closed the middle drawer, opened his bottom desk drawer and took out a chrome-plated pistol. Jud held up the gun for him to see.

"Know what this is?" Jud said.

"Katie Kane's .38," he said, instantly.

§

The next day, down in Twofer County, the rain showers fell fast and furious, slowed to a patter, drizzled awhile, and then abruptly stopped. Then came the heat wave and the broiling humidity—stewed.

Aretha licked Stanford's face, and he brushed the big head away. Franklin sat at his feet. He reached down and picked Franklin up in his arms.

"You know, QueenBee, when I see another set of baby bull mastiffs around, it makes me so sad."

"Well, Son, we all gotta leave away from here. Aretha and Franklin, they are both seven, going on eight. They are healthy dogs. But none of their ancestors reached ten. And it takes those two about a year and a half to break in their replacements. Even now, poor Aretha, she's already ornery and getting worse after each full moon. Bullheaded heifer."

"So, Shelley did kill his stepfather," Stanford said.

"Beat me to it," QueenBee said, her rocking chair at rest.

He sat listening to QueenBee tell how she'd been hypnotizing Shelley since he was a boy, about the Vietnam War, about the Miami Assassin, about the Chaserville Massacre, and on and on.

He said, "so when David Harte erased your post-hypnotic suggestion for Shelley to come back to Twofer County, he triggered Shelley's killing spree. Is that right, QueenBee?"

QueenBee nodded. "I'd rather believe that. Whether it's true or not. It's easier to swallow that way."

QueenBee looked almost tiny.

She said, "Shelley, he had nothing to do with killing Stacey and Christopher. That's a whole different ball game. You talked to Katie Kane's niece—what's her name?"

"Candice. Candice Bergens. Colt's got her stashed at the back of the cemetery. She'll wait until I show up to get her."

QueenBee sighed. "You suppose Stanley and Jocelyn are back from their sightseeing, so we can get on with this?"

§

Stanford and Jocelyn sat at a table in QueenBee's greenhouse, eating apple pie and homemade ice cream.

Stanley joined them and tried to get his hands on the keys to Jocelyn's Jaguar, so he could take it for a spin. But the teenager settled on sitting behind the wheel and blasting the 240-watt sound system to his eardrums content.

"The keys are in the ashtray," Jocelyn told him.

They watched Stanley leave.

QueenBee rattled the dice. "Jocelyn," she said, "why do some folks call you reporters, talking heads and such?"

His grandmother spoke in a bewitching tone. He recognized that as her first shot fired over Jocelyn's bow. It had started, the beginning of the end of his search.

Jocelyn knew gunfire when she heard it, too and her beguiling smile lost half its charm. Jocelyn studied his face as if she expected him to rescue her from QueenBee's aggression. Not seeing him throw a life preserver her way, Jocelyn shifted her eyes back on QueenBee and slipped the charm back into her now smaller smile.

Jocelyn's hands became worry beads.

QueenBee rattled the dice. The sound unnerved Jocelyn, and her neck seemed to shrink a few inches down into her shoulders.

"Jocelyn, who's Alice Cooper?" QueenBee said.

The ambush shook Jocelyn. Disbelief zipped across her brow like a burning arrow. But she was a professional at beating back attacks, and few people were better at it than she was. She slipped easily back into character like the player she was.

Jocelyn cleared her throat.

"Alice Cooper." Jocelyn cleared her throat again. "Well, Queen-Bee, that was my name before I changed it to Jocelyn Slade."

Jocelyn spoke confidently, but she threw Stanford another worried look. "Then I joined the army, and that's when I burned my past behind me. Not much of a past, I admit though."

"Huh-huh," QueenBee said. She stopped rocking and leaned forward, the bones jumping in her fist.

"Why did the army kick you out?" QueenBee said.

Jocelyn jerked her attention back to QueenBee, pain filling her eyes to the brim. Stanford knew about the army, but not the boot.

"How—"

Jocelyn looked over at him again, then back at QueenBee. "If you know about that then you also know I slugged a senior officer. The Army tried to crap on me. But, I got me a civilian lawyer and got my honorable. The colonel got sacked. End of story."

Jocelyn glanced over at him again then turned back squinting at QueenBee. "It was sealed. How did you find out? It was sealed."

QueenBee rocked back, stopped, rocked forward, stopped, and then the pitch of the dice grew into a steady singsong.

"Why go to Butte, Montana, for college?" QueenBee said. "That's a whole different world out there."

Jocelyn's lower lip trembled. "How did you get behind a sealed court document? I wanna know. It was sealed."

QueenBee rocked forward in the rocking chair and stopped, the steady singsong of the dice grew agitated and then increased to the high pitch of a rattler set to strike.

"If you're Alice Cooper, then, tell me, who in tarnation is C. C. Ryder?"

Gasping, Jocelyn's hands flew to her throat. She fell back in the chair as if that one question had two fists that delivered a one-two punch right between her startled eyes.

The name made him squirm, and he didn't have a clue as to why the name made him squirm. He had never heard the name before, that he could remember. So why did the name make him squirm? And why did the name leave Jocelyn Slade in wide-eyed shock?

QueenBee rocked back in the chair and glared at Jocelyn.

"Get a hold on yourself," QueenBee said. "Now why Butte, Montana, instead of, say...Opp, Alabama?"

Jocelyn's gaze locked down on her busy hands.

"I, ah—," Jocelyn stuttered. "I went to Butte to get away. I went to Butte to shed what I was, who I was. I went to Butte to bury my past. I went to Butte to make a new me." Jocelyn ignored her hands long enough to look over at him. "I went to Butte because I was a nothing and a nobody."

Jocelyn turned her gaze back on QueenBee, then she looked over at him again before she looked back down at her squirming hands.

"I went to Butte, Montana, so I could learn the social graces in an out-of-the-way place so people wouldn't be laughing at me. I went there so I could read big books, so I could take drama training, so I could take speech classes and dance and art classes in such an out-of-the-way place so people wouldn't be laughing at me. I was nothing and a nobody, so I went there to change nothing into something, to change a nobody into a somebody."

Jocelyn looked at him again. "Isn't that what every girl wants— to rise above her poverty and her shitty start in life?"

She studied his face with passion. "Isn't that what we all want— to rise above being a nothing and a nobody?

"Everybody everywhere wants to be somebody somewhere."

Jocelyn went back to staring down at her busy hands, then her shoulders rolled back, and her worrying hands fell apart to lie still in her lap. Slowly, almost reluctantly, she lifted her head, jaw set and jutted, her eyes now blocks of smoking dry ice.

"I went to Butte because I needed privacy to tear down the old me," she bragged. "To rid me of my southern drawl, to bury my Appalachian twang. After serving a two-year, self-imposed exile in Butte, I left Montana to become a quick study at the University of Louisville. I took a degree in broadcasting and a minor in sociology and psychology. After a two-year hitch in Louisville, I got the hell out of Kentucky for good. I struck out for the Big Apple where I scratched and clawed for four years in NYC. Although the Big Apple did keep the doctors away, it came with its own demons. But, me, I blew that town in the nick of time. I landed in Atlanta where I hit my stride. I became the new anchor for the number-three TV station in town. In seven months of cutthroat competition, I ended on top. I used every trick I learned in the trenches of NYC to slice and dice my way to the top in this city too busy to hate, and too laid-back to keep a go-getter down for long.

"And, me, I've been the cream of the crop in Atlanta TV News ever since."

Jocelyn squinted over at him with a look of triumph.

"Not so bad for a lil' ol' orphan from the Kentucky coal mines, huh, Stanford?"

65

TWOFER COUNTY

THURSDAY, JUNE 30

RAIN WAS POUNDING nails down in the ground, as the old folks used to say, when Stanford and Jocelyn left the homeplace.

The wind blew mightily through the forest of tall reedy pine trees, playing a tune that rose and fell in pitch as the wind rose and fell in strength. Angry raindrops splattered the windshield while the wind howled through the pine needles like wolves.

Stanford steered the Jaguar under the Twofer County Dirt Beds arch and parked. Wind gushes rocked the car like swells rocked a rowboat, and swept the driving rain across the tombstones as if it were a broom sweeping away leaves and debris.

He killed the engine, slid out the ignition key and palmed it.

Jocelyn gave him a curious look but otherwise sat unflustered in the eye of the thunderstorm whirling all around her.

"It's ugly out there," Jocelyn said and squeezed his hand.

He stiffened at her touch but smiled in her face. The conflicting signals were not missed by Jocelyn, who knitted her brow.

"What is it, Stanford? What's wrong?"

Jocelyn followed his gaze out the window, and she squeezed his arm. The touch of her fingers felt like tentacles.

He cleared his throat. "Jocelyn, who's Norman Gene Bates?"

Jocelyn's hand fell from his arm; she looked genuinely hurt.

"Stanford, why are you doing this? Don't you care for me?"

He repeated his question. "Who is Norman Gene Bates?"

Tears swelled in Jocelyn's deep eyes. "I'm sorry, Stanford. Miss Perfect, I'm not." Her sniffles made her lips pout and quiver.

The wind blew sheets of rain at the car, rocking it like a cradle.

Jocelyn molded her palms together prayerfully beneath her chin.

"Stanford, does one mistake make me a bad person? Does one little mistake disqualify me from loving you, and you loving me? Does one mistake make such a big difference in our lives?"

His eyes circled Jocelyn's face. His clashing emotions had him so tangled up inside that her words registered in his mind only because they were not the words he wanted to hear.

"Tell me about Norman Gene Bates, Jocelyn. Tell me now."

Jocelyn sat, her head cocked; she was twirling a clump of hair around a finger, and studying his face now, looking for clues.

Finally, Jocelyn nodded as in a gesture of self-approval.

"Okay, Stanford," Jocelyn said. She rubbed her temples before she looked at him with eyes as bright as crystal. "I owe you that.

"Norman Gene and I, we met in New York City eight years ago. Norman Gene, he was like an agent for starry-eyed, horny-assed, wet-behind-the-ears news readers like yours truly back then, like me. Norman Gene was streetwise and flashy. Me, I was just one bug-eyed country hick running fast and loose in a big city oozing with all sorts of crazy pleasures, whatever your crazy pleasure may be. Until then in my young fledging career, it was the same sorry story. Country girl meets city boy. NYC had it all.

"New York City was one hotbed of young exuberant talent. And I mean everybody was knee deep into dicks and pussies and coke and uppers and having one hell of a good time in the cultural heartland of America. NYC was a place for dreamers and doers. Everywhere you looked around the Big Apple, you saw territorial studs leaning on lamp posts on each street corner. I mean those guys looked good enough to take home to momma. Super studs they were. Big dicks. Big egos. Big bucks. Endless lines of coke. And to ride that gravy train all a woman had to do was to spread a little stanky stuff around to soothe the oversized egos of those coke heads, which took all of two minutes, if that long. And for a few minutes of your very plentiful downtime, you bought yourself one hell of a good time for the rest of the glorious night, the rest of the next eye-popping day, the rest of the eight-day week."

A gush of wind roared beneath the wheels and rocked the car as if they were babes in a cradle.

"On the job, me, I was an okay news reader, that's all. Not the best news reader but okay enough to keep a job. But I can tell you what I was. Stanford, I was a realist. Oh, boy, if Jocelyn Slade was anything, Jocelyn Slade was a realist. Hey, I had good looks, but being just average in the brains department was a big shortcoming in my business. You can only screw your way so far up the ladder before you run clean out of rung to hold onto.

"Stanford, once you get so high up there in the so-called board room, those old coots couldn't long appreciate a steady diet of a young women like yours truly. I never fooled myself about the racket I was in. My graces, my schooling just didn't take root deep enough for me to pretend, for me to put on airs I didn't have.

"I could have bullied my way to the top on just pure survival instincts, my only motivation being to stay the hell away from where I came from. I was born and raised in Eastern Kentucky, for Christ's sake. I grew up in that other world you people only read about in comic strips and in hillbilly books. I was close kin to Lil' Abner, for crying out loud. I was a nothing. I was a nobody."

Jocelyn's eyelids seemed to roll up under her brows. Her eyes bulged from her head as if extended on eyestalks.

"My peers were mostly big-city folks, and those Ferrari asses— that's what I called them, Ferrari asses—they ran laps around the hick kid from the Blue Grass State, I'm here to tell you. Me, toot-tooting around in my new Model T."

Jocelyn gazed down into her hands as if they were deep buckets filled to the brim with her grief and her pain. Then she hitched up her head to study his face with deep feelings in her round eyes.

"You know, Stanford, I learned a very valuable lesson about this country of ours back then. I learned that your past, it went a long ways in deciding your future unless you had lots of money or loads of talent. Average people like me, we are an aberration in this business. Me, I was not only penniless but a small talent to boot. I was no one special. Now, I'm only one rung away from latching onto the big times, one rung from reaching the top of my profession. Folk in the business would kill for this chance. Well, Stanford, I don't want it that bad anymore. I just want to be loved."

He understood that. He didn't want that. But he understood it.

"I do want you to love me, Stanford. I want you to love me, love me, love me. I dare you to try to love me more than I love you, Stanford. I don't want to be the best me anymore. I just want the best us that we can be—together, me and you, Stanford. That's all. Just the best us, so we, you and I, we can be together and we can stay together, Stanford. I want you to love me, Stanford. I want you to love me, love me, love me."

The sky darkened. He heard hunting dogs baying in the distance.

"Stanford, I've always had to scratch and claw for a job. In NYC, I was a ten-dollar talent hanging out in a hundred-dollar body, and I was stressed out like you wouldn't believe. Still, I woke up every morning and thanked my lucky stars I was living and fighting in NYC, and not living and not fighting back home in Eastern Kentucky. Each day was gut-check day for me. I got stressed out like you would not believe. Before long, this country kid was lost."

Jocelyn chuckled horribly. "I was standing on very shaky ground back then, Stanford, let me tell you, very shaky ground."

She rubbed her eyes. Black clouds moved in on the horizon.

"Sure, I was a party girl. But I didn't screw around. Sure didn't. Not even a titty feel. And, boy, when word got around the chitling circuit that old Jocelyn Slade wasn't screwing nothing, I became a marked woman—a trophy to be bagged."

Jocelyn chuckled.

"The dicks and the clits, God forbid, they all came screwing up out the woodwork—studs and superstuds; butches and dykes, all hustling this starry-eyed kid from Eastern Kentucky. But, I hung in there. I hung tough against that onslaught of inhumanity. But the pack, they soon wore my tired behind down, for real. Was the peer pressure too great, or was I too weak? A moot point, really."

"What about Bates?" he said.

"I'm getting there," Jocelyn said, eyes glistening with memories. "Under those stressful conditions, into my sorry life walks handsome Norman Gene Bates."

Jocelyn's eyes dimmed as if the fun had gone out of her life.

"Norman Gene Bates never even reached first base with me and he, kind of, I thought at the time, threw me to his buddy, Bryce Boyd. You know you men just love passing along to your so-called friends, us women you men considered to be cold fish. Hell, me— I was more than a cold fish, I was Arctic salmon, let me tell you.

But I had it all figured backwards about Norman Gene Bates and Bryce Boyd. You see, Bryce, he did the siccing. He sent Norman Gene Bates to see what I was about and to report back to him."

The blowing rains abruptly stopped with a shudder. The air rippled as the clouds wrung out the last few raindrops.

"And Bryce Boyd," Jocelyn said, "he was an Adonis. By comparison, good-looking Norman Gene looked like a toad. The girls, and some guys, they went all gaga, goo-goo over this handsome man, Bryce Boyd. Me, I just stood off to the side, soaking it all in. But I secretly lusted after the prettiest man I'd ever seen in my life. I just didn't see how any man could look any better than Bryce looked. Hell," she chuckled, "it was only later that I learned Bryce had even more brains than he had looks—a deadly combination. But he just couldn't keep it in his pants. Often enough."

Overhead, the tall, dark clouds sank lower to the ground as if eavesdropping on the goings-on down below.

"Between Bryce and me, things jumped off from the get-go. And it was all good. Hey, one day I'm so burdened and on the verge of cracking up. But the next day I'm not that way at all. I'm telling you, Stanford. It was like I'd been living in the Dark Ages in a cave all that time, and then Bryce Boyd, he came along to flick the light on, so I could see. For the first time in my life, I had fun. I started loathing sleep, and I kept pinching myself to keep from dozing off and missing something. I was so wired. My life was so grand with Bryce. It was all good.

"Bryce and I, we became a New York City item; can you believe it? Me. Bryce and I, we went places—expensive, faraway places. Bryce and I, we did things—expensive and daring things. Bryce, he shaped me into the ultimate professional I am today. Bryce, he made me improve my small talent, drove me like a madman, made me work my butt off. Bryce, he made me care. I mean he made me really care, Stanford. He turned this piece of a coal-town girl into a diamond in the rough just by being nice to me, and letting me be free. He never smothered me, Bryce didn't.

"Bryce, he...he even built me this private little broadcast booth, and he—and he made it soundproof, so I could practice my craft twenty-four hours a day in a real-time broadcast booth, the whole nine yards, the works. And then Bryce, he did something I never expected him to do. After all of this attention and devotion and expense, Bryce, he faded into the background of my life. Bryce Boyd, he left me standing alone on my own two feet."

The sky quickly blackened as the tall dark clouds on the horizon flattened out and rushed in.

Jocelyn's eyes floated behind a rising tide of tears.

"Stanford, Bryce stepped back so I could step up. And soon, the kid was feeling pretty darn good about herself. My confidence hit the roof; the way my heart swells in my throat when you know you're in love with the right man, like I know I'm in love with you, Stanford. I'm so tired of being alone, Stanford. I want you to love me, Stanford. I want you to love me, love me, love me."

He opened the car door. "I'll be back," he said, and closed the door. He limped past Stacey's and Christopher's graves and up the asphalt until he had limped completely out of sight of the Jaguar.

The clouds burst into rain.

§

Jocelyn squinted up through the windshield, trying to see through the pounding rain. The woman had appeared from behind the rain like a ghost. She was now bouncing toward the car like a runway model. Her hips were swinging from side to side.

Jocelyn bent closer to the windshield, her nose nearly touching the glass. She squinted harder, but the driving rain made it impossible for her to clearly see the hip-swinging woman's face.

Jocelyn rubbed her eyes, squinting harder. Suddenly, she jerked back from the image. But her eyes stayed locked on the ghostly figure marching her way, sashaying up and down like a fashion model bouncing along the runway at a fashion show.

The hip-swinging woman drew closer, quicker. Jocelyn sat sucking air and whining like a trapped animal. Then her composure broke down completely, and shattered.

Jocelyn Slade lost touch with reality.

Time and place abandoned her.

She screamed.

"Shelllleeey!"

66

STANFORD'S KNEES BUCKLED when hot, molten pain shot down his spine. But he stiffened his knees to break his fall. His legs trembled, but he stayed on his feet.

He was twenty yards away from the Jaguar. He could see Candice standing in front of the sleek luxury automobile, peering down through the windshield at Jocelyn. The long walk away from the Jaguar had left Stanford barely able to lift his feet off the ground without suffering paralyzing pain.

Shuddering and grunting, he dragged his left foot even with his right one. More pain cut across his hip, and violent muscle spasms sent shivers all through his body. He stood paralyzed, trembling, and hurting. He could drag himself no farther.

§

The sniper's purse dangled heavily from her shoulder. She stared down through the windshield into Jocelyn Slade's twisted face. When Stanford recruited Candice to play this role, he wouldn't tell her what the game was about. Stanford simply told her to let Jocelyn see her face, and then she would know what to do next.

But all Candice saw was one terrified chick, who looked more than a little whacked out. The chick was a nut case, no doubt.

Jocelyn screamed up into her face. "You're dead, and he's mine! Mine! Go away! Leave me alone! Go away!"

Boy, was she bent.

A light clicked on in Candice's head. What it revealed hiding in the shadows of her mind iced her blood. She slid the key Stanford had given her into the door lock. She turned the key—the latch popped up. Jocelyn scrambled from under the wheel and backed up against the passenger's door, whining fiercely up at her.

When Candice opened the driver's door, Jocelyn shrank away, lifted her legs and started kicking her feet, the woman's legs churning like pistons in an engine.

Candice grabbed one leg by the ankles and tried to yank Jocelyn out on the ground. But the scowling woman kicked her foot free, and kept kicking at her face. No longer whining, Jocelyn snarled and hissed. She was much stronger than she looked. But Candice wanted her prize. She made a promise she intended to keep.

Twice more, Candice grabbed one leg and, twice more, Jocelyn kicked her leg free. But the third time Candice got two good hand-holds on one leg and yanked with all her strength. She dislodged Jocelyn from the passenger side of the car over to the driver's side where the hellcat grabbed the steering wheel. With a mighty jerk, she broke the woman's hold and dragged her out on the ground on her butt. But the spitfire bounced up off the ground like her butt was spring-loaded, and the ground was a trampoline.

Candice felt a cold panic. The scene was so unreal. She might have to shoot the bitch. But that was as far as her thinking got. Jocelyn sprang at her like a cat, and attacked her with the fierce strength of a wild animal.

She tried to fight the woman off, standing toe-to-toe with her, slugging it out with her. Their arms flailed, trying to maul each other's face with their nails. Jocelyn's insane strength was overwhelming Candice. The intensity of the newswoman's attack was nonstop. Candice ducked one wild punch, and she ducked another wild punch, but the third wild punch got through. The fist struck her jaw, and the next thing she knew she was looking up at Jocelyn from the ground and seeing many of her. She shook her head to clear away the cobwebs and rolled to her stomach. She struggled up on her hands and knees; and, she heard dogs baying in the distance. Then the crazy woman leaped on her back and rode her back down to the ground. The punches kept raining down on her head like someone playing knock-knock jokes on fast-forward.

Candice tried covering up, but still too many blows were getting through to her head.

"No! No! No! You're dead, he's mine! You're dead, he's mine!"

Candice twisted and turned, squirming, and fought back up on her knees and hands. She bucked and snorted, trying to unseat Jocelyn, who had locked her legs around Candice's waist and kept pounding down on her head unmercifully, riding her like she was a mare.

Candice kept bucking until finally an extra vigorous leap off the ground dumped Jocelyn off her back and on her butt. But the newswoman bounced back up and slammed into her like a stiff rubberband connected them at the hip. Candice fought desperately, trading blow for blow with the hellcat, standing toe-to-toe with the crazy woman, and losing badly.

Again she hit the ground on her butt, but this time she bounced right back up, driven by pure adrenaline and the strong will to live. It was kill the crazy bitch or die trying to kill the bitch.

§

Stanford had taken only baby steps in the past three minutes. One very slow, very painful half-step at a time, he dragged himself. He could see the Jaguar and hear the fighting women. Another sharp pain pierced his rib cage and buckled his knees. He grunted, shivered and held on. Raindrops started falling on his head.

More spasms moved through his gut like cockscrews as he kept inching along toward the Jaguar. He took one awkward step and stumbled to one knee. He tried to stand but his legs simply trembled from the effort. Water puddled around the depression his knee made in the soft dirt. He slowly let his other knee sink to the ground as well. No way he could stand. He braced his palms on the ground, down on all four, and tried crawling. But his limbs only quivered at his command to move. The effort sent more pain cutting from his hip up to his shoulders and neck. His arms gave out and he fell back down to the ground with a splat. He lay there, resting his cheek in the cool mud as more spasms wrestled down his spine and ended as a sharp pain in his tail bone.

Raindrops peppered his face; water puddled around his cheek.

§

The two women kept slugging it out. Jocelyn's fierce, nonstop attack drove Candice back on her heels, and kept driving her backwards. Candice threw a vicious punch that landed on Jocelyn's temple.

Instead of the blow toppling the newswoman, it only intensified her savage counterattack.

Jocelyn hit Candice another jaw-jarring punch that sent the sniper sprawling back to the ground, the side of her head striking a headstone. She lay on her back, unmoving.

§

Desperation drove Stanford's fingers clawing down into the mud. But his arms lacked strength to pull him. He rolled painfully on his back. The raindrops washed his face. He found the pain of laying on his back was worse, so he struggled until he was able to roll back over on his stomach to rest.

He had to get there; he was supposed to be there with Candice.

His mind fought for a solution to his problem, and finally it found one. When he rolled over from his stomach to his back and back to his stomach, he had moved closer to the Jaguar.

Stanford rolled again over on his back, rested, then over on his stomach and rested. He kept it up in a slow and painful roll toward the Jaguar, now so close but yet so far away.

§

QueenBee and Big Bertha McConico materialized from the rain like ghosts, the bull mastiffs swaggering at their heels. All four came splashing through the water puddles, kicking up spray.

The Jaguar lay between them and Stanford. Neither could see the other. QueenBee stopped the procession. The bull mastiffs danced at her ankles. She pointed at Jocelyn and barked an order.

"Tree Franklin. Sic 'er!"

Franklin yelped and hit full sprint in two great leaps.

Aretha crouched slow, almost on her belly, and started slinking away toward the action.

"Stay."

Aretha growled and reared on her hind legs, but she stayed put, snarling at the injustice and tapping out a war dance near Queen-Bee's feet, whining and watching Franklin work.

§

Jocelyn saw the big powerful dog in full gallop, and she ran for her life. Franklin was already on her flank, trotting alongside and snapping at her heels and growling and snarling. Jocelyn's head swung back and forth as she ran. She hopped and skipped her way across the cemetery and over the tombstones. The snarling bull mastiff snapped at her heels, herding her.

Jocelyn kept stumbling, twisting and turning back toward the Jaguar. Shrieking, she bunny-hopped across the tombstones, legs flapping to the sides like flippers. She was ten feet from the Jaguar when she took a running leap up on the hood, landing with both feet planted, and sprang up on the roof without breaking stride.

Growling deep in his throat, Franklin stopped and reared up in front of the grille, snapping his powerful jaws and spraying the air with drool. The bull mastiff's powerful front paws scratched and clawed deep ruts in the delicate skin of the Jaguar.

Wide-eyed and hysterical, Jocelyn Slade squatted on the roof like a frog on a lily pad. She was screaming maniacally down at the snarling Franklin, her cries one with the bluesy mood spreading out all across the Twofer County dirt beds.

"Heel, Franklin." QueenBee whispered the words.

Aretha yelped and leaped into the air, landed and gave out three quick yelps.

"Thanks, Aretha, old girl," QueenBee said. "I needed that."

Franklin wheeled around and galloped back to QueenBee's side, huffing and puffing and drooling, chest extended—satisfied.

§

Covered in grit, Stanford continued to roll toward the jaguar. He was within five car lengths of the Jaguar when he stopped again to catch his breath and to let the pain ease somewhat. He heard the commotion between the bull mastiff and Jocelyn, but the Jaguar blocked his view of what was going on. He saw Candice lying on the ground near a headstone, and her shoulder bag laid on the ground beside her. Then he saw Jocelyn squatting on top of the Jaguar. Jocelyn turned her head, limp hair matted to the shape of her skull, and she saw him from on high.

He whispered Jocelyn's name, unable to hear his own words.

Jocelyn rested her chin on her knees, looped her arms around her legs and looked down at him.

Stanford lay his head on his arm, cursing himself. He'd been so naive, and so easy to manipulate. There was something broken inside that woman. She was totally off her fucking rocker. She'd hired the murderer who did the actual killing, and then she killed the murderer she'd hired—It was all so…so damn cold-blooded.

Stanford lay helpless on the ground, loathing himself.

Jocelyn unraveled her arms from around her legs and reached down to him like she was inviting him into the arms of a messiah. Her words floated down to him as if they came down in a dream.

"I love you, Stanford. I want you, Stanford. You want me, don't you, Stanford? I need you, Stanford. You need me, don't you, baby? Oh, don't you just need me, baby? I want you to love me, Stanford. I want you to love me, love me, love me."

He wanted to cover his ears, but his arms were useless. He could not block out the noise. And neither could he block out the truth.

"I want you to love me, Stanford, love me, love me, love me."

That awful and pathetic truth.

"I want you to love me, Stanford, love me, love me, love me."

He didn't hate Jocelyn Slade.

"I want you to love me, Stanford, love me, love me, love me."

He loved Jocelyn Slade.

"I want you to love me, Stanford, love me, love me, love me."

The grief.

"I want you to love me, Stanford, love me, love me, love me."

The anguish and the guilt.

"I want you to love me, Stanford, love me, love me, love me."

This just couldn't be happening to him.

Jocelyn leaped to her feet, prancing on the roof like a brat. She threw her arms all about her head like she was fighting off a cloud of gnats, her contorted face, at last, a true reflection of her twisted mind.

"Stop whining, damn you!" Jocelyn screamed down at him.

Jocelyn glared down at him, her face as stern as a marine drill sergeant chewing ass up and down the line. "Look at me, Stanford Rome! Feast on me!" She poked out her chest. "Look at me!" Her finger pounded her chest. "Feast on me!"

Jocelyn's ranting sent the bull mastiffs into a frenzy.

"Heel, you mutts," QueenBee warned the dogs. "Keep still."

Thunder exploded ferociously overhead.

The powerful blast trailed behind swift lightning bolts streaking across the sky ahead of the roar. The bull mastiffs, bundles of high-strung energy, whined their impatience to get on with it.

Jocelyn stopped prancing in midstride and turned her angry gaze up at the sky as if God had pissed her off, and she was giving God a piece of her mind. Then she lowered her wide cross-eyed gaze back down on him. The rain was now a steady downpour as if the weather wanted to shield prying eyes from the goings-on down there amongst the Twofer County dirt beds.

Jocelyn burst into tears.

She buried her face in her hands, sobbing, shoulder-shaking grief and sadness spilling out of her. Uncovering her eyes, she threw her palms up to the sky, spilling her tears out into the rain.

"Help me, Stanford. I'm so alone, and I'm lost. Oh, Stanford, I went looking for a love, and I lost my way. Help me, Stanford. I don't wanna lose you. I need you, honey. I love you, baby. I want you to love me, Stanford, love me, love me, love me."

Her pretty words, her anguished plea twisted Stanford's stomach into knots he couldn't even begin to untangle.

"I want you to love me, Stanford, love me, love me, love me."

Wind gushes whipped about the graveyard, the force pounding the rain into twirling flurries of mist, the silvery spray sweeping across the tombstones like teardrops—and a crying shame.

"I want you to love me, Stanford, love me, love me, love me."

Stanford saw Candice stir. She was tugging weakly at the strap of her shoulder bag, reeling it in while Jocelyn was talking down to him. But Jocelyn latched onto his line of sight before he could look away, and Jocelyn saw Candice fumbling inside the shoulder bag.

With the wail of a wildcat, Jocelyn leaped down to the ground with the lightness and the dexterity of a feline.

Candice drew the .380 from the shoulder bag a moment too late. Jocelyn was on top of her in a flash. Jocelyn's vicious kick connected with the back of Candice's head. The stunning blow sent the sniper sprawling over on her back.

Jocelyn snatched up the .380 and spun around on her heels. She leaped back up on top of the car using leg strength alone and swung the .380 around on QueenBee. She snapped off a shot. Bertha leaped in front of QueenBee and took the bullet in the neck, her throat exploding in a mist of red.

The impact of the bullet knocked the big woman backwards off her feet. Bertha collapsed on top of QueenBee, pinning the eighty-three-year-old matriarch to the ground under her dead weight.

Stanford saw the gun. He heard the shot. He tried to stand, but the crippling pain drove him back to his knees; his body quaked in spasms. Jocelyn swung the gun around on him and fired a second time. The bullet kicked up mud inches from Stanford's feet.

QueenBee struggled to free her gun.

"Kill, Aretha! Sic 'er!"

Aretha yelped and became a blur of speed.

Jocelyn spun around. The 120-pound bull mastiff was already in full flight through the air when Jocelyn fired the gun point-blank. Aretha yelped, crashed and bounced off the trunk of the Jaguar. The big dog slammed into the ground in a whimper of death—a bullet between the eyes.

QueenBee freed her arm and her gun just as Jocelyn swung the .380 around on Stanford again. QueenBee was leveling the barrel when the Jaguar trunk lid popped up. Stanley rolled out, right in QueenBee's line of fire, a gun in his young hands.

Stanley fired the gun.

The bullet struck Jocelyn between her shoulder blades.

Jocelyn grunted and stumbled a step. Her body stiffened and bucked. Her left arm went behind her back, hand groping around for the bullet that hurt her. Turning, Jocelyn saw Stanley, and she swung the .380 toward the wide-eyed boy.

Stanford leaped up, crashing through his pain, and threw himself toward the Jaguar, yelling out to Franklin as he moved.

"Kill, Franklin! Sic 'er!"

The bull mastiff's powerful leap forward left ruts in the mud. In one second Franklin was airborne, sailing over Stanley's head, his vicious growl freezing Jocelyn's trigger finger, unnerving her aim.

Stanford's desperate hand locked around Jocelyn's ankle at the same instant Franklin's huge canines ripped into her throat.

Jocelyn and Franklin tumbled in tandem off the roof of the Jaguar entangled like lovers in the midst of a kiss.

The big thick-backed bull mastiff stood astride Jocelyn's body, the powerful jaws nearly wrenching her head off her shoulders.

The sun winked obliquely through the clouds.

EPILOGUE

"IT'S GONNA BE hot and sticky today, folks," barked the weatherman, gasping into the mike. "Jungle heat all-day long down here in the South Georgia Deep—"

Click!

Stanford rested an arm on Stanley's shoulder as they stood looking out the window of QueenBee's Twofer County hospital room.

Yesterday at the cemetery had done his grandmother in. His fingers kneaded Stanley's shoulder muscles. "You okay, Son?"

Stanley nodded. "I'm just bored."

QueenBee rattled her throat then rattled her dice.

"Stanley," QueenBee said, "you look plum bored. Why don't you go terrorize a nurse. Let me talk to your daddy a minute."

Stanford pulled a chair near the head of the bed and sat with their faces only two feet apart.

"Stanford, Emma and Isaiah Whitfield, those two weirdos had another child. Four years younger than Shelley was. A girl."

QueenBee paused and rattled her throat weakly.

"The girl, her name was Claudia Chester Whitfield, was adopted by Faye and Benjamin Ryder. From over in Harlem, Georgia. Near Augusta. The girl changed her name from Claudia Chester Whitfield to Claudia Chester Ryder. When Benjamin Ryder died, his widow, Faye Ryder, she put Claudia in an orphanage when she was five. She said with her husband dead, she couldn't care for the girl. The girl left the orphanage when she turned seventeen. Claudia changed her name again when she joined the army. Not

405

only changed her name, but changed her identity, too."

QueenBee rattled her throat again.

"Claudia, she took another girl's identity. In fact, Claudia became that other girl is what I'm saying to you, Stanford."

QueenBee's roving eyes steadied to meet his searching ones.
"You don't get it, do you, Son?"

Stanford shook his head. He didn't get it. "I sure don't."

"Do you remember what happened when I asked Jocelyn if she was Alice Cooper, then who was C. C. Ryder?"

He nodded. "Yes, she looked as if you'd slapped her."

"Do you remember her answering the question?"

"No, she never answered it."

"Hold that thought," QueenBee said.

"Did you notice when she got mad her lower lip trembled?"

He nodded, his mind impregnated with a thought he had never thought before. When his mind gave birth, he was stunned.

"Ahh, man," he said, thinking: see-see.

"You got it. She had to go off the air for two months because she started suffering migraines and having seizures."

"Ahh, man," he repeated, thinking: see-see.

"Son, I told you, in the beginning, about that woman."

Stanford remembered that day, a month and a half ago, the day Jocelyn Slade had cornered him in the Twofer County Dirt Beds.

"You did. I remember your exact words. You said, 'It's those eyes, I tell you. It's those eyes. They're troubling to me.'"

"Her trembling lower lip was a dead giveaway," QueenBee said.

"Ahh, man," he said again. "They both had seizures. They both had migraines. They were both crazy as hell… Ahh, man."

"Stanford, what was that saying Shelley had about blues and jazz; you know, when you boys teased him about his sullen ways?"

He smiled, remembering.

"There's a thin line between your jazz and my blues."

He laughed, thinking: see-see.